The Bread Maker

a debut novel by

Moira Leigh MacLeod

Suite 300 - 990 Fort St
Victoria, BC, V8V 3K2
Canada

www.friesenpress.com

First Edition — 2016

ISBN
978-1-4602-7217-6 (Hardcover)
978-1-4602-7218-3 (Paperback)
978-1-4602-7219-0 (eBook)

1. *Fiction, Literary*

Distributed to the trade by The Ingram Book Company

To Gary…for Believing

Give Us This Day Our Daily Bread

Saturday, October 29, 1933

She watched as the last lonely leaf let go and ended its fanciful journey at the toe of her muddy shoe. She picked it up, eyed it carefully, and twirled the stem back and forth. "Ya were the strongest one of all. Ya put up a good fight."

Her da, teetering unsteadily in the doorway, greeted his daughter more warmly than usual. "Mabel!" She jumped.

"Who the hell ya talkin to now?" he asked.

She shoved the leaf in her pocket. "Yer home early, Da."

"I told ya, stop yakkin out loud when there's nobody round to hear ya. Neighbours say yer strange in the head. That ya should be put in the crazy house. Hell, I might even put ya there myself."

"Ya heard me, Da. So, I guess I wasn't talkin to myself."

He raised his hand to slap her, but didn't. He'd eat first.

Mabel knew his words were an idle threat. She put the food on the table, the coal in the scuttle, and the whiskey in his belly.

"Hungry, Da?" she asked, stirring the pot of cabbage soup atop the coal stove.

"Do ya think I came home for the great company? And why the hell are ya home? Better notta gotten yerself fired."

Mabel ladled the soup into a shallow bowl and put it in front of him, next to a plate of buttered bread. "No, Da. Mr. Cameron had an appointment in town. He closed up early and insisted on drivin me home. He told me I was doin real good," she said, returning to the stove to fetch her own soup.

"Yeah. He's a real gem," her father snorted.

Mabel had no idea why her da didn't take to Mr. Cameron, but knew better than to ask.

"Ain't no meat in it, or steam off it," he mumbled. "Don't know why I bother to come home. Dumb, ugly girl can't cook for shit. She'd have no place to stay if it weren't for me."

Mabel turned toward her father. "Da, yer talkin to yerself again. People are gonna think yer strange and that ya should be locked up in the –"

The bowl caught her above the right eye. Mabel stumbled back into the stove. The blood dripped down her nose, creating a pink pool around the splayed white shards and pale limp cabbage on the linoleum floor.

"Clean it up," he said, slamming the door and storming out.

She looked down, thinking what a waste of good cabbage. She wiped her face with the hem of her bloodstained shift, put a cold washcloth to her forehead, and eased down on her bed.

Sunday, October 30

CHAPTER I

She woke, feeling first the cold, then the pain across her head, and finally the lack of cabbage soup in her belly. She sat up for a moment, felt dizzy, and slunk back against her ma's pillow. "Stupid! Stupid! Stupid!" she said, vowing never to taunt her da again. She sat up, knowing it was time to head off to Mr. Cameron's Bakery and Dry Goods Emporium and make the best bread ever for the families of Number Two.

The shack was dark and cold; colder than usual. "The dumb arse didn't bank the stove when he came home," she muttered, as she wrapped her blanket around her and made her way down the hall to the kitchen, promising to watch her foul tongue. When she passed her da's room, she knew he hadn't come home. He always slept with the gas lamp on, and there was no amber glow shining from under his door. She'd bet her last penny he was back at that woman's on York Street. One thing she knew for sure, he wasn't where he should be; in church, begging God's forgiveness.

She had no idea of the time. The one clock they had, unreliable as it was, sat on a steamer trunk next to the cot in her da's room, and nobody went in there without his approval. And Da wasn't home.

She entered the moonlit kitchen, crumbled up some paper, stuffed it down the belly of the stove, and thought of how lucky she had been to get her first real job; and with such a kind man for a boss. Work had been pretty scarce until Mr. Cameron had hired her. Roddy, her da's big shot brother-in-law, helped her get the odd stretch of work washing the soot off the white walls and high ceilings of the homes of the *la-di-dahs* at the British Imperial Coal Company, but then he and Aunt Amour packed up and headed for Boston. And her friend, Mary Catherine, helped her get what had looked like a promising job at the local fish plant, but the bloody place burnt down three weeks after she'd started. Stunk up the town and turned me off fish for a good while, she thought. She felt around for the matches. Her mind turning to old Mrs. Greene. Poor woman had kept her busy for a while. Mabel shook her head, remembering the time she found the rather buxom Mrs. Greene walking around without any bottoms, not even her bloomers, belting out a song that certainly wasn't English. Maybe Gaelic? Imagine, Mabel thought, she normally couldn't get around without help, and yet, there she was dancing up a storm and shaking her bare arse in the air. Took nearly a half hour to get her dressed and back in bed.

Mabel always wondered if Mrs. Greene had gone strange in the head because of her advanced age, or because they found her half-naked son beaten to death in the alley behind his own da's shoe repair. She made the sign of the cross, and chided herself. She should be kinder and remember him by his name. David. She hadn't known David well. Talked to him once or twice at Mendelson's Market where he worked from time to time, always rearranging things that didn't seem like they needed rearranging. She smiled, thinking of him in his funny little cap, still puzzled by why it never toppled off.

Mabel made the sign of the cross again as she thought about his poor mother. She'd had to bury her only child one week, and her husband, found hanging from the rafters in the rear of his shop, just three weeks later. And then there was all that nasty talk that Mr. Greene had killed his own son. "Nonsense. He hung himself out of grief, not guilt," she hissed, nervously looking around to make sure her da wasn't lurking about in the dark.

She added some kindling to the stove, and looked in all the usual places for the box of wooden matches. They were nowhere to be found. Bastard took them with him, she thought, and quickly ran barefoot back to her room for the spare box she always kept on hand. She opened the top drawer of her dresser, relieved he hadn't found her hidden stash. She was about to close the drawer, when she reached back into the far corner, pulled out a small satin satchel, and gently eased its contents into the palm of her hand.

She sat on the edge of her bed remembering the day she had shown up at Mrs. Greene's, and the local barrister, Samuel Friedman, pressed the pretty cloth bag and a five dollar bill into her hand with word the dear old woman had passed on. Mabel ran her fingers over the small star-shaped brooch. She had wanted to wear it to Mrs. Greene's wake, but never got the chance. Mrs. Isaac Greene, nee Sophie Dubinski, aged fifty-three, was buried the very next morning on a patch of cindered ground between her husband and her only child, a far distance away from the rest of the graves. You were a kind woman, Mrs. Greene, who bore more than your fair share of grief, she thought. She blessed herself for the third time in as many minutes, recalling her da's reaction when she told him Mrs. Greene died from an attack on the heart. *It's a heart attack, stupid girl*, he'd said, as the back of his hand came across her cheek.

Mabel returned the bag and its treasured contents to its hiding place, leaned into the cracked mirror above her dresser, and examined the latest evidence of her da's black moods. "Wasn't no need for it, Da," she said, scratching her fingernail along the stubborn, brown crust surrounding the open wound.

"Enough mullin over the past. What's done is done," she whispered. She walked back to the kitchen, struck a match across the side of the box, and brought it to the edge of the pink butcher paper. She watched the small orange and blue flames grow and lick the sides of their narrow cavity. She stood there warming her hands as the kindling crackled, and the fire cast a pretty, flickering glow around the dark room. "Better get my arse in gear if I'm gonna have a half-dozen loaves risin by seven," she said, and reached down for the coal scuttle. It was empty. "Fuck! Ya couldn't even fill the fuckin bucket," she yelled. So much for watching my foul tongue, she thought. But she'd loved the sound of the word from the very first time she heard her da describe her baby brother as a *fuckin beaut.* She'd thought it was Gaelic for good, or pretty. Sure sounded Gaelic. She started to laugh. "Thank God for Mary Catherine. Imagine! If she didn't tell me it was a swear word, I mighta told Father Vokey his sermons were fuckin inspirin."

Time's-a-ticking, she reminded herself. She'd promised Mr. Cameron she'd never be late, and it was a promise she was going to keep. Just as she had done from her very first day on the job, she was going to go in early every morning, stay late every night, and make bread that would melt in yer mouth. "Count yer blessing," she said, thinking they were many. "Hell, I musta used up my share of misery by now. I'm due for a stretch of luck."

All hopes of imminent good fortune quickly faded when Mabel opened the front door to refill the scuttle. "Jesus, Mary n' Joseph!" she yelled, as a fluffy, white knoll fell inward onto the floor of the shack. "Shit! It's too early. It ain't even All Saints Day. And I got no boots," she hollered. She eyed her shoes. "Fuck! Yer no good to me. I shoulda picked up a new pair when I surrendered my old pinchers to Mary Catherine. Boots!" she yelled. "Boots!"

The best she could come up with was doubling up a pair of her father's heavy pit socks with a pair of her own, and stuffing the toes of his never worn work boots with the butcher paper from the hambone she'd brought home from Mendelson's. She drew the laces extra tight at the top, where her pale, bare legs clashed with the black of the boots. They were way too big and too loose. She thumped awkwardly across the floor, gave her face a good wipe to get rid of the dried blood that clung around the creases of her nose, and threw on her thin coat..

She opened the door and peered out. It's not that bad, she thought. She looked up at the bright moon, hoping it would help her find her way around the drifts. She lifted her leg to step over the first hurdle that blocked her way and fell forward. "Jesus! It's like I got fuckin anvils for feet," she said, pushing her hands into the snow and clumsily bringing herself upright. She blew on her hands and looked out to see open patches of bare ground. "I'll just walk around the drifts. And it ain't that cold," she murmured, as if saying the words aloud would convince her they were true. Remember, ya love to walk and it ain't that far.

Mabel plodded along in the dark, thinking of her warm oven, and thanking God for Mr. Cameron. If it weren't for him, she'd have no job to go to. She thought of his mean wife, who had whispered that Mabel wasn't old enough. That there were other women more qualified. That she wasn't a good Christian. "Like I'd be making Holy Communion and servin it up at High Mass, or somethin," Mabel said.

She dug her hands into her coat pockets, recalling the morning of her interview, and the look on Mrs. Cameron's face when she told her she wasn't quite sure how old she was. Like I'd know. I had no cause to know and no one to tell me, in any event. Not like I was going to ask Da a second time. First time I asked, he threw his tea at me, yelling not to ask stupid questions. Wasn't any point in asking a second time, I'd just get the same answer. Mary Catherine told me that all girls get their monthly when they're thirteen, so I figured seventeen was about right.

Mabel shook her head, thinking of Mrs. Cameron's ridiculous questions and her own equally ridiculous answers. She pursed her lips, turned up her nose, and began mimicking the snooty old witch.

"And how old are you, Miss Adshade?"

"Pretty sure I'm seventeen, Mrs. Cameron."

"*Pretty sure?*" Mrs. Cameron repeated, more as a question than an understanding reply.

"Maybe eighteen."

Mrs. Cameron turned and gave her husband a disapproving look. Like I was the only person on earth who didn't know when they were born.

"You don't know?"

"Not entirely, Mrs. Cameron. Up till now, never had cause to."

"And what about your schooling?" she had asked.

"That, I'm sure of. I attended St. Anthony's from time to time. They put me in grade three. I wish I could tell you I can read good, but that wouldn't be entirely true. But I know how to measure flour, get a good rise, and make a good batch of bread. And I'll work hard–"

"And church, Miss Adshade? I assume you attend regularly?"

"Actually, practicalities usually get in the way."

"And what kind of practicalities would keep you from God and his church?" she asked, with her hands clasped tightly in front of her, and her hair perfectly set upon her head.

"Food and rent."

"I assume you brought letters of reference?"

I told her Mr. Toth didn't speak good English, so likely couldn't write good either, but I'd inquire. Mrs. Greene couldn't very well provide one, since she's dead. And the fish plant burnt down three weeks after I started, so I never got a chance to stand out from all the other gutters.

Mabel recalled looking at Mr. Cameron. He was smiling. Mrs. Cameron wasn't. Her piercing stare and turned down mouth made her beautiful face look ugly. Then, Mr. Cameron went and asked something about the rent Uncle Roddy charged for staying at the shack and I just rambled on like a fucking imbecile. "I tend to the cookin and cleanin, Da to the finances. I'd love to go to church if I didn't have a job that called me at that very same time Father Vokey rings the bells for service. If I got the job, I'd gladly go to mass on Sunday, but I'm pretty sure Da wouldn't be comin with me."

Then, the old bat chimed back in. "Perhaps you could bring your young man then?"

I had no young man, so just smiled and looked at Mr. Cameron. I'll never forget how his kind eyes clashed with those of the cold woman standing beside him. *Mr. Nice married to Mrs. Nasty.*

"You do have a young man, Miss Adshade? Pretty, young girl like you?" she asked, kind of snide-like.

Then I started rambling again. "Thanks for sayin so, Mrs. Cameron. But I'm not what you'd call pretty. Passable, maybe? But certainly not pretty. I don't have a suitor and don't want one. Most of the eligibles I come across either smell of coal or fish, and I ain't partial to either. I just want to make bread, maybe some scotch cakes and pies. Da loves my pie."

All of a sudden, Mr. Cameron called his wife to the back of the store. I figured I didn't have a chance in hell of getting the job and was glad I hadn't told Da I was looking into it.

Finally, Mr. Cameron walked back in the room and told me I start at seven the very next day. That he'd see how the bread sold after a month and, if it all worked out, I could stay on permanent. Then old Miss Priss comes up from behind. I resisted the urge to stick my tongue out at her, just grinned from ear to ear, and told Mr. Cameron I'd have my first batch rising well before seven. I was about to tell the crotchety old bird I'd see her in church on Sunday, but she walked straight past me and Mr. Cameron, and went upstairs.

That was the day my luck finally changed. Da'd be in a better mood knowing his whiskey supply would be secure, and there'd be more meat and less fish. And I got the best job in town doing what I love most, despite lying to Mr. and Mrs. Cameron, not once, but twice. Imagine, Da saying he loved my pie. Closest thing to nice he'd ever said to me was, 'Don't be spreadin yer legs and bringin home no little bastards.' He must have figured someone would want to do *the nasty* with me, she thought, recalling the details Mary Catherine shared with her one morning while they were gutting cod. Then, there was the big lie about skipping church to pay for food and rent. Food, whiskey, and Da's gambling money was more like it, but I couldn't very well tell them that.

Mabel stopped to tighten the laces of her da's boots. Her hands were stinging as she struggled with the icy knots. On days like this, it would be great if we lived closer to Mr. Cameron's, she thought. But then we'd have to pay for our lodging, and Da'd have no appetite for that. We're luckier than most. If it weren't for Uncle Roddy and

Aunt Amour we'd still be paying a small fortune for that dump in Number Three. Hard to believe they let us move into the shack and never looked for so much as a cent of rent. No small wonder, given that Roddy was known to walk with his head down, scouring for lost pennies. Can't say I blame them for packing up and leaving so abruptly. They just got one too many threats from an angry miner, or a grieving widow swearing to burn them out. The scorched wall at the rear of the shack, proof that at least one of those threats was not offered idly.

Given the weights on her feet, Mabel was making reasonable progress when the sleet started. She stopped again, pulling her collar up around her neck, and her sleeves down over her frozen fingers. She looked across the street in the direction of Matthew Toth's company house, and wondered how he and the boys were getting along. She hadn't seen them since she got the job at the bakery and surrendered her weekend child care duties to Mary Catherine. Poor man, she thought, always wandering the cliffs along Table Head. Came all the way from Hungary. Hardly had time to settle his young family into their new home when his pretty wife dies of some sort of growth, leaving his three boys with no ma, and one still on the teat.

She wondered about the time, thinking it was still early. There wasn't a light on anywhere in sight. *God it's cold.* She looked down at her feet, then across the field. Then it hit her. *Christ, I forgot to change my fucking frock and I got a gash above my eye. What am I going to tell Mr. Cameron?*

She turned and looked back in the direction she had come. It was too cold and too late to head back to the shack. She had no choice but to keep going. She decided her apron would cover the blood on her dress and that she'd tell Mr. Cameron she slipped on the ice leaving the house, or fell out of bed. "I'll tell him I lost my fuckin footin on the fuckin floorboards and fell into the fuckin table," she said. A gust of wind nearly knocked her over. "Fuck!" she screamed, steadying herself. Hell, it doesn't matter what I come up with. Like everybody else in town, Mr. Cameron knows Da takes easy to rage.

He'll probably see through whatever I tell him.

She was almost halfway there, lost in planning her lie. She didn't see him coming, but she heard him. He bounded out of nowhere and knocked her to the icy ground. Fritz, the MacLeod's dog, normally tied to a tree, was loose and angry. He snarled and snapped at her head. Mabel could feel his hot breath on her face. She buried her head in her arms, twisted sideways, and began kicking wildly in the direction of his face. He caught her left foot between his teeth, bared down, and began violently thrashing his head from side to side. Eventually Da's loose boot, along with the butcher paper that held the scent of a two-day old hambone, gave way. Fritz, the poor dog she'd always wished free of its tether, was now set upon tearing at least one of her Da's good boots to shreds. She crawled along, her hands and elbows breaking through the hard snow. She tried to stand, but fell headfirst, before finally scrambling to her feet and stumbling forward. She didn't dare look back. She just kept repeating "Dear Jesus! Dear Jesus! Dear Jesus!" And with every *dear Jesus* she muttered, the wind grew a little louder and the freezing rain a little harder.

By the time she reached the top of Caledonia Street, she was exhausted and her bootless foot felt like it was encased in ice. Her da's pit sock, weighed down by what seemed like a million miniature snowballs, felt heavier than the foot carrying her lone clunker. But she could see Cameron's. "Damn dog! Damn butcher paper!" she cursed, as she dragged her bone-chilled body closer to the promise of her warm oven and kneading table.

When she got to School Street, she could see that the wooden shutters covering the store's windows were still firmly secured. She tried to run to the door, but slipped and fell on her side. She got up and hobbled the rest of the way. She tried to knock, but her hands were too cold. She pounded on the door with the side of her fist. "It's Mabel. Mr. Cameron! It's me! Mabel! Mr. Cameron, are you there?" She banged harder. "Mr. Cameron! It's Mabel!" She looked up to the apartment above. Nothing. She banged and hollered louder, before realizing she was no match for the howling wind and the hard, noisy sleet pelting down around her.

She looked up and down the street. Still, there wasn't a light on. She must be way too early. She needed a place to get out of the wind and freezing rain that was ripping into her skin. She ran around to the back of the store, waded through a knee-high drift, and pulled on the icy handle of the back door. Again no luck. She was walking back around the front when she eyed the coal shed. She could climb in and out of the pelting rain, but it was too high. She spotted the corner of an empty apple crate jutting out from the snow. She dug at it with her bare hands like a dog with a treasured bone, thinking this is what Fritz was doing to her da's partially consumed boot, if he hadn't already polished it off. "Damn dog!" She knelt down, wrapped her numb fingers around the open slats of the rough crate, yanked hard, and fell back empty handed.

More digging. More pulling. Despite the cold, she felt like she was sweating. Finally, the crate broke free. It was heavier than she thought. She dragged it alongside the store, flipped it upside down, stepped up, and quickly realized it wasn't high enough for her to hoist herself up into the shed. She turned the box on its side. It was now too high for her to step onto.

She fell to her knees, frantically pulling from a drift behind her to build a mound of frozen snow. She managed to step on top of the slippery crate. It teetered a little, but not enough to keep her from clawing away at the snow-crusted lid that was frozen shut. With as much anger as desperation, she began pounding on the shed's icy cover. If finally broke loose. She lifted it up and rested it against the outside wall. She then swung her numb, bootless, bare leg up over the side, and hurled her frozen body down onto the hard rock below. She knelt on the black coal, reached up for the lid that would shield her from the pounding ice pellets, eased it back down, and curled into a ball. "I think I'll die here," she said, through her chattering teeth. "I hope Mr. Cameron knows I got here early."

CHAPTER 2

Stanley looked out the window and wondered if the weather would let up enough to harness Walter and Winnie, two pit ponies he rescued from an unhappy ending after the manager of Number Two mine deemed them unfit to serve. They were old, slow, and skittish around the automobiles that were starting to crowd the local streets, but people still needed their coal, and they still had a purpose. They were Stanley's closest companions. No matter how slowly they plodded along, or how much hay he had to feed them, he'd have paid five-fold the outrageous price he'd been charged for saving the British Imperial Coal Company the cost of two bullets.

He opened the door of his half of the company house, while the widow MacNeil and her eight children slept crowded together in their half, as much for warmth as lack of space. He walked to the barn, lifted the latch, and entered. His two tiny ponies stirred and slowly stood to attention. Stanley struck a match and brought it to the wick of his gas lamp. "Not a great day for deliveries, I know. Just a couple of stops, I promise," he said, patting Winnie's nose and reaching into his pocket. "Mrs. Lowry's, the Demont's, and then home."

He gave them each a cube of sugar, put their halters on, hitched the wagon, and brought them unhappily out front. He then put a blanket on the frozen wooden seat that would be his helm, jumped up, and headed to the Number Two pithead to load his wagon. It was slow going, and the trio got bogged down several times, but the freezing rain had let up, the skies cleared, and the temperature inched up, making the journey easier.

Their deliveries complete less than two hours later, they headed home with a wagon still half-full of coal. Stanley decided to ease the burden of his weary haulers and drop the remaining coal off at the Cameron's. He pulled up alongside the shed, jumped down, and mounted the back of the wagon. He was about to pick up his shovel when he spotted the discarded apple crate on its side, and then the lid, wiped bare of snow. He lifted it up and saw her motionless body curled into a ball. Her skin was white, and her lips blue. She looked frozen to death. He knew he couldn't get her out on his own. He jumped down, ran to the front of the store and began pounding. James Cameron was in the kitchen preparing tea. "What in the world?" he said, making his way to the door. More pounding. "Hold your horses!" he hollered. When he opened the door, Stanley was frantic.

"The girl! She's in the shed!"

James had no idea what he was talking about, but knew he had to follow him, and be quick about it. They both climbed onto the back of the wagon and looked down. "Jesus!" James said, wondering how Mabel had ended up in the shed, and how long she'd been there. Stanley eased himself down beside her, gently picked her up, and placed her in James's outstretched arms. He then jumped back on the wagon and down to the ground. James returned her to Stanley, who held her tight to his chest and followed James around front.

"Take her to the kitchen, where it's warm!" James shouted. James ran upstairs into his room and tore a blanket off the bed Margaret had just made. He then started for the door, turned back, and grabbed the quilt off the dowry chest at the foot of their bed.

"What are you doing? And what was all that pounding?" Margaret hollered.

James ran out without saying a word, descended the stairs three at a time, and rushed back into the kitchen, laying the quilt on the kneading counter. He felt for a pulse.

"Hurry! Take the car! Find Dr. Cohen!" he barked at Stanley.

Margaret walked in a few minutes later. Her husband was standing over Mabel, brushing her wet, stringy hair away from her forehead.

"What did she do now?" she asked.

CHAPTER 3

Stanley sped along the rutted dirt roads, praying Dr. Cohen was either at home, or at the synagogue. As he approached Dr. Cohen's, he could see his red Buick backing out. Stanley was back at the store in less than fifteen minutes, with Dr. Cohen close on his heels.

James looked down from the top of the stairs. "She's up here."

"How is she?" Stanley asked.

"I'm not sure. Her colour looks better," James said.

Stanley watched James greet Dr. Cohen and disappear out of sight. He then turned to the window and looked out at his restless ponies, still hitched to their wagon. You earned your room and board today, he thought. Better get you home.

James led Dr. Cohen into the room that was once a nursery. Mabel was lying on top of the bed, covered with a heavy patchwork quilt. Dr. Cohen dropped his well-used black bag on the floor, removed his hat, and placed it on the seat of a child-sized rocker in the corner.

"Sorry for interrupting your day, Thomas," James said.

Dr. Cohen unbuttoned his coat and draped it over the footboard. "No need to apologize, James. It's all part of the job. Stanley said you found her in the shed. Any idea how long she was there?"

"No clue."

"Nasty cut. Has she woken up?"

"No. But she let out a couple of moans. Mumbled something. I couldn't make it out. She keeps throwing her covers off even though she's shivering."

Dr. Cohen bent down, undid the straps on his bag, retrieved his stethoscope, and wrapped it around his neck.

James's anxiety grew as he watched the all-too-familiar scene play out before him. "She was only wearing one boot," he said. "A pit boot. Her sock was a block of ice, so I took it off. The toes on her left foot look bad."

Dr. Cohen put his hand to Mabel's forehead, then looked back at James. "Why don't you put on some tea?"

"Of course," James said. Mabel once again began to shiver and push her covers aside. James pulled them back over her. "Will she be alright?"

"I'd be more concerned if she *wasn't* shivering. I'm sure she'll be fine," Dr. Cohen replied. "We need to keep her warm. The tea will help."

Dr. Cohen pulled the blanket up from the bottom of the bed so he could assess the damage to Mabel's legs from the knees down. He could see they were red and swollen. He pressed his fingers into her toes. They felt spongy. He placed the blanket back over her legs, reached in his bag, and took out a bottle of alcohol. He poured some on a piece of gauze and daubed the open cut on her head.

Mabel flinched and opened her eyes.

"Sorry, Mabel. I'm just going to put in a couple of stitches so you won't scar so much."

He pulled his wire-rimmed glasses from the pocket of his herringbone suit coat, threaded a needle, and gently brought the sides of the raw wound together.

Mabel shivered, pressed her eyes tight, and bit her bottom lip.

"Sorry. Almost done," he said, putting his finger in a jar. He excised a good smattering of sticky salve, spread it over the stitching, and taped a clean strip of gauze over top. "Mabel? Can you sit up?" She opened her eyes, but closed them almost immediately. "I'm sure you're going to be just fine, but I need to listen to your chest. Is that okay?" She nodded. He pulled the blanket down from her chest and began undoing the buttons on her dress. He was at her waist when he saw the bloodstains. "Mabel? Do you think you can sit up?" She opened her heavy eyelids, slowly put her arm down to push off the bed, winced, and plopped back down. She pointed to her shoulder. He bent down, wrapped his arm around her back, and pulled her into him so she could rest her head on his chest. He slipped her dress off her shoulders. She had a sizeable contusion on her upper right arm. "I'm just going to make sure nothing is broken." He felt her shoulder, bent her arm at the elbow, and gently pulled on her wrist. He put the stethoscope to his ears, laid it on her chest, and then on her back. "You passed the test. You need your rest, but you'll be your old self in no time."

James entered, carrying a tray with three cups of tea. He placed the tray on the nightstand, and watched Dr. Cohen ease Mabel's head back down on her pillow.

"James? Can you see if Margaret might have a warm nightdress for Mabel to wear?"

Margaret was in their bedroom doing needlepoint. "Thomas is here. He's looking for a nightdress for Mabel."

Margaret walked to her chest of drawers, pulled out a long, flannel nightgown trimmed with lace, handed it to James without saying a word, and returned to her needlepoint. He was disturbed that she never asked about Mabel, but knew no good would come from sharing his feelings. He returned to see Dr. Cohen standing over Mabel. "Everything okay, Thomas?"

"Mild case of hypothermia and frostbite. Nothing too serious. Why don't you wait downstairs? I'll only be a few more minutes," he said.

"I'll just wait in the hallway. In case you need me," James said, making his way to the door, before turning back and looking at Thomas.

"James, she'll be fine," Thomas assured him.

James smiled and pulled the door closed behind him.

"Okay, Mabel. Let's get you into something more comfortable. Can you lift your bottom?" She didn't open her eyes. "Mabel? Can you lift your bottom?" he repeated. Her eyes fluttered open and she lifted her pelvis enough for him to quickly reach under and tug her dress free. Dr. Cohen put his arm under her back, brought her into a sitting position, and carefully swung her legs over the side of the bed. He then slipped Margaret's nightgown over her head, slowly easing one arm through its sleeve, and then the other. Her nightgown fell into a ball on her lap.

"I'm almost done. If you can you just lift your bottom one last time?"

She complied again. She was swaying back and forth with her eyes closed when Dr. Cohen made the grisly discovery. He looked up at her, then back down. "There. All done," he said, easing her back on the bed, and wondering how she ended up with a hole in her leg. She was asleep again the moment her head hit the pillow. Dr. Cohen opened the door. "You can come in now."

Dr. Cohen handed James Mabel's bloodstained shift. "There's more to her story than we know," he said.

James looked at the untouched tea. "She's okay, though? Isn't she?"

"She'll be fine. Lungs are clear. I suspect it's mostly exhaustion. Her legs are coming around nicely, but we'll need to keep an eye on her toes. Skin is still intact, which is a good sign. She'll be tired and sore for a few days, but no broken bones or long-term damage that I can see. I put a couple of stitches in her forehead. The best thing for her now is rest. So, tell me again how she ended up in your shed?"

James looked from Mabel to Thomas. "I have no idea. She must have been trying to get out of the storm."

"And the cut on her forehead?"

"I know she didn't get it on the way here." James looked down at the dress in his hands. "Her dress has blood on it, but her coat doesn't. I figure she was trying to get away from Johnnie and came here. I know he beats her. I've seen the bruises."

"Did you ever talk to her about it?"

"Tried. More than once. She makes up excuses. Says she's naturally clumsy. But you don't get bruises on your cheeks from being clumsy. Christ! He must have been in a rage."

"Or a hole in your leg," Dr. Cohen said, peering at James over the rim of his glasses. Mabel said something they couldn't make out. "Just keep her warm and leave her here for the night. And try and get some warm fluids into her. I'll stop in tomorrow afternoon to check on her. I'd be in big trouble at home if I didn't look after the best bread maker in town."

Mabel opened her eyes and saw Dr. Cohen packing up his black bag. She wanted to cry. The best bread maker in town, he'd said. *The best bread maker in town.* She closed her eyes and went back to her dream.

Her ma, sitting near the stove, was pulling out breakfast for the wide-eyed baby in her arms. Her skin was pale, but her eyes were bright. She was smiling at Mabel, then at the baby who latched onto her and sucked loudly. Then nothing. Nothing but thud, thud, thud. The sound of wet mud hitting the top of a giant apple crate covered in daisies.

CHAPTER 4

Johnnie Adshade was pissed to the gills when he staggered toward the shack. There were no lights on. Fuck, where the hell is she? Place better be warm. It's fuckin freezing out. He opened the door, entered the dark room, tripped over one of Mabel's shoes, and fell on the floor. "Fuck. I'm gonna kill ya, ya bitch," he said, stumbling to his feet.

He walked across the black room and felt for the lamp, almost knocking it to the floor. There was no food on the table, and it was just as cold inside, as it was out. "Mabel! Where the fuck are ya, girl?" he yelled, as he made his way to the kitchen, and flopped down hard onto a chair that wobbled under his weight.

For a moment, he thought he might have thrown one too many dishes at her and she'd left for good. "Wouldn't do that stupid girl? Would ya? Wouldn't leave yer da to fetch his own supper? Christ, ya better notta run off," he slurred, his breath visible in the cold air. He leaned forward, stretched his arm across the table, and put his head down. He thought of going to his room. He slowly raised his bobbing head and looked around the bleary shack. "Better notta fuckin run off, cause I ain't goin down no fuckin pit! I'll throw myself off the cliff before I go fuckin underground," he said. He put his head back down. "Just like Matthew Toth," he mumbled, before passing out.

CHAPTER 5

"Mabel. Sit up and have some soup. Your father must be worried about you," Margaret said, tugging impatiently on Mabel's sleeve. Mabel opened her eyes, nodded, and then closed them again.

James interrupted. "Let her be, Margaret. She's exhausted, and she's not going anywhere tonight. Put the soup back on the stove and let the poor girl get some sleep."

"James, she's nothing but trouble. I don't know why you hired her over Mrs. Ferguson. You know, when I mentioned to Gladys you were going to be engaging a baker, she counted on getting the job. And then you go and hire a scatterbrained girl, with no experience, and not a single reference. Gladys has barely spoken to me since."

"Margaret, I told you, Mabel's mother and I were good friends. And you can't complain about her baking. Her bread is already bringing in new traffic to the store," James said.

"Yes, James. You mentioned she's the daughter of an old friend. And Gladys was my friend, at least until you hired *her*."

James walked away from Margaret, rolled his eyes, and took a deep breath.

"I want you to take her home. Tonight!" Margaret said. "We don't need people gossiping about her staying on."

"Margaret, unless you tell Gladys Ferguson, I think our reputations are safe," he said. He handed her the tepid soup, put his hand under her elbow, and led her to the door.

"Her trial period isn't up yet. You could let her go. I'm sure Mrs. Ferguson would —"

"Please, Margaret! I already told Mabel the job was hers for as long as she wanted it." He looked at Mabel, hoping she was oblivious to his wife's plea.

"Without talking to me?" Margaret shot back.

"Keep your voice down. Look, it's been quite the day. Go on downstairs. I'll be down shortly."

"James," Margaret said more quietly, trying to contain her mounting anger, "I was going to let this wait for a more appropriate time, but you should know, she's been stealing from us. I saw her leaving with a loaf of bread and some canned goods yesterday."

"Enough already! I told her to take the bread. And I wanted her to have the sardines, but she insisted on paying me."

"Why would you do that? You pay her a fair wage."

"Because I wanted to! That's why," he said harshly. He looked toward Mabel, then back at Margaret. She was glaring at him. "Margaret," he said, calming his voice, "I don't want to argue about this now. Let's talk about it later."

She turned and left.

James returned to Mabel's bedside, pulled up a chair, and sat down. He felt like he was back in time, looking at Ellie. He reached over and peeled away a hair that had become glued to the sticky substance that oozed from the gauze above her eye. "I bet Johnnie did this to you," he whispered. He clenched his fist, thinking of the only man he could say he truly hated. Johnnie Adshade was both a bully and a coward. For as James was given to think — and he was a thoughtful man — they were one and the same. Johnnie was nothing but a loud mouth drunk, known to bed any woman horny enough to spread her legs, and stupid enough to bear his fists in the morning. Man enough for that, but not man enough to strap on his boots and go underground with the rest of the men and boys, even when work was plentiful. Lazy coward, couldn't even hold on to the soft job Roddy got him at the Company Store. You could've gone back underground and provided for Mabel, James thought. But no, not you, Johnnie. You don't give a damn about anyone but yourself. You selfish bastard.

Mabel woke three hours later. James was sitting on a wicker chair in the corner, reading *The Post.* She pushed the quilt forward and looked at her long, white sleeves trimmed with lace.

James put the paper on the floor. "You're awake," he said smiling. He sat on the edge of her bed. "How are you feeling?"

"Good," she lied.

"Hungry?"

"No," she lied again, not wanting to impose any more than she knew she already had.

"How about some soup? Dr. Cohen was by. He said you should have some warm fluids."

"I'm good, thanks," Mabel said, wondering if she had really heard Dr. Cohen compliment her bread, or if it was just a dream.

"Some tea then?"

"No. I'm good."

"You really should have —"

"Mr. Cameron? Did you find me in the shed?"

"No. It was Stanley. Stanley MacIntyre."

"Ya mean the old, deaf guy who's always sittin on the crates in the store, smokin his pipe, and starin at ya like ya got two heads?"

James smiled. "He's not deaf. He can't hear much out of his right ear. But his left one works well enough. And he's not old. He's younger than me, you know."

Mabel had a moment of panic, wondering if Stanley heard her talking to herself. Maybe he heard her when she said his pipe stunk and he looked kind of creepy.

She looked at James. "Well, I certainly don't think yer old. Not a bit," she said, hoping she hadn't insulted him.

"Well, neither is Stanley. And if it weren't for him thinking folks might need a top up of coal with the weather turning so cold, so fast, you might have frozen to death."

"I'll make him a coupla double loaves for sure. Of course, I'll pay for the ingredients."

"I'm sure he'd like that. Dr. Cohen took a look at your legs and feet. You've got a mild case of hypothermia and frostbite, and a good bruise on your arm. Anyway, he says you'll feel some tingling in your legs and feet for a while, but that's to be expected. He's coming back tomorrow to check on your progress." He pointed to her forehead. "How did you get the cut?"

"This?" she said, putting her fingers over the puffy white bandage.

"Yes," he said. He waited for her answer.

"I was just walkin through the MacLeod's field and didn't see Fritz. He came at me from behind. He's their dog. He's normally tied, but he wasn't when I came through. He just knocked me down. And there was this stick that was stickin outa the ground. It was kinda hard and sharp. I just fell right into it."

James knew she was lying. "What time was this?"

"I'm not sure. Maybe, five-thirty or six. It was early for sure."

"And what, may I ask, were you doing in the MacLeod's field in the middle of the night during a storm?"

Mabel looked at Mr. Cameron. She thought his soft eyes had turned hard. Her lower lip began to quiver. "It's the quickest way to the bakery."

James put his head down. Mabel started to well up, sensing she had disappointed him. James, seeing she was upset, decided the rest of his questions could wait till morning. "Get some rest for now," he said. He reached forward and dimmed the light.

"But I gotta get to my table!" Mabel said, throwing her legs over the side of the bed.

"Mabel. You're not baking now."

"But I must be late. What time *is* it?"

"It's just past eight."

"Then I'm two hours late," Mabel said.

"Mabel, it's not eight in the morning. It's eight at night."

"Ya mean I missed a whole day?" she said loudly.

He was helping her back in bed. "No, Mabel. It's Sunday. It's your day off."

Mabel wasn't sure whether to laugh or cry. She was glad she'd kept her promise never to be late, but she also gave Da plenty of reasons to be angry. And most times, he didn't need one. *Christ, I didn't even know what fuckin day of the week it was. And Da would have come home to a cold shack and bare table. No boiled dinner with brisket to soothe his ugly mood or calm his sour belly. Dear Jesus, I hope Da forgot it was Sunday, too.*

"Mabel," James said with a note of authority, "you're staying here until Dr. Cohen says it's okay for you to go home." In fact, James was intent on making sure she stayed until he had a word with her father.

Mabel could feel her burning legs and sore foot. "I'd be grateful to spend a few hours before startin my bakin. And I'll gladly pay ya for my room and board. I've gotta good boss who pays a good wage," she said, smiling.

James pulled the quilt back over her. "Okay, then. Lay back down and get some rest. I'll see you in the morning. And, Mabel, there'll be no baking tomorrow. We can survive a day without bread. Good night."

"Good night. Thank you, Mr. Cameron," she said, knowing that no one could survive more than one day without fresh bread from Mr. Cameron's Bakery and Dry Goods Emporium.

James walked into the hall, pulled the door closed, and momentarily rested his forehead against it. He turned, slowly slumped to the floor, and buried his face in his hands. He began to cry. He sat there for several minutes before wiping his wet face and getting to his feet.

He had no idea Margaret had been peeking out from behind their bedroom door, seething in the firm knowledge her husband had betrayed her.

CHAPTER 6

James was bone tired. Despite the exhausting events of the day, he knew sleep wasn't about to come easily. His mind was racing as he crawled into bed next to his wife. He knew Margaret didn't like Mabel. She never missed an opportunity to complain about the crude way she spoke, the way she dressed, the amount of butter she wasted, her annoying laugh, her unkempt hair, her nonstop talking. As far as Margaret was concerned, *that girl*, as she was wont to call her, had not a single redeemable quality. God, what happened to us, he thought, already knowing the answer. She used to be the most loving, generous, and forgiving woman he'd ever known, but she had become cold, bitter, and judgemental. They used to do everything together. Take long walks, go dancing, skating, visiting friends. They used to have candlelit dinners with fine china. They used to make love. Even their conversations had become mundane accounts of the weather, what was for supper, who passed away. They used to share a loving home. They now shared a cold house. He began a silent prayer asking God to grant him patience and to forgive him for his many failings.

Margaret leaned over his shoulder. "James? What does that girl mean to you?" she asked.

James's eyes flew open. "I thought you were asleep. What do you mean?"

"Why did you insist she stay the night?"

James turned quickly to face her. "It was Dr. Cohen who said she should stay. And, Margaret, she had a pretty rough day. No harm is being done. Her father —"

"I saw you crying outside her door."

"Margaret!" he replied in a tone she was not used to hearing, "I would expect that you, of all people, a good Catholic, would feel badly for her circumstances." He roughly threw his covers back and sat on the edge of the bed. "You saw the cut on her head. Christ, she almost froze to death trying to get here. Her father beats her for goodness sakes. She's been tormented so much she didn't even know it was her day off. Jesus! Thomas even said she has a hole in her leg. Why you're spying on me, or what you're accusing me of is beyond me."

"James! Do not take the Lord's name in vain."

James turned and glared at her, got up, and quickly pulled on his pants.

"Where are you going?" Margaret asked, her voice matching her cold stare.

"God damn it, Margaret! What difference does it make?" he said. He grabbed his shirt from the bedpost and walked out, closing the door more roughly than he intended. He made a fist and wanted to pound on it. Instead, he put his hand on the knob, turned it, and pushed it open just a crack. He walked away slowly, more certain than ever that the woman he had married was gone and never coming back.

CHAPTER 7

Margaret stared at the door realizing her instincts were right. Whatever doubts she might have had vanished at the sight of her husband crying outside the room Mabel intruded upon. She had suspected it from the day James hired that *crude* girl. And her suspicions had grown every day since. She saw how her husband doted on her. She heard him laughing with her over tea, raving about her bread, and offering to drive her home — and the greatest irony of all — asking her to join them at Sunday Mass.

And she saw Mabel. Always smiling at him. Telling him how much she loved baking. How he was the best boss ever. She never shut up. Talked incessantly, either saying something frivolous, or asking stupid questions, as James hung on her every misspoken word. She couldn't even let them have one day in peace, disrupting the solemn quiet of their Sabbath.

Margaret knew the intimacy she and James had once shared had waned. But it wasn't her fault. After two miscarriages and the loss of baby James, she couldn't bring herself to fulfill her duties as a wife. No woman could have. Why James couldn't understand this was beyond her. But he had promised before God to love and cherish her in sickness and in health, and it was a promise she would make sure he kept. Tonight, she would let him sleep on the sofa alongside her disdain. Tomorrow, with God on her side, she would rid her home of that vile girl. She reached for her Bible and turned to Hebrews, Chapter XIII.

Marriage is honourable in all, and the bed undefiled: but whoremongers and adulterers God will judge. Let your conversation be without countenance: and be content with such things as ye have. For He hath said, I will never leave thee, or forsake thee.

Margaret turned off the gas lamp, closed her Bible, and then her angry eyes. She laid there for some time, thinking about her latest confrontation with James. Her eyes flew back open.

"What did he mean she had a hole in her leg?" she whispered.

CHAPTER 8

James, unsure of his wife's accusation, his own angry response, and the God who never seemed to answer his prayers, descended the stairs from the apartment above the store, walked to the room in the back, and took a can of MacDonald's tobacco down from the shelf. He rolled himself a makin. He had given them up years ago due to the same breathing issue that had forced him out of the pit after the war, but tonight he didn't care. He needed one, and he was damn well going to have it. He lit one after the other and thought about his troubled marriage. It wasn't just the lack of intimacy that created the growing gulf between them. He understood the anguish Margaret had felt after they'd lost the baby. He also knew she needed time to grieve and heal. They both did. And, in the three years that had passed since, he'd never once complained that she slept with her back to him. But he was beginning to think time alone would never make things better. Margaret's capacity to love had died with their son. There was no going back. And, for James, there was no going forward, as long as Margaret was happy being miserable. He put his head down, and thought about the first time he saw her.

She had been selling fudge outside a dance to support the families of fallen soldiers. Next to Ellie, she was the most beautiful girl he had ever seen. Her honey-coloured, shoulder length hair, and big smile had garnered the attention of a lengthy line of potential suitors, all eager to satisfy more than their sweet tooth. He waited impatiently as she wrapped her wares in wax paper and deflected the advances of more than a few young men who had beaten him to the front of the line.

"How much is the fudge?" he remembered asking.

"Not a penny more or less than what the sign says," she said, pointing to the large cardboard sign above her head. "Ten cents a square."

"Seems like highway robbery, given the pieces are so small," he teased.

"A bargain at twice the price, given it will do your heart good to support a good cause."

"What kind is it?"

"Maple. You look a little thin. Maybe you should buy a few?"

"If I do, will you dance with me?" James had asked.

"I'm not going to the dance. Just here to sell fudge."

He eyed the half dozen pieces left on the table. "Looks like you're almost sold out," he had said.

She lifted the table skirt to expose two large pans of what would be a major impediment in his mission to free her of her charitable duties. "Hardly," she said, grinning.

"So, if you sell all your fudge, will you come inside and dance with me?"

She started to laugh. "I doubt that will happen."

He reached into his pocket and took out his last two five dollar bills. "Will this do?"

She smiled up at him, packaged up the remaining fudge, and they made their way inside. She danced all night. He mostly watched. He got the first dance and the odd one in between, but there were plenty of other guys waiting their turn to be seen with the prettiest girl there. He couldn't take his eyes off of her. He'd be patient, because he already knew the last dance would be his.

He walked her home through the Scotch mist that hung in the cool air; a good five miles apart from the uneasy quiet of the lonely house on Caledonia Street he'd once shared with his parents. Despite having just met, there was no awkwardness between them. She talked easily and smiled often. She worked part-time doing administrative duties at the middle school. She wanted to be a teacher, loved children, and hoped to have a dozen of her own someday. Her father had lost an arm working at the steel mill, and her mother did some sewing and took in boarders to make ends meet. She had a brother who had survived the war, but had come home damaged. Her brother's plan to marry his childhood sweetheart had been quickly abandoned, as much by him, as by her. He made and sold the odd piece of furniture, but rarely left home.

James tried to slow their leisurely pace, wanting to keep her with him for as long as he could. When they reached their destination, he felt a moment of anxiety. He wanted to kiss her. But apart from the time Lizzie MacNeil had asked him to walk her home after a church social and gagged him with a surprise tongue plunge, he had never really kissed a girl before. He also worried it was too soon. It would have to wait. He handed her the remains of the packaged fudge.

"Here. Take it for the kids at school."

"But you paid so much for such small pieces," she said, elbowing him.

"I'd have paid more if I had to. Please! Take it. I honestly don't have much of a sweet tooth."

"That's too bad. I sell fudge at all the dances."

"So, if I want to see you again, I need to buy ten pounds of maple fudge?"

She put her hand on his forearm, leaned in, and kissed him on the cheek. "That won't be necessary," she said. She turned, opened the door to her parent's modest home, and left him on the front step with a smile that stretched from ear to ear.

After six makins, James felt queasy. He reached for the empty Crisco can he kept on hand for the remains of Stanley's pipe, butted his cigarette, and vowed it would be his last. He stood on the stool to hide the evidence of his lapse of willpower from Margaret and spotted the dusty rum bottle on the top shelf.

"Might help me sleep," he said. He rolled another makin. After two rums, his mood began to lighten. He would tell Margaret everything. He pulled the white string overhead, turning the room to black, and slowly crept along to the stairs.

When he got to their bedroom he pushed on the door. It didn't budge. He tapped lightly, but heard nothing. He whispered her name. Again nothing. He turned the knob, but it was locked. And for the second time that night he slid to the floor. Ten minutes later, he crawled up on the short, horse-hair sofa in the parlor, and for only the second time in their married life, slept apart from his wife. The first time, was not out of anger, but grief. This time, it was both.

Monday, October 31

CHAPTER 1

Mabel woke with a start. Her eyes darted around the unfamiliar room. The images of the storm, Fritz tearing at her da's boots, and the coal shed, all tumbled out of her foggy mind. Her legs felt like they were being jabbed with needles, and her right foot was hot and tender. She flipped the quilt back and pulled her nightgown up to her waist. Even in the dimly-lit room, she could see her legs were swollen. She stood, carefully walked over to the heavy drapes that covered the icy window fronting School Street, and peeked out.

"Still black as night," she said, and sat back on the edge of the bed. She reached over and turned up the lamp to more closely examine her tingling legs. They were swollen for sure, and red. She gasped when she saw how white the toes on her left foot were. "Fuck, I hope I don't lose ya," she said, blessing herself.

She surveyed her surroundings. Her freshly washed shift was draped over a chair, along with her da's clean pit socks. His lone boot was cast off to the side, like nobody knew what to do with it. "Oh, well. Ain't like he was ever gonna use them." She put one pit sock on, and slowly eased the second over her sore foot. She then fixed the bed to appear as if it had never been slept in, and folded Mrs. Cameron's flannel nightgown, like it was being readied for the window display at *Marshall's Fine Ladies' Wear.*

Apart from being so hungry she could eat a horse and chase the driver, she felt pretty good. Good enough to get to work, and put in a few extra hours to repay Mr. and Mrs. Cameron for their kindness.

Mabel opened the door and tiptoed into the hallway, and with every step she took, she whispered, "fuck." She felt her way along, her hand stretched out into the dark, searching for the newel that would lead her downstairs. She had no idea that James was lying awake in the dark, thinking about her, her mother and father, and the damn war.

Mabel smiled when the dark kitchen lit up. She loved this time of day; the quiet and the peace. It was when she felt most productive. She lit the coal stove, and began preparing her dough and greasing her pans. "Careful," she said out loud, mimicking Mrs. Cameron, "use the butter sparinly." She thought of Mrs. Cameron watching her every move. Pretty woman, for sure, but never smiles. Mabel kneaded her sticky dough, thinking of what an odd pairing Mr. and Mrs. Cameron were. Kind of like Aunt Amour and Uncle Roddy, she thought. She pictured her aunt in her hand-me-down coat with the frayed collar, always trailing behind Roddy in his expensive bowler and leather gloves. He looks like an undertaker with his lanky frame and pointy nose. And Amour's so pretty. Da always said he and Amour got their good looks from granny Adshade, but they skipped a generation when I came along. And Ma was pretty, too. Mabel closed her eyes and tried to remember her mother's face, wishing she had a photograph. She'd seen one, once. It was under a doily in Da's room. It was a nice picture, she thought. Me on Ma's lap, and Da standing off to the side with his hand on her shoulder. Be nice if we were smiling, but it'd still be a lovely keepsake. I'd have it hanging on my bedroom wall so I could look at Ma every day. Now, I can barely remember what she looks like. But I remember she was pretty. Real pretty. Imagine, all that pretty in one family, and I got none of it. She ran her hand over the gauze above her eye. "And this sure ain't gonna help," she whispered.

"I'm sorry, did you say something?" James asked, surprising Mabel from the doorway.

Mabel could feel her face get hot. "Oh, don't mind me, Mr. Cameron. I sometimes talk out loud. Crazy I know. Been a bad habit of mine my whole life. Da ain't too fond of it. Can't say as I blame him. I do my best not to, but sometimes my mouth charges right past my brain."

James smiled. "I sometimes do the same. You know, I thought I said there'd be no baking today?"

"But I'm fine, Mr. Cameron. Shoulder's a little stiff, but the kneadin actually helps."

"And your head and feet?"

"All good, Mr. Cameron. I swear. And thank ya so much for rescuin me and callin in Dr. Cohen. I'd have perished for sure, if it weren't for you. And of course, Mr. MacIntyre. And Mrs. Cameron, too. I imagine they must think I'm pretty daft, comin to work on my day off, and endin up near froze to death in yer coal shed. I'm bakin all week and don't expect my wages."

"Mabel, you'll be taking your wages," James said, reaching for the kettle. "Did you have anything to eat?"

"I'm afraid I ate the better part of yer first payment," she said, nodding toward a sticky jar of molasses and the remains of a double-loaf of freshly made bread. "I'm certainly gonna be fixin the bill with Dr. Cohen. That's fer sure."

James changed the subject. "Mabel, your father likely doesn't know where you are. When Stanley comes by, I'll ask that he let him know you're here, safe n' sound." James knew Johnnie couldn't care less about his daughter's whereabouts or well-being, but figured it best not to give him another excuse to use his fists.

"Honestly, Mr. Cameron, no need to trouble Mr. MacIntyre any more than he's already been. I'm sure Da's fine. I'll see him when I get home and explain it all to him." She tensed at the thought of another flying bowl incident when he found out she was so stupid she went to work on her day off, and in the middle of a storm to boot.

"All the same, Stanley can drop by when he does his deliveries and let your father know you're here."

James left to take off the shutters and let the day's business begin. When he opened the door, Stanley was running up the steps. Mabel could see the two talking in the doorway. She brushed her floured hands against her apron, and walked toward them so she could properly thank Mr. MacIntyre for saving her life.

"I came early to check on the girl, and to tell you the Toth boys are orphaned. Matthew fell off the cliff yesterday," Stanley said.

"Dear God," James said, wondering if it was a fall or a jump that left the boys without their only living relative on this side of the ocean.

"The boys!" Mabel cried, putting her hand over her mouth. "Dear God."

James pulled Mabel into him. "Stanley, would you mind gathering up some bread, some canned goods, flour, sugar, and whatever else you think might be needed, and take it to the Toths." He reached in his pants pocket and handed him the keys. "Take my car. Oh, and grab a couple bags of penny candy for the boys. And, Stanley, if you don't mind, could you stop by Mabel's on the way back and let her father know she's here, and she's alright," James sputtered.

Margaret, hearing the commotion below, looked down from her perch atop the stairs to see James cradling Mabel in his arms, and brushing his chin against the crown of her head.

"James!" she seethed. "What's going on?"

"Margaret. Matthew Toth fell off the cliff yesterday. Remember? Mabel used to care for his boys."

Mabel pulled away quickly, blessed herself, and returned to the kitchen. Stanley went off to gather the supplies. Margaret glared down at her husband. "You know, James, there are worse things than orphaned children who have each other and the church to tend to their needs."

James closed his eyes and dropped his head. "And what would that be, Margaret?"

"A mother who buries her son."

"A *mother* who buries her son," James repeated, wondering if she blamed him for their son's death. She measured everyone else's pain against her own, and no one suffered like she did. "I miss him, too, you know?" he said, looking up. She was already gone.

He walked to his room in back of the store and prayed for Matthew Toth and his orphaned sons, and for baby James. He then lifted the lid off his the can of MacDonald's tobacco, rolled himself a makin, and wondered if there really was a God.

CHAPTER 2

James was outside filling the coal scuttle when Stanley pulled up. James could see he was agitated. “You okay, Stanley?”

“The girl’s not safe with him! He said he was going to kill her. Accused me of doing things to her. Came at me with a pan shovel. Would have taken my head off if he wasn’t still drunk.”

James dropped the bucket. “C’mon,” he said, grabbing Stanley’s arm. “I’m gonna kill the bastard.”

“You might want to hold off on that,” Stanley said. “I clocked him. I figure, between that and the booze, he won’t be moving for quite a while. But when you do go, I’m going with you. He’s crazy!”

James smiled, knowing Stanley, with not a pinch of fat to spare, could pack a punch. He could have made good money as a pro boxer. Thirty-four fights, no losses, and one draw that went eleven bare-knuckle rounds before he and his opponent both surrendered. He had talent alright, too much for his own liking. He almost killed Willie Morrison in what was supposed to be a friendly sparring match to help Willie prepare for a run at the national middleweight title. But Dirty Willie, as he was better known, kept gouging Stanley’s eyes and punching him well below the belt. Stanley finally snapped and landed a powerful body blow that brought Willie to one knee. Willie was getting to his feet when Stanley pounded a hard left into the right side of his head. Willie’s head bounced off the canvass and he began twitching. He never fought again. Neither did Stanley.

Mabel peeked out from the doorway of the kitchen and approached Stanley. She held out a grease-stained paper bag containing two loaves of warm bread. "I want to thank ya for what ya did for me! I'd have surely perished if ya hadn't come by," she hollered.

James covered his ears. "Geez, now I'm deaf," he teased.

Stanley took the bag from her. "Smells good. Thank you."

"It is good. Ain't it, Mr. Cameron?"

"Of course," he said, immediately sensing Mabel was disappointed by his lukewarm compliment. "Actually, it's very good. Hands down, the best bread in town."

"If ya say so, Mr. Cameron? It must be true," she said. She turned to Stanley who had his nose in the bag. He looked up at her. "It's a lot of bread for one person," he said.

"Ya'll be glad of that once ya taste it. Anyway, ya look like ya could use some fattenin up. Ya both do," Mabel said, and headed for the kitchen. *It's a lot of bread for one person*, he'd said. She wondered if his words were more than a statement of fact. When she reached the doorway she turned back. Stanley was smiling at her. It was a sad smile, she thought, as she made her way to her kneading table.

James suddenly felt like an awkward intruder. "So, Stanley, we'll go see Johnnie in the morning. I'll pick you up at eight."

"No need. I'll walk."

"You sure?" James asked.

"I'm sure. I like to walk."

"Good then, I'll see you here tomorrow at eight," James said. He wondered what Margaret's reaction would be when he told her Mabel would be staying another night.

CHAPTER 3

Mabel rolled, pulled, pushed, and patted her sticky dough. And with each roll, pull, push, and pat she whispered the name of Matthew Toth and his three boys: Luke, Mark, and John. She repeated their names over and over again, wondering how much hardship God could pile on one family. She was thinking of Mary Catherine and the boys when Mrs. Cameron walked in carrying the nicest pair of boots she'd ever seen.

"You'll need these, Mabel, for your walk home this evening. They might be a little big, but they're certainly better than the one boot you arrived with."

"Thank you, Mrs. Cameron. They're beautiful. I'll get em back to ya tomorrow, all buffed up."

"No, Mabel. Keep them…as a reminder of my generosity."

Mabel thought her tone betrayed her kind offer. She looked at Margaret. Margaret was glaring back.

"But never, my dear, mistake my generosity for naiveté. And know this! You will never, *ever* leave my home with anything that belongs to me. Do you understand me?"

Mrs. Cameron turned on her heels and walked out as quietly and as quickly as she had come in. Mabel stared down at the boots, thinking of the bright orange leaf that had danced in the air, and landed at her feet. She had childishly thought it was a sign of good luck. Now, it seemed more like a bad omen dressed up in a pretty colour. The flying bowl, the early storm, no boots, the stupid butcher paper, Fritz, forgetting it was her day off, Matthew Toth. And now, Mrs. Cameron, who was mad at her for something. God, she prayed, don't take this job from me. And God, please let Da pass the night on York Street.

CHAPTER 4

Mabel was lost in kneading her bread when her face appeared out of nowhere. Her words, as soft as ever, like they were just whispered in her ear. The silhouette of her kneeling at the side of her bed.

"Come, Mabel. Pray with me."

"What are we prayin for, Ma?" Mabel had asked, kneeling beside her mother, and putting her small hands together.

"For forgiveness and strength. They're the only things worth asking for. The only things you and God can work on together."

The beautiful, clear image in Mabel's mind vanished as quickly as it had appeared, when Mr. Cameron walked in.

"Let the oven cool down, Mabel. You've done enough baking for the day. How are the legs and feet holding up?"

"Hardly give em a thought," Mabel lied, looking down at her pit socks and wondering if her toes were still white. "Mrs. Cameron was kind enough to bring me some boots for my walk home."

"Well, you're not going anywhere tonight," James said, firmly. He momentarily wondered if Margaret's generous offer was motivated by kindness, or anger. He decided it must be the latter. "Dr. Cohen still hasn't come by, and he's expecting to see you. Probably still doing his rounds."

"But I'm feelin great. And Da'll be worried," she said, lying for the second time in less than as many minutes.

"Mabel, your father's in an angry mood. Stanley had a chat with him earlier today. I don't want you to go back I 've had a word with him and I'm convinced he'll do you no harm."

"Oh, Da ain't no trouble," Mabel said, unconvincingly.

"Just the same, I'm going to speak with him before you go home. I want to make sure he knows you're not to blame for not getting home last night."

"But what about Mrs. Cameron?" Mabel began, not sure of what else to say.

"Mrs. Cameron will be fine with you staying another night." This time, it was James who sounded unconvinced. "I need to pick up some supplies in town tomorrow. I'll drop in and speak to your father on the way back. For now, why don't you go upstairs and get washed up for supper."

"Thank you, Mr. Cameron, but I'm more tired than hungry," Mabel lied, again. "Maybe I'll pass on eatin."

"You can eat later then," James said, relieved to know Mabel and Margaret wouldn't be sitting across from each other during the evening meal.

Mabel swept the floor one last time and surveyed the kitchen. Satisfied everything was in order, she made her way to the stairs. She stopped at the bottom, praying Mrs. Cameron was in her room, and that her bedroom door was closed.

James went to the back of the store. He needed one last makin before checking on Margaret. He hadn't seen his wife since the morning. She was usually in and out of the store and the kitchen a dozen times by now. No doubt she had her head buried in her Bible or needlepoint. No doubt still mad at him for any number of reasons. He was butting his cigarette when he heard the front door open.

"Sorry I'm so late. Hope I'm not disturbing your supper?" Dr. Cohen called out.

"Not at all. Just glad you're here," James said, pulling the door of the back room shut.

"Took longer to do my calls than I thought. There's something going around that's hitting a lot of people. Flu of some sort."

"A bad one?"

"No such thing as a good one. They had to take two men up from Number Six last night. They were too weak to swing their picks. I also heard the six o'clock trams were a lot lighter in Number Two and Number Twelve. At first I thought it was some kind of union action, but I'm seeing too many people, women and children included, with the same kind of symptoms. Although I'm pretty sure it's not as virulent as the one that hit us three years ago," Dr. Cohen said. He looked down at the floor for a moment, before raising his head and looking at his long-time friend. "I'm sorry, James. That was careless."

James waved his hand. "Don't worry, Thomas. Mabel's upstairs. Go on up."

Thomas looked up to see Margaret coming down the stairs.

"Hello Margaret," he said, easing past her.

"Thomas," she acknowledged. She fixed her gaze on her husband and walked toward him.

"Margaret! I was just about to check on you. I thought you would have started supper by now. Have you had anything to eat today?" James asked.

"I'm not hungry."

He could tell from her tone that neither her Bible nor her needlepoint had softened her mood.

"I don't think it's wise that Dr. Cohen, who has seen so many people exposed to whatever it is that's going round, should be here. Who knows what kind of germs he and *that girl* are bringing into our home?"

"You can't *catch* frostbite. And Margaret, she's not exposing us to anything. We run a business, for goodness sake. People are coming and going all the time. If we're going to catch something, we're going to catch it."

"But who knows what Thomas has been exposed to. And if it wasn't for —"

"Margaret! Keep your voice down. And why, in the name of all that is good and holy, do you dislike her so much? First you're worried about our reputations. Now it's our health. What has that sweet girl done to you other than help pay for that pretty new blouse you're wearing?"

She heard him plain as day.

"James! I want that *sweet girl* of yours gone. I want her out of my home. Tonight! I won't have people gossiping, sullying our reputations. People will talk."

"Well, let them talk," he snapped, throwing his arm in the air. "Let them damn well think and say what they please. And, Margaret? You know who'll be doing the talking? Spreading the ugly rumours? The *holier-than-thous*, like Gladys Ferguson. Folks who go to Mass on Sunday, throw a few pennies on the collection plate, and think that's what makes them a good Christian." He couldn't help himself. "And you, Margaret. You'll never be happy until everyone else is as miserable as you are."

Margaret stared at her husband. He had never spoken to her so harshly. James closed his eyes and put his hand to his forehead. "I'm sorry, Margaret. I didn't mean that. I shouldn't have said... I haven't been sleeping well. And the events of the past couple of days...well, they've taken their toll on—"

"Well, James, I pray to God you sleep well again, tonight. Back on the sofa." She hitched her skirt and quietly returned to her room.

James wondered if his latest exchange with Margaret carried upstairs and their private matters were no longer so private.

Dr. Cohen came downstairs twenty minutes later. He showed no outward signs he was aware of James's argument with Margaret; immediately reporting Mabel would be fine. "She's tough. Her toes are looking better. But she should limit her walking for a while yet. I'd give it at least a week. And for God's sake, tell her to stay away from the MacLeod's dog."

"So, did she tell you how she got the cut on her head?" James asked.

"She did. But she wasn't being truthful. Said she fell on a stick. But the lump and bruising around the gash makes me think she was hit in the head, and that she's lying to protect whoever is responsible."

"It's been a rough day, Thomas. You up for a glass of rum?" James didn't see much of Thomas socially, but he enjoyed his company. He had been a godsend when the baby got sick. He came by every morning and every night, despite his own physical exhaustion. And when the baby died, Thomas continued to drop by to check on Margaret, encouraging her to eat and keep up her strength. Suggesting she get out more, perhaps give more of her time to the church. He'd gently remind her that there was still time for her to have another child. Maybe more than one. But James's prospects of a happy future with Margaret, and a home full of kids, had died on the day they buried their only child.

Thomas could see his friend needed a friend. "It's late… but what the hell. A quick one won't hurt."

James and Thomas went to the back of the store, where James retrieved his bootleg rum from the top shelf. He left to get two glasses. By the time he returned from the kitchen, Thomas was smoking a makin, and rolling another.

"Didn't know you to smoke, Thomas," James said.

"Not as a rule. But every now and then. Hope you're not smoking. You know you've got sensitive lungs and these things don't help."

"It's a rare treat," James replied, thinking he was *treating* himself a little too much lately.

"Thomas? What did you mean when you said Mabel had a hole in her leg?" he asked, handing him his drink.

"Well, not exactly a hole. More like a deep puncture. Real deep, and quite wide. Like she was stabbed with something, and it was twisted about. Whatever it was, it tore away a good chunk of flesh, if not part of the bone. Anyway, it's ugly to look at for sure, but nothing to be worried about."

"So, it's an old wound?"

"Oh, yes. I'd guess it happened years ago."

"Do you think it was an accident?" James asked.

"Doubt it. Can't imagine how you'd end up with a hole that size above the knee. And if it was an accident, no one bothered to tend to it, at least not properly," Thomas said, taking a drink.

"Did you ask Mabel about it?" James asked.

"I did. She seemed embarrassed by it. Claimed she couldn't remember and that it didn't bother her. Hard to imagine she could forget an injury that would have been so painful. Anyway, she quickly changed the subject. So I let it go."

James shook his head in disgust. "I know it was her father. Miserable bastard."

"Wouldn't surprise me in the least," Thomas said. "So, how is Margaret doing? She looks good."

"She's doing much better," James lied. "And Eileen?"

"Same as ever. Busy with Home and School. Always doing this or that. I think she puts in more hours volunteering than I do on the job. Anyway, I'm sure she's home now and wondering where I'm at." Thomas drained the last of his rum. "And I've got another busy day ahead of me tomorrow."

"Understand completely. Say hello to Eileen for us," James said, passing him his hat.

Thomas was walking to the door, then turned around. "That reminds me. Eileen mentioned she'd like to have you and Margaret over for supper. Maybe after the flu settles down and I can get home at a decent hour. And, James. This time, no excuses."

"Sounds wonderful. I'll mention it to Margaret," James said.

"Oh, and bring your wallet so you can settle up your account. You're one of the few I can count on to pay with real money. God knows, I have enough chickens and eggs to put Larry Mendelson out of business," he laughed.

"I will. But, here! Take this," James said. He reached for the bag of bread on the counter and passed it to Thomas. "Mabel made me promise to give it to you."

"Now *this* I can use," Thomas said. "Supper. Don't forget," he repeated.

James watched from the doorway as he drove off, thinking Margaret would once again decline his invitation to supper. He considered calling it a night, but didn't feel tired enough to sleep. He returned to the rear of the store, smoked another makin, poured himself another rum, and thought about the hole in Mabel's leg and his latest argument with Margaret.

It was three in the morning when he woke, slumped over the counter with his head resting on his numb, outstretched arm. He stood and slowly arched his stiff back. He was heading upstairs when he noticed the light in the kitchen. Mabel was greasing her pans.

"Mabel! What are you doing?"

She jumped when he called her name, dropping the pan to the floor. "I'm so sorry, Mr. Cameron," she said, quickly picking it up. "I was tryin to be real quiet. Did I wake ya?"

"No. I fell asleep out back. I was doing the ledger and just woke," he said, worrying he was getting accustomed to lying. "Leave everything as it is and go back to bed. It's way too early to be up."

"I'm not tired. Slept most all a Sunday. Thought I'd get an early start on the bread. Maybe make a few pies for a change with the apples out back. Would that be okay?"

"No," he said, rubbing his eyes.

Mabel didn't expect his answer and her face showed it.

"I mean, yes. Yes, you can make some pies. Just not at this hour. C'mon. You're going back to bed." James put his hand on her elbow and led her to the stairs. "Shush," he said, placing his finger to his lips. "We don't want to wake Margaret."

The caution wasn't necessary. Margaret was sitting in her chair, wide awake. Sleep wasn't about to come to her knowing her husband and that vile girl were downstairs doing things to each other that would see their souls condemned to eternal damnation.

James waited for Mabel to get settled in, then headed to his bedroom. As he feared, the door was closed. For the second night in a row, he climbed onto the short, stiff sofa, praying sleep would come, and he could escape to his dreams.

Tuesday, November 1

CHAPTER 1

James came downstairs feeling groggy. More from the rum he figured, than the uncomfortable counter and sofa that had doubled as his bed. Mabel was already up, with her apples peeled and her pie crusts laid out.

"Good mornin, Mr. Cameron. I got some tea brewin."

"Morning, Mabel," James said. He opened the cupboard and grabbed a cup.

"I could only find three pie tins in the pantry. Do ya think there's any more about?"

"How many pies do you plan to make?"

"As many as I can."

James poured his tea. "And what are we going to do with all those pies, Mabel?"

"Whatcha mean, what are we gonna do with em? We're gonna sell em of course," she said, laughing and shaking her head.

"You can barely keep up with the bread orders. So, are we going to sell less bread?"

"Heck no, Mr. Cameron. We can sell both. And I won't be cuttin back on my bread bakin. No chance of that. I'd just like to try the pies. See how they go over. Ya could probably make more sellin a pie than a double loaf."

"I'll ask Margaret if we have more pie tins. Just go slow for now. Put the pies you're making on the counter. Charge what you think is a fair price, and we'll take it from there."

"I was thinkin that in the summer we could get some berries… some cherries, blueberries, strawberries. I could make all kinds of pie. I could make pumpkin, rhubarb and—"

"Let's stick to the apple and see how that works out," James interrupted. He marveled at the thought of her excitement at the prospect of more work for the same wage.

Margaret appeared in the doorway.

James felt his anxiety grow. "Good morning, Margaret." He was hoping they were not about to have another scene. Mabel wasn't sure what to do.

"Good morning," Margaret said, without looking at either of them.

Mabel walked to the stove and reached for the teapot. "Good mornin, Mrs. Cameron. I made some scones. And I gotta pot a tea on. Can I get ya a cup?"

"I'm perfectly capable of pouring my own, Mabel," Margaret said, breaking the end off of a scone and buttering it.

"Of course," Mabel said, pulling her hand away from the teapot. The tension in the room made her nervous. She wondered why Mrs. Cameron disliked her so much. And what did she mean never take anything that belonged to her? I only ever stole one thing my whole life, and I'm not about to do anything that stupid again, she thought.

"Mrs. Cameron? Mr. Cameron said I could make apple pies to sell."

"Did he now?"

James was waiting for his wife to explode, but she just poured her tea, ate her scone, and watched Mabel roll out her pie crust.

"I told Mr. Cameron I found three tins. But I got enough apples to make a coupla dozen. Do ya think ya might have any more I could use?"

"I'm afraid not."

"Well, I got a few at home. I'll bring em here."

Mabel knew Mrs. Cameron wasn't in the mood for small talk. She put her head down and focused on her baking.

"I'm volunteering at the guild this morning, James. I'll need you to drive me to the parish after breakfast," Margaret said.

He was surprised her voice was so level. "And what time will I pick you up?"

"By one."

"Stanley is coming by this morning. We have some errands in town and we're going to stop by Mabel's to let Johnnie know she's doing fine and will be home after work. We'll drop you off and pick you up on the way back."

"And who's tending the store?" Margaret asked.

"Douglas. He should be here any minute."

Margaret left without saying another word. She met Stanley and her sinful husband at the car fifteen minutes later. Stanley opened the front door for Margaret to sit beside her husband. She stepped in back. Stanley, immediately sensed the rift and tried to fill their awkward time together with talk of the weather and rumours of a strike. He and James were both grateful when they arrived at St. Anthony's.

"Have a good day, gentlemen," Margaret said, getting out of the car.

They both knew she didn't mean it.

Fifteen minutes later, Stanley and James were on Commercial Street. They decided to do their business in town before stopping at Johnnie's. James didn't want to have to drag him out of bed. Stanley went in one direction, and James in the other. James stopped at the savings and loan, Ferguson's Formulary, and then Mendelson's, the only place in town to buy good lamb. They met up an hour later across from Isaac Greene's boarded up shoe repair.

"Wait here a minute, Stanley. I'm going to run into the clerk's office. I won't be long." James crossed the two-lane street, climbed the narrow stairway, and walked in. Lizzie MacNeil had her head down and was rummaging through a pile of papers. *Christ*, he thought, *not her*.

"Hello, Lizzie. How are you?"

"Well, look at you, Jimmy," she said, smiling. "Ya haven't changed a bit. Yer as handsome as ever."

Lizzie was the only one who ever called him Jimmy, and he hated it.

"Thank you," James said, resisting the temptation to return the compliment. Lizzie was nice enough, and very attractive, but he didn't want her to get any ideas. He cringed as he thought of the night she shoved her tongue down his throat. She was still single and growing even more desperate to shake the title of old maid.

"This a personal or professional visit?" she asked, resting her elbows on the counter and smiling.

"I'm looking for a birth record," he replied, sensing her disappointment.

Lizzie straightened up. "Well, ya came to the right place. I'm in charge of records. Birth records, death records, marriage records. You name it, and I'm yer girl."

James gave her a look to show he was impressed. "That's fabulous."

"And whose record are ya inquirin about?"

"Mabel Adshade's."

Lizzie had no idea who Mabel Adshade was, but was curious why Jimmy might be asking. "Is she a relation?"

"No. She's my employee and a friend of Margaret's," he lied. He felt it couldn't hurt to remind her he was married. "Miss Adshade asked if I'd stop in and check on her record of birth."

"Not sure she was born?" Lizzie said, laughing at her own joke.

James smiled awkwardly.

She slapped her hand over his. "Wait here," she said, and disappeared down the hall. She came back a few minutes later wearing a fresh coat of bright red lipstick, and carrying a well-used tome. "What's her mother's maiden name?"

"Ellie… Eleanor MacKinnon," James said, thinking her garish

lips detracted from her otherwise pretty face.

"And her father's?"

James paused. "John Adshade."

"Date of birth?"

"She didn't give me that. Do you need it?"

"Makes it easier. But since it's you, Jimmy, let's see what comes up," she said, winking. He thought she was making a sexual innuendo, but wasn't quite sure.

"Adshade. Adshade. Adshade," Lizzie repeated, as she ran her finger down the long yellowed page. "Good thing it's not a common name round here. If it were a 'Mc' or a 'Mac', we'd be here till the cows come home. Here it is. Mabel Grace Adshade. Born to John F. Adshade and Eleanor M. Adshade, née MacKinnon. I'll write out the official record of birth fer ya."

"Thanks, Lizzie. I really appreciate your help. Is there a fee?"

"Not for you, Jimmy."

He put a dollar on the counter. "For your help."

"Drop by any time," Lizzie hollered, as James quickly descended the stairs. When he reached the bottom, he looked at it more closely. Mabel Grace Adshade. Born, Nov 24, 1915, Pleasant Bay, Victoria County.

Mabel was seventeen, soon to be eighteen. He'd surprise her with a cake on her birthday. When he left the clerk's office, Stanley was waiting exactly where James had left him, talking to Dirty Willie.

James waited for the cars to pass, watching Stanley reach into his pocket and hand Willie a bill he could ill afford to part with. When they met up, James gave his good friend a pat on the back. "Let's go and have a heart-to-heart with Johnnie."

They were there in less than five minutes. James knocked on the door several times before he began pounding. "Johnnie! It's James Cameron! I want to talk to you about Mabel. Johnnie! Open up! I know you're home. Johnnie! I can see the smoke from the chimney."

Johnnie swung the door open, revealing two shiners and a broken nose. "What the fuck do ya want with my daughter?"

"Calm down. No one's looking for any trouble."

"Yeah? Then why ya got the goon with ya?" He looked at Stanley. "I was just gettin ready to go and report ya to the police for assault, ya miserable piece of shit. Don't think yer not gonna pay for showin up at my house and comin at me like a fuckin maniac," he said, glaring at Stanley.

James looked past Johnnie, wondering where the pan shovel was. "Johnnie? I'm not going to mince words. I know you beat Mabel. And it's going to stop or you'll be the one the police will be investigating."

"Fuck you, Jimmy!" It was the second time in the same day someone called him the name he hated. "What the hell's up with you and my daughter? Not getting it at home anymore? That ugly wife of yers not spreadin her legs for ya, so yer goin after the young ones? That's it. Ain't it, Jimmy? Couldn't jab the mother, so yer jabbin my daughter."

James lowered his head and tried to control the rage washing over him.

"And, here, I had ya figured as a pussy who likes to stick his thin, little dick into little boys' asses. Hell! I had ya pegged for killin that queer Jew boy."

James, thirty pounds lighter and a good four inches shorter, charged at Johnnie like it was the final scrum for the Caledonia Cup and he was the team captain. He screamed, and with a fury, drove Johnnie back from the doorway to the far wall. He held him by the neck of his filthy undershirt. "Listen to me, you miserable bastard. If you so much as raise your voice to that girl again, I'll kill you with my bare hands."

Stanley stepped through the doorway as Johnnie hurled a hawker in James's face.

"Get outa my house, ya fuckin arsehole!" Johnnie screamed at James.

James shoved Johnnie hard against the wall, picked up a rag on the counter, and wiped the runny snot from his face. "Actually, Johnnie," he said evenly and calmly, "this is my house. Bought it from Roddy more than three years ago. Ever wonder why your cheap brother-in-law never comes looking for his rent? Because he doesn't own this place. I do."

"Yer full of shit."

Johnnie never saw James's fist coming, but he certainly felt it. And for the second time in just a little more than twenty-four hours, Mabel's da hit the floor like a sack of potatoes.

James turned to Stanley. "Let's get out of here."

"Sure am glad I didn't come up against you in the ring," Stanley said, clearly impressed with his friend.

"No worries, there. I must have brittle bones. I think I broke my hand."

CHAPTER 2

James pounded his fists against the steering wheel, before screaming and throwing his already swollen hand in the air. He was angry he let Johnnie get the better of him. He knew he should never have told him he owned the house. Sooner or later, Johnnie would want to know why he let him stay there and never charged rent. "Idiot! Idiot!" he said, this time banging his head against the steering wheel.

"James? Did I hear you tell Johnnie you own the place?" Stanley asked.

James put the car in gear and drove off. He made Stanley swear he would never tell another living soul, then filled him in on why he let a man he hated so much live rent-free in a home that he owned. It wasn't Johnnie he wanted to help, but Mabel.

Stanley thought of his friend's circumstances. James made a living that most men in town would envy, but he certainly wasn't a rich man. And while he always knew James to be generous, he never fully realized the lengths James would go to quietly help someone in need. Stanley remembered his Aunt Geraldine quoting the Bible. *When you give to the needy, do not let your left hand know what your right hand is doing, so that your giving may be in secret.*

As they approached the parish hall, James nodded in Margaret's direction. "I think my day is about to get worse." Margaret was out front, pacing back and forth. She looked fit to be tied.

Stanley opened the door to let Margaret in the front, but she once again got in the back. He immediately decided he'd rather walk the short distance home than sit in the car a minute longer.

"I'll walk from here," he said, giving James a sympathetic look.

"You're sure?" James asked.

"I'm sure," Stanley said. He stepped out of the car, closed the door, and wondered where all the smoke was coming from.

CHAPTER 3

"You're late," Margaret huffed from the back seat.

James glanced at his watch as he maneuvered his way onto Dominion Street. "It's only ten to one."

"Gladys barely acknowledged me."

James looked at his wife. He knew she was hankering for a fight, but couldn't help himself. "Lucky you."

"She's my friend."

"Gladys Ferguson's a bitch."

"How dare you say that! She's a God-fearing woman who does a lot of good in this town," Margaret spat.

"As if spreading rumours and causing trouble is God's work."

"It's your fault, you know?"

Exasperated, James threw his swollen hand into the air. "I did you a favour. She's an ugly woman in every—"

"What did you do to your hand?" Margaret asked.

"It's nothing. I was helping Larry Mendelson move some crates. I jammed it." Christ, it hurt. Maybe it *is* broken.

"Is it broken?"

James slowly extended his fingers, then brought them into a fist. "Feels fine," he lied, again.

"All the same, you better have Thomas take a look."

James thought she sounded genuinely concerned and decided to try and lighten the mood. "Stanley said it's fine. He used to be a boxer. He'd know." He turned his head to look at her. "That reminds me, Thomas and Eileen invited us to supper again."

"You can go if it pleases you. But I won't be going."

"I can't go without you! How would I explain your absence? I don't understand why you don't like them. They're fine people."

"I don't mind him so much, but I don't care for her."

"But why?"

"I have my reasons."

"What reasons?"

Margaret turned her head to the side and looked out the window. "It doesn't matter. She just rubs me the wrong way."

James decided to leave it at that, wondering if it was because Eileen married outside the church. They drove the rest of the way in silence. When they entered the store, Margaret proceeded directly upstairs, adding to his bleak mood. Douglas peeked out from the kitchen, waved, then ducked back in behind the doorway to renew his banter with Mabel. James slowly unbuttoned his coat and looked about. He wondered what his parents would have thought of all the changes he made to their modest home, hoping they'd have approved.

He closed his eyes and pictured the pale green paint in the living area that his father loved and his mother hated. He could see his father in his armchair, and his mother sweeping their braided oval rug. He could see the upholstered footstool with the burnt orange flowers that had been his favourite perch. He opened his eyes, turned to his right, and walked over to one of the few visible reminders of his youth, laying his hand over the handle of the door that once led to his bedroom— the place he would go with his books to escape the worried whispers of his parents— who constantly feared there might be another cave in and the mine would be shut down for good.

He turned the knob and pushed the door forward, looking past the array of empty boxes and crates scattered about, imagining his narrow bed against the far wall. His melancholy weighed on him. He pulled the door closed and looked to where his parents once slept in their large wrought iron bed. A wide landing leading upstairs to an open parlour, the master bedroom, a one-time nursery, and a bathing area, had replaced their lair. Little of anything of their original home remained. The small, one-story bungalow he had once shared with his parents now extended outwards and upwards in anticipation of a large family, and a livelihood earned outside of the pit. James's chest tightened as he looked at the long counter adorned with Mabel's bread and samples of his wares, and the floor-to-ceiling shelves that were too slow to empty. He thought of the day Douglas's father, Nelson, had helped him mount the hard maple countertop on top of its huge wooden posts; cutting in half the area he and his father once sat discussing sports and union politics.

Douglas emerged from the kitchen, walked behind the counter, and put two double loaves on the counter. James smiled at him, thinking of how much Douglas looked like his father, and how proud Nelson MacGuire would be that his son had grown into such a fine young man. He missed Nelson's hearty laugh and big smile, recalling the day he had heard that his overturned fishing boat had washed ashore twenty miles up the coast.

"They'll be gone in no time," Douglas said, hovering over the glistening mounds, and inhaling their warm, buttery scent.

"You can head home now. Oh, and take a loaf for your mother," James said, remembering how generous Douglas's father was with both his brawn and his fresh catch.

"Ma'd love that. She hardly ever has time to bake anymore since she started at the Stamp and Post."

Mabel peeked out from the doorway. "Mr. Cameron? I can't keep up with demand."

"I see that. Douglas told me that as fast you put the bread out, it's gone."

"Did he also tell ya that we sold three pies for thirty cents each? Oh, and I told folks they only got the pie if they promised to bring their tin back tomorrow," she said proudly.

Douglas, with one arm in his coat sleeve, raised his eyebrows, and nodded in James direction, confirming Mabel wasn't lying. Mabel smiled her appreciation to the young man who made her laugh and ducked back in the kitchen. James saw Douglas out, then joined Mabel. She had both hands buried in a large, gold-coloured bowl. "Mr. Cameron? I was thinking we should charge extra if they use our tins, and we'd give em their money back when they return em. Maybe five cents. Whatcha think?"

James was thinking the margins on the bread and the pies weren't great, but they were certainly increasing traffic in the store and the balance on the ledger was finally moving in the right direction. "I think it's a wonderful idea, Mabel. It'll bring customers back, for sure," he said. He walked to the counter and reached for the kettle.

"That's what I was thinkin, too," Mabel said, looking back at him over her shoulder. "I was wonderin—" She jumped when the kettle hit the floor, its thin blue lid rolling under the table.

James was cradling his swollen hand.

"What happened to yer hand? It looks broke," Mabel said, quickly picking up the kettle and putting the lid in place.

James was not about to tell her his hand didn't look half as bad as her father's face. He'd let Johnnie do the explaining. He knew one thing for sure; Johnnie wasn't about to tell Mabel, or anyone else for that matter, that *the pussy* put the dukes to him. "Mishap at Mendelson's."

"Must be good n' sore? Can I do anythin for ya? Want me to make ya some tea?"

"Have you ever rolled a makin?"

"Roll em all the time for Da."

James walked out of the kitchen, turned to his left, and opened the door to the long, narrow room that had become his refuge. This is where he came to think, pray, and cry. And lately, he thought, it was where he came to get away from Margaret, to smoke, and drink. He pulled the overhead string that lit up the windowless room, with its foot-wide counter, wall of drawers and cupboard doors, and creosote aroma. He then reached for the familiar green and white can with the image of a smiling young woman wearing a red tam. Mabel walked in behind him, pulled a stool out from under the counter, and sat down. James handed her the can and packet of thin papers, and watched her expertly fashion the tobacco leaves into tight, thin cylinders.

"You were about to ask me something," James said, as Mabel licked the sticky sides of the paper.

"Oh, yeah. Just wonderin if it'd be possible to take one of the pies over to Mary Catherine's? That's Catherine with a C. She's lookin after the Toth boys, and I know she's hurtin, too."

"Then bring her a pie and anything else you think they might need."

"Ya won't have one for supper tonight since we sold the other three, but I'll make more tomorrow and be sure to set one aside for you and Mrs. Cameron."

"Why don't you make one for Stanley while you're at it? And, Mabel, I'll drive you home tonight. Dr. Cohen said you should limit your walking for at least a week."

"Really, Mr. Cameron. I'll be fine. I got the lovely boots Mrs. Cameron gave me. And I won't be cuttin through the MacLeod's field no more, that's for sure. If Fritz doesn't kill me, Dr. Cohen will."

"All the same, I'll take you home tonight. And I've made arrangements with Stanley to get you back and forth for the rest of the week. But there's one condition. You start at seven-thirty. We can't ask Stanley to pick you up before the sun comes up."

"Then, I'll just have to stay late," Mabel said, smiling. She turned on her heels and headed for the kitchen.

James returned to the front of the store, relieved a slow but steady stream of customers kept his mind from thinking too much about the past. He looked at his watch. It was going on three and Margaret hadn't come out of her room since they arrived home. He walked upstairs to check on her. Just as he thought, she was in their bedroom doing needlepoint.

"Margaret? Can I get you anything?"

"No."

"Okay, then. Just wanted to check. I forgot to mention, I picked up some fresh lamb at Mendelson's this morning. I'll make supper. I'll drive Mabel home and get things started when I get back. Hope you don't mind waiting?"

The needle went into Margaret's finger, but she didn't flinch. And she didn't look up.

"I'll come get you when it's ready, then," he said, pulling the door over. He heard the chimes announcing a new customer. He stopped halfway down the stairs. It was Stanley. James immediately knew something was wrong and rushed toward him.

"What's wrong? Is it your aunt?"

Stanley shook his head. "No."

James put his hand on his shoulder. "What is it? What happened?"

Stanley tried to talk, but couldn't bring himself to say the words out loud. Tears ran down his face. James led his friend to the rear of the store, opened the rum, and poured it into the two sticky glasses he and Thomas drank out of the night before.

"The ponies... the ponies are gone. Fire." Stanley wiped his face with the back of his hand.

James sat down heavily, pulled a second stool out for Stanley, and handed him his rum. "Dear God. I'm sorry."

Stanley tried to collect himself. "There...there wasn't anything in the barn to cause the fire. Took the kerosene lamps in this morning to refill them. They're still on my kitchen table."

James thought of Johnnie's warning to Stanley, wondering if he had anything to do with it.

"Neighbours couldn't get the ponies out, but kept it from spreading to the house. Barn is completely gone. Mrs. MacNeil's side is charred in the rear."

"I'm so sorry, Stanley."

The two sat across from one another without much talk. Stanley, heartbroken for his ponies. James, heartbroken for his friend. When the next customer entered the store, Stanley headed for the door.

James begged him to stay, but Stanley would have none of it. James then tried to convince him to let him drive him home, but again, Stanley refused, insisting he needed the air.

"Stanley. I'll pick you up tomorrow at seven so I can get back to the store and start the stove for Mabel. I have a few odd jobs I was putting off. You can give me a hand. And, I don't want any guff, I'm paying you."

Stanley nodded and walked out. James finished up with his latest customer, then went to tell Mabel about the fire.

"What'll he do now?" Mabel asked, blessing herself.

"I'm hoping he'll help out at the store. Lots of things need fixing. Thought I'd put up more shelving. Maybe expand the hardware section." James had always wanted to make improvements to the store, but put it off knowing he would have to take out a loan, something he was always loathe to do. A strike, or another cave in at one of the mines, could bring financial ruin. He thought of Stanley's circumstances and weighed the consequences of his decision. It was risky for sure, but a risk worth taking.

"Or maybe the bakery?" Mabel said.

"What?" James asked, as he thought of his meagre balance at the savings and loan.

"Instead of expanding the hardware section, why not expand the bakery?"

"It's time for you to call it a day," James said.

For the first time since she started the job, Mabel didn't protest. She'd normally stay as long as should could to avoid her da and the shack, but tonight she knew there was another hardship to face. She was going to see Mary Catherine and the Toth boys.

James looked up and down the street in the event another customer might be in sight. "You've' got two minutes before the train pulls out of the station," he yelled into the kitchen. He flipped the cardboard sign hanging on the door announcing the store was closed for the day.

"I'm here."

He turned. Mabel was wearing his wife's boots and holding her pie-to-go. "If it's not outa yer way, can ya just drop me off at the Toths? It's only a hop, skip and jump from there to the shack. I promise I won't be doin hardly any walkin. Cross my heart," she said, making the sign of the cross.

As they neared the Toths, James looked at Mabel. "Mabel, if your father so much as raises a hand to you, you have to tell me. You have to swear you'll tell me."

"Da ain't as bad as ya think, Mr. Cameron," she lied.

"Just the same, if he tries to harm you in any way, you need to tell me. You need to promise me, Mabel?"

Mabel made a point of keeping her promises, but wasn't sure this was one she could keep. She closed her eyes and crossed her fingers. "Yes."

"Remember, Mabel! A promise is a promise."

She stepped down from the car and looked at her handsome chauffeur. "Mr. Cameron," she paused, looking for the right words. "Yer a good man. A kind man. Thanks for always lookin out for me."

"Good night, Mabel. See you in the morning."

Mabel cried on the way into the Toths. Mr. Cameron cried on the drive home. Both for different reasons.

CHAPTER 4

James anxiety grew as he drove back home. He'd tell Margaret everything and hope she'd understand and forgive him. He'd bought the lamb knowing it was her favourite. He immediately started the evening meal, careful to use his sore hand sparingly. Boiled potatoes, some carrots, and braised lamb. He set the table using the china normally reserved for guests or special occasions, and lit the candles. They used to always have candles at supper. That had stopped three years ago, too. The only candles lit since, were in church. He surveyed the room, hoping it would help lighten her spirits. He opened the oven to check on the lamb. Supper was just minutes away. He went upstairs to let Margaret know.

"Margaret," he said. "Everything's ready to go. Just waiting on you, dear."

She was lying in bed, with the covers partially covering her head. "I won't be eating."

"Is it another headache?"

"No."

"But I have the lamb. And you haven't eaten anything all day?"

"I've had my fill."

"Fill of what, Margaret?"

"Fill of you," she whispered.

James stood there absorbing the venom of her words, staring at his wife, draped in her sorrow, self-pity and anger. He turned slowly, walked to the door, and pulled it behind him, without shutting it completely. He made his way to the top of the stairs, put his hand on the banister, and looked down. He felt deflated. Then, he heard the door close. He turned and looked back, remembering the promise they had made to each other when they were first married. No matter how angry they were, they would never close their bedroom door on one another. Tonight, for the third night in a row, he doubted it would ever open again. He started his descent. When he neared the bottom, he flopped down hard, put his elbows on his knees, and his head in his hands. He no longer questioned whether his wife still loved him. He knew the answer. He looked around the store thinking he should sell it, give Margaret the money, and move on. He shook his head, knowing he'd never do it. He could smell the lamb. He got up, walked into the kitchen, blew out the candles, and watched the black smoke drift upward. He felt numb as he took the roaster from the oven, and returned the table to its unadorned state. He then shut the light off, thinking it was symbolic of what had happened to their marriage. He started to head back upstairs to the sofa, but stopped. Instead, he went to the room in back, where he'd find his rum, and hopefully some relief.

He poured one, then another, as he drew in the harsh smoke from the makins Mabel had rolled for him. He picked up his ledger and tried to focus on the numbers, but tossed it to the side. He looked at the rum bottle, wondering if he should have another, and thought about the time he had had his first drink. He was with Percy and Ellie. He smiled, recalling how happy he had been back then. How the three of them did everything together. Swimming at the Gut, skating on Nash's pond, picking blueberries behind the Dowe farm. They had a special bond. They were inseparable. Each an only child in a neighborhood full of families of five or more. Each wishing they had a sister or brother. But they'd had each other. He remembered Percy saying that if they had come from big families they wouldn't have become the Misfits, the name he dubbed them on one of their first outings together. Ellie argued that God intended for them to be together, and that it had nothing to do with the fact they didn't have brothers or sisters. It's all part of God's grand plan, she'd said. Percy, James thought, was like a big brother. And, Ellie, the sweetest, most beautiful girl in the world.

"Fuckin war," James said, picturing Percy's big grin as he waved his good-to-go papers in the air. 'Can't be any worse than the pit,' he recalled him saying.

James closed his eyes and thought of the final hours they spent together. Ellie and Percy, sitting on their side of the booth, held their straws between their fingers, their mouths at the ready. "No cheating, James," Ellie warned, as she started the countdown. "One… two… three." They sucked their chocolate malt dry in record time, Percy showing his appreciation with a large belch that resulted in a derisive look from their waitress and a playful swat on the arm from Ellie.

James opened his eyes, picked the rum bottle up and brushed it with the back of his sore hand. He started to cry as he remembered the three of them walking from the Five and Dime to the brook. "Look what I got," Percy had said, reaching in his jacket and holding up the half-empty bottle for inspection. "Da gave it to me on the condition Ma never find out. Said if I'm man enough to go to war, I'm man enough to drink." The rum was gone as fast as the chocolate malt. This time it was Ellie who burped. The three of them had started to laugh, lightly at first, and then with abandon. Then, the quiet crept in with the cold and Ellie began to cry. They got up and walked back to Number Two, hand-in-hand-in-hand, with Ellie in the middle. James remembered Ellie squeezing his hand, tighter and tighter, as they approached his front step. "Well, James, this is where we say good-bye. But just for now. Right?" she had said.

"You're not coming to the station in the morning?"

"I'd be a snotty mess. Promise me you'll write."

"I promise."

"And promise me you'll be careful and come home safe."

"I will."

James put his hand to his cheek, remembering the feel of her lips as she stretched up and kissed him. "I love you, James Cameron," she'd said. Then, she turned, rested her head against Percy's shoulder and the two of them walked off, still hand-in hand. He wanted to keep walking with them. He wanted to run back to the enlistment office and say it had all been a big mistake. "Bye, Ellie. I love you, too," he whispered, as the silhouettes of the two people he loved most in the word disappeared into the darkness.

James topped up his rum and lit another makin. He could still picture his mother and father, and Percy's mother and father, Rita and Joe, standing next to each other, waving to them from the platform. Their fathers looking proud, their mothers like they were ready to burst into tears. Then, she appeared in her pretty yellow coat, standing out from a sea of black and grey. She'd said she wasn't going to come, but there she was, holding two bouquets of freshly picked daisies. He recalled whistling and waving, and shouting her name. But neither he, nor Percy could be heard over the throngs of well-wishers, flag wavers, and the noise of the train that had already started to pull out. James remembered how he and Percy ran from one open window to the next, elbowing others out of their way, and calling her name. She didn't see them. But they could see her, until Johnnie walked in front of her, dwarfing her small frame. James kept looking until the platform was out of sight. Percy was already sitting down, opening his grandfather's old pit can. "Ya know, those flowers were for me?" he'd said, grinning and taking a huge bite of his baloney sandwich.

James, his eyes closed, swayed unsteadily on his stool. It'd be the last time he'd see his father. And it would be years before he'd see Ellie again. He felt himself falling forward and opened his eyes, throwing his foot out to keep himself upright. "Fuck you, Johnnie! Miserable bastard."

CHAPTER 5

Mabel left the Toths feeling like her body and mind were worn out. Her friend was heartbroken. Mary Catherine wanted to take in the orphaned boys, but had no means to care for them. Her father's meagre salary barely provided for his small family, let alone three growing boys; one still a baby.

Mabel walked home, thinking about what she could do to help. When she neared the shack, she looked up to see smoke coming from the chimney, and light escaping the kitchen window. "Damn," she said. She began to tremble. She stood there for several minutes trying to get her shaking under control, and her mind in order. She remembered the promise she made to Mr. Cameron, walked up to the door, and went in.

The place was full of smoke. She thought the coal stove must have backed up. She ran into the kitchen. It wasn't the stove. Da and two of his buddies were chain smoking makins, and draining the last of two bottles of whisky and a bottle of rum.

"Da! What happened to yer face?"

"Well, if it ain't my long, lost daughter. Where the fuck you been? Ya been out screwin around? Better notta been out there spreadin yer chubby, little legs for that goon."

"Da, what happened to ya?"

"Got jumped by a bunch a niggers from Aberdeen. I might not look too pretty, buy ya should see *them*. Must have been six or seven of em against yer old man. I left three or four of em black and blue. Not that ya'd ever be able to tell. Hey, Billy? Did ya get it? I left the niggers black and blue."

Billy was sitting at the table with his head in his hands. Johnnie whacked him with a dishcloth.

Billy opened his eyes. "I heard ya."

"Dumb arse can't hold his liquor," Johnnie said.

"I got it, Johnnie," Eddie slurred.

"Sure, Eddie. Nothin escapes you. Ya got a mind like a fuckin steel trap."

Mabel knew Eddie was simple and didn't pick up on her father's mean humour. "Did ya go to the police, Da?"

"Now, why'd I do that? They're useless."

"When did it happen?"

"Last night. Just mindin my own business and attacked outa nowhere fer no reason."

Mabel wondered why Mr. Cameron never mentioned anything to her about her da's appearance. Probably didn't want to upset her. Not that someone putting the pucks to her da would upset her that much. She blessed herself for having such a mean thought.

"Mabel? What's here to eat? Me and the boys are starvin."

"There's sardines. I'll make up some sandwiches."

"I love sardines," Eddie said.

"Ya just love free food," Johnnie said, shoving him.

Mabel put a plate of mustard and sardine sandwiches on the table, took one for herself, and went to her room, grateful Da didn't punish her with his fists for not cooking his Sunday supper.

She had no idea Johnnie was telling the boys that the washed-up old boxer who nearly killed Dirty Willie was fuckin his good-fer-nothin daughter.

Wednesday, November 2

CHAPTER I

Mabel woke with her head pounding, her body aching, her nightgown pulled up past her waist, and an empty rum bottle on the floor. She squeezed her eyes shut and brought her hand up to the side of her head, running it across a huge lump. She then spread her legs and looked down at the bloody sheet; physical proof of what she already knew.

She leaned over the side of her bed, threw up the remains of her sardine and mustard sandwich, and began to sob. She screamed, sat up, and turned her anger on the bloodstained pillow that was evidence of her shame. She thrashed at it until her arms were sore. She picked it up and threw it hard against the wall, knocking a picture of Jesus off the wall. She jumped off the bed and began wildly clawing at her nightgown, before slumping to the floor in exhaustion. She stayed there until the dark sky turned grey, and for the first time in her life, didn't care about being late for work.

She knew her da didn't do it. As vile as he was, he would never touch her in that way. Apart from the slaps, punches and odd kick, he'd never touched her inappropriately. She wondered if it was Eddie the simpleton, Billy, or God forbid, both. No, Da might not have done the deed, but he was responsible for it. "I'm gonna kill the fuckin bastard," she cursed, not caring if he was within earshot.

She got up, felt faint, and sat back down on the floor. She then turned onto her knees, laid her head against the side of her bed, and prayed. Dear God in heaven. Why? Why Lord? Tell me what I did to offend you. I won't do it again. Forgive me God, and give me strength.

She thought she heard a knock on the front door. She listened. It was louder this time. She slowly got to her feet, walked to the mirror, ran her hands under her eyes, and combed her hair with her fingers. The knock came again, this time with more urgency. She walked down the hall and through the kitchen where Da was sprawled out over the table. There was no sign of Eddie or Billy, just the remains of the damage they'd done the night before. She walked to the door, pulled back the sheer curtain, and peeked through the small window. She opened the door a crack.

"You okay, Mabel?" Stanley asked.

"I slept late. What time is it?" she asked hoarsely.

Stanley didn't respond.

"What time is it?" she repeated.

"Just a little past seven," he said.

Mabel didn't feel like making bread today, but she also knew she couldn't stay home with her da, fearing she'd take her bread knife to him. "I'll just be a minute."

Stanley thought she looked like she had been crying. "Maybe I can come in while you get ready?" he asked, moving forward and placing his hand on the door.

"No! I'll just be a minute," she said, pushing the door closed. She ran down the hall, took off her soiled nightgown, and poured some cold water on a washcloth, running it over her face and the lump on her head. She twisted the cloth over the basin and watched the clear water turn pink. She then gently rubbed it against her burning, violated parts, and threw it roughly into the basin. She rinsed her mouth, gently brushed her hair, and briefly studied the image the tiny mirror reflected back; her swollen eyes and bandaged forehead. She rushed back to her room, and quickly put on some clean undergarments and a frock. She made her way down the hallway, hesitated, then returned to her bedroom. She shoved some clothes into a tote that had belonged to her ma and headed for the kitchen. She stopped and looked down at her da slumped over the table. "Bastard!" she said, pushing him off his chair and onto the floor. He barely stirred.

Stanley thought he heard a thump. He was about to open the door when Mabel pulled it open and rushed past him, throwing her bag on the seat, and climbing in beside it. He instinctively knew not to talk, or ask any questions. He also knew Johnnie didn't heed James's warning. He just quietly drove along, his fists clutching and unclutching the steering wheel. He looked at Mabel. She was staring out the passenger window with her arms resting over the black and green floral brocade bag on her lap. He could see the flat, damp mass on the side of her head, and a tinge of pink below her left ear. He was going to kill her father.

James was opening up the shutters when he saw them approach. He opened the door for Mabel. "You're late," he said, his tone conveying surprise, not disappointment.

"Sorry. I slept in. Won't happen again. I promise. I'll stay late," she said.

"No need for that. Just glad you are here. I was beginning to worry the car might have broken down. Coal stove's lit and the oven is already piping hot."

James looked at Stanley, his eyes asking if everything was alright. Stanley just shrugged. He considered telling James about the blood in her hair, but feared his friend would do something stupid. And if anybody was going to do something stupid, it was going to be him.

Stanley and James went out back to discuss James's plans to expand the store. James offered Stanley the job, but Stanley declined. James persisted, swearing it was something he had been planning for a long time. "You need a job, and I need a job done. It works out for both of us," he insisted. Stanley finally agreed.

"Take the car and go home for now," James said. "You can come by later to take Mabel home. We'll get a start on things as soon as I secure the loan."

CHAPTER 2

Stanley arrived home to find the widow MacNeil's oldest son, Angus, examining the charred remains of the barn. Angus took off his flat cap. "Sorry bout yer ponies," he said.

"Thanks," Stanley said, his eyes focused on the rubble that used to be his barn, and home to his ponies. "Tell your mother I'll replace her burnt shingles."

"Me and the boys can see to that. Any idea how it started?"

"No. My lamps weren't even in the barn."

"I got my suspicions."

Stanley turned sharply toward Angus. "Did you see someone around the property?"

"Just before I saw the smoke, I passed a coupla guys. Nobody I recognized from the neighbourhood. Then someone yells fire and one of them takes off. Then the other guy chases after him. Seemed odd to me, that while everyone else was runnin toward the fire, they were running in the opposite direction."

"What they look like?"

"One had a limp. Looked kinda simple. The other guy was about six feet. Had dark, greasy hair. Figure they were both in their early twenties."

Stanley knew right away that Angus was describing Johnnie's lackeys, Eddie and Billy.

"Ring any bells?" Angus asked.

Stanley shook his head. “None.”

“Think we should go to the police?”

“No,” Stanley said, shaking his head again.

“Ya know, they coulda burnt down the whole place,” Angus said, pointing to the singed shingles on the back of his mother’s half of the house. “Might be worth filin a report.”

“It’d be a waste of time. They’re useless.”

“Anyway, let me know when yer ready to start the cleanup and I’ll gather up the boys.”

“Appreciate that, Angus,” Stanley said, dreading the gruesome task ahead of him. He watched Angus disappear around the corner of the house and stood alone, surveying his heartache. He reached down to move a large blackened timber and saw the scorched rump of what he instinctively knew was Winnie. He took off his hat, knelt down, and moved his hand slowly down her shank to the small shoed-hoof poking out of dusty, the grey ashes. “You were a good girl. A loyal friend. You too, Willie,” he whispered as he patted her. “Don’t worry. I’ll get the bastards who did this to you,” he choked.

CHAPTER 3

By two o'clock, Mabel had only put out three double-loaves and not a single pie. She'd made five batches, but burnt two. She was having difficulty concentrating. Her head was still pounding from the rum bottle that had struck her head, her stomach sour from the violation that ensued, and her heart sick, knowing that, from now on, she was dirty. She felt the lump on the side of her head. At least she hadn't been aware it was happening. She wondered if Da pulled up a chair and watched. She couldn't bear to think about it.

She needed to think of something, anything else. She thought of her ma.

They were back in their rented farm house in Pleasant Bay. Da'd be off fishing and gone for days. It was just her, Ma, and her baby brother, Jonathan. They were happy. Ma'd be baking or doing dishes in front of the kitchen window. She'd pull the stool over beside her and say, 'jump up.' They'd look out over the crab apple trees, the blue water beyond, and the two clumps of daises in the backyard.

Ma'd point out each daisy and call them by name. Daisy Jane, Daisy Mae, and Dudley the Daisy. They all came to life through her mother's words, taking Mabel to far off places she couldn't wait to visit when she grew up. Mabel remembered her whispering her secrets for making melt-in-yer mouth bread and playfully shushing Mabel as she peeked around to make sure no one else was listening. Then she'd ask Mabel to recite the alphabet, to measure out the flour, or to draw a picture of the cheery tree they were going to plant. And when the baby was settled in for the night, she'd read passages from her well-worn Bible, telling Mabel what the words meant and urging her to sound them out.

CHAPTER 4

James thought Mabel was unusually quiet. Normally, she was always talking. Sometimes, even when there was nobody around to talk to. He noticed the burnt bread.

"How are you feeling, Mabel?"

"Thinkin Sunday's events finally caught up to me. I'm a bit tired, even though I slept in. Sorry about the bread," she said, turning her head toward the blackened loaves.

James thought it was more than that. "Everything quiet at home last night? Your father didn't give you any trouble, I hope?"

Mabel thought of her bloody sheets and put her head down.

"No, Mr. Cameron. No trouble. But someone gave him some. He was all beat up. You and Stanley saw him yesterday. Ya musta seen the mess of him. How come ya didn't tell me?"

"I'm sorry, Mabel. I should have," he said, pretending like he was looking for something in the cupboard. "I just figured you had enough on your plate and you'd find out soon enough. Anyway, your father can look after himself."

"Yeah. Not like it was the first time he was on the receivin end of someone's fists."

"So, did he say what happened?"

"Said he was jumped by some coloureds, night before last."

Leave it to Johnnie to come up with that, James thought.

James went back to the store, and Mabel, back to her kneading.

She closed her eyes, her hands folding the sticky dough over and pushing it roughly forward. She felt tormented, like the day she heard her mother's scream and rushed into her parents' room. Ma was standing over Jonathan's crib, thrusting her tight fist into the air, and bringing it down hard on her chest. She was yelling at God and wailing. Mabel remembered watching, unsure of what to do as her ma fell to the floor. She ran barefoot to the Anderson farm. By the time she arrived back at the house with Mrs. Anderson panting behind her, Ma was in the living area rocking Jonathan, trying to sing to him between sobs.

"Mrs. Adshade? Why don't you let me have the baby?" Mrs. Anderson said, her arms outstretched.

"He hasn't had his bath yet," Ma'd said, cradling Jonathan. She walked to the sink and ran a basin of water, topped it up with warm water from the kettle, and swished her hand around to make sure it wasn't too hot, or too cold. Mrs. Anderson, unsure of what to do, stood off quietly to the side. Ma placed Jonathan in the basin and ran a soapy cloth over his small, round head and slippery body. Tears streamed down her face, dripping off her nose and into the water. "Mabel," she'd said, nodding to the counter. Just as she had done on so many happy occasions in the past, Mabel unfolded a towel and spread it out for Ma to place the squirming bundle. Only this time, Jonathan wasn't squirming. Ma patted him dry, picked him up, wrapped him in the towel, and held him to her chest like he was sleeping. She then put on what was to be his christening gown and his bonnet and booties.

"Mabel? Say goodbye to your baby brother," Ma had said, holding him out. Mabel remembered thinking he looked ready for church and kissing his forehead. "We'll bury him on the knoll," Ma said. She turned, passed the tiny, lifeless bundle to Mrs. Anderson, returned to her bedroom, and closed the door.

Ma was in her bed. Da was off fishing. Mabel lay curled up on the floor and, for the first time in a long time, sucked her thumb. It was near dark when she heard the door open.

It was Mrs. Anderson, again. She had an armful of food. “How’s your Ma?” she’d asked. “Oh. There you are, Mrs. Adshade.”

Ma was standing in the doorway that lead from her bedroom to the sparse living room. Her eyes were red. “Life goes on, Mrs. Anderson. As hard as it is.”

“I brought you some supper. I’m afraid it’s not much. A few lobster sandwiches and some chicken soup. I just pulled from what I had about,” she said, placing her offerings on the table. Mabel remembered being hungry, but not wanting to eat, either.

Ma smiled at Mrs. Anderson. “Thank you. And thank you for coming over this morning.”

“Martin is just sandin down the box…” she hesitated, before awkwardly correcting herself. “The coffin. He burnt the image of a bunny on the top. He plans on lining it with a spare quilt we found. It’s mostly blue. I hope that’s good by you?”

“That’s very kind. Please thank him for me.”

“He also made a small marker and started digging where you said you’d like the burial. Told me it has one of the prettiest views of the bay. That it’ll get at least eight hours of sun, even in winter. Any idea when your husband will be back?”

“I’m afraid not.”

“It’ll be a terrible shock to him, I’m sure. Only son and all.”

“I’m sure.”

“Well, no need to worry about arrangements. We’ll keep…*the baby* with us for as long as you like”

“No, Mrs. Anderson. We’ll bury Jonathan in the morning.”

“Of course. I’ll let Martin know. Any time you want to—”

“At sunrise.”

“We’ll see you, then. And, Mrs. Adshade, please try and eat something and get some rest. You’re gonna need your strength to get through all this.”

Jonathan Garfield Adshade, not yet three months old, was laid to rest the next morning as the sun came up. Mr. Anderson read a passage from the Bible. Mrs. Anderson cried softly. And Ma stood dry-eyed, staring off in the distance.

Da arrived home three days later. Drunk as a skunk.

CHAPTER 5

"Mabel," Mr. Cameron called out. "Douglas's mother is here. She heard about your pie and wants to try one."

"Sorry. No pies today. I barely kept up with the bread. How bout tomorrow?"

Mrs. MacGuire walked up beside Mr. Cameron and poked her head into the kitchen. "That'd be grand. Mabel? There's a letter at the Stamp and Post for your father. Pretty sure it's from your Aunt Amour, because it's postmarked Boston. Want me to drop it off on my way home from work tomorrow?"

Mabel was struggling to control her emotions. "That'd be great, Mrs. MacGuire."

"I'll drop it off when I come for my pie, then," Mrs. MacGuire said, waving and walking out the door.

James worried that Mabel hadn't kept her promise. He entered the kitchen. "Mabel, Stanley will be by any minute to take you home. So I guess if you have no pies for the customers, you don't have the one you promised me, either."

Mabel couldn't stop from welling up. "Um…um sorry, Mr. Cameron," she said, knowing it was another promise she hadn't kept.

"It's okay, Mabel. I can wait for my pie," he said.

She started to sob.

James was surprised by her reaction. "I'm sorry," he said. He walked over and hugged her. "You're not yourself today. Tell me, what's got you so upset?"

"Get out of my house!" Margaret hissed from the doorway.

"Margaret," James said, turning to see his wife's angry face. "For God's sake! This isn't what you're making it out to be. Mabel's not at fault here. Neither am I, for that matter. You're—"

"James," she said, before storming out, "I was talking to you."

James looked down at his feet.

Mabel knew she was responsible for Mrs. Cameron's anger and Mr. Cameron's pain. She dabbed her eyes with the hem of her apron. "Um sorry, Mr. Cameron. I know Mrs. Cameron doesn't like me. I think she thinks I'm stealin from her. But I don't steal. Stole once. Won't never do it again. I'll look for another job," she said.

Stanley arrived to see them both waiting on the step. "You've got two passengers tonight," James said. "Take Mabel home. Take me to Murphy's Inn."

It was another quiet drive, until Mabel spoke up. "Can ya just drop me off at the Toths. I'm gonna stay there tonight and help Mary Catherine with the boys." She prayed they were home.

"You mean Mary Catherine's with a C?" James said, hoping to lighten the mood.

"Yes," she said flatly.

"Mabel. Mrs. MacGuire will be by for her pie tomorrow. I expect you to be at work at your usual time."

"But, Mr. Cameron? What about Mrs. Cameron?" Mabel asked. She clutched her mother's tote, wondering if Mr. Cameron was making the right decision and trying not to burst into tears, again."

James turned to face her. "Just leave everything to me," he said, without a clue as to how he could convince Margaret that she was wrong about Mabel.

Stanley dropped Mabel off at the Toths and headed to Number Two.

"Stanley," James hollered, "you're going the wrong way."

Stanley pretended he didn't hear him and kept driving.

"Where are we going?"

"It's not Murphy's, but I got a spare cot, a bottle of rum, and a can of tobacco."

CHAPTER 6

James drank and smoked, as Stanley puffed on his pipe and listened to him lay his sadness bare. Despite knowing each other for almost ten years, neither spoke much about their past. Stanley was distracted and struggled to hear what James was slurring, but he picked up on most of it. James lost his best friend to the war, and the woman he loved to Mabel's father. James told him he and Percy were best friends from the moment they met. Similar interests in reading and fishing. Neither particularly good at athletics.

"Did I tell we signed up the same day? Joined the 25th Battalion, off on our big adventure. Duty to king and country, and all that shit. Christ, I miss him. Shoulda got a special medal of honour just for bein such a good guy. Seriously, of all the men I ever knew, he was the finest. Ya woulda liked him, Stan. Hey, I like that. That's what I'm gonna call you from now on, Stan," James said. He dropped his makin on the floor and bent over to pick it up. "Sorry bout that. So, whatcha think? You hear anythin I've been sayin?"

Stanley smiled and nodded.

"Anyway, I was thinkin earlier today how much Percy woulda liked you. Cause yer a good guy, too. A real good guy. And Ellie woulda loved ya, too. She loved everybody. Pretty as all get out. Actually, there were prettier girls than Ellie. Like, they had the looks, but not the whole kit n' caboodle. There was just somethin about her. Oh, and that smile. Seriously, Stanley, it could bring ya to yer knees. Hey, Stanley… Stan. How about rollin another makin?" James said, holding up his swollen hand.

James poured himself another drink. "How ya doin, my friend? Christ! I'm sorry about the ponies. Ya doin okay?"

"I'm fine," Stanley said, digging his hand into the tobacco can and dropping the dry brown leaves into the paper cradled between his fingers.

"Did I tell ya we served together in the same company? Me and Percy."

Stanley turned to face him. "You never speak about the war."

"Ain't like it's somethin ya want to think about. Anyway, we stayed close through the first six months. Then, they decided Percy had a knack for… for wirin and stuff. Detonation. Yes, that's it, detonation. Anyway, we ended up gettin separated. I was never so afraid in all my life. I was scared shitless when we were together, but I was fuckin terrified when we were apart. Finally, my unit's going to Ypres, and I'm happy. Not like I wanted to go to Ypres for the hell of it, but I knew Percy was there. So I arrive, jump off the truck and see this corporal crossin names off a sheet. And I say, hey bud, any idea where I can find Percy MacPherson from 25th Battalion. And he points to the dress tent. It was fuckin awful. Guys with legs and arms blown off. Bandaged from head to toe. Stink of burnin flesh would make your stomach turn," James said, butting his makin. "Cauterizin, I guess. But the worst, Stanley, was the moanin. God, it was awful. I don't mean to offend ya, my friend, but it woulda been a good time to be hard of hearin. I can still hear those moans. Saw some pretty bad stuff in the field too, but then your adrenaline's pumpin so fast, and your so caught up in stayin alive, ya don't take it all in. Remember seein this one kid, though. He was hangin off a wire fence with his arms stretched out." James threw his arms off to the side. "And he had one foot stuck in the mud and one leg bent up like this." He tried to stand and demonstrate, but fell forward onto the floor.

"Jesus, I'm drunk."

Stanley helped James to his feet and back to his chair.

"Anyway, I couldn't help myself. Bullets were flyin everywhere, but I just stopped and stared at the kid. Thought if you took his helmet off and put a crown of thorns on his head it would be just like Jesus on the cross. Still think of him every time I see a crucifix. Anyway, I left the tent, and I go back up to buddy and tell him Percy ain't there. He shrugs. So I go back in again and ask one of the nurses, and she points out a guy on a cot with a missin leg.. He was wrapped from head to toe in oozin gauze. I must have passed by him a dozen times. It was Percy all right. Cause I saw how he welled up when I stood over him.

James picked up another makin. Stanley dragged a match against the side of the box and leaned in to light it.

"Stanley? How come you didn't sign up? Was it your hearin?" he asked, dragging on his makin.

"I was too young."

"Yeah, of course. Fuckin war. Fuckin God damn war."

"How's your hand?" Stanley asked.

"Oh, it's fine. Good as new. See," James said, stretching his stiff fingers slowly in and out.

"It's getting late. Your cot is ready," Stanley said, pointing to the far wall.

"Am I borin you? Can you hear me okay?" James asked, slapping Stanley's knee. "How bout I finish my rum? Cause I want to finish my story. I *need* to finish my story."

Stanley looked at the clock, then at his friend, teetering back and forth as he topped up his rum, getting more on himself than in his glass.

"I'm listening," Stanley said.

"Percy and Ellie woulda loved ya. Where was I?"

"You found Percy."

"Yes. That's it. Ya know, ya hear pretty good for a guy that can't hear so good. Better than most people I know. Yeah, Percy woulda liked you. Anyway, he was bandaged from head to toe. Could barely talk and everythin was a mumble. Nurse tells me he was gassed first. Fuckin Krauts with their fuckin chlorine. Tried makin his way back to the trench. Got within about twenty yards or so. Then gets hit by a shell. Nurse smiles at me and says he was one of the few to come to back alive. Like he was lucky or somethin. Woulda been better off if he died on the field. Wouldn't have suffered so much."

James's head was bobbing and his eyes filled up. "Anyway, that was that. I stayed with him all night. Every now and then, he'd just look at me. I just sat there, tryin to be strong, and not cry. Fell asleep in the chair at some point. Nurse wakes me up and told me he was gone. He was barely twenty. It was the worst day of my life. So nurse tells me she's sorry about my friend. And I tell her he was my brother. She hands me his personal belongings. A partially written letter to his mother, a few coins, a picture of Ellie flanked by me and Percy in our uniforms, and this," James said, reaching under his collar and pulling out a St. Christopher's medal. He started to sob.

Stanley leaned forward and put his hand on his shoulder. "C'mon bud. It's going on nine."

"But I wanna tell ya about Ellie? Mabel's mother. I love em both, ya know?" James said. His eyes were barely open.

Stanley didn't know if he meant Percy and Ellie, or Ellie and Mabel. He was pretty sure James didn't either. He helped his friend to his feet and onto the cot near the coal stove and put a blanket over him. He returned to his chair, puffed on his pipe and waited until James's breathing fell into a slow, steady rhythm. He then put on his jacket, quietly opened the door, and walked out, into the pouring rain.

Thursday, November 3

CHAPTER I

James felt a blast of cold air, opened his bleary eyes, and pulled the blanket up around his chin. "What time is it?"

"Almost one. Go back to sleep."

Stanley sat on the edge of his bed and unlaced his muddy boots. He rested his elbows on his knees and his head in his hands. He thought about Mabel in the coal shed and the dried blood on the side of her head, his charred ponies, his sick aunt, and Willie lying on the canvas in spasms. He thought of Clair and wondered what happened to her. One day they were planning their future together, and the next, she's gone. He thought of Johnnie's bloody face.

He stretched out over his bed and dozed on and off. He could hear James snore. He sat up, lit a match, and checked the time. It was almost five-thirty. He got up to fed the hungry belly of the still warm stove.

He turned as James stirred.

"Did I sleep late?" James asked.

"No. It's not quite six."

"I don't feel good. What time did I go to bed?"

"Just before nine," Stanley said.

"You should have cut me off after two." James stood unsteadily, arched his back, and stretched his arms wide before flopping down sideways. The springs of Stanley's cot making a noisy squeak. "I kept you up late, rattling on about the past. I'm going to pay for it today," he said, running his hand over his forehead and squeezing his eyes shut. "Another reason for Margaret to be mad at me."

Stanley watched the kindling spark to life, added some coal, put the lid back on, and placed a pot of water on top. The two drank tea and ate some of Mrs. MacNeil's oat cakes without much talk. James was relieved Stanley didn't have much to say. It was an effort to think, let alone talk.

"Shit. I feel awful," James said. "Might as well drop me off first so I can open the store, then you can get Mabel. You okay, Stanley? You look like you never slept a wink."

"Slept fine."

The two walked out into the brisk air and onto the hard, packed dirt. James paused and leaned on his mud-caked Plymouth. The buttered oat cake he just put down felt like it was about to come back up. "I'm not feeling very good," he said, again. He slumped into the passenger seat and closed his eyes. He leaned forward and put his hand on the dash, as the car bounced along. "Christ! The roads are a mess," he said, hoping Stanley would slow down. But Stanley kept his pace, weaving the car around the pockmarked road the rain and freezing temperatures conspired to create.

When they approached the store, James looked up to see the familiar black wagon out front. "Is that the paddy wagon?" he asked, sitting up.

"Looks like it," Stanley said.

James felt a rush of panic. "What are the police doing here?" Something happened to Margaret, he thought, until he saw her at the door greeting Sergeant McInnes. He turned to Stanley. "I must have been robbed."

Stanley said nothing. He stopped long enough to let James out, then went to get Mabel.

James walked toward Margaret and Sergeant McInnes. Margaret saw her husband approach and quickly disappeared into the store. "Sergeant? What's going on?"

"I'm looking for the Adshade girl."

Another moment of panic. "Why? What's wrong?"

"Her father's dead."

"Johnnie's dead?" James couldn't believe his ears.

"Yeah. Body was found in a ditch along Brookside Street this morning. I went by his place to notify his daughter, but no one was home. Neighbours said she works for you. Any idea where she is?"

"She's staying at the Toths on Union Street. Stanley just went to pick her up. What happened?"

"Not sure yet. Ten-After-Six found him when he was out walking. Captain Collins just told me to go find the next of kin."

James always had a soft spot for Ten-After-Six. He could be seen walking day or night, no matter what the weather. Everyone in town knew him. But no one called him by his real name, Peter Boyd. Poor guy walked bent over from the time he was a trapper boy, working the ponies in the pit. He was so scared, he'd bend over even when there was plenty of head space for his small frame. Left the pit after a few years to work above ground, but kept walking that way. No one was sure if it was out of habit, or if he'd done permanent damage to his spine.

Sergeant McInnes interrupted his thoughts. "Anyway, he musta been beaten to death. Apparently his face is a mess."

James's head shot up. A stabbing pain radiated across his forehead, causing him to bring his hands to his temples. "Beaten to death?" he repeated, squeezing his eyes shut.

"Yeah. Anyway, the body should be with the medical examiner by now," McInnes said. He placed his hands under his armpits and bounced on his toes to keep his feet warm. He nodded at James's hand. "What happened to your hand?"

James looked down at it. "I jammed it between some crates in the store."

"Did you know him well?"

"What?" James said, still struggling to absorb the news and

feeling guilty the unexpected news brought him relief, not regret.

"Did you know *Adshade* well?" Sergeant McInnes repeated.

"Knew him well enough to say that, like everybody else, he wasn't my favourite guy."

"Where were you and Stanley comin from just now?"

James was taken aback by his question. He paused before answering. "Stanley's. I stayed there last night. Played some cards and just decided to spend the night." James knew it wasn't exactly the truth, but he didn't think it was any of Sergeant McInnes's business that Margaret threw him out.

"Were you drinking?"

"Might have had a dram or two," he confessed, thinking McInnes could probably smell it off him and he might throw up at any minute.

"Where'd you get it?"

"I didn't buy it. It was a gift," James said, deciding it was a small lie he could get away with.

"Mind if I wait inside? It's freezin out here?"

"Come in." The store wasn't much warmer, so James started the coal stove. He looked up the staircase and immediately knew his night away from Margaret hadn't softened her mood. He looked back at Sergeant McInnis. "Perhaps it would be better if I broke the news to Mabel."

McInnes shrugged. "Suit yourself."

James excused himself, saying he was going to open the shutters. When he got outside, he went around the side of the store, bent over, and spewed the contents of his rum-sick belly onto the ground. He rested his hand on the side of the store, wondering if it was just a momentary reprieve from the nausea, or if it would return and continue to add to the misery of his day. He stood, walked out front, and watched as his Plymouth approached. He could see Mabel eyeing the ominous, black wagon. He went to help her out of the car. "Mabel, the police are here. I'm afraid I have some sad news. I'm sorry, dear. Your father died last night."

"What did ya say?" she asked, giving him a confused look.

"Your father. They found his body this morning. I'm sorry, Mabel."

James turned toward Stanley. He looked away.

"Da's dead?" she asked, her head down. "But how? What happened to him?" she asked softly. James put his arm under her elbow and guided her to the store. "We're not sure. Come inside. Sergeant McInnes is here. He'll tell you as much as he knows."

Sergeant McInnes walked toward her when she entered the store, but Mabel ignored him and went directly to the kitchen. James followed close behind. She was standing beneath a picture of the Virgin Mother that was hanging on the wall above the kitchen sink. Mabel was surprised she felt sad. Yesterday, she'd wanted to take her bread knife to him. Today, she got her wish and he was gone. She felt ashamed for wishing him dead. As bad as he was, he was still her father. He had his demons for sure, but he'd treated her decent enough before Ma and his only son had died. He just didn't know how to deal with his grief. And he came for her after she got into that mess of trouble and had nowhere to go. He didn't have to. But he did, even though it meant he had to quit fishing. Sad, she thought, how she never remembered a single kind thing he did, until now. She bowed her head and prayed. Dear Father, forgive Da of his sins and look to the goodness that existed within him. I know there was some. May he rest in peace with Ma and baby Jonathan. And, Lord, forgive me for my shameful thoughts. I'd also appreciate ya tellin Da I'm sorry I wasn't a better, more understandin daughter. Oh, and God? Please grant me strength and forgiveness. She blessed herself.

James put his head down, realizing he'd intruded on what was meant to be a private moment. Mabel smiled at him as he stretched his hand out to her. The two walked arm and arm back into the store; Mabel sad for her da. James sad for Mabel.

Mabel's conversation with Sergeant McInnes didn't last more than a minute. There weren't a lot of details to share. The death was suspicious. They'd know more after the medical examiner had a chance to examine the body.

"Thank you, Sergeant," she said, and turned to re-enter her sanctuary.

James followed her into the kitchen. "Mabel? Why don't I take you home? Or, maybe to see your friend, Mary Catherine?"

"Thanks, Mr. Cameron. But I always thought it best to work through your sorrow, not wallow in it." James was surprised that Mabel, who had suffered her father's fists and hateful treatment, would feel sad. But he could see that she did. "Besides, I gotta make Mrs. MacGuire's pie. And the bread orders are backed up with the batches I burnt yesterday." She looped her apron over her head and began tying it in the back.

"If you're sure? And, Mabel. I'll get a cable off to Amour and Roddy and make whatever arrangements are needed."

Mabel lifted her head and smiled.

James's throat tightened as he saw both her strength and her sadness. He turned, walked into the store, and looked at the stairs. Margaret must have gone back to bed. He nodded for Stanley to join him at the back of the store.

"Honestly, James, the world is better off without him. At least we know he won't be taking his fists to Mabel anymore," Stanley said.

"I know. But they think he was beaten to death. I know he had his enemies, but who hated him enough to kill him?"

Stanley sat on the stool next to James. "I'm sure there were more than a few."

"McInnes said his face was a mess. But we both know it was a mess before last night. Maybe he died of natural causes. Maybe it was a heart attack or something and they think it is suspicious because of what we did. Do you think we should tell them?"

Stanley chewed on the stem of his pipe. "No. I don't think that's wise. Next thing you know, the police will be hauling us in for questioning."

"You know, I feel badly for saying it, but I can't say I'm sorry he's gone either," James said. He peeked around the corner and looked toward the stairs. "Can you keep an eye on the store? I'm just going to check on Margaret." He handed him the butt-filled Crisco can.

James put his hand on the banister and looked up. He took a deep breath. "God help me," he whispered. The door to their bedroom was closed. He knocked softly. There was no answer. He knocked again, this time a little louder. He turned the knob, but it was locked. "Margaret? Let me in." He was about to start pounding, when he heard her unlock it. She swung it open, immediately turning her back to him. She returned to her high-backed chair and picked up her needlepoint. James's plan to calmly reason with his wife gave way to anger. "I assume Sergeant McInnes told you why he was here?"

She looked at him sternly. "Yes."

"Yes? That's it? Just yes?"

"What do you expect me to say? I didn't know the man."

James walked to the closet, opened the door, and put his good hand on his large brown suitcase. He pulled on it, but it didn't budge. He grabbed it with both hands and tossed it hard onto the floor.

The thud startled Margaret.

"What are you doing?"

He shot her a look that made her sit up straight. "What does it look like? I'm packing!" he said, tearing at the bindings, his damaged hand throbbing.

Margaret's anger began to give way to concern. She had never seen James so angry.

James roughly threw the top back, reached in, grabbed the heavy quilt that lay inside, and tossed it aside. Mothballs flew out in every direction, noisily bouncing across the wide-planked floor. James retched. The stench of the small round balls adding to the nausea he was struggling to contain.

"So, you're leaving to be with her? I knew it! I knew it was just a matter of time before you—"

"Before I what?" James snapped, throwing his arms in the air and turning to face her. "Before I got fed up from being shut out of your life?"

The thought of divorce and the scandal that would ensue terrified Margaret. Shame him, punish him, and save him from damnation, yes, she thought. But not lose him.

James's heart, head, and hand were pounding. He tried to calm his emotions. "Margaret! I don't know what you think is going on, but whatever it is, you're wrong. Dead wrong! The only interest I have in Mabel, is in her welfare."

"My eyes and ears tell me differently. I see how she looks at you. And you at her. I know you have needs, James. Needs that I would hope you would—"

"What I need, *Margaret*, is for you to listen to me." He walked over and squatted in front of her chair. She turned her head to the side. He grabbed her arms. "Look at me!" he said, bringing his face within inches of hers. Margaret! Look at me!" he repeated more sternly. She fixed her eyes on his. "Margaret! I have never touched Mabel and have no desire to. I don't want to be with her. I want to be with you."

Margaret began to doubt her suspicions. This was his chance to leave. Yet, here he was saying he wanted to be with *her*. "If you're not in love with Mabel, why does she have such a hold on you?"

"I told you. Her mother was a dear friend. I made a promise to her just before she died. I'm just trying to make amends for failing her. That's all."

"James you were crying outside her door, for goodness sake."

He let go of her arms and dropped his head. "I felt I failed Ellie. I felt I failed Mabel. Margaret, I felt I failed you. I knew you would expect me to keep my word to a dying friend. Margaret, Mabel's had a horrible life. I could have, *and should have*, done more to help her."

"I also heard the two of you come upstairs together in the middle of the night. What could you have possibly been doing downstairs together?"

He raised his head. “Not what you must have been thinking. Look! You were mad at me. I had a drink. Actually, I had a few drinks and fell asleep out back. I woke up and Mabel was getting things ready to start baking. She wanted to get an early start so she could repay us for letting her stay the night. And for calling in Dr. Cohen. I made her go back to bed. When I got to our room I saw the door was closed. So I slept on the sofa.”

“Why didn’t you just tell me about Mabel’s mother and your promise?” she asked in a pleading tone.

“Trust me, I tried. I was hoping to tell you everything over dinner the other night. That’s why I bought the lamb. Let’s face it, Margaret, you and I haven’t really talked to one another in months. *Years.* And we both know our troubles started well before Mabel arrived on our doorstep. We haven’t lived as man and wife since the baby died. I know you’re not happy. And frankly, neither am I.”

She bowed her head.

“Margaret? Do you still love me?”

She didn’t look up.

“Do you still love me?” He waited. “It’s a simple question, Margaret. Yes or no?”

“Of course,” she said, as her eyes filled up.

James dropped his head and let out a sigh of relief. “Good. Because I still love you. I’ll always love you. But is it asking to too much for you to show me? We used to do things together. We used to laugh and be happy. You’ve shut me out of your life. It’s like you look for reasons to push me away. Honestly, sometimes it feels as if you blame me for what happened to the baby.”

Margaret burst into tears, startling James. He reached over and drew her close to him. He waited for her to stop sobbing.

“I don’t blame you! It’s my fault he’s gone! I don’t deserve to be happy!” she said loudly. She pushed him away and reached across the night table for her handkerchief.

He sat back and looked at her. “What are you talking about? It wasn’t *your* fault.”

She snapped her head in his direction. "It was!" she screamed. "If I hadn't been parading him out for everyone who came by the store. I let people touch him. Pick him up. I should have known better. I knew people were getting sick," she said angrily.

"Margaret! You did what any proud mother would do," he pleaded. "There were lots of mothers and their babies in and out of the store at the time. Lots," he said, caressing the side of her head.

"But he was fussing and I just ignored it. I should have summoned Thomas sooner."

"Babies fuss all the time," he said more softly. "If you're to blame, then so am I. I didn't see it coming, either. It all happened so fast. Listen to me. It wasn't your fault, or mine. It was God's will."

She tried to collect herself as he pressed on. "You're not honouring his memory by denying yourself happiness. No one, not me, not your friends at church, not God, or even baby James, expect you to wear the burden of your grief forever. Finding pleasure in life doesn't mean you've forgotten him. The best way to honour his memory is to remember that it's the love we have for one another that brought him to us. Promise me you won't blame yourself anymore? Promise me you'll try to be happy again?" he pleaded, holding her hands in his.

Margaret thought he was asking too much of her, but she also knew it wasn't possible to go on without him. She wiped the tears from her face and made an effort to smile.

"Will you at least try, Margaret?"

"I'll… huh… huh... I'll try," she said, trying to catch her breath.

"That's all I ask. I'm glad we had this talk. I'm just sorry it didn't happen sooner. Why don't you come downstairs and have something to eat? I'll get Mabel to set aside a fresh loaf."

"She's here? I mean… I mean….huh….huh… with news of her father, and all."

"Yes. She won't go home. Wants to keep working."

"How is… huh… huh is… is she coping?"

"Despite how he treated her, she's sad."

"He was her father, after all," Margaret said, lowering her head in an attempt to hide her shame.

"So, will you come down and have something to eat?"

"Yuh... yuh... yes" she said, not looking up at him.

"Good then," James said, standing to leave. He waited for her to look up at him. When she did, he saw her eyes were no longer angry. They were sad. She started to cry again. He crouched back down and wrapped his arms around her.

"I'm sorry, James. I'm so sorry. I've been so—"

"We're going to be okay. We're going to be okay," he said, rocking her back and forth just like on the day they lost their son.

James eventually let her go and stood up. "Margaret, there's more bad news. Stanley's ponies died in a fire yesterday."

She moved the handkerchief back and forth under her nose. "Oh dear. He la... la loved those ponies. Wha... wha... what hap... happened?"

"Not sure."

"Wha...what will he do for... for work?"

"I've got a few things he could help out with around the store. It'll keep him busy in the short term. Maybe he'll go back underground. I left him tending the store and should get back."

"James," she said. "I'll try har... har... harder."

James brushed his hand along her cheek. "Thank you," he said, hoping her words of contrition were a sign they could once again be happy.

He pulled the door after him, careful to leave it open just a crack.

CHAPTER 2

Stanley was bent over the counter reading *The Post* and puffing on his pipe when James came downstairs. "Thanks, Stanley."

"You okay?" Stanley asked.

James nodded, relieved he and Margaret had finally spoken about their feelings for one another, and hopeful for better days ahead.

"And Margaret?"

"She's…she's doing better."

"Good. Well then, I need to go and see about buying some shingles," he said, closing the paper over.

"Take the car."

"Are you sure?" Stanley asked.

"I'm not going anywhere," James said.

Stanley grabbed his cap, slapped James on the arm, smiled, and left.

James walked into the kitchen, cursing himself for not talking to Margaret sooner. If he had, perhaps they wouldn't have been so miserable for so long. Mabel was kneading her bread. Three double-loaves were rising on the counter. She's where she wants to be, doing what she wants to be doing, he thought.

"Doing okay, Mabel?"

"Doin fine, Mr. Cameron. Can't undo what's already done, no matter how much ya will it."

They were sitting at the table having tea when Margaret came around the corner. Mabel could feel her heart pound. She kept her head down, afraid to look up at the woman who despised her.

"Mabel. I'm very sorry to hear about your father. If I can help in anyway, just let me know."

Mabel brought her head up, hoping the look on her face didn't reveal her shock. "Thank you, Mrs. Cameron. That's very kind of ya. I feel like I already owe you and Mr. Cameron so much."

"Just the same, if either of us can help, please let us know. And, of course, you're welcome to stay with us for as long as you like."

Mabel wasn't sure she heard right. She looked at Mr. Cameron. He gave her an encouraging nod. "Thank you, Mrs. Cameron," Mabel said.

Margaret walked toward the stove, stopped briefly next to James, and put her hand on his arm. *Thank you,* James mouthed. Margaret rewarded him with a smile. She then poured her tea, buttered a biscuit, placed them on a tray, and started for the door. She stopped, turned, and looked back at Mabel. "I'm truly sorry, Mabel. For *everything*."

James tried to assure Mabel that she had meant what she said. "Her behaviour towards you had little to do with you, and more to do with me. She's just been going through some tough times. But we had a good talk. Once you get to know her better, I know you'll like her."

As much as Mabel wanted to believe him, she doubted her relationship with Mrs. Cameron could be anything more than cordial. *Imagine, taking to that frosty old bird.*

James stood at the sound of the chimes and went back to the store.

"Hello. Anyone here?"

"There you are, Mr. Cameron," Mrs. MacGuire said. "I just wanted to drop off the letter I spoke to Mabel about. Poor girl must be sick at heart with news of her da."

"She's here," he said, tilting his head in the direction of the kitchen. Mrs. MacGuire gave him a surprised look. She walked in and hugged Mabel. "Douglas told me about your father. I'm very sorry, dear. My deepest sympathies."

"Thank you," Mabel said, handing Mrs. MacGuire her pie.

"Oh my! I didn't think I'd be getting my pie today. Just came in to drop off the letter I mentioned yesterday. See," she said pointing. "It's from Boston. Poor Amour is going to be devastated to hear about her dear brother. Anyway, let me know if there's anything Douglas or I can do for you."

"That's very kind of you." Mabel looked at the envelope addressed to her father and put it in her apron.

James walked Mrs. MacGuire to the door and returned to the kitchen. "Mabel. You should stay here for the night."

"Thanks again, Mr. Cameron. But I gotta face the shack sometime. Now's as good a time as any."

"Maybe you could ask a friend to stay with you, or go back to the Toths with Mary Catherine?"

Mabel starting flouring her board. "I'll be fine, Mr. Cameron. Likely just go home, have a bite to eat, wash up, and crawl in bed. Been an eventful few days," she said.

"Sure has," he said, not knowing the half of it. He left her to her baking.

It was going on five when Stanley pulled up front. James walked Mabel to the car, holding the door open for her. "I'll see you tomorrow. Try and get your rest. Oh, Stanley? Wait a minute." James ran back into the store and returned with the pie Mabel had set aside for him. "Mabel made this for you." He winked at Mabel before she could protest.

They were in the car heading toward the shack when Mabel remembered she'd forgotten the letter in her apron. She'd get it in the morning. She thought of how hard it would be for Amour. She hadn't seen her brother in over three years and, now, she'd never see him again.

CHAPTER 3

"Pie smells good. Thank you," Stanley said. Mabel just nodded and looked out the passenger window. Stanley sensed her sadness, reached over, and placed his hand on hers. Surprise, not revulsion, caused her to pull it back quickly. Stanley assumed it was the latter. They didn't say another word to each other for the remainder of their journey. When she got out of the car, Stanley smiled at her. "Good night, Mabel."

"Night," she said, thinking there's that sad smile, again. She watched the car disappear out of sight. The world is full of bad men, she thought. "But you ain't one of em," she whispered.

Mabel entered the cold, dark shack. She walked to the kitchen, and stood over the chair she had knocked her da off the morning before. She lit the stove, went to her bedroom, and looked down at the bed where she had been savagely mounted. She thought of Billy's greasy hair and filthy nails as he reached for his sardine sandwich, and of Eddie's simple mind and bad leg. Her eyes watered and her body shuddered. She spotted the crusty pool of yellow vomit on the floor, gagged, and threw up, again. She flopped down on the bed, picked up her mother's pillow, and hugged it tight, rocking back and forth. Tears streamed down her face, until exhaustion took over.

She woke two hours later as the heat from the coal stove surrendered to the cold. She crawled under the covers, wondering what she had done to displease God so much. All she ever wanted was to have a family of her own, a steady job, and to learn to read and write.

Why can't I have that? Why can't I have more than a few fleeting moments of happiness? Is it because I stole from a poor family? Or skip church to walk at the brook? Is it because I taunted Da too much? Because of my foul tongue?

She closed her eyes as memories of him came flooding back. He was baiting her hook and showing her how to cast. He was handing her a tiny package wrapped in pretty paper. He was teasing Ma as they washed dishes together. He was ripping up an old shirt and dressing her bloody leg.

Mabel wasn't sure if the images in her head were real, or if it was God's way of telling her to forgive him. Maybe he wasn't such a bastard. Ma had seen some good in him. She loved him. And as far as Mabel could remember, he'd only ever hit Ma that one time. It was over the daisies.

It was the only time Mabel ever remembered her ma being really angry. She'd looked out the window at the two barren patches of earth. "My daisies," Ma had screamed. "Mabel did you pick my daisies?" she had asked, grabbing her by the arms

"No, Ma."

Then, Da walked up behind her and handed them to her in an empty milk bottle. Ma grabbed the bottle from him and threw it to the floor. "I prefer my daisies alive and in the ground, not withering on the shelf," she'd said. Da's eyes grew angry. He slapped her, called her an ungrateful witch, and stormed out.

It was just before baby Jonathan died.

Mabel pulled the covers back, stepped over the vomit, and walked down the hall clutching her pillow. She stood before the unopened door to Da's room. No more glow from under the door, she thought. Her fingers were shaking as she reached for the knob. She had always been afraid to step in without his approval. But he was gone now. Still, she hesitated. She looked down the hall, then slowly pushed the door open.

The room was surprisingly tidy. She walked to the steamer trunk, lifted the greying doily, and stared down at the sepia faces looking back at her. She shivered, pulled the covers back off her da's bed, threw his pillow to the side, and replaced it with her ma's. She put her head down and pulled the blankets up to her chest, clutching the yellowed photo containing the last remaining image of her parents. She thought about Pleasant Bay, when they were happy. When they were a family. Her weary eyes fell shut just as the sun started to rise, sleep bringing only a brief reprieve from her torment.

Forgive Us Our Trespasses

Friday, November 4

CHAPTER 1

James woke knowing Margaret must be exhausted. She had cried most of the night. He eased his arm from under her head. She stirred and opened her eyes.

"It's way too early. Go back to sleep. I have to get Mabel's oven started, or there'll be hell to pay," James said, buttoning his shirt.

Margaret sat up. "I'm sorry. I know I kept you up."

"Are you feeling any better?" he asked.

"A little."

He reached for his pants. "You'll feel even better after a few more hours sleep."

"James? We're going to be okay, aren't we?"

"Yes, Margaret. I believe we will," he said, and smiled.

James's heart quickened when she smiled back. He forgot how beautiful she was when she smiled. He walked over and kissed her on the cheek. He was walking to the door when he turned back. "In fact, Margaret, I know we will." He put his head down and walked out.

Margaret got up and walked to her dresser. She reached down and picked up the sterling silver hairbrush her parents had given her as a wedding gift. They would both be dead within the year. She ran her fingers over the bright floral inlay with its opalesque border. She had planned to hand it down to a daughter, or daughter-in-law, on her wedding day. She brought it to her head and began running it through her hair. She looked at the image reflected back. Her red-rimmed, puffy eyes, this time, evidence of regret, not self-pity. It was the first time in three years Margaret had cried herself to sleep, not because of her own suffering, but because of the suffering she had caused others. She placed the hairbrush next to its matching hand mirror, opened the bottom drawer, and looked at the blue blanket she had knit for her baby boy. She picked it up, smelled it, wrapped it around her hairbrush and mirror, and gently placed the bundle back in the drawer. She pulled up on the wooden knobs, hesitated a moment, then pushed the sticky drawer shut, hoping to hide the daily reminders of a future she knew she could no longer have. She stood up and looked back in the mirror. "God forgive me. And grant me strength," she whispered.

CHAPTER 2

Sergeant McInnes was at his desk when Billy Guthro and Eddie Lynch walked in. They knew who'd killed their friend. They proceeded to tell him about Johnnie being jumped by a gang of niggers three nights ago. They said there were eight to ten darkies who put the boots to him, but Johnnie beat them off, leaving a few of them pretty banged up.

"Happened somewhere near Commercial Street. Johnnie swore he was gonna kill em, one by one," Billy said.

Eddie couldn't contain himself. "Looks like they got to him first."

Sergeant McInnes was a little skeptical. Coloureds usually kept to their own end of town. And while Johnnie was pretty good with his fists, McInnes didn't have him figured as someone who could fight off eight or more men. Just the same, he was determined to restore the constabulary's reputation after all the talk following the Jew boy's murder. Faggot got what he deserved, McInnes thought. He gathered up a few of his officers and headed to Number Six, where they hauled every coloured man and boy over the age of thirteen into the station and made them strip down to their underwear. Nine were found to have suspicious cuts or bruises. They were interrogated for more than eight hours. Sergeant McInnes didn't find any good leads to follow up. He did, however, find a way to ramp up racial tensions in the town.

CHAPTER 3

James was opening the shutters when Stanley and Mabel pulled up. "How'd you sleep, Mabel?"

"Not bad," she lied, rushing past him.

"And how are you, Stanley?"

"I'm okay."

James immediately sensed something was wrong. Mabel certainly didn't seem herself, and both she and Stanley seemed distant and uncomfortable with one another.

James looked at Stanley. "Everything okay with you two?"

"What do you mean?"

"I just… never mind. Not important. I'm going to head to town. Take a look around and see how we can make better use of the space. Margaret's looking after the store and will get you whatever you need.

James's first order of business was to stop at the telegraph office to get the wire off to Amour and Roddy. He was the only one there, besides the young man who typed his message.

> *Dear Amour and Roderick. Stop. I write to notify you of the sudden death of your dear brother and brother-in-law. Stop. Few details at this time. Stop. Mabel doing fine. Stop. Deepest condolences. Stop. James Cameron.*

He then went to the police station to talk to Sergeant McInnes, but was told he was tied up all day in interrogation. James then spoke to a junior officer who said Johnnie Adshade's body was still with the medical examiner. He was on his way to the savings and loan when he heard the familiar voice.

"Jimmy! Jimmy Cameron!"

Even though they were separated by a road two bulky Chevrolets could easily share, James was, once again, taken aback by the bright red lipstick of the town's record keeper. Lizzie MacNeil was waving him over with one arm, the other firmly crooked around that of a well-dressed man he hadn't seen before. James reluctantly obliged and crossed the street.

"Jimmy. This is Michael Donnely. He just arrived from Boston," she said, proud as a peacock. "Michael, this is an old beau of mine. Jimmy Cameron. One of the town's most successful proprietors."

James winced at the old beau reference, as well as his success as a businessman. He hoped his embarrassment wasn't too obvious. The two acquaintances shook hands.

"Mikey, here, is gonna stay on and help manage the coal company's head office," Lizzie said, looking up at him with wide eyes and a big smile. "Go ahead, Mikey. Tell him yer title."

Michael Donnely smiled. "Really, Lizzie! I don't think that's—"

"Well, Jimmy. Suffice it to say, he's not just good lookin, he's real important."

Donnely closed his eyes and dropped his head.

"Have you been in town long, Mr. Donnely?" James asked, sensing Lizzie's new friend wanted to climb into the nearest hole.

"Barely forty-eight hours."

James figured that was plenty of time for Lizzie to have stuck her long tongue down his throat.

"I just happened to be at the station when I saw this big, handsome guy lookin round like he didn't know which way to turn. So, I just popped over and introduced myself. And we've been best friends ever since. Oh, listen to me goin on about our encounter," Lizzie said. She reached over and clutched James's sleeve. "Anyway, I just wanted to pay my condolences to ya."

"Condolences, Lizzie?" James asked, screwing up his face.

"On the passin of yer brother."

"*My brother*?" James said, laughing.

"Yeah! Yer brother. Well, half-brother. Johnnie Adshade."

James put his chin down and raised his eyes to her, suggesting it was the most ridiculous thing he had ever heard.

"Ya did know, Jimmy—"

"Lizzie," he interrupted. "What are you talking about? Johnnie Adshade's isn't… *wasn't* my half-brother."

"Sure was. At least, that's what the records say. And I keep real good records." She looked up at her new beau. "I'm in charge of keeping all the official records. Births, deaths, marriage. You name it."

Michael Donnely looked up the street, wishing he was anywhere else.

"Lizzie! I don't care what the records say, Johnnie Adshade was *not* my half-brother." James knew there was a tone in his voice.

Donnely interjected. "Perhaps, it's just a misunderstanding? These things happen."

"Not on my watch," Lizzie said, giving her latest arm-holder a playful swat.

"Remember, Jimmy? Ya came lookin for the Adshade girl's birth record. When I got the notice of Mr. Adshade's tragic death, I decided to see if he might be a relative of hers, being it's not a real common name round here. And lo n' behold, he's her father. So I dug out his record of birth to see if there were any other relatives in these parts and come to find Johnnie Adshade was the son of one Henrietta C. Appleton. That's yer ma, right? Well, she had a baby boy. Born a coupla years before you came along."

James was reeling as Lizzie prattled on.

"No father listed in the records. Old Mrs. O'Neil who comes in to help out in accountin from time to time was a friend of Mrs. Adshade. Apparently, she and her husband, Frank, I think it was, tried havin a baby for years with no luck. So, they scooped up Johnnie shortly after he was born, and whata ya know, they're with child nine years later. Had a baby girl. Funny how things work out like that. Ain't it? Oh, listen to me. I'm sorry, Jimmy. I just assumed ya knew."

James felt sick. It couldn't possibly be true. Johnnie Adshade, his mother's bastard child, Ellie's husband, the man he detested, was his half-brother. Not a chance, he thought. Then it hit him like a ton of bricks. He'd come home from school complaining about Johnnie beating up kids half his age and less than half his size. He was in the kitchen with his mother. *Ma, he's a filthy pig. He punched Percy today. He was born of the devil. Me and Percy are going to give him a taste of his own medicine. I hope he goes to the pit and it caves down on him.*

He remembered his gentle, soft spoken mother walking toward him, glaring down, and slapping him hard across the face. It was the first, and only, time she ever raised a hand to him out of anything but love. And it was the last time he'd ever say another word to her about Johnnie Adshade.

"You okay, Jimmy? I just thought ya woulda known. Shame you guys didn't know ya were brothers before he passed. I hope I didn't upset ya, or anythin. Ya sure yer okay?"

"Yes. Yes, I'm fine. Lizzie? I'd appreciate it if you don't mention this to anyone."

"Of course not, Jimmy. Ya know me. I'm very professional and *always* discreet."

James turned to Donnely. "Nice meeting you. I'm running late." He walked back to his car thinking about Lizzie's news and his mother's angry eyes. "Born an innocent bastard, died a miserable one," he mumbled. He needed a drink.

He didn't remember the drive home. If there were any other automobiles on the road. If he stopped at any intersections. When he walked into the store, Margaret was finishing up with a customer who was asking if there were any pies.

"James? Did you get the blood pudding?" she called to him.

He walked past her and straight for the rum. He drained the last of the bottle into a sticky tumbler that was on the counter. Margaret looked at the door leading to the back room, then at a young man standing in front of her, eyeing the penny candy. "Take what you want and leave the money on the counter," she said, rushing to James. He was sitting on the stool, with his head down, holding his empty glass.

"James! It's not even noon," Margaret said.

When he raised his head, tears were running down his pale face.

"James? What is it? What's wrong? You're not sick, are you? You don't have the flu?"

He tried to speak, but instead just waved his hand in front of him.

She walked over, put her arms around his neck, and brought his head to her chest. "James? What is it? Tell me! What's wrong?"

James began to sob. Margaret rubbed his back while he tried to gain his composure.

"Margaret, I need to lie down. If I'm not up in two hours, come and get me," he said and abruptly headed for the door.

"But, James? What happened? You have to tell me what happened. I want to help."

"I will, Margaret. Just not now. Tell Mabel I wired Amour and Roddy." He walked out.

Margaret followed him into the store and watched him slowly mount each stair like he was carrying a ton of bricks on his back. What could have made him cry like that, she thought, recalling how stoic he was when their baby died? Stanley came out from the storage room, taking in Margaret's worried expression. He followed her gaze and looked up to see James disappear out of sight. She turned, offered Stanley an awkward smile, then toward the indecisive young boy who was still hovering over the candy display, unable to decide between the licorice, chicken bones, or honeymoons.

Stanley walked up to the counter. "James alright, Margaret?"

"I'm afraid not. Something happened while he was in town that upset him. He went to lie down for a bit."

Stanley began to worry it had something to do with Johnnie. He left the store, telling Margaret he'd be back in an hour.

Mabel walked out of the kitchen and deposited two fresh loaves on the top of the counter. She looked at Margaret and immediately sensed something was wrong. "Is everything alright, Mrs. Cameron?"

"Yes," she said, turning quickly toward her. "James told me to tell you he wired Amour and Roddy."

"Oh, my God. I forgot about the letter." Mabel reached into her apron pocket and pulled it out, pausing to admire Amour's beautiful handwriting before carefully unsealing it. It would be the last letter ever addressed to Da. She wondered if she should even read it. He was very particular about his privacy. But it had to be important, Amour hardly ever wrote.

> *Dear Johnnie:*
>
> *I'm returning home without Roddy. I'll explain everything when I see you. Hope to stay with you and Mabel. I arrive around 8pm on the sixth. No need to meet me at the depot. I'll hire a ride. Looking forward to seeing you both.*
>
> *Love Amour.*

"Jesus, Mary, n' Joseph!" Mabel blurted, quickly covering her mouth, and nervously turning to Mrs. Cameron. "Mrs. Cameron? Do ya know what day it is?"

Margaret was distracted. "I'm sorry, Mabel?" she said, looking toward the stairs and worrying about her husband.

"I was wonderin, if ya know what day it is?"

"Friday," she said.

"Sorry. I mean the date?"

"I believe it's the fourth."

Mabel studied the letter. Amour had no idea sleeping arrangements were no longer a problem. With Da not coming home, she'd have a room to herself. She'd clean it up and make her a pie. Maybe a Jiggs dinner. She dreaded the thought of breaking the news to her. She needed to make sure no one passed on their sympathies before she got a chance to tell her. Christ, she thought, people are going to think she came home for the burial and, here, she doesn't even know her brother's dead.

CHAPTER 4

James flopped down on his bed and closed his eyes, wondering if his father knew of his mother's shame. He pictured the black coal embedded in his father's cuticles, the dark lines under his green eyes, and his big smile. He remembered him walking into the house after working the back shift, sitting at the kitchen table, and devouring his favourite morning fare of liver and onions. He was not an educated man, but he was smart and kind.

James thought of the day he came home from school early and watched his parents waltz around the kitchen, oblivious to his presence. His father was singing in his mother's ear. She had her eyes closed and her arm wrapped around his neck. James had never seen them like that before. And while he was too young to know what love between a man and a woman felt like, he knew from that moment on what it looked like.

An hour went by when James finally got up, splashed some cold water on his face, and returned to the store. "Margaret. I'm going back to town. I'll check on the blood pudding. I won't be long."

"Are you sure you're alright? You look terrible. I really wish you'd tell me what's going on."

"I'm fine, Margaret," he said, quickly putting on his coat. He walked up and kissed her on the cheek. "I just received some troubling news. It's nothing for you to worry about. I'll tell you all about it when I get home."

He was out the door before she got a chance to tell him she'd like to come with him.

CHAPTER 5

Margaret was pouring her tea and watching Mabel pricked the tops of her pie crusts with a fork. "I'm startin to make more pies than bread," Mabel said. "If we wanna keep our bread customers happy, I gotta slow up on the pies, or I'm gonna need another oven. Oh, and I'm gonna need more apples. Come to think of it, I'm runnin low on butter and yeast cakes. And they gotta be Royal yeast cakes, cause like the box says, *they're the most perfect made.*"

"I'll let James know," Margaret said. She put her tea down, hauled a chair over to the sink, and stood on top of it. She opened the overhead cupboard, pulled out a box, and stepped down.

"These are for you," she said, handing the box to Mabel.

"For *me?*" Mabel said. She lifted the lid and looked inside at three shiny pie tins, pulled one out, and examined it as if she had just been given a beautiful piece of jewelry. Mabel's mouth was hanging open when she looked up at Margaret. "They're brand new," she said.

"They were a gift. But I've never been much of a baker," Margaret confessed.

"Thank you so much." Mabel put the box down and surprised Margaret with a hug. "They're beautiful."

Margaret hesitated, then lifted her arms from her sides and brought them around Mabel's back. She closed her eyes and smiled, pleased that her small act of kindness had made Mabel so happy. "I'm glad you like them," she said. The two quickly separated.

Margaret picked up her tea and walk back into the store. Mabel knew Mrs. Cameron wasn't much of a baker. She was beginning to think she might not be that much of bitch, either.

CHAPTER 6

James left Mendelsons, walked to his car, and tossed the blood pudding on the seat. He crossed the street to the savings and loan, filled out the paperwork for his advance, and headed off to see Dr. Adams, a childhood friend of his mother and Percy's dad.

"Well, look at you. Jesus, James, you look worse than half the bodies I'm tending to," Dr. Adams said, extending his hand to his unexpected visitor.

"Hi George. It's been a while. How are you?"

"Busy. As you can see, the bodies are piling up," he said, looking around at the white sheets covering a half dozen cadavers. "That's Matthew Toth," he said, pointing to the table against the back wall. "Guess he couldn't handle his heartache. Shame about the kids." He walked to another table, lifted the sheet, and looked down. "And this one. A young Polish guy they brought in from Number Six this morning. Didn't stand a chance. Overhead beam collapsed, crushing his skull. His father was working a few feet away and saw the whole thing. Poor bastard dug him out with his bare hands, but there was nothing anybody could do for him."

James looked toward the door, thinking he had made a mistake in coming.

"If that isn't bad enough, I got Johnnie Adshade out back. Between the rigor mortis and the freezing temperature, he came in as one *stiff,* stiff. Now, there's a body I don't mind cutting into. You boys must have been around the same age?"

"He was a few years older."

"And how old are you now? Thirty-two?" he asked, gathering up some sharp implements and wrapping them in a white towel.

"Thirty-six."

"*Thirty-six*? Time sure flies, doesn't it?"

"It sure does," James said. He looked around the crowded room, anxious to find out what Dr. Adams knew and leave him to see to the dead.

"Well, it won't be flying by for Johnnie anymore. But you won't see me shed a tear. He just picked on my boy one too many times. Tim was so terrified of Johnnie, I'd have to drag him to school by the scruff of the neck. I finally went to see Johnnie's father. For all the good that did." Dr. Adams shook his head. "He just looked at me and asked, 'What did the little bastard do now?'"

James pinched his eyes closed at the word *bastard*. "Actually, I just dropped in to find out if you know the cause of death. His daughter, Mabel, works at my store, and she obviously wants to know what happened. Sergeant McInnes mentioned something about him being beaten to death."

"From the looks of him, you'd think so. But the bruising on his face is obviously ante mortem. At least one or two days prior to death. I'm figuring he got into a fight and, sometime later, someone ran him down. Hell, if he walked into my path, the brakes on my old Ford might not work too well, either," he said, chuckling. "In fact, if I had my Brownie handy, I'd take a photograph and hang it up as a reminder he's gone. Not sure if it's your cup of tea or not, but if you want to see the body?"

"Actually, I would," James said, not expecting the offer to be made, or his answer. They entered the cold room in back. Dr. Adams walked up to Johnnie's outstretched body and roughly pulled the sheet back. "Good riddance," he said. He looked up to see James remove his hat and bow his head. Dr. Adams quietly left the room and closed the door behind him.

James looked down on Johnnie's still handsome, but bruised, face. How did you get so mean? Why'd you beat Mabel? Abandon Ellie? Did you set Stanley's barn on fire and burn his ponies alive? Why? You had a good home. You were good looking. Better educated than most. God knows, your mother… our mother, was a good woman with a kind heart. What made you so miserable?

James knew Johnnie had nothing to offer. Instead, he contemplated the answers to his own questions. Did you know you were adopted? That your mother abandoned you? Did you feel you didn't fit in? That you were a bastard? That you had a half-brother?

He knelt down on one knee and bowed his head. Dear Lord, forgive this man for his sins on earth and grant him your everlasting glory in heaven. Bring him to his loving mother and may they both rest in eternal peace. He blessed himself, stood, pulled the white sheet over Johnnie's broken body, and opened the door. "Thank you, George. All the best to you and the family," he said, quickly walking past him and out onto the street.

He stood outside the Medical Examiner's Office, tilted his head back, closed his eyes, and drew the cool, salty air up his nose and into his lungs, desperate to rid himself of the stink of death. When he opened his eyes, huge black clouds were approaching from the west. He wondered if they would bring rain or snow. He pulled his coat around him, folded his arms over his chest to fend off the dampness, and watched as young and old alike aimlessly shuffled about, condemned to life in a place with so little to offer.

He then looked at the imposing stone wall that wrapped around the perimeter of St. Agnes Church. Hardly a welcoming sight, he thought, as he took in the bare earth on either side of the rough-hewn planks leading to the church that offered worshippers relief from the mud on rainy days. In the two years since St. Agnes's held its first Mass, not a single blade of grass had taken hold, despite the efforts of many determined elders and the impassioned pleas of the faithful. James had only been in the church three times. Each time for a funeral. And each time, the elderly priest prayed as hard for grass as he did for the souls of the dearly departed. Even the occasional sprinkling of holy water came up dry. Unlike many who believed the infertile ground was the work of the devil, James believed it was because the large stone fence and massive image of Jesus impaled on the cross blocked the sun.

The crucifix, a gift from the town's Italian immigrants meant to endear them to their fellow parishioners, instead created dissension within the flock. Many insisted it be taken down. Others were equally adamant it stay. James had heard that the issue had become so divisive, the two camps were now sitting on opposite sides of the church during Sunday worship. Ironic, he thought, that an image of God could create so much acrimony. He looked up at the white alabaster image and upon His face, His crown of thorns, His spiked hands and feet, and considered how that same image caused him so much internal conflict.

For God so loved the world that he gave his only begotten son, and whosoever believeth in Him shall have everlasting life.

How could *You,* a loving and merciful God, take my son from me? *Why*? He felt himself well up, knowing the answer. Knowing God hadn't failed him. Knowing he had failed God. He closed his eyes. "Forgive me Lord. Give me strength. Restore my faith," he whispered. His moment of reflection was abruptly dispensed with.

"Michael!" And louder. "Mikey!"

James watched Michael Donnely pick up his pace and walk steadfast in the opposite direction of the familiar voice. Everyone stopped dead in their tracks to take in the embarrassing scene that only Lizzie MacNeil seemed oblivious to. Finally, Lizzie screamed his name so loud even Ten-After-Six seemed to bolt upright. James felt sorry for Lizzie as he watched her latest prey point to his watch and then at the building he desperately wanted to escape to. His pursuer, however, was not to be deterred. Lizzie was at his side in no time, slipping her arm around his, and running her tongue over her ruby lips.

James's solemn mood grew as he walked past the boarded-up shoe repair, the yellowed curtains hanging in the dirty window of the Five and Dime, and the pimple-faced boy standing in the doorway of the empty telegraph office. Every building in town, including the church, was either grey or black. The only splashes of colour; compliments of the Union Jack flying atop the British Imperial Coal Company office and the stained glass windows of St. Agnes Church. It was more practicality than bad taste, he thought. It was, after all, a town fueled by coal. Any bright colour applied to the exterior of any one of the dozen or so drab structures that lined Commercial Street was destined to turn black as chimneys spit their filthy remains in the air.

"Mr. Cameron," Mrs. MacGuire called out from behind. "Just wanted to tell you that Mabel's pie was to die for." She momentarily stopped at his side, bent over, and took a deep breath. "I'll definitely be stopping by for another. I'm late as usual. Gotta run," she said, quickly waddling ahead with her purse dangling from the crook of her arm, and her hand waving high in the air.

"I'll let Mabel know. Thank you," James hollered, spotting Willie Morrison outside of Mendelsons. He was bobbing and weaving, and jabbing at his phantom opponent to the amusement of a group of scruffy kids who mimicked his every move.

James was almost to his car when the black clouds burst open, sending everyone scurrying for cover. He ran and climbed in. The rain pelted hard against his windshield, blurring any evidence the town existed. He put the wipers on, but they did little to help. He turned them back off, bent over the steering wheel, and sobbed. He sat there for some time before realizing the torrent had subsided. He sat up and looked out at the aftermath, his eyes following the dirty water that flowed along the mini rivulets the rain had carved into the brown earth. Dear Jesus, he thought, why did I come back to this godforsaken place?

CHAPTER 7

"Looking after the store again, Stanley?" James asked, wiping his muddy feet on the mat.

"Margaret's in back with Mabel."

"Thank you. Don't know how we'd manage without you."

"Everything alright, James? Your mood seems as dark as the weather."

"Not really. But this too shall pass. I'm glad it's rain and not snow. You ready to take Mabel home?"

Stanley wasn't sure, given the awkwardness that had passed between them since he'd reached for her hand. "Whenever she is. Oh, and I left you a little something on the top shelf," he said, gesturing to the back of the store. "Looked like you might need it."

James smiled, knowing Stanley had paid a visit to Iggies. "You're a good man, Stanley," he said, thinking his friend could ill afford to be spending what little money he had on others.

Margaret walked toward them, relieved to see James looking more collected. "Everything okay, dear?" she asked, resting her hand on his arm.

"Everything's fine, Margaret. We're in luck," he said, forcing a smile. He held up the blood pudding.

"Mabel's just finishing up. She won't be too much longer. Supper should be ready in about a half hour," she said, and retreated to the kitchen.

James looked at Stanley. "Follow me." The two walked into the back room.

"Something's weighing you down," Stanley said. "Anything I can do to help?"

James pulled the stools out from under the counter. "Found out today… Johnnie was my half-brother."

Stanley's eyes widened. "Johnnie Adshade?"

"Yeah. Johnnie Adshade. I always said he was a bastard." James reached into his can of tobacco, pinched a few leaves, and dropped them into the thin paper awkwardly cradled between his thumb and forefinger. Stanley reached over. "Here? Better let me do that," he said, nodding at James's swollen hand. He rolled it swiftly, handed it to James, and struck a match on the underside of the counter. James leaned forward and sucked the smoke into his lungs.

"Where the hell did you hear that?" Stanley asked, thinking it couldn't possibly be true.

"Lizzie, from the clerk's office. She flagged me down this morning to pass on her condolences. She told me my mother had Johnnie and gave him up to the Adshades."

"Your *mother?*" Stanley said, jerking his head up.

James nodded.

Stanley couldn't believe Johnnie and James were in any way related, let alone half-brothers. "Gotta be a mistake."

"Afraid not."

"Jesus Christ, James," Stanley said. He reached for the rum bottle. "I don't know what to say. Mind if I help myself?"

"Pour a good one. I'll have one, too."

Stanley passed James his glass. "Any news on what killed him?"

"George said it looks like a hit and run."

Stanley put his head down. "A hit and run?" he repeated, reaching into his pocket for his pipe.

"Apparently he has lots of broken ribs and a cracked skull," James said.

"What are the police saying?"

"As far as I know, they still think he was beaten to death. No doubt because of the mess we made of him. We need to go and tell them we paid Johnnie a visit."

James waited for him to reply. Stanley held a match to his fresh bowl of leaves, sucked on his pipe, and waved his hand in the air to extinguish the small, orange flame. "So, if you're Johnnie's half-brother, I guess that makes you Mabel's—"

"Mabel's what?" she asked, surprising them from the doorway.

James stood quickly, wondering what she had heard. "We were just talking about your bread. How it's the best in town."

Mabel turned to Stanley, "I just wanted to tell ya, ya don't have to drive me home tonight. Thought I'd walk. My legs and feet are as good as new and I could use the exercise."

"Sorry. But Dr. Cohen said no walking for a week. And the week's not up. That's an order," James said. "Besides, Stanley's been waiting to take you home."

"But I feel good. Real good," she said, hoping to avoid another awkward encounter with her driver. She began hopping from one foot to the other. "See. All good."

"Doctor's orders. Your drive awaits," James said, resting his hand on Stanley's shoulder.

"Ready?" Stanley asked, tapping his pipe against the Crisco can.

"Not quite. I need to tidy up," she said, and returned to the kitchen. She hauled the huge bag of flour away from the counter and put it in its assigned place in the pantry, did one last wipe down of her kneading table, and looked around the large kitchen that made her feel at home. She reluctantly picked up her coat and put it on, wondering why her driver made her feel so nervous. It wasn't like she feared him. After all, he helped save her from certain death. It was something else. He was too quiet. And that hand grabbing thing. What was that about?

Stanley watched her from the open doorway as James poured another rum. "Keep the car for the night. You can pick Mabel up in the morning. Then we'll go see Sergeant McInnes."

Stanley turned to face him. "Isn't that getting a little ahead of ourselves? You know what those guys are like. If they find out we both had a run in with Johnnie within forty-eight hours of him ending up dead, they'll jump to conclusions. Assume we had something to do with it."

"That's crazy. It was a hit and run. And besides, we were together the night Johnnie died. We have nothing to worry about. And it's the right thing to do."

"I really think it's better if we just let Dr. Adams tell them it was a hit and run before we get involved. I just don't trust them," Stanley said.

James was initially surprised by Stanley reluctance, but conceded he didn't trust the police, either. "You may be right. Actually, I found Sergeant McInnes's questions a little unnerving."

"What questions?"

"Where we were coming from? If we were drinking? How I hurt my hand? What I thought of Johnnie? Wasn't sure if he suspected us of something, or if he was just being nosy."

Stanley reached back into his pocket, took out his pipe, and began chewing on the stem.

"So, what did you tell McInnes about your hand?" he asked.

"I told him I hurt it moving some crates."

"So, if you go to him now and say you hurt it when you punched Johnnie in the face, he'll be all over you like shit on a hot shovel."

James dragged on his makin and looked down at his sore hand, weighing Stanley's warning.

"I'm ready," Mabel said, reappearing in the doorway, and sensing the unease that had crept into the air.

CHAPTER 8

Stanley started the car. They were more than halfway to the shack before Stanley finally spoke up. "Must be hard for you going home to an empty house?"

"Must be just as hard for you? I'm really sorry about the ponies."

"Thanks," he said. "I'm sorry for you, too. Although I gotta admit, I didn't care too much for your father."

"Can't say he was everybody's favourite. Hell, can't even say he was mine."

Stanley pulled up to the dark shack. He wanted to go in with her to make sure everything was okay, but thought she might misinterpret things, again. "Thanks, Stanley. See ya Monday." She was about to close the door, but swung it back open. "Ya never said how my pie was."

He cupped his ear.

"How was my pie?" she asked louder.

"Didn't try it."

"Ya didn't try it?" she said, her voice high and her eyes wide.

He just leaned across the passenger seat, exposed the hint of a smile, pulled the door shut, and said, "Nope."

Mabel stood there with her mouth hanging open as he drove off.

CHAPTER 9

James washed up while Margaret prepared supper. He turned his head from side to side, examining the grey hair that was quickly creeping away from his temples and up along the sides of his forehead. The image of Johnnie's jet black hair came to mind. "We were nothing alike," he said, flopping down on the bed. He wanted to pull the blankets up over his head and stay there for the night. He couldn't bear the thought of telling Margaret about his shame. But he also knew he couldn't avoid it any longer. He got up, walked out the door, and made his way downstairs. Margaret heard him approaching.

"Don't come in just yet."

"What are you up to?"

"I'm fixing supper."

"How long?" James asked.

"Twenty minutes at most."

James was thankful for the delay. He went to the rear of the store, poured himself a short rum, and lit a makin. He was devastated by Lizzie's news, confused by his own reaction to Johnnie's death, yet happy Margaret was coming around.

"It's ready," Margaret hollered from the kitchen. James snuffed out his makin and downed the last of the black rum he hoped would settle his nerves.

The kitchen table was topped with white linen, two crystal

glasses, fine china, and four tapered candles. "I thought we should celebrate a fresh start," she said.

James looked at his wife and felt his chest tighten. The silence in the room returned, neither sure of what to say. They stood awkwardly apart from one another, like teenagers on a first date.

James nodded his pleasure. "This is nice. Really nice."

"Mabel helped," she said. She reached down to tug on the corners of the tablecloth, and nervously ran her hand over the top, as if wiping away a crease.

"I see she also made my pie. Didn't think I was ever going to taste the hottest commodity in town," James said, hoping to dispatch their shared anxiety. His heart was pounding. Margaret's was, too.

"First things first. Come and eat."

James walked around the table and pulled her chair out. "So, what's in the glasses?" he asked, settling Margaret in before taking his place across from her.

"Vermouth."

"*Vermouth*?"

"Yes. Vermouth. Compliments of Mrs. MacGuire. It's medicinal."

He grinned. "So is rum." He reached down and picked up his cloudy, red drink, smelled it, and took a sip. It must have been medicinal. It tasted as bad as any tonic he'd ever had.

"James. I've been worried about you all day. I need to know what happened to make you so upset."

"I'm sorry."

"You also promised to tell me about Mabel and her mother."

James nodded. "I'm just not sure where to begin."

"We've got all night. I want to hear everything, from beginning to end."

They sat across from one another at the small round table. James took a good mouthful of his medicine and began with memories from his past he'd never shared before. About how he had been lonely growing up. About Percy and Ellie, who were also from one-child families. About the war, finding Percy in the dress tent, and the St. Christopher medal he always wore. About how everything had changed when he came home from the war, including him.

He then told her how Ellie had married Johnnie Adshade, the guy he and Percy hated so much, and moved away. How she'd promised to write during the war, but hadn't sent a single letter to either of them. How, years later, he was sure he saw her in town with a young child and called out to her, but she hadn't acknowledged him. How much it hurt, and how he felt as lonely as a grown man, as he had as a child. And how, after many years without hearing from her, he finally got a letter asking if he would come to see her in Pleasant Bay.

"They were living in a rundown farmhouse, with not a neighbour in sight. And she was sick. Her skin was grey and she was very weak," he said.

Margaret was glad James was finally opening up to her, but disappointed in him for not sharing any of this with her before now. She realized it was as much her fault as his. She looked at him, with his head down, crushing his fork into the uneaten blood pudding that formed a black mass on his plate. "What was wrong with her?"

"Don't know. She hadn't seen a doctor. Probably cancer." He finished his vermouth. "Then she drops a bombshell…tells me Mabel is Percy's daughter."

"Johnnie's not Mabel's father!" Margaret said, stunned by James's revelation.

"No."

"And Mabel has no idea?" she asked, refilling his glass.

James shook his head. "No."

"You have to tell her."

"I know. I just have to find the right moment," he said, dreading the thought. He took a forkful of the black pudding and looked down at his plate. He wasn't hungry.

Margaret wasn't sure she wanted to hear the answer, but she needed to know. "James? Were you in love with Ellie?"

He lifted his head and leaned back in his chair. "I was young. I thought I was… until I met you." She reached over and squeezed his hand. He turned his palm upward and clasped hers.

"I was just hurt. I felt Ellie betrayed Percy and me. He should have known he had a daughter. I should have known he and Ellie were more than friends. We never kept anything from one another. Nothing. At least, that's what I believed."

They sat quietly, each warmed by the other's touch. Each wondering what the other was thinking. James looked at her and smiled. "I know it sounds childish, but I felt as if they shared a secret and kept it from me." He let go of Margaret's hand, reached for his glass, and took a healthy swig. "When Ellie told me Percy was Mabel's father, I wanted to leave. But I also needed to know why she married Johnnie. Why she didn't write."

"Was Mabel there?" Margaret asked.

"She was mostly outside playing. When she did come in, Ellie introduced me as an old friend from school. She might have been seven or eight."

"Where was Johnnie?"

James waved his hand dismissively. "Maybe off fishing. Probably off on a bender."

"So, why did she marry Johnnie?" Margaret asked. She reached for a piece of Mabel's bread, thinking of how quick she had been to judge her.

"Because she wanted to keep the baby. As an unwed mother, she knew the baby would be taken from her. She said she'd rather marry a man she didn't love, than give up her child. Percy's child."

Margaret watched James pick up his fork and push his food around. "Her parents wouldn't help?"

"Ellie's parents were pretty much by the book. And her father wasn't what you'd call the forgiving kind. She felt she had no options if she wanted to keep the baby."

Margaret took a sip of her Vermouth. She knew how hard it was to lose a child. She thought of her own baby, and how she would have done anything in the world for him. "But why Johnnie?"

she asked.

"Ellie said if it wasn't Percy, it didn't matter who it was. She said her wedding day was the saddest day of her life, until the day she heard Percy had been killed. Said she wanted to die, but Mabel kept her going."

"Do you think Johnnie knew he wasn't Mabel's father?"

"No. Not then, at any rate. I seriously doubt he ever found out. As far as I know, I was the only one she ever told."

"But the baby would have come early. He never put two and two together?" she asked. She ran a buttered knife over the bread and passed it to James.

He took the bread from her and laid it next to his uneaten pudding. "Apparently not. She actually walked to the old couple's farm next door when her water broke. Johnnie was nowhere to be seen. He came home and the baby was just there. Ellie said the first words out of his mouth when he walked in and saw the baby were, 'I was hoping for a boy.' Only thing he asked, was who helped with the delivery."

Margaret thought of the night she had given birth to her baby. The pain was almost as excruciating as her worry. She had already suffered two miscarriages, was terrified the baby wouldn't survive, and that she and James would once again be devastated. She looked down at the table and closed her eyes.

James watched her closely, worried their conversation was upsetting her. "Let's leave it there for now," he said, reaching over, and touching her shoulder.

She lifted her head and looked at him in a way that assured him she was okay. "No, James. Go on," she said. "And, please, eat your supper."

He sat back in his chair. "Anyway, Ellie and I sat at her kitchen table and talked for a couple of hours. She told me she wasn't happy, but not miserable either, and that she had many blessings to be grateful for. Talked about how strong and resilient Mabel was, with a natural curiosity to learn. Said she marveled at how Mabel found joy in simple things. Ellie wanted her to go to school and get proper lessons, but the school was too far and there was no way to get there, so she taught her as best she could with what she had on hand. Said Percy would have been proud of his daughter. She also said she and Johnnie had a baby boy named Jonathan. But he died. Apparently, Johnnie didn't take to him any more than he did to Mabel.

Margaret's eyes began to tear up. "Poor Mabel. She never knew her real father. Lost her mother and baby brother while still a child herself. And lived with a man that beat her. Yet, you'd never know she's had such a miserable past. She's been so strong… and I've been—"

James looked at his wife. She had her head back and was brushing away a tear. "Margaret, everyone deals with tragedy differently."

Margaret bowed her head. "Clearly some, much better than others." She pushed James's plate toward him and looked down at her own. She picked up her fork. But it was his story she needed more of, not the blood pudding.

"Do you think Johnnie beat Ellie?"

"No. I think he actually loved her, in as much as he could love anyone. But he didn't treat her well, either. She should have seen a doctor. He should have forced her to go. *I* should have forced her to."

"She knew she was dying?"

He nodded.

"It must have been hard for you?" Margaret said, taking a sip of her vermouth.

"It was harder for Ellie," he said.

Margaret was anxious to get to the events that made him so upset earlier in the day, but decided it would come soon enough. "So *why* didn't she write?"

"She said she wrote almost every other week, but didn't post the letters. Claimed she couldn't bring herself to mail them. Saw no point in it, given her circumstances. And she was afraid Johnnie would find out. She told me she somehow knew in her heart Percy would never come home, but if he had, she would have left Johnnie. She also admitted she heard me calling after her on one of her rare trips to town, but couldn't face me. She was ashamed she married Johnnie, sorry she didn't write, and afraid facing the past would be too painful."

"So, she contacted you to say her goodbyes?" Margaret said. She picked up their plates and walked to the sink.

"Yes. And to put her affairs in order. She wasn't afraid of dying, but of leaving Mabel with Johnnie."

James started to well up and took his time before continuing. "She …" his voice cracked.

Margaret walked back to the table and moved her chair closer to his.

"She wanted me to check in on Mabel when I could. She also had some war bonds her father had left her after he died. She figured Johnnie would just use them to buy whiskey. So, she gave them to Samuel Friedman, along with her last will and testament, stating I was to be Mabel's trustee. That's why she was in town the day I saw her." He started to cry.

Margaret rubbed his arm. "Ellie obviously loved you."

"But that's just it," he said, abruptly standing and scratching at his forehead. "Margaret! I failed her. And I failed Mabel."

"How can you say that? She's here. You gave her a job. You're looking after her as best you can. Ellie would be proud of you."

James shook his head. "I doubt that."

"Well, I don't." Margaret stood up, handed him her napkin, and walked out of the kitchen. When she returned, he was wiping his eyes and blowing his nose. She was holding the rum bottle. "I saw Stanley sneak it in earlier today," she said, uncapping it and pouring a healthy amount in his empty glass. She picked up her own, dumped the remains of her vermouth into the sink, walked back to the table, and picked up the rum. "Just this once," she said, and poured a small amount for herself.

James smiled and returned to his chair. "I failed everyone."

Margaret shook her head back and forth. "I really don't understand how you can say that."

"I only went to check on Mabel once. After I got the letter from Friedman asking me to come settle up Ellie's estate."

"Well, it wouldn't have been easy. They lived a good distance away. And you had no car back then."

"That's not a good reason, Margaret. I just didn't do it. Always found an excuse."

"But you did go back and check on her. Most people wouldn't have even done that much."

"I went. But I never saw her. When I got to the farmhouse, I could tell nobody lived there. So I walked to the nearest neighbor. They told me they didn't know where Johnnie and Mabel were living. Said they knew Ellie, but not Mr. Adshade. The old woman told me she and her husband had helped bring one of Ellie's children into the world and buried the other."

James looked at Margaret. "I'm sorry, dear," he said. "I know this must be upsetting."

"Go on," she said. She brought her glass to her mouth and felt the warm, burning sensation of the rum against the back of her throat.

"The old woman said she knew Ellie wasn't well and that her husband was rarely about, so she would check in on them from time to time. Then, one day, she walked in and found Ellie all bundled up on the sofa with a few withered daisies on her chest. Mabel was sitting on the floor next to her, holding her hand. The old woman said… she said… she said Ellie had been dead for several days."

Margaret put her glass down and brought her hand to her mouth. James went over and knelt down beside her. "I'm sorry. I think that's—"

"No, James. I don't even know what happened today. There's a lot you still haven't told me."

He went back to his chair, his rum, and his story. "Johnnie was nowhere to be seen, so the neighbours took Mabel home to stay with them and buried Ellie next to her son on the hill. Then,

Johnnie shows up looking for his wife and daughter. The old lady said he never shed a tear when he found out his wife was dead. He just grabbed Mabel and left. They stayed in the farmhouse for about another week. Then they were gone. She told me she thought Johnnie only visited the gravesites once, and that was to pull Mabel away. Said she had no idea where they went after that. She saw Mabel about a year later with a family she didn't know, but didn't get a chance to talk to her. When I asked her how Mabel seemed…" James lips started to quiver, "she said, 'thin.'"

"I'm so sorry, James. I only wish you had shared this with me before," Margaret said, welling up. "I feel terrible about how I've behaved toward you *and* Mabel."

"Margaret. I couldn't bear to think about it, let alone speak of it. It haunted me for years. Then we had the baby and things got better for a while. When we lost the baby, it all came flooding back. I felt God was punishing me for my failures," he said.

"James," she said gently, "why didn't you cry when the baby died?"

James looked at his wife and swallowed hard. "Margaret, I cried all the time. Still do. Just not when you're around. I thought I was going to lose you, too. You were so depressed. Not eating or leaving your bed. I was just trying to be strong for you."

"James. I never questioned your strength. I questioned your heart. I didn't know you suffered as much as you did. I should have spoken to you about it. We need to promise one another to talk more and …to lean on each other more."

"We also need to promise we'll never close our bedroom door on each other," he said.

Margaret smiled and nodded, then reached for the rum to top up her glass.

"Margaret," he blurted. "Johnnie Adshade, was my half-brother."

Margaret let her hand slip from the bottle.

"That's why I was so upset today," he said.

"But that's preposterous! Where in the world did you hear that nonsense?"

"Lizzie MacNeil. Manager of records. She waved me down when I was in town this morning to pass on her condolences."

"Well, I don't believe it. The two of you are nothing alike, in looks or in manner."

"But we shared a mother."

"Your mother!" Margaret said, her voice and eyes revealing her shock.

"Yes," he said, feeling his revelation was also something of a betrayal. It was a secret his mother had taken to her grave.

"And you believe this…this Lizzie?"

"I do," he said, telling Margaret about the day his gentle, soft-spoken mother had slapped him.

"Still, James. I'd want to see the records for myself."

"Lizzie would have no reason to lie."

"Who's Johnnie's father?"

"Records don't say. According to Lizzie, the Adshades took him in shortly after he was born. He probably never knew he was adopted."

"So, Johnnie died not knowing who his real parents were, or that he wasn't Mabel's father."

"Or that he had a half-brother. I called him a bastard all my life, not realizing he was my mother's bastard."

"I'm so sorry."

"There's more."

Margaret's shoulders slumped and her arms fell loosely to her sides. "Dear God."

"I own the Adshade property. At least, it's in my name. But it belongs to Mabel. I'm sorry. I had no right to keep this from you." James expected her to be angry. It was one thing to keep the secrets of others from his wife, but this one was his.

"I thought it belonged to Roddy and Amour," she said, curious as to how James came to own it.

"They did. But when I heard they were leaving for Boston, I went to see Roddy and bought it from him on the condition he keep quiet about our arrangement. I found out Johnnie and Mabel moved back to town when Roddy gave him a job keeping the books for the Company Store. Even though Johnnie was doing better than most folks, he and Mabel were living in a dump. Johnnie, being Johnnie, drank most of his earnings and didn't give a damn where they slept. I knew Ellie would want Mabel to have a decent roof over her head, so I used the money from the war bonds to buy it from Roddy."

"And Johnnie had no idea?"

"Not until the other day, when Stanley and I paid him a visit to tell him what happened to Mabel. Anyway, we had an exchange. I let him get to me. I blurted it out, then clocked him," he said, holding up his hand.

"I didn't think you were being truthful about how you hurt your hand," she said, looking down at it. "So, why let Johnnie stay on? Why didn't you just sign the house over to Mabel?"

"There would have been no point in that. Johnnie would have forced her to sell it to cover his drinking, or gambling habit. And it would have just opened up a huge can of worms."

"But, James? She deserves to know the truth now that Johnnie's gone."

"I know. I'm just not sure how to tell her, or when."

"The sooner the better."

"She's gone this long without knowing. A little while longer won't hurt. Let her bury Johnnie, first. Hard as it is to believe, she's sad he's gone. And it's not going to be easy to tell her her real father's dead, too. And that she was born out of wedlock."

"Is that it, James? Is there anything else I need to know?"

"Isn't that enough," he said, deciding to keep his suspicions about Johnnie burning Stanley's ponies alive to himself, for now. He'd divulged enough for one night. He was spent.

"I'll say," she said, still trying to absorb everything she'd heard. "You hardly touched your supper. At least try some pie?"

"Well, I'd better. They keep disappearing on me."

Margaret approached with their pie. "Hope it tastes better than it looks," James said, breaking off a sizeable chunk and putting it in his mouth. He pursed his lips, squinted his eyes, leaned forward, and spit it into his napkin.

"Are you okay?" Margaret asked.

"Good God! It's like I ran my tongue along a salt lick," he said, reaching for his tea. He was putting his cup down when he saw Margaret bent sideways in her chair. "No, you try it," he insisted, twisting his fork under the crust and peering in. "On second thought, don't. Mrs. MacGuire said it was to die for. I didn't think she meant it could kill you."

Margaret started to howl. "I… I…" she said. She tried to stop laughing long enough to finish her sentence.

James started to laugh, too, unsure of what was so funny.

"I must have mistaken….mistaken the salt for sugar," she roared.

"*You* made this," James said.

"Tried to."

James picked up his fork, broke off a third of his pie, and shoveled it into his mouth. He bravely crunched into the disgusting, salty mush, "Actually, it's really… really…bad." He, once again, spit it into his napkin. "Sorry," he said, thinking as much as he hated Margaret's pie, he was loving the moment.

Margaret was still chuckling when they walked to the sink. "Mabel wanted to help, but I insisted I make it on my own. I think I'll stick to my needlepoint and leave the baking to her."

"Did I tell you lately how much I love your needlepoint," he said, reaching for a dry rag.

She poked her head into his chest. "You're tired. I'll get the dishes."

"The dishes can wait," he said. He reached for her hand.

"You go up. I'm right behind you."

James stopped in the doorway leading from the kitchen to the store, and turned around as Margaret was dumping the remains of her pie into the trash.

"Thank you, Margaret."

She smiled. "Just leave the door open. I'll be up shortly."

James got into bed, feeling the rum and relief wash over him as the grief and anger that had kept him and Margaret apart, let go. He was glad he'd finally shared his past with her and, that for the first time since they lost the baby, they had opened up to one another. He felt the barriers were finally coming down and silently thanked God.

He drifted in and out of sleep several times before Margaret crawled in bed and leaned into him. "James," she whispered. "There *are* worse things than being a mother who buries her son." He turned to face her. "There's a mother who buries her son and leaves another child behind."

James closed his eyes and kissed her softly on the lips. When he opened them, she was looking back. He hesitated a moment, then pressed his mouth against hers. And for the first time in over three years, they loved one another.

Saturday November 5

CHAPTER I

Stanley and Mabel arrived at the store at seven to find it was still closed. "That's odd. Mr. Cameron's normally up by now with the shutters off and my oven heatin up," Mabel said.

She and Stanley sat quietly, waiting for some sign of life. Mabel shivered as she looked at the coal shed and wondered what would have happened if she hadn't been discovered.

Stanley reached behind him and pulled a blanket off the back seat. "You need a warmer coat," he said, draping it over her shoulders. To Mabel's relief, James finally appeared in the doorway.

"Sorry. We slept in," he said, pulling his robe around him.

Mabel entered the kitchen. Margaret was holding the kettle under the tap. "Good morning, Mabel."

"Mornin, Mrs. Cameron."

"Mabel? I'd like you to call me Margaret."

"But that wouldn't be right, Mrs. Cameron."

"Margaret, please? Mrs. Cameron makes me feel old."

"So, *Margaret*… how did Mr. Cameron like your pie?" Mabel asked.

Margaret pointed to the pail in the corner with the remains of her pie. "I'm afraid I don't have your talents."

"But yer so smart at other things. The way ya talk. All the books ya read. And yer needlepoint is so beautiful. Only thing I'm good at, if I do say so myself, is bakin."

"Don't sell yourself short. You're very bright for someone with so little schooling."

Mabel looked at Margaret thinking she looked different. She studied her for a moment, before realizing that Margaret had smiled at her. Not a forced smile hiding a different meaning, but a real one.

"Mabel? I'd like to ask you something."

"Sure. What is it?"

"James mentioned you had a hole in your leg. I was curious as to how it happened?"

Mabel paused, thinking of what she would say. She didn't want to lie to Margaret now that they were getting along better, but she also didn't want to have to admit to what she had done to deserve it. She put her head down, before bringing her eyes up to Margaret's. "Truth is, I got caught stealin. It was my punishment."

"What did you steal that would warrant that kind of punishment?"

Mabel dropped her head, again. "A can of Carnation."

Margaret looked at her in disbelief. "When was this?"

Mabel reached for her apron. "A long time ago. It don't hurt none."

"How long ago?" Margaret asked softly.

"I dunno. I musta been round seven or eight. Can't tell ya exactly. Cause.... well you know... I ain't exactly sure how old I am. Just know it's somethin that happened a while back."

"Did your father do it?"

"Oh, no. It was his cousin Frankie. Da sent me to live with him and his family after Ma died. I went to help out, since they had six kids n'all, and Delores, that's Frankie's wife, was havin another baby. Anyway, I got what I deserved for stealin from a family with so little to begin with. I was just real hungry, given I only got what was left over, and there usually wasn't much. Can't blame Frankie. The Carnation was for the little ones. Funny thing is, I no sooner got it down when it came right back up. Still can't look at a can of Carnation without my stomach churnin."

"But… the hole? How did you get the hole?"

"Scissors."

CHAPTER 2

James smiled at the chatter in the kitchen, relieved Margaret and Mabel were getting along much better. It was a good day, one of the best he could remember in a long time. He welcomed a steady stream of customers, many who placed bread or pie orders for the following week, while Stanley cleaned out the clutter in the storage room. He felt like a million tons of doubt and worry had been lifted off his broken spirit, and that maybe God needed him to bare his soul in order for life to begin to align itself. He was about to close the store for the night, when one last customer stopped by. It was Michael Donnely.

"Hello, Mr. Cameron," Donnely said, extending his hand. "We met—"

"Yes, of course, Mr. Donnely. I remember. What brings you to this part of town?"

"I am invited to a dinner tonight and thought I'd see about your pie. I hear they're quite good."

"I doubt there are any left, but I'll check with my baker. Mabel," James hollered into the kitchen. "Do you have a pie back there?"

"Just one. And it's yers. It ain't for sale."

James poked his head around the doorway. "Mabel? I have a customer going to a dinner."

"Sorry. But you haven't even tried my pie yet. It ain't goin to nobody but you."

"But, Mabel?" he whispered. "He's a very influential man around town. If he likes your pie, it could bring in more customers."

"It's yer pie, Mr. Cameron. So I guess if you don't want it, it's yers to do what ya like."

James walked over and picked up the pie. "You can make me one any time."

"Tell him I want my tin back," she said, giving James an exasperated look.

Michael Donnely left with the pie, thinking he suddenly felt famished.

CHAPTER 3

Mabel and Stanley were on the way to the shack. The quiet between them unsettled Mabel. He's not much of a conversationalist, she thought. "Whatcha do with yer spare time? Got any hobbies?" she asked.

"I like to sketch and read."

"Ya like to read?"

"Yeah. Does that surprise you?"

"Sorta."

He glanced toward her. "So, what do you do when you're not baking?"

"I like to walk. Also, gotta get caught up on my washin and cleanin. Just chores n' stuff. I go to church when I can. Da wasn't too keen on it. I'll go more now," she said, looking down at her feet. "Do ya go to church?"

"I go to funerals."

"But ya believe?"

"I guess."

"Whacha mean? *Ya guess*. Either ya do, or ya don't."

"I believe in God. Just not the church."

"That makes no sense. The church is just people who gather to pray and do God's work."

"That's just it. I know too many folks who go to church but who aren't necessarily what you'd call good people. Got tired of seeing the big shots around town showing up in their fancy suits and throwing a buck or two on the collection plate and feeling smug about it. The same folks that run the coal company and the Company Store. Bunch of mean, miserable hypocrites, forcing hardworking families to live in squalor."

"So, yer punishin God cause ya don't like some of the folks who go to church?"

"I don't think of it like I'm punishing God."

"Better hope he doesn't either," she said, as the car came to a halt. "Thanks for drivin me home. Guess it's the last time. Dr. Cohen says I can start walkin next week. See ya Monday."

Stanley looked in the rearview mirror as he pulled away. She was standing on the pathway to the shack and looking in his direction. He wondered what she was thinking.

"Damn. I forgot to ask him about my pie," she said.

CHAPTER 4

Margaret wanted to kick herself. She should have left well enough alone. Instead, she ruined the lightness of the day by plowing ahead and telling James how Mabel got the hole in her leg. She might have known he would find a way to blame himself. It didn't matter what she said, James believed that if he had gone to Pleasant Bay sooner, it would never have happened.

James placed his teacup on the table. "I'm going to bed, dear."

"James, don't be so hard on yourself. You're a good man with a kind heart. I know that. Mabel knows that. And so did Ellie."

James looked at her like a man who couldn't be convinced. He pushed his chair back and took his plate to the sink. He had his back to her looking out the window. "Margaret, never doubt how much I love you."

She felt a wave of sadness grip her. She stood, walked up behind him, wrapped her arms around his waist, and leaned her head against his back. "James," she said, struggling to find the words she hadn't spoken for so long. "I've been a complete fool. Thank you for giving me another chance." James turned, embraced her, and kissed the top of her head.

They were both crying.

Sunday, November 6

CHAPTER I

Stanley arrived well before nine to take James and Margaret to church. He knocked several times, each time louder than the next, but there was no answer. He returned to the car and waited another thirty minutes, before finally giving up and driving to the brook. He'd check back in an hour.

When he got to the brook, he shut the car off, and tamped his pipe. He sat up when he spotted her walking along the other side. He watched her for a while, knowing she had no idea he was there. He finally stepped out of the car and walked toward the brook that separated them.

"Pretty cold day to be out walking," he said, startling her.

"What?" she asked.

"I said it's a pretty cold day to be out walking."

"It ain't that cold," she said, shoving her hands into her pockets.

He cupped his good ear, so she said it again, louder.

"Still," he said, "Mr. Cameron and Dr. Cohen wouldn't be too happy with you right now."

"My feet are fine and I missed my walks. Besides, who's gonna tell them?"

He heard her, but pointed to his ear, then at the foot bridge that crossed about fifty feet before the mouth of the harbour. They walked together on opposite sides of the brook and met in the middle.

"Yer not gonna tell them, are ya?"

"Tell who? What?"

"Mr. Cameron and Dr. Cohen. Bout me out here walkin."

"No," he said. He took out his box of matches and lit his pipe.

"What brings ya here? Not spyin on me, are ya?" Mabel asked.

"No," Stanley said, chuckling.

"So, ya just happened to show up when I'm here?"

"Yep."

"Did ya try my pie yet?"

"No."

"It won't be any good by the time ya get round to it. Ya got eat it in a coupla days, or the crust gets all mushy. What's wrong? Ya don't like pie?"

"Love pie."

"Well, eat it up and get the tin back to me, so I can make one for somebody who'll appreciate it."

"I will," he said. He didn't tell her he'd polished it off in one sitting.

"So, what are ya doin here?" she asked.

"I was supposed to take Margaret and James to church. They must have decided to go to a later Mass, so I'm just killing time."

"Killin time. Never understood why people feel the need to kill time. Makes it seem like there's too much of it or somethin. I never think there's enough."

He walked to the other side of her so she would be talking in his good ear.

"Did ya hear what I said about killin time?"

"Yes."

"Well, it's a terrible thing. Like wastin the time God gave ya on earth. It could end any time, ya know." she said, thinking of her ma, her baby brother, and her da. "Every minute counts. Mind ya, I like some minutes a lot more than others. Like when I'm bakin or walkin. I love that. But when ya think that ya sleep through half of them, there's none to spare. Do ya like walkin along the brook?"

Stanley leaned over the wooden handrail. "One of my favourite places."

"See, then. Yer not killin time. Yer doin somethin ya like."

"Can't argue with that."

"How'd ya lose yer hearin?"

"What?" he asked.

"How did ya lose yer hearin?"

"What?" he repeated.

"Ya heard me the first time," she said, swatting his arm.

"Boxing. Used to hear pretty good in both ears until about eight years ago. Lost the hearing in this one after a match. The other one still works pretty good."

"Ya were a boxer? Ya don't look like a boxer."

He turned sideways to face her, resting one elbow on the railing. "No. Why do you say that?"

"I dunno. Ya just don't look like any boxer I ever saw."

He straightened up. "So, what *do* I look like? A coal hauler?"

She studied him for a moment. "A teacher."

"A *teacher?*"

"Don't go flatterin yerself. It's just the pipe. Sure didn't have ya pegged as a boxer, that's all. Were ya any good?"

"I won a few bouts."

"Why'd ya quit?"

"Just got tired of it," he said. He closed his eyes, thinking of Dirty Willie twitching on the canvass. "Any idea on when you're going to bury your father?" he asked, as anxious to change the subject as he was to see Johnnie in the ground.

"My Aunt Amour is comin in from Boston tonight. She was Da's only livin relative outside of me. Least I know of. She doesn't know he's gone. She should have a say in the burial."

They both let silence hang in the air as a group of kids make their way up the side of the brook. They were breaking the thin ice that clung to its frosty banks with the heels of their boots.

"I feel awful bout the ponies. They helped ya save me. I woulda liked to have met them."

"You would have loved them."

"Are ya havin any kinda special burial?"

"No. Nothing special. I'm just gonna clean up where the barn was and plow it over."

"I'd come if ya were, ya know?"

"Need a drive back home?" he asked, this time trying to get his mind off his ponies.

"No. Not goin there, in any case."

"Where are you heading?"

"Goin to finish my walk." She turned and walked away, before spinning back around, "Don't forget my tin," she hollered.

He waved, puffed on his pipe, and never took his eyes off her till she was out of sight. He lingered, thinking about how much he hated her father, how much he liked her, and how much they were nothing alike.

CHAPTER 2

Stanley drove back to the store wondering how much he should tell James. He knew that if James went to the police and told them about Johnnie's busted up face, McInnes would be banging on his door in no time. He loved James like a brother, but he hadn't told him he knew Johnnie was responsible for killing his ponies, or about the blood he saw in Mabel's hair. Little good, he decided, could come from unburdening his guilt, by weighing down his friend. For now, at least, he'd keep things to himself.

When he pulled up to the store, James came from around the side of the store with a bucket full of coal. He waited for Stanley to get out of the car. "You look deep in thought," James said.

"Not really. I was by earlier to take you to church. Figured you must have walked, or decided on a later Mass."

"Sorry. Slept in again. Hope we didn't hold you up from anything?"

"No. I just took a drive to the brook. I ran into—"

"Into?"

"An old friend," he said, remembering his promise to Mabel.

"We're not going to church. And I have no plans to go anywhere in the morning, so keep the car if you like."

"Thanks. Do you have time to talk about the plans for the store?"

"Sure. Want some tea? Something to eat?"

"Any pie?" Stanley joked.

"Afraid not. Mabel's day off," James said. He peeked around the corner. "And you don't want Margaret's."

"I was thinking about what you said about the hardware section," Stanley said.

"Yes?"

"Well, I hear Larry Mendelson's considering doing the same. And he gets a lot more traffic than you do."

"I didn't know. Sounds to me as if you're trying to talk yourself out of a job."

"No. I just think I might have a better idea. Instead of expanding and selling what practically everybody else is selling, why not sell what none of the others have?"

"And what's that?"

"Bread and pies."

James gave him a puzzled look. "Everyone's selling bread and pies."

"Not Mabel's."

"Did she put you up to this?" James asked.

"No. I swear," Stanley said, blessing himself. "Honestly, James, it makes more sense. If you expand the bakery you won't have to knock down the wall to the kitchen. There's lots of room back there for another stove. And lots of space to add another work table and more storage."

"Might not be a bad idea. But Mabel can't do all the baking herself. And God knows, Margaret's of no use to her."

CHAPTER 3

Mabel left the brook and approached the shack. Mary Catherine was sitting on the stoop. She had a plate, wrapped in a tea towel, resting on her lap. "I heard about your da. I brought you some sandwiches." She reached into her coat pocket. "And here's a Mass card from Ma."

Mabel hugged her friend. "C'mon. I'll make some tea."

"How are you doing?" Mary Catherine asked.

"I'm good. Aunt Amour is comin home tonight. A bit worried about breakin the news."

"She doesn't know?"

"No. She was plannin on comin home before it happened. She wouldna gotten the telegram Mr. Cameron sent along."

"Oh, dear. Coming all this was to see her brother, only to find out he's passed."

"I know. It's gonna be hard to tell her," Mabel said. She slid the lid lifter under the round iron plate, moved it off to the side, crumpled up some paper, and shoved it into the belly of the stove. She then added some kindling and struck the match. She waited to make sure the fire had a good burn, before adding some coal, and putting the lid back in place. Mary Catherine started to unbutton the heavy brown coat she got from the consignment shop.

Mabel turned to her friend. "Jesus, girl. Leave yer coat on, or you'll fuckin freeze to death."

Mary Catherine pulled her coat around her. "So is it true your

Da was beaten to death by a bunch of coloureds?"

Mabel reached for the kettle. "Where'd ya hear that?"

"It's all over town."

"Da told me the same thing before he got himself killed, but I didn't believe him. I figured he got into a fight cheatin at cards, or got caught with another man's wife. Wouldn't be the first time. Ain't like the coloureds to come round these parts. And Da certainly wouldna been caught dead in their neck of the woods."

"Well, there's plenty of people who believe your da wasn't lying. Heard some folks outside church this morning talking about burning them out."

Mabel thought back to her conversation with Stanley at the brook; how he didn't go to church because of all the hypocrites. "Jesus, Mary n' Joseph. Leave it to the God fearin to jump to judgement. Sure hope it's just hot air. Town's ugly enough without all that," Mabel said, wondering if her Da was about to create as much trouble dead as he did when he was alive. Mabel added water to the kettle, placed it on the stove, and joined Mary Catherine at the table. "So, how are the boys doin?"

"Not bad. Luke is a little quieter than I'd like. But the younger two are adjusting pretty good. Church has been helping some. Collecting clothes and dropping off food. But Da fears that we can't count on that for much longer." Mary Catherine's face showed her worry.

"Ya know, I can help out now that I only got my own mouth to feed and don't pay no rent," Mabel said.

"I can't expect you to do that."

"It's not about expectin anythin. I care bout those boys, too, ya know," Mabel said.

Mary Catherine started to cry.

Mabel put her hand on Mary Catherine's back. "I thought ya came here to cheer *me* up," she teased.

"Looks like it's the other way around," Mary Catherine said. She brushed her hand over her wet cheeks, then started to laugh.

"Don't worry. We'll work things out," Mabel said.

Mary Catherine pulled a hanky from her pocket and blew her nose. "If only I could get steady work. Ma said she'd mind the boys. She and Da have already taken to them like they're their own."

"So, how are ya at bakin?" Mabel asked.

CHAPTER 4

Mabel replenished the stove and surveyed the shack one last time before heading to the bus station. She had one of Mrs. Cameron's boots on and was reaching for the other when she heard the knock.

She wasn't expecting anyone. She tensed. Again, the knock. This time louder. She stood and tiptoed unevenly to the kitchen to retrieve her bread knife.

"Who's there?" she hollered. There was no answer.

Again, the knock.

"Who is it?" she yelled louder.

"It's Stanley."

"Just a minute," she said. She returned the knife to its rightful spot and opened the door. "What are ya doin here?"

"Figured you'd need a drive to pick up your aunt."

"I was expectin to walk and hire a ride back. But since yer here n' all."

Mabel quickly shoved her foot into the other boot and grabbed her coat. "Guess Mr. Cameron still doesn't want me walkin?" she said, jumping into the passenger seat.

"Guess not," Stanley said, smiling to himself.

"He's a very considerate man."

"Can't argue with that."

"I gotta make him his pie, for sure. Did ya eat yers yet?"

"Afraid not."

Mabel turned and looked at him. She wasn't happy. "Well, it ain't no more good. Might as well toss it out. Waste of flour and good apples," she huffed.

Stanley had his eyes fixed on the road. "It wasn't wasted."

"I ain't the deaf one, ya know. Ya just said ya didn't eat it."

"Had some friends in. They ate it."

"And?"

"And what?"

"And did they like it?"

"They never said."

Mabel turned her head to look out the passenger window. "Well, I'm not makin ya another one."

"Never asked you to."

"Fine then."

"How long is your aunt staying?" Stanley asked, thinking there was no need to continue tormenting her.

"Don't know. Never said."

They didn't speak the last five minutes of the ride.

Mabel jumped down from the passenger seat. "Thanks," she yelled, walking in front of the car.

Stanley shut the engine off and stepped down from the driver's side.

Mabel gave him a queer look. "What are ya doin?"

"I'll wait with you and take you home."

"Ain't no need for that."

"Mr. Cameron's orders," Stanley lied.

The two entered the small depot and waited for the bus to arrive. Stanley sat on a narrow bench that stretched the length of a whitewashed wall, splashed with posters advertising everything from *Emerson's Auto Parts* to *Auntie Stella's Fabulous Knitted Wares*. The local jobs bulletin hung bare, as did the lost and found notice. The bus was already a good forty minutes late. He looked at Mabel. She was pacing and moving her lips. She seemed to catch herself and looked over at Stanley. Mabel knew he caught her talking to herself.

Her face got hot. She could see him stand from the corner of her eye. He was making his way over.

She turned her head toward an older woman standing beside her with a kerchief tied in a tight knot under her chin, idly pushing a large black stroller back and forth. Stanley walked past them and up to a four-by-four foot advertisement made of tin and bolted to the wall. A cartoon-like character doffing his blue cap proclaimed *Ernie's Bus Service. Always on Time… So You're Never Late!* Stanley started to chuckle when he read the message forever etched into Ernie's proud pronouncement. *Ernie's a fuckin liar.*

Mabel glanced at Stanley, then back at the woman beside her. "How old's the baby?"

The kerchiefed woman, with an abundance of facial hair, pulled the carriage into her and brought a filthy yellow blanket up to the baby's chin. "Four months and some."

Mabel wondered if she was the child's mother or grandmother.

"Girl or boy?" Mabel asked.

"Boy."

Mabel thought he resembled her baby brother, Jonathan. Same nose and eyes. "He's beautiful."

"He's a retard. Probably not long for this world. God willin," the kerchiefed woman said.

Mabel put her head down and thought of her mother on the day Jonathan died. She began to tear up when the doors finally opened and anxious greeters rushed to meet their delayed arrivals. She wiped away any appearance of her sudden rush of sadness, dabbing her runny nose on the end of her sleeve. She stood on her toes, looking over and between the shoulders of those who blocked the entrance, scouring the now crowded room for her aunt.

It was Amour who found her.

"Hello, Mabel."

Mabel turned quickly toward the familiar voice. She couldn't believe the woman who had appeared beside her, was her aunt. She seemed a lot taller in her three inch heels, and looked like a million dollars in her mink stole and skintight, elbow-high leather gloves.

"Amour! Oh, my God. Look at ya! Yer so beautiful," Mabel said, wrapping her arms around Amour's neck. Mabel pulled back, shaking her head in disbelief. "I coulda tripped over ya and stopped to give ya my apologies without ever knowin it was you. Ya look like ya oughta be on the cover of a fancy magazine. Geez, I gotta get myself to Boston."

"Mabel. You don't need Boston. You're as pretty as ever." The two hugged again. "So, is your father here?"

Mabel had rehearsed the scene over and over again. She wanted to wait till they had some privacy before telling Amour the news of her brother. "He ain't here," she said, hoping to keep her lies to a minimum. "Ya must be tired," she added, and nervously scanned the room.

"Looking forward to seeing Johnnie and getting to bed. It's been a long day. Train was on time, but the bus certainly wasn't. By the way, who's that standing over there? The tall, handsome man in the camel coat, holding his fedora?" Amour asked, nodding in his direction.

Mabel turned. "No clue. Never saw him before. Looks rich. Anyway, I got us a ride home," she said, looping her arm through Amour's and pulling her toward the exit.

"I told your father I could find my own way back," Amour said. She stopped and slid her arm out from around Mabel's. "Mabel! I can't very well leave without my luggage."

"Oh, yeah. Yer luggage," Mabel said.

Amour pointed to the bandage above Mabel's eye. "What did you do to your forehead?"

"Oh, it's just a scrape. I'm as clumsy as ever." Mabel looked back at the arrival door. A red-faced Ernie was dragging a huge, blue trunk along the brown, paint-chipped floor and hollering, "Clear the way."

"That's mine," Amour said. "And I have two other smaller bags." Mabel looked at the massive trunk, thinking her aunt must have planned on staying a good while.

Stanley walked toward them. Mabel looked flustered. Her eyes darted to him, then back at Amour. "Amour, this is… this is…" She couldn't think of how to describe him. "This is my friend, Stanley. He's gonna drive us home."

"Hello, Stanley."

"Hello. Nice to meet you." He looked at the trunk. "Is this it?"

"No. I'm afraid there are two more," Amour said, as Ernie, struggling under the weight of Amour's remaining bags, dropped them with a thud next to the trunk.

Stanley shook his head. "Nothing breakable I hope."

Amour smiled. "Thankfully, no."

Stanley stretched his arms across the length of the trunk, gripped the handles, effortlessly hoisted it up, and made his way to the door. Mabel quickly reached down, grabbed Amour's remaining bags, and began chasing after him, ignoring Amour's pleas to let her help. Stanley loaded the trunk in the back seat, took the bags from Mabel, and placed them on top. Mabel rattled on about the weather.

"Sure hope ya brought along warm clothes. Yer gonna need em, for sure. It's been cold. Real cold. Coldest fall I can remember. Not even a single leaf on the trees. Ain't it the coldest fall ever, Stanley?"

"One of them for sure," he said, wondering what Amour made of Mabel's mile-a-minute chatter.

Mabel left the front seat for Amour and crawled into the remaining space in the back. She was still going on about the weather when they neared the shack.

"Mabel, I'll be fine. I brought plenty of warm clothing," Amour said, tugging on the tips of her glove and sliding it off her arm. "So, how long have you two been a couple?"

Mabel shot forward. "*A couple*?" she shouted, as if it were the most ridiculous thing she had ever heard. "We're not a couple. We know each other from the bakery, that's all. Geez, why'd ya think that?"

"Oh! I just assumed by *friend,* you meant *boyfriend.*"

Stanley heard the horror in Mabel's voice. He felt deflated.

When they arrived at the shack, Stanley followed Mabel and Amour inside, deposited the bags at the door, and went back for the trunk. Mabel held the door for him. "Put it in there," she said, pointing to the door that led to Da's old room. Her heart began to pound thinking the moment of truth was upon her. She watched as Amour looked around the room.

"It's exactly as I remember," Amour said.

Stanley walked from the bedroom to the door. "Good night, ladies," he said, placing his hand on the knob.

"Oh, Stanley? Just a moment," Amour said. She picked her black clutch off the table, unsnapped it, and pulled out a dollar bill.

Stanley looked at her. "Thank you. But I've already been paid for my time." He nodded to them and left.

"I like him," Amour said. "So, where's your father?"

Mabel closed her eyes. Her well-practised lines escaped her. "The morgue."

Monday, November 7

CHAPTER I

Mabel was back to her old routine and at the store by seven the next morning. Mr. Cameron greeted her, asking how Amour had taken the news.

"She was devastated. Cried most of the night. Had nothin to eat. Just had some tea and went to bed."

"Does she know his death is suspicious?"

"I told her everythin I knew. Which ain't much."

"Is Roddy coming home for the funeral?"

"I asked if we should wait for him, but she said no. Said she just wants to get on with the burial."

"You know, you don't have to be here today. Maybe you should go home and spend the day with her?"

"I told her I was sure you wouldn't mind me skippin work, but she didn't want me to. Said she had some stuff in town to look into and would be gone all day, anyway."

"I'll drive you home this evening, and stop in and pay my respects."

"Oh, and Mr. Cameron. Thanks for sendin Stanley to take me to the depot. I told him he didn't have to wait and take us home, but he said you insisted. That was very kind of you."

James was about to protest, but decided against it. “And Stanley, too,” he said, wondering why his friend gave him credit for the idea.

CHAPTER 2

Amour's first stop was St. Anthony's where she lit a candle for her brother. She was kneeling with her head down, when Father Vokey walked across the altar to the credence table.

"Good morning, Father."

He turned toward the voice, but didn't recognize the woman before him. "Good morning. Don't let me disturb you."

"Actually, Father, I was hoping to see you."

He narrowed his eyes, put his hand to his forehead, and peered out. "Is that you, Amour? I'm sorry. I didn't recognize you." He walked off the altar, knelt down beside her, and laid his hand on her back. "I'm so sorry for your loss, dear. How are you coping?"

Amour raised herself from her kneeling pad and sat back against the pew.

"Thank you, Father. Still trying to come to grips with Johnnie's passing."

"I'm sure it came as a terrible shock," he said, struggling to rise off his knees.

"Yes, Father. I hadn't seen him in over three years. I was looking forward to seeing him again. I know…" she paused to think of what to say about her brother. "I know Johnnie wasn't what you would call a *good Christian.* But he was always good to me. I'm going to miss him."

"Your brother had his struggles for sure, and his detractors. But he was a child of God. And, as we know, God is all forgiving. Did you want to see me about the funeral?"

"Yes, father. But there's something else."

"By all means, dear child. Tell me what I can do for you."

"You can help me have my marriage annulled."

CHAPTER 3

Stanley stood under the stairs in the dark alley and watched all manner of town folk climb the rickety steps to the second floor, leaving a few minutes later with their stash hidden under their coats, or in the baby carriages that transported their well bundled porcelain charges. At least a dozen people had come and gone in the hour that he had hidden himself from view. He was no one to judge. He had climbed those stairs on many occasions himself, as recently as two days ago. He knew it was just a matter of time before his prey showed.

Another hour passed as he watched and waited in the cold. The last to come and go, two members of the local constabulary. Neither, he knew, there to enforce the law. It was well past eight. He'd give it another hour. If they didn't show, he'd come back again, and again, and again; for as long it took. He blew into his cupped hands, reminding himself that patience was a virtue. He was about to give up when he heard their familiar voices. Billy and Eddie mounted the stairs, unaware they were being watched. A few minutes later, their transaction complete, the two happy customers started down the stairs. Billy stopped halfway down to light a makin. Stanley peered through the stair treads at the heels of Billy's boots. Johnnie's lackeys restarted their descent. When they reached the bottom, Stanley was there to greet them.

"Evenin, boys."

Eddie looked at Stanley, then Billy. He turned and tripped, as he tried to run back up the stairs.

Stanley grabbed the back of his jacket and yanked him back. "Why are you running, Eddie? I don't want to hurt you, son. Just need you to answer a few questions."

"What the fuck do ya want?" Billy asked.

Stanley held tight to Eddie's collar. "Come on, Billy. You know what I want."

"I know ya want trouble."

"Billy, you know damn well why I'm here."

"I don't know what the fuck yer talkin bout."

"Bet you do, Eddie," Stanley said, pulling him closer. "So, Eddie, tell Billy why I'm about to beat the shit out of him, or I'll beat the shit out of you."

Eddie started to whimper.

"Keep yer mouth shut, Eddie," Billy said. He reached into his pocket, flicked his wrist, and flashed a blade. "I'm gonna carve ya up, ya piece of shit."

"That all ya got?" Stanley asked. He threw Eddie to the ground. Eddie's whisky bottle flew out of his jacket pocket, releasing its golden contents over the hard, brown earth. Billy was swiping wildly at Stanley, who jumped back, before lunging forward and punching him square in the face.

Billy fell backward to the ground. Stanley walked up to him and kicked the knife away.

"Ya broke my funkin nose! Ya prick!" Billy said, covering it with his hand.

Stanley hauled him back to his feet and hit him a second time in the mouth. Billy was back on the ground.

"Eddie! Tell Billy why I'm here, or you're next," Stanley said, reaching down with one hand and lifting Eddie back up. He held him by the throat and cocked his fist back. "Tell him, Eddie."

"Was it the—"

"Shut the fuck up, Eddie!" Billy screamed.

"C'mon, Eddie," Stanley repeated.

"Fuck, Eddie! Keep yer fuckin mouth shut!"

Eddie could feel Stanley's grip tighten "Is it cause of the girl? I swear…I—"

"Shut up, Eddie! Shut the fuck up, ya fuckin idiot! It's not the girl!"

Stanley loosened his grip on Eddie's collar, not sure of what he meant by, 'the girl.'

"Yeah. It's the girl, Eddie," Stanley said. "Tell me about the girl."

"Eddie! For Christ sake! It's the fuckin ponies, ya fuckin arsehole."

"Tell me about the girl, Eddie," Stanley repeated, his voice more threatening. Billy leaned forward and struggled to get to his feet. Blood streamed from his nose and mouth. Stanley held the neck of Eddie's jacket, roughly hauled him toward Billy, reached down with his other hand, and grabbed Billy by the hair. He pulled Billy's neck back, causing the blood to pool at the back of his throat.

Eddie looked at Billy, then at Stanley. "I just watched," he said.

"Shut up," Billy choked.

"Don't leave anything out, Eddie," Stanley warned.

Billy closed his eyes, resigned to the fact he couldn't stop the simpleton from digging their graves even deeper.

"I… I… I just watched," Eddie said, between sobs. "Billy… Billy got on her. I didn't. I promise," he cried.

Stanley's mind flew back to Mabel opening the door and the matted blood on the side of her head. He felt sick. He was hoping he was wrong and that they weren't talking about Mabel. "Where was Johnnie?" he shouted at Eddie.

"He… he… was passed out. I promise. I didn't touch her. I … I just… watched."

"You just watched," Stanley said. He pushed Billy back down, turned, and plunged his fist into Eddie's face. Eddie dropped as if he'd been shot dead on the spot. Stanley turned back toward Billy, who was crawling along on his hands and knees, swearing he'd never lay a hand on the girl again.

Stanley grabbed him by the collar and hauled him up. Billy's legs were like rubber and he was swaying back and forth. He was pleading with Stanley to let him go. Stanley smashed his fist into Billy's face a third time. "That was for Walter and Winnie," he said, as Billy collapsed next to Eddie. He grabbed them up by the arms and dragged them to where he had waited for them in the shadows. He looked around, reached into Billy's inside pocket, took out his recently purchased pint of whisky, uncapped it, and took a long swig. He poured the rest over Billy. He then reached in his own pocket, took out his pipe, and tapped its head against the staircase that had served as his blind, ridding it of its spent ashes. He retrieved his packet of fresh leaves, tamped his pipe, and struck a match that illuminated the two motionless, bloodied bodies at his feet. He held the flickering flame over Billy and watched as it made its way down the thin, narrow stick, closer to his numb fingers. He then held it to his replenished bowl of MacDonald's tobacco. The smoke warmed his mouth and scented the cold air. He puffed on his pipe, as he thought of Mabel and his two charred ponies. He then unbuttoned his pants and pissed in Billy's gaping mouth.

"And that was for Mabel," he said.

CHAPTER 4

Despite a long, emotional day that included attending the burial of Matthew Toth, Mabel was grateful she had had a productive day, and that she had put a good dent in the backorders. She was dead tired, but her restless mind kept leaping from one thing to the other. She sat up, turned on her side, doubled up her thin pillow, and put her head back down. She was worried about Amour. She'd hardly said a word when Mabel arrived home from work. She seemed to be taking things a lot harder than Mabel expected. Wouldn't eat the brisket Mabel had made, barely touched her tea, and went directly to bed. Must be a combination of being tired from her long trip and dealing with the shock of hearing about her brother. Mabel would make corned beef hash for supper tomorrow night and they could talk about Da's arrangements. They needed to get the body out of the morgue and into the ground.

"Not fair to Da to keep him waitin much longer," she said. She blessed herself, thinking he wouldn't be happy that she's still yakking out loud. She lay awake, staring at the grey wall adorned with a picture of Jesus with his open palm resting under his heart, the other stretching out in her direction. I wonder if he made room for Da, she thought.

She closed her eyes and ran the tips of her fingers over the raised, red gash above her eye. Dr. Cohen came by the bakery in the afternoon to remove the stitches and said it was healing nicely. Still,

Mabel worried her lumpy forehead would be a constant reminder of Da's rage. She wanted to remember him differently, but wasn't sure she could. She provoked him. She should have known better. "Was as much my fault, Da, as it was yours," she whispered. She hoped the scar would remind her more of her own failings, than his. "Gotta learn to be more thoughtful and think before I put my big mouth in gear."

Mabel's mind turned back to Matthew, his boys, and the morning's events. He was buried without a viewing, or church service. Just her and a handful of people at the graveyard. Mary Catherine, her parents, the boys, Mr. Cameron, Stanley, and a reluctant Father Vokey who, though not convinced Matthew's death was an accident, gave a lovely send off just the same. She thought of how nice it was for Mr. Cameron and Stanley to come along, and for Mrs. Cameron to stay behind and look after the store. There is no one kinder than Mr. Cameron, she thought. The church offered up a free plot for the burial, but it was nowhere near Matthew's young wife, so Mr. Cameron purchased the one next to her.

One burial down and another to follow in its wake. She thought of Mary Catherine's dilemma. Mabel would give her a third of her earnings till things got sorted out. She'd also look for an opportunity to talk to Mr. Cameron about having Mary Catherine help at the bakery. Only made sense for him to hire another baker. She'd tell Mr. Cameron he could cut her wages and, that with some extra help, he could easily double his bake sales. Mary Catherine was also clever enough to cover the store from time to time. And it sure wouldn't hurt to mention how it would help the boys.

It was well past eleven before Mabel finally closed her eyes for the night. She dreamt of ponies running through a giant field of daisies. She woke with a start as the ponies careened off a cliff into a river of fire and empty rum bottles below. She turned up the lamp and looked at the clock she had retrieved from Da's room. It was not quite four o'clock. Still too early to head to the bakery, but way too late to return to her dreams. She'd try and read the book Mrs.

Cameron had dropped off at her bread counter.

> *It was the best of times, it was the worst of times, it was the age of wisdom, it was the age of foolishness, it was the epoch of belief, it was the epoch of incredulity, it was the season of Light, it was the season of Darkness, it was the spring of hope, it was the winter of despair, we had everything before us, we had nothing before us, we were all going directly to Heaven, we were all going directly the other way...*

Mabel put the book on the floor. "It's a waste of time, is what it is."

CHAPTER 5

It was still dark when Billy stirred with a terrible taste in his mouth, an aching nose, and a missing tooth. He was covered in blood. He sat up and put his hand on the ground to steady himself. His hand brushed the neck of his empty whiskey bottle. He picked it up, threw it hard to the side, and slowly stood up. He looked down at Eddie, curled up in a ball. His first instinct was to kick the idiot in the head and finish him off. Instead, he slapped him to get him to come to.

"Wake up, ya fuckin idiot. Wake up."

Eddie opened his eyes and rubbed his jaw.

"Get up, ya pussy. Get up," Billy said.

"I thought he was gonna kill me," Eddie whimpered.

"Yer lucky I don't. Whatcha go and tell him about the girl for? Fuck yer stupid."

"I'm sorry. I figured he was gonna beat me to death. I thought he knew—"

"How the fuck would he know bout the girl? He came after us cause of the ponies."

"How'd he find out bout the ponies?"

"How the fuck do I know? Christ, yer fuckin stupid."

"Do ya think he's gonna report us to the police? I don't wanna go to jail," Eddie said.

Billy cuffed him on the head. "Get up, ya fuckin waste of air."

"But I can't go to jail, Billy," Eddie cried.

"We're not gonna jail, ya dumb ass." He smacked Eddie in the head, again. "Get up."

Eddie got to his knees, put his hands on the ground, and struggled to get to his feet. Billy put his foot on his back and kicked him back down. "I said, get the fuck up."

"I'm tryin, Billy."

"Well, try harder," Billy said, grabbing him roughly under the arm and dragging him to his feet. "Let's get the fuck outa here. And ya better listen to me and listen good! Or, so help me God, *I'll* kill ya."

Tuesday, November 8

CHAPTER 1

Traffic in the store was steady first thing in the morning, but died down by midday. James brought his tea to the counter and opened the thin paper that informed the town of the two-day old news already making the rounds at the Five and Dime and Mendelsons. The first article to catch his attention was about Johnnie.

> *Police report that the death of thirty-nine year-old, John Adshade, whose body was discovered off Brookside Street last week, is suspicious. Sergeant Dan McInnes advised that the investigation is ongoing and that there are no suspects currently in custody. When asked, McInnes refused to confirm the police are investigating a number of coloureds from New Aberdeen who were believed to have had a previous encounter with the deceased.*

James's heart began to pound as he thought back to his conversation with Mabel. Christ, Johnnie told her he was jumped by a bunch of coloureds. He must have told others. I should have gone to the police. God knows the coloured folks have a hard enough time in this town without being fingered for killing a white man. He had to get Dr. Adams and go to the police. He'd leave Stanley out of it for now. He closed the paper over and was about to get ready to head to town, when he saw a familiar face staring back at him. It was a photo of Roddy MacPherson, alongside a wire story reposted from the Boston Globe.

> *Boston Police have a thirty-eight year-old man in custody on charges of gross indecency, involuntary confinement, and assault. Roderick MacPherson, Vice-President, New England Steel and Coal, was arraigned on Thursday, Oct. 24th, without bail, after the fifteen year-old son of one of MacPherson's colleagues alleged the accused tied him up and repeatedly subjected him to indecent acts over the course of a six-hour period. The boy, who escaped through an open window of a vacant warehouse on Cambridge St., said he was lured to the site by MacPherson, who said he wanted to show him the location of a promising new area in the south end he hoped the boy's father would help him develop.*

He then read the sidebar.

> *Roderick MacPherson had previously served as Vice-President of the British Imperial Coal Company and continues to hold the deeds to several local properties.*

"Jesus," James muttered. "Mabel!" he hollered into the kitchen. "Did Amour mention why Roddy wasn't coming home?"

She came around the corner, wiping her hands in a tea towel. "No. Just said he wasn't comin."

"She didn't say anything else?"

"No. Why?"

He wasn't sure if she should show her the article or not. He decided it was Amour's place to tell her. "Just wondering, that's all. I have to go to town. Can you manage your baking and keep an eye on the store till Margaret comes home from the Guild?"

"Sure, Mr. Cameron. I—"

James grabbed his coat and was heading out the door. He turned back and scooped up the paper.

Mabel looked at him. "What's going—"

He was out the door before she could finish her sentence. Mabel had a feeling it wasn't anything good.

CHAPTER 2

James raced into the medical examiner's office, but didn't see Dr. Adams anywhere. He hollered his name, then swung open the door to the back room. Dr. Adams was standing over the body of a young boy.

"James! Anything wrong?" he asked, surprised by his second visit in less than a week.

"Did you see the paper today?"

"No. Been busy here. Flu and a couple of cases of meningitis taking its toll on—"

"Did you talk to the police about Johnnie?"

"No. But it's not through lack of trying. I went to the station. They told me to leave my report on McInnes's desk."

"We have to go there. Now!" James said, the urgency in his voice putting Dr. Adams on edge.

"But—"

"Grab your coat. I'll fill you in on the way."

Dr. Adams was about to leave, but turned back to pull the sheet over the latest casualty to come his way. On the drive to the station, James told Dr. Adams he was right and that the bruises on Johnnie's face were a couple of days old. He said he was responsible, but didn't provide the details of their encounter. He never said anything about Stanley breaking Johnnie's nose.

"I won't judge you for putting your fist in his face," Dr. Adams said, despite being curious as to the reason.

"Look! I'm really afraid this thing with the coloureds is going to blow up. You need to tell them it was a hit and run. And I need to own up to my part in all of this."

The two arrived at the police station to talk to Sergeant McInnes, but were advised he was out on a case. They asked to speak to someone else, but were told it was Sergeant McInnes's investigation. They waited for over an hour before McInnes finally walked in with his latest perpetrator in cuffs.

"Stanley!" James said, jumping up and rushing toward his friend. "What the hell's going on?"

"James. I'll need a lawyer," Stanley said.

"Shut up," McInnes hissed, walking in front of Stanley. He then barked at Constable McEwan. "Take him out back and lock him up. No visitors."

James ran up to McInnes and held his hands in front of his chest. "Just a minute, Sergeant. Why are you arresting Stanley?"

"Assault."

"*Assault*? Assault on whom?" James asked, turning to see McEwan roughly spin Stanley around and drag him down the hallway.

"Can't see why it's any of your business," McInnes said.

James wondered why he was being such a bastard. "Look, Sergeant, he's my friend. I'd like to talk to him."

"You heard me. No visitors."

"But he's entitled to see a lawyer."

McInnes looked around the room. "I don't see any lawyers here. Do you?"

James called out to Stanley. "I'll get Samuel Friedman." He clenched his sore hand as he looked at the young upstart smugly smiling back at him, but thought better of striking him, knowing he couldn't very well help his friend if he was locked up, too. "Listen, Sergeant. He's a good man and a good friend. This must be a big mistake," James said, hoping a level voice would bring McInnes to reason.

"No mistake at all. Had two guys come in this mornin who are badly beaten up. They both claim he's their assailant. They also claim he's responsible for Johnnie Adshade's murder. And I gotta say, I believe them."

"Johnnie Adshade's murder?" James yelled, throwing his hands in the air and laughing at the inanity of such a thought.

"Yeah. Johnnie Adshade's murder," McInnes said, walking past him.

James darted in front of him, stopping abruptly, and blocking his way. "That's ridiculous. Stanley doesn't have it in him to hurt a fly."

McInnes moved to the side and pushed forward. "Tell that to Dirty Willie."

"But I already told you he was with me the night Johnnie died. He couldn't have done it. Neither did the coloureds. That's why Dr. Adams and I came to see you." He turned frantically in the direction of Dr. Adams.

"James is right. It's all in my report. The deceased died as a result of subcutaneous injuries and a ruptured spleen. He also had a fractured skull, brain hemorrhaging and a shattered patella. And, as I told James, the bruising on his face predated the time of death. I believe his injuries are more consistent with an accident involving a motorized vehicle, than a beating."

McInnes turned his attention to Dr. Adams "So you're sayin there's no possibility Adshade was beaten to death?"

Dr. Adams looked at James. He hesitated, then turned to McInnes. "Well, it's not exactly a precise science. But my medical experience leads me to conclude Adshade likely died from a hit and run." He looked back at James who was urging him to go on. Dr. Adams put his head down for a moment. "I suppose it's possible he may have been on the receiving end of a two-by-four, or some other heavy object. But again, the nature and location of the injuries, suggests to me he was hit by a car. And the force of any blows would have to be—"

"So, *it is possible*," McInnes interrupted, satisfied Dr. Adams would make a good witness for the prosecution.

"This is absurd," James implored. "I told you. I was with Stanley. He couldn't have done it!"

"I remember ya tellin me as much. Playin cards and drinkin. Fell asleep. Well, I got a dead guy covered in bruises who didn't die of natural causes. Two witnesses who claim MacIntyre beat the shit out of them. And two signed statements claimin MacIntyre threatened, then admitted to killin Adshade. If I were you, Mr. Cameron, I'd be very careful before I jumped to your buddy's defence," McInnes said.

"Are you calling me a liar, Sergeant?" James seethed.

The two stared each other down.

"Just sayin, keep it up and MacIntyre might not be the only one needin a lawyer." He turned to face Dr. Adams. "Can't wait to read your report," he said and walked away.

James hollered after him. "How do I go about posting bail?"

McInnes kept walking, "Gotta wait for the arraignment."

"When's that?" James yelled.

"Whenever Judge Kennedy gets around to it."

James turned and stormed toward the door. Dr. Adams ran behind trying to catch up. "Sorry, James. I didn't mean to—"

"It's okay, George. You did what you had to do."

"Thanks. Gotta say, the dead give you a lot less trouble than the living."

CHAPTER 3

By the time James got home, Mabel had hung the closed sign on the door and left for the day. He latched the shutters and entered the store. He was relieved Margaret was upstairs. He needed to pull his thoughts together. He walked in back and poured a rum and smoked a makin. He wanted to hire Samuel Friedman, but he wasn't available. He'd tried two other lawyers, but both declined, saying they didn't have the time to take on what could be a lengthy trial. James thought it had more to do with their fear of taking on the local prosecutor. He'd had to settle for Samuel Friedman's young son, who had just received his licence to practise. He had wanted someone with more experience, but there wasn't anyone. Hopefully the kid's eager and has something to prove, he thought.

James knew in his heart that Stanley hadn't beaten Johnnie to death. Yet, he was troubled by two thoughts. He was certain Stanley shared his suspicions that Johnnie was responsible for the fire, but he hadn't mentioned it to him, or gone to the police. He also thought he remembered waking up in the middle of the night and Stanley telling him to go back to sleep, but wasn't sure if he didn't just dream it.

"Not a chance," he mumbled.

"Not a chance of what?" Margaret asked from the doorway.

"Not a chance Stanley murdered Mabel's father."

"Of course not, James. What are you talking about?"

James stood up and gave her a hug. "It's been another eventful day. I've got a lot to tell you."

CHAPTER 4

Mabel entered the shack and could immediately tell Amour had been crying again. She was sitting on the upholstered occasional chair in the corner of the living room with a copy of *The Post* on her lap.

"Mabel, I'd like to bury your father the day after tomorrow. I spoke to Father Vokey. If you agree, I thought we would just hold a graveside service at nine."

"I saw Father Vokey at Matthew Toth's burial this morning. He told me you two had a chat. It's fine by me. I'd rather Da's departure be private. Better that, than disappoint him with a lousy turnout," Mabel said.

Amour started to cry again, feeling guilty that she had her own reasons for not wanting a church service. She knew news of her disgrace was making the rounds of the town, and that the church would swell with gossip mongers who would come, not to mourn Johnnie, but to mock her.

"I'm so sorry, Amour. Must be hard losin yer only siblin. And the shock of it all. You comin home for a visit, only to find he's gone for good."

"Mabel, I'll miss your father. But there's another reason I'm upset."

Mabel walked over and knelt beside Amour's chair. "My friend, Mary Catherine, Catherine with a C, tells me I'm real good dealin with sad. So, if ya wanna tell me, I might be able to help ya through it."

Amour brushed the side of Mabel's cheek with the back of her hand and handed her the paper. Mabel's mouth dropped open as she stared at a grainy picture of Roddy. Amour left Mabel to read about her shame and started the water for tea. Mabel knew her uncle was in a mess of trouble, but didn't understand the charges.

The tea was poured and Mabel was still looking at the story.

"Now, do you understand?" Amour asked.

"Can't say as I do. What was Uncle Roddy doin with the boy?"

"Come, and I'll explain it to you."

They had several cups of tea before Mabel understood the gravity of the news. No one had ever talked to her about men doing such things to one another. The only nasty she had ever heard of was between a man and a woman. She tried to figure out how two men could even do it. "So, what's gonna happen to him?"

"I suspect he will be going to jail for a very long time."

"What are you gonna do?"

"I can't go back to Boston. I was hoping to stay here with you. At least for a while."

"Stay with *me*? More like me stayin with you. You and Uncle Roddy own the shack."

"Apparently, Mabel, we don't. The shack belongs to James Cameron."

CHAPTER 5

James told Margaret about the day's events. Margaret had a million questions, but mostly let him continue uninterrupted. "You don't actually believe Stanley killed Mabel's father?"

"Of course not. He's a good man, not a violent one."

"But what about all that talk that he nearly killed a man?"

"Margaret, that was in the ring. He was a boxer. He didn't mean to hurt Willie. He just got caught up in the moment. And he quit boxing after that. He rescued pit ponies for goodness sake. And he's so good to his aunt. I just know it's not in him. And don't forget, I was with him the night Johnnie was killed."

"So that's, that. You just tell the police—"

"I tried," he said, sounding exasperated. "And there's more."

"I'm afraid to ask."

"Mabel's uncle, Roddy, has been arrested for gross indecency and assault on a young boy in Boston."

Wednesday, November 9

CHAPTER I

Mabel survived another restless night. She was tired, but anxious to get her da buried, and to find out why Mr. Cameron let them stay in the shack all this time without looking for so much as a penny. She knew him to be kind and generous, but was puzzled by Amour's news. It was no secret Mr. Cameron didn't care much for her father, so why did he let them stay in a house he owned and not charge rent. He must have his reasons for keeping it a secret, she thought, as she made her way down Brookside Street, wondering where Ten-After-Six found her da's body. Remember, she reminded herself, don't go blurting anything out to Mr. Cameron about the shack.

James opened the door when he heard her climb the front steps. "Good Morning, Mabel."

"Mornin, Mr. Cameron."

"Thought we could have a chat before you start your baking."

She took off her coat and walked into the kitchen. "Ya know, I can do both?"

He followed her in, pulled a chair back from the table, and indicated for her to take a seat.

Mabel hesitated. "Am I in trouble for somethin?"

"Not at all," James smiled. "Mabel, you have to stop thinking you're responsible for everything that goes wrong."

"Well, I ain't normally in the middla anythin that goes right," she said.

"You did nothing wrong, " James said, reaching over and putting his hand on her arm.

She was relieved, but curious. "So, whatcha want to talk to me about?"

"A couple of things, actually."

"Is it about you ownin the shack?" she asked, unable to keep the words from pouring out.

James sat back in his chair, completely taken aback.

Mabel saw the shocked look on his face. "Amour told me."

"Well, that wasn't what I wanted to talk to you about. Let's put that aside for now. Let's just deal with one thing at a time."

"So what is it?"

"I thought you should know the police arrested Stanley yesterday."

"Fer what?" she scoffed.

James walked to the stove, picked up the teapot, and poured two cups. "He's been charged with aggravated assault against two men."

"Who?"

"I don't know yet."

"But why?"

"I don't know that either." James handed her her tea.

"Is he in jail?"

"Yes," James said, reaching for the sugar bowl.

"Should I bring him a pie?"

"Not yet," he said, putting his hand over hers, and thinking Stanley needed a good lawyer more than he did a pie. "I'm going to head to the station shortly. Margaret's still in bed with one of her headaches. So, I'll need you to cover the store while I'm gone. It could be a few hours."

"I'll be fine, Mr. Cameron. I'm good with numbers."

"Mabel? There's something else."

"What's that?"

"Stanley's also being held as a suspect in your father's death."

Mabel looked dumbstruck. "Why would the police think Stanley had anythin to do with Da's death?"

"The two men Stanley assaulted claim he told them he did it. I'm sure it's just a big mix up and that the charges will be tossed out in no time."

"So, he'll be alright?"

"I'm sure of it," James said. "He's a good man, Mabel. One of the finest I've ever met. I know he didn't do it."

"Mr. Cameron. If my da came back from the dead, stood before me, and pointed his finger at Stanley, I'd say he was a liar. We both know Stanley ain't no murderer and that Da was more sinner than saint. He probably got caught cheatin at cards or somethin. He wasn't much at makin friends, but he sure was good at makin enemies."

James smiled, grateful she didn't think Stanley could do such a thing. "Anyway, I just thought you should know. And I wanted to be the one to tell you. God knows, it'll be all over town before you know it."

"Well, I won't pay no mind to it," she said, shaking her head.

"Good then," James said. He stood to leave.

"Oh, and Mr. Cameron? Amour and I talked last night. We're gonna bury Da tomorrow at nine. No funeral Mass or anythin. Just want to set him on his final journey. Not sure what direction he'll be headin, but he can't stay at the morgue forever. I'm hopin to take the mornin off. I'll stay late."

"No, Mabel. After the internment, go home and spend the day with Amour."

"If it's all the same to you, I'd rather come back after the burial. I'd prefer to be bakin, than sittin round thinkin bout things I can't do nothin bout."

James knew there was no point in arguing. "I'll leave the decision to you. Just know it's not expected."

"Mr. Cameron?"

"Yes."

"Do ya really think Stanley's gonna be okay?"

"Yes, Mabel. I'm sure of it."

CHAPTER 2

James sat on the hard bench along the wall of the narrow hallway of the police station, looked at his watch, and then at Sam Friedman, sitting to his left and scribbling notes. James had hoped this morning's trial was just a case of first-time jitters. He could tell Stanley's young layer was visibly nervous, and that made James nervous. Sam's mouth was bone dry and his hand shook every time he took a sip of water. Even though the young lawyer had prevailed in the end, James feared he'd need a lot more victories under his belt before he could take on the local prosecutor. Christ, he thought, if this thing goes to court, Mannie Chernin's going to make minced meat out of the kid. James looked at his watch a second time. He had hoped to be back at the store by now with this whole mess behind him. He'd agreed to pick up Sam at the courthouse at ten, after Sam argued his first case, but it dragged on much longer than expected. It had taken another hour for the case to be heard and for the judge to render his decision.

James stood and began to pace. It was now going on two and he still hadn't spoken to Stanley. The door finally opened. Constable Dunphy emerged and looked at James. "It shouldn't be too much longer," he said. Dunphy then picked a notepad off the front desk and disappeared back behind the door.

Stanley was sitting at a large rectangular table in the dimly-lit interrogation room. Sergeant McInnes sat across from him, while

Constable McEwan leaned against the side wall. Dunphy walked in, whispered in his sergeant's ear, and put the notepad on the table in front him. He then resumed his place beside McEwan, and watched him wedged a large plug of tobacco into the inside of his cheek.

"Stanley? Yer in a shitload of trouble," McInnes said. "Judge takes one look at Billy and Eddie and he's going to throw the book at ya, along with his gavel. Jesus, it looks like they had a tussle with a train. Billy can't even see out of his right eye. And his nose is broken in more than one place. So, let's not drag this out any longer than necessary."

Stanley looked at McInnes. "I don't know what you want me to say. I admit it. I put a pounding on them. They burnt my barn and my ponies. I wanted to put the fear of God into them, but things got out of hand. Billy came at me with a blade."

McInnes started to laugh. "So you've said. Billy says he doesn't even own a knife."

"He's lying. I kicked it out of his hand. It's probably still there."

Dunphy spoke up, offering to go look for it.

"Stay where you are," McInnes shot back, giving his young constable a disapproving look.

"Your word against two others. Eddie says there was no knife."

"He's lying," Stanley said flatly.

"Stanley? I really don't give a damn about the assault. It's what you did to Johnnie that interests me. Christ, ya even admit to hitting him two days before he ended up dead in a ditch. And the boys tell me you said..." he checked his notes, "keep yer fuckin mouths shut, or I'll do to you what I did to Johnnie."

Stanley shook his head. "They're lying."

"I guess they're lying about the girl, too?"

"They are. I told you. I didn't touch her."

"C'mon, Stanley. Ya were fuckin Johnnie's young daughter. The two of ya had words. He warned ya to leave her alone, so ya threatened, then killed him."

"Boys are lying through their teeth. I never touched Johnnie's daughter."

"But you have no alibi for the evenin they claim they heard the threat."

"What can I say? I live alone. Look! They burnt my ponies. Go ask Angus MacNeil. He'll tell you he saw them just after the fire started, running in the opposite direction. I knew Johnnie put them up to it. It was pay back after I broke his nose for coming at me with a pan shovel. But I'm not involved with his daughter, I never threatened him, and I sure as hell didn't kill him."

"See, Stanley. This is the thing. I remember you just drivin off when I was at the store the mornin of the third. And I witnessed a lot of strange behaviour. Suspicious behaviour, if you ask me. And, well the boys' story is pannin out to be true. And yers isn't. So, why not just admit ya killed Johnnie, and let's put all this behind us. The Crown will likely go easier on ya if ya just come clean. Hell, I might even put in a good word for you."

McInnes pushed the notepad toward him.

Stanley pushed it back.

"Suit yourself," McInnes said, sitting back in his chair and hooking his thumbs through his belt loops. "Ya know, Stanley, they hang ya for murder." McInnes turned sideways in his chair, put his hands around his throat, rolled his eyes back, and stuck his tongue out ghoulishly to the side. Constable McEwan started to laugh, quickly bringing his sleeve to his face and wiping away the black juice that rolled down his chin. McInnes turned back to Stanley. "She must be an awfully good fuck," he said.

Stanley lunged forward.

McInnes quickly pushed his chair back, steadying his balance. Dunphy and McEwan rushed toward Stanley, pushing him back down onto his chair.

"See, boys. Told ya he had a temper," McInnes said, brushing his hands over the front of his shirt. "Cuff him."

Dunphy removed the cuffs from his belt and approached Stanley with an apologetic look. He lifted each of Stanley's arms off the table, slid the bracelets over his wrists, and clasped them shut.

McInnes stood, dragged his chair back in place, and started to laugh. "Tell me, Stanley? Did ya set your own ponies on fire as a diversion? That way, if the boys reported what they knew about you and Johnnie's daughter, ya could claim they started the fire. Hell, not like two half-dead, blind ponies would be much of a loss."

Stanley glared at McInnes, his jaw muscles taut with anger.

McInnes stood and looked down at him. "Looks like we're done for now, boys," he said. He headed for the door, followed by Dunphy and McEwan. He turned back to Stanley. "I'm gonna nail ya to the cross," he said and walked into the hall.

Sergeant McInnes smirked at James. "He's all yours. Say your goodbyes. Won't be long before ya see him danglin from a noose."

Constable McEwan pulled up a chair, placed it outside the door, and sat down. "Sergeant's orders," he said, fixing his attention to the second shirt he'd ruined in as many weeks.

Samuel Friedman Jr., or Sam, as he preferred, grabbed James's coat sleeve. "What did he mean about the noose? You said Stanley was charged with assault."

"He is," James said, looking down at Sam's hand gripping his arm. "He hasn't been charged with anything else. They mentioned something about Johnnie Adshade's death. They're just blowing smoke. It won't amount to anything. C'mon. I'm anxious to get this done and get back to the store."

James and Sam walked into the interrogation room.

"I brought you some tobacco," James said, reaching in his pocket and putting it in front of Stanley.

"Stanley, this is Sam Friedman. I just watched him win his first case," James said, patting Sam on the back.

Sam held out his hand, looked down at Stanley's cuffed wrists, then pulled it back. "Mr. MacIntyre," he nodded.

"Call me Stanley," he said. He turned to James. "I thought you'd bring a pie."

"Mabel wanted me to."

Stanley then looked at Sam, thinking the kid didn't look old enough to shave.

"So, how are you managing?" James asked.

"Room and board aren't bad, but the company stinks."

"We're working on getting you out of here. Right Sam?"

Sam looked up from his shiny black valise, a gift from Rabbi Goldberg for passing the bar. He pulled out some loose papers, shuffled them into an organized pile, and tapped their uneven edges down on the table. "That's right," he said, looking at Stanley and placing the neat stack beside him.

"Appreciate that," Stanley said.

"So, who was it you allegedly beat up?" James asked, hoping it wasn't true.

"No alleged about it," Stanley said, describing his conversation with Angus MacNeil, waiting outside Iggies for Billy and Eddie to show up, kicking the knife out of Billy's hand, and their claims that he threatened, and then admitted to killing Johnnie. He didn't mention anything about what they had done to Mabel.

"Are you sure they started the fire?" James asked.

"Well, I didn't beat them up for being ugly and stupid. They admitted it."

Stanley and James watched Sam's elbow come across the table knock his neatly stacked pile of papers onto the floor.

"Sorry," Sam said, pushing his chair back. He jumped down and crawled on his hands to collect them off the scratched, grey floor. He poked his head up from under the table and looked at Stanley. "I'll need to know how to find Angus MacNeil."

Stanley gave James a worried look. "Anyway, James, you know what the police are like. They don't investigate anything. They build a case against the first person they suspect. They don't even believe Billy pulled a knife on me."

Sam crawled back up on his chair. "I don't get it. Why would the boys want to set fire to your barn?" he asked, pulling a hankie from his pocket, and brushing the dust off his hands.

"Johnnie Adshade put them up to it after I broke his nose. Vain bastard," Stanley said before he could stop himself. He looked at James who had his head in his hands. There's that word again. *Bastard.*

"This is all my fault," James said. "If I hadn't asked you to go see Johnnie—"

"Don't be ridiculous. This isn't your fault," Stanley insisted.

"Wait a minute. Did you say you broke the deceased's nose?" Sam asked.

"Yes," Stanley replied.

Sam's head shot up. "When?"

"Couple of days before he ended up dead," Stanley said matter-of-factly.

Sam looked nervously toward James, then at Stanley. "Why?"

"Johnnie swung a pan shovel at his head," James said, filling Sam in on why Stanley paid Johnnie a visit.

Sam looked back and forth between James and Stanley. "Geez, guys. This is a lot more than I bargained for."

"It'll be fine," James said, hoping to reassure Sam, as much as himself. "Stanley wasn't the only one to punch Johnnie in the face. I hit him, too. And I certainly didn't kill him."

"You hit him, too?" Sam said. "Tell me it wasn't two days before he died?"

"No. It was the day before," James said, holding up his sore hand.

"So, you both hit Johnnie within a couple of days of his death?"

"Yes," James said.

Sam turned to Stanley. "And where were you the night Johnnie was murdered?" he asked tentatively.

"At home."

"Can anyone verify that?"

"I can," James answered.

"Let me get this straight. You both have a run in with Johnnie within hours of his death, *and* ...you're each other's alibis?"

"That's right. I know it doesn't look good, but neither of us had anything to do with it," James said.

Sam looked like he was ready to pass out.

He looked at James. "So, what do we have to go on?"

"The truth," James said.

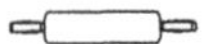

CHAPTER 3

James and Sam left the police station and drove to the Five and Dime to confer. James ordered two teas. Sam sat sideways in the booth, his legs extending into the aisle. He slapped away at the dusty remains of the interrogation room floor that clung to the knees of his new black suit. "Mr. Cameron. I'm more than a bit worried I don't have the experience for this kind of case. I think you should find someone else."

"Don't be ridiculous. I saw you in court this morning. You're a natural," James lied.

"But I didn't sign up for a murder trial."

"Stanley's not charged with murder."

"Not yet," Sam countered.

"Let's take this one step at a time. Billy and Eddie are just trying to send the police off in another direction so they don't get charged with arson."

Sam picked up his tea and blew on it. "You're sure Stanley didn't threaten Johnnie? Kill him?"

"I'm sure."

"Honestly, Mr. Cameron. I really don't think I'm cut out for—"

James "James, please?"

"James

"Sam? Stanley's a good man. We just need to discredit Billy and Eddie. Prove they're lying. We know Angus MacNeil saw them in the area just before the fire. And we have Mabel. She'll vouch for Stanley. She'll tell the police Stanley didn't touch—"

James and Sam both turned as Dirty Willie burst through the door.

"There's a mob heading to Number Six," Willie shouted, excitedly pointing up the street. "They're gonna burn the niggers out!"

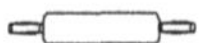

CHAPTER 4

James and Sam arrived at the scene to find a mob of about one hundred people, including women and children, carrying sticks, shovels, and bull reeds soaked in kerosene. They were chanting, '*Out with the niggers,*' A small band of coloureds held hands as they faced the angry crowd, nervously looking back and forth at one another; knowing they were significantly outnumbered and outarmed.

"What's taking the police so long to get here?" Sam asked.

"They're probably waiting for the Number Six day shift to finish up so they can join the crowd," James said, thinking his assessment was probably bang on. Two police wagons finally pulled up. Sergeant McInnes stepped out of the lead car and walked slowly toward the front of the unruly mob, his hand perched on his revolver. A posse of about a half dozen constables stood off to the side. They were slapping their batons into their open palms, eyeing the coloureds in the event they stepped out of line.

"Okay, folks. Party's over," McInnes shouted. "Darkies aren't responsible this time. We got the man responsible for Adshade's murder in custody. Ya can all go home now."

Sam turned to James. "Sure sounds like they're going to add murder to the assault charge."

A voice from the back yelled, "We know it's the niggers. They beat up Adshade before he was killed."

"That was all a big misunderstandin," Sergeant McInnes yelled.

"Yer full a shit," a young, torch-carrying woman said from the front.

The mob started chanting again, moving closer to the terrified fathers and mothers who pushed their children behind them and eyed their tarpapered shacks. A lone chant soon grew into a loud chorus. '*Burn em out! Burn em out!*' James and Sam watched one lit bull reed touch the head of another. Black smoke clouded the air and the smell of gas, hung thick.

"What's he waiting for?" Sam asked.

Sergeant McInnes finally unsnapped his holster, pulled out his pistol, and fired into the air. The crowd quieted. "I'm telling ya. Go home. Coloureds didn't murder Adshade."

"Liar. They beat em. Then came back to finish him off," an old man waving a shovel yelled back.

The crowd started to push forward. McInnes's posse moved in to keep the black and white camps apart. James began elbowing his way to the front, anxious to acknowledge he was responsible for Johnnie's initial beating.

"Johnnie told Billy the niggers jumped him," someone to James's left shouted.

"Billy was wrong," Sergeant McInnes hollered back.

James turned toward the young man who mentioned Billy and pushed his way to him. "This Billy you're talking about. What's his last name?"

"What's it to ya?"

"Just tell me his last name," James said impatiently.

"Guthro. Billy Guthro."

James thought it odd that the same guy who accused the coloureds of murdering Johnnie was now pointing the finger at Stanley.

"Go home," McInnes shouted again, pointing his gun in the air. "We got Johnnie's murderer. And he's not a coloured."

James rushed to find Sam. "Sam! Sam! You're not going to believe this," he said, sharing his discovery.

Eventually, the crowd began to peter out. A few lingered about, shouting slurs at the small band of coloureds folks who looked resigned to the fact that their small part of town, just got a lot smaller. The white folk, James thought, just looked disappointed.

James and Sam approached Sergeant McInnes as he was about to pull away. James knocked on his window. McInnes rolled it partway down.

"So, your key witness in the case against Stanley, also accused the coloureds of murdering Johnnie. Doesn't sound like a reliable witness to me," James said. Sam smiled at this side.

"No worries, boys. We know we got the right guy this time. By the way, Mr. Cameron, I still got a few questions for you. Feel free to take along yer young buck," he said, nodding at Sam. "Yer gonna need a good lawyer," he laughed. "I'm late for my supper." He rolled the window back up and drove off.

James began to walk back to his car. "C'mon, Sam," he shouted. "Let's go to Iggies."

Sam ran to catch up. "But, I don't drink."

James stopped and waited for him. "We're not looking for booze, Sam. We're looking for the knife."

It took the two of them less than ten minutes to find the knife. Sam spotted it sticking out from a patch of dry weeds under a bramble bush. He bent down to pick it up. James reached down and put his hand on his arm. "Wait. Let the police find it. We can't just walk in and say we found this knife at the scene. They'd never believe us."

"You're right," Sam said, standing and looking about. "Kind of scary to think they didn't send anyone to look for it."

"I know. But not surprising," James said. "I'll stop in to see McInnes in the morning and ask about the knife. If I have to, I'll shame him in to sending some to the scene."

"I'll come with you. After all, I am Stanley's legal counsel."

"Yes, you are," James said, wishing it was the boy's father.

CHAPTER 5

James returned from Iggies to see the lights still on. A customer he didn't know was leaving with a pie and a bag of goods. It was well past six. The store was rarely open this late. He walked into the kitchen.

"Sorry I'm so late. You should be home eating supper by now," he said to Mabel.

"All's good here. We had a real good day. I'm almost caught up with my backorders. Just need to finish tidyin up."

"That's great. I'm going to have to give you a raise," James said.

"A raise? Shake yer head, Mr. Cameron. I still gotta make amends for Dr. Cohen's fees. And I haven't fergotten about the three years in back rent I owe ya fer—"

"Has Margaret been down?" James interrupted, not wanting to have to get into any long explanations.

"No. I checked on her a few times. Brought her some tea and bread. She barely drank the tea and didn't have so much as a bite to eat."

"Her headaches are brutal. Thankfully, she doesn't get them often. So you managed okay by yourself?"

"Actually, I had some help. Mary Catherine came by with the boys for a coupla hours. Boys reorganized yer canned goods. And Mary Catherine did a fabulous job on the register. I could tell the customers loved her."

"I'll be sure to pay her for her help," James said, peeking around the kitchen doorway into the store. "Shelves look great."

"I had em turn all the cans so the labels are facin out. I paid them in penny candy. Hope that's okay?"

"That's fine, Mabel. It never occurred to me to do that. Great idea."

Mabel cursed herself for not giving Mary Catherine credit for the *great idea.*

"Did ya see Stanley?" she asked, hoping Mr. Cameron had good news and that he wasn't still in jail.

"I did. He's doing good, all things considered."

Mabel was dragging her bag of flour back to the pantry. "So, he's still in jail?" she asked.

James rushed to help her. "Yes. But I am hoping not for much longer."

Mabel lifted her head and smiled.

"I'm just going to peek in on Margaret. Then, I'll drive you home."

"No need, Mr. Cameron. I can walk."

"No, Mabel. You're not walking home. I'll just be a minute."

James mounted the stairs and quietly opened the door to their blackened bedroom. He walked over and whispered her name. He could see the covers were over her head and decided it was best to leave her be. He touched her shoulder gently and tiptoed out. It would be morning before she was over it. When he returned to the kitchen, Mabel was holding a pie and grinning.

"Yer finally gonna get to try my pie."

"I can't wait. Seems like I'm the only one in town who hasn't," he said. He helped her on with her coat.

James filled Mabel in on the day's events on the drive home. He told her Stanley didn't deny beating the two men, but as far as he was concerned, he had good reason. They had set fire to his barn. He also told her about Angus seeing them just before the fire.

"But why would anyone want to hurt Stanley and his ponies?"

James decided now was not the time to bring Johnnie into the picture. She was still mourning and likely blame herself for what happened. "Not sure. Maybe they just get their kicks from starting fires. Anyway, I don't blame Stanley for what he did. Heck, I'm a peaceful man, but I might have done a lot worse."

"Well, if they did the likes of that to me, I'd sure as hell be sharpenin my bread knife," Mabel said.

James started to laugh. "Anyway, I'm sure the Crown will see they're not reliable witnesses."

"Sure hope so," she said, thinking of the day she and Stanley talked at the brook.

They turned onto Minto Street. "I thought I'd come in for a moment and pay my respects to Amour."

"Sure, Mr. Cameron. Amour could use some cheerin up. I'm sure she's gettin sick of just seein my ugly face."

CHAPTER 6

Amour looked at the clock. It was going on seven. She was expecting Mabel to be home by now. She was hungry, but would wait and eat with her. Her mind turned to her encounter with Mr. Donnely. She knew he looked familiar, but was still surprised when she was led into his office to discover that they had met at a reception in Boston. She thought she had prepared herself for the ridicule that would inevitably follow the news of her husband's perverse proclivities, but today proved otherwise.

She practically ran out of Mr. Donnely's office when he mentioned he had worked with Roddy before coming here. He must think I'm daft, she thought. I didn't even get to the business of why I stopped in to see him. Just excused myself and walked out like he had insulted me in some way. I'll have to face him again before too long. I'll just tell him the truth; that I'm embarrassed and ashamed I married a man so evil.

She was putting the soup back on the stove when Mabel walked in, with James close behind. James reached out and took Amour's hand and placed it between his.

"I just wanted to stop in and tell you that I'm sorry for your loss, and your troubles."

Amour instinctively knew, that unlike most people in town, he wasn't judging her for Roddy's actions.

"Thank you. It's been a difficult few weeks," she said.

"Mabel told me about the service tomorrow. I'd like to come, if that's all right? I could pick you and Mabel up around eight-thirty?"

"Of course you can come. I'm afraid there will only be a handful of us there. And it's very kind of you to offer to drive us. Thank you."

"Please? Come in and have some tea. In fact, why don't you stay for supper? I've got plenty of —"

"Thank you, but it's getting late and Margaret's at home. She's not feeling well. I just wanted to pay my respects. "

"I understand," Amour said.

"So, I'll see you in the morning." He looked past Amour. Mabel had her head over the pot of soup. "Good night, Mabel."

"Good night, Mr. Cameron. Thanks for takin me home."

As We Forgive Those Who Trespass Against Us

Thursday, November 10

CHAPTER I

"Ashes to ashes and dust to dust," Father Vokey bellowed into the crisp air, as if trying to be heard over a large crowd. A gravedigger, standing off to the side with his hands resting on top of his shovel, waited patiently for the handful of mourners to say their goodbyes so he could get started on the next hole.

"Dear Lord, we commit the body of John Adshade to the ground and commend his soul to your eternal glory. Lord, bless him and keep him. Make Thy face shine upon and be gracious to him. Lord, lift up your countenance upon him and give him everlasting peace."

Mabel walked in front of James, Amour, and Mary Catherine to the pine box awaiting its decent into the partially frozen grown. "Bye, Da. I hope ya find more peace where yer headin than what ya had here on earth. I'm sorry I wasn't a better daughter to ya." She put her hand over the box, wishing she had some daisies. She felt James's arm wrap around her shoulder.

"You okay?" he asked.

"As bad he was, he was still my da," she said, through misty eyes.

Father Vokey and the four mourners walked over the brown, crisp, uneven grass toward the car. James looked across the expanse of crumbing headstones to the far side of the cemetery and thought of his own father, buried next to his mother. He then thought of Mabel's father, buried in a communal grave, far from home, far from his family, but far from forgotten.

CHAPTER 2

Margaret approached Mabel from behind the counter. "I'm sorry, dear," she said, awkwardly hugging her.

"Thank you, Mrs… Margaret. Da's finally on his way. How ya feelin?"

"Much better. Thank you for checking on me yesterday."

"Hope the boys didn't disturb you?" Mabel asked.

"What boys?"

"My friend, Mary Catherine, Catherine with a C, came by with the Toth boys."

"Look, Margaret," James said. He pointed to the canned goods. "The boys turned the cans around so all the labels are facing out."

"How clever of them."

"Actually, it was Mabel's idea," James said.

"Come. I made some tea and you must be chilled to the bone," Margaret said. She led them into the kitchen.

Mabel was unbuttoning her coat and watching Margaret pour the tea when she spotted it. "Mr. Cameron!" she yelled, causing Margaret to jump and spill the tea over the table. "Ya didn't try my pie. It ain't as good now."

"Sorry, Mabel. I came home and went straight to bed," he lied, recalling the two rum and four makins he enjoyed before crawling in beside Margaret. "I'm sure it's fine. I'll have some now."

"Not this one," she said. "This one's headin for the discount counter." She turned to Mr. Cameron. "Ya gotta eat my pie the day it's made. That's when it's best."

James and Margaret exchanged glances, trying not to laugh.

"I'll have my tea after I change," James said.

When he got to his room, he sat on the edge of the bed, kicked off his shiny black shoes, and shed his well-worn funeral jacket. He then pulled his suspenders off his shoulders and stepped out of his grey and black pinstriped pants. He put on a clean, pale blue shirt and casual pants that hung loosely on his hips. He grabbed a belt and eased it through its loops. He pulled the strap back, edged the pin into its favoured notch, and slipped the tongue through its keeper. He looked in the mirror and restarted the process, pulling the belt back another notch. Margaret is right, he thought. I *am* losing weight. He patted his flat stomach, thinking he had little fat to spare. He decided it was time for a full breakfast for a change, with back bacon and eggs.

James cracked his eggs into the cast iron pan that angrily spit its sizzling fat back at him. "How long before my pie is ready?" he asked.

"Every pie is different. I don't tell it when it's done. It tells me," Mabel said, closing the oven door. "I like to see the sticky juices bubble up over the sides."

James sopped up the last traces of bacon grease and egg yolk with a crust of bread, popped it in his mouth, and marveled at the care Mabel took and the speed she worked. She would closely examine the dimpled mounds of dough bursting out of their narrow tins and gently tap their sticky heads with the tips of her fingers. She quickly peeled, cored, and cut her apples, then expertly tossed them in a large bowl, each piece as generously adorned in their sweet coating as the next. Her pie tins, lined with a pale, thin sheet, would welcome equal amounts of their candied filling, before being draped in a delicate blanket of creamy-white pastry.

Mabel held her pie in front of her. Her outstretched fingers deftly balancing her latest creation above her kneading board. She scraped her knife along its side. Her excess pastry, falling into a neat pile below, would be set aside for the next pie.

Mabel looked at James. “Yer making me nervous.”

“I don’t mean to. I was just thinking how good you are at your job. You don’t waste anything.”

She reached into the oven to pull out her latest golden creation. “Try not to waste my time, my money, my emotions, or my pastry,” she said.

She placed the pie on the cooling rack, next to her rising bread.

James bent over it and inhaled its sweet, warm vapors. “So, that’s my pie?”

“Yeah. It’s yer pie,” Mabel said proudly. “But ya gotta wait for it to cool down.”

“Smells great,” James said. He picked up a tea towel, wrapped it around the pie, and headed for the door.

“Where ya goin with it?” Mabel hollered after him.

“Putting it somewhere where it won’t disappear on me.” He retreated to the back of the store, put his coat on, and peeked around the corner to make sure Mabel wasn’t watching. He then picked up the pie, winked at Margaret standing behind the counter, and tiptoed out the door.

CHAPTER 3

James and Sam approached the officer on the front desk. "Brought me a pie did ya?"

"Sorry. It's for one of your guests," James replied. "We're also hoping to have a word with Sergeant McInnes."

"It's his day off."

"Who's handling the MacIntyre case in his absence?"

"That'd be…no one."

"Well, who's in charge here?" James asked sharply.

The cocky young officer nodded to the room to his right. James and Sam approached the open door. James was relieved when he looked and saw Captain Collins. James didn't know him well, but he did know he was one of the few honest cops, among a lot of mean, incompetent, brutes who liked to use far more force than necessary.

"Captain Collins."

Collins looked up. "Yes."

James balanced the pie in one hand and extended the other to the Captain. "James Cameron. And this is—"

"Sam Friedman," Collins said. "You're the spit of your father." He shook Sam's sweaty hand. "And Mr. Cameron, we've met before. I believe it was at the forum."

"We did. I wasn't sure you'd remember."

"I'm pretty good with names and faces. An asset in my line of work. What can I do for you gentlemen?" he asked, pointing to the hard wooden chairs across from him.

"We're here about the MacIntyre case. Stanley MacIntyre. He's been charged with assault," James said, taking his seat and resting the pie on his lap.

Sam walked to a bookshelf and peered at an impressive array of law books.

"I've heard," Collins said. "Anyway, I'm afraid that I can't help you. Case is being headed up by Sergeant McInnes and I'm not privy to the details."

"Yes. We wanted to speak to him, but he's off today. There's a matter we believe needs urgent attention," James said.

"And what would that be?"

James told Collins about Stanley's ponies, Angus MacNeil's observations, and that Stanley's accusers pretty much admitted to Stanley they set fire to his barn. That it ruined Stanley's livelihood, damaged the company house he shared with the widow MacNeil, and that it could have been a lot worse. James said Stanley had wanted to put a scare into the boys, but things heated up when Billy came at him with a knife, which hadn't been located. He also told him Billy first claimed the coloureds from Number Six were responsible for Johnnie Adshade's death, but that he's now claiming it was Stanley.

"I'm still not sure what you expect me to do. Sergeant McInnes is heading up the investigation," Collins said. He knew his rogue sergeant wasn't about to share details of his case, especially with him.

Sam turned away from the bookshelf and walked toward Captain Collins. "We would expect that there be a thorough investigation and not a rush to judgement. Your officers have accepted the word of a suspected arsonist. Moreover, they have dismissed outright the word of a good man who acknowledged his actions and who acted in self-defence. It will look poorly on your good office when it comes out that Sergeant McInnes failed to even survey the crime scene to search for said knife, or any other evidence that might corroborate the testimony of my client."

James turned and looked at Sam, surprised and impressed by his eloquent argument, thinking he too might have rushed to judgement.

"Are you telling me that no one went to see if there was a knife on the premises?"

"Yes, that's exactly what I'm saying," Sam said. He looked over at James, hoping he won his approval.

Captain Collins excused himself, walked into the hall, and hollered for Dunphy.

Dunphy stuck his head out from an office down the hall. "Sir?"

"Tell McEwan to bring the wagon out front."

"On it, sir."

"Thank you, Captain," James said, standing and extending his hand.

CHAPTER 4

Stanley was laying on his back with his eyes closed. He was thinking of Donnie Wilson, the former load superintendent at Number Two. Wilson's fourteen-year old daughter had been raped several years ago by the beloved choir director at St. Anthony's. When charges were laid and it became public, she became the focus of derision; shunned by her friends and schoolmates and mocked by her fellow parishioners. Her rapist ended up with a slap on the wrist, she ended up slitting hers, and Donnie Wilson ended up an unemployed alcoholic.

James and Sam stood beside Dunphy as the young constable reached for the huge key ring dangling from his hip and noisily opened the cell door.

"We caught a couple of breaks," James said.

Stanley propped himself up on his elbows. "See you brought me Mabel's pie."

"It's all yours, my friend," James said. He handed it to him.

"If it tastes as good as it smells, I'd get myself locked up for one, too," Sam said.

"No need for that. I'll make sure you get one," James offered.

The two amateur sleuths filled Stanley in on the last twenty-four hours. How Billy and Eddie told the police a group of coloureds were responsible for Johnnie's death. That he and Sam went to the scene and found the knife Billy had said didn't exist, and that Captain Collins was now taking an interest in the case.

"When they find the knife, I'll use it to further discredit Billy," Sam said. "I'm starting to feel like we have a pretty good case after all."

Stanley didn't share Sam's optimism. He also couldn't stop thinking of what Billy and Eddie had done to Mabel. "James? How's Mabel?"

James walked to Stanley's cot and sat down beside him. "Good. She's glad to have Amour home and happy her pies are flying off the shelf. Obviously anxious for you to get out of here."

Stanley smiled and put his head down.

James put his hand over his shoulder. "You know, I've been thinking about Billy and Eddie. I'm starting to think they might have something to do with Johnnie's death and they're just trying to finger you."

"But what would be their motive?" Sam asked.

"I don't know. But there's something we're missing," James said.

Stanley knew the answer to Sam's question, but wasn't about to say. "I have a question," he said.

"What's that?" James asked.

"Can one of you boys fetch me a fork?"

CHAPTER 5

Billy's skinny, shirtless father was at the kitchen table running his hand up the dimpled leg of the oversized woman sitting on his lap and nuzzling his neck.

Billy ran his hand through his greasy hair, pacing back and forth. "Fuck! Imbecile probably got lost on the way."

Billy's father reached for his whiskey. "Why don't ya bugger off and give us some privacy."

"How bout you two go to the fuckin bedroom," Billy shot back.

"Cause it's my fuckin house! That's why. Ya better watch yer foul tongue. What's got ya so riled up, anyway?"

Billy pulled the yellow, water-stained curtain back and looked out the window. "Eddie shoulda been here by now."

"Eddie couldn't find his way out of a cardboard box," his father said.

Eddie flew through the door. "I got it, Billy. I got it!"

"Give it to me," Billy said, grabbing it.

"What are ya gonna to do with it?"

"I'm gonna cut ya to fuckin pieces if ya don't fuckin calm down," he said, swiping it back and forth in front of Eddie's face. "Anybody see ya?"

"No. I was real careful. Just like ya told me," he said, hurt that his friend was so ungrateful.

Billy slapped him lightly on the side of the head. "Ya did good, Eddie."

"I did. Didn't I, Billy?"

"Yeah, Eddie. Ya did real good. Now let's get the fuck outa here."

CHAPTER 6

Captain Collins and Constable McEwan were digging in the bushes outside Iggies.

"It ain't here, Captain," McEwan said, blowing on his red hands and eager to get back to the warm station.

"Keep looking," his captain shot back, as he moved along on his hands and knees, patting the sharp grass and thinking about the night at 'The Y' when Stanley had sparred with Willie Morrison. There was no question Stanley snapped. But he had also seen Stanley's reaction when his opponent fell to the canvass. Stanley had sat on his stool, with his head in his hands, and wept. Not the reaction of a naturally violent man, Collins thought. He liked him. In fact, he thought, he liked Stanley almost as much as he disliked McInnes. Only one of them was a mean brute. And it wasn't the accused. He also knew McInnes to be sloppy when it came to police work. He was quick to point the finger and slow to see evidence that didn't substantiate his assumptions. He was also far from discreet, often sharing confidential information with anyone willing to listen to him boast about his *superb* investigative skills.

Collins closed his eyes. He could still see the freshly polished shoes of his good friend dangling in the air. He knew McInnes was responsible for practically everyone in town believing Isaac Greene killed his son. I should have done more to protect my friend, he thought, recalling Isaac pleading with him. *Teddy. I'd never do anything to hurt my boy. I loved him. Teddy, ya know I wouldn't do anything so horrible. Ya got to help me. Sophie is beside herself. She won't leave the house. Teddy! Ya got to tell them. I loved my David.*

James and Sam were leaving the station when Collins and McEwan walked in.

"Any luck?" James asked.

"Sorry guys. We scoured the area. No knife," Collins said.

Sam gave James a nervous look.

"You're sure, Captain?" James asked.

"Positive. We looked in every nook and cranny. Nothing there."

"But that's—" Sam started.

James gave him a reproachful look. "That's not what we expected. Someone must have found it. I know Stanley's telling the truth."

Collins sensed James's disappointment. "Maybe the boys picked it up before they left." He was heading to his office when the image of Isaac's bloated face, the purple ligature marks around his neck, and his clenched, white fists flashed in his mind. He turned back and looked at James and Sam walk past the front desk.

It was too late to help his friend, but not too late to help another good man in need.

"Dunphy! Go fetch Eddie Lynch… and find me a switchblade."

CHAPTER 7

James and Sam drove from the police station to Iggies to see if Captain Collins had missed the knife. Sam jumped out of James's Plymouth and ran to where he had seen it the day before. He pushed the bushes aside. James walked up to him. "Find it?"

"It's not here," Sam said, swiping his hand over the dry grass.

"You sure?" James asked, bending down for a closer look.

"Positive. It was right here," Sam said. "The boys must have come back for it. What now?"

"I'm not sure. Let's go. I think better over tea," James said.

The two drove the short distance to the Five and Dime and sat at a booth in the back.

"James? What if they charge Stanley with murder?"

"I was with Stanley the night Johnnie was killed. We both know Billy and Eddie are lying. We need to prove they set the fire. I'll go see Angus MacNeil and have him talk to Collins," James said.

"And I'll check to see if Billy and Eddie had any prior arrests," Sam said. He looked at James, hesitating before asking. "James? How come you didn't tell the police you struck Johnnie?"

James smiled and shrugged. "I meant to. When I read about them suspecting the coloureds, I went to the station to tell them. That's when they hauled Stanley in. Things just began to unravel. McInnes wouldn't listen to reason. He already had his mind made up about Stanley, despite Dr. Adams saying it was a hit and run."

"You look worried," Sam said, as their waitress approached.

"Not really. Just wish I hadn't lied to Sergeant McInnes about how I hurt my hand."

Sam leaned into James. "What are you talking about?"

The young waitress smiled at Sam and put two teas on the table. James waited for her to leave.

"The day McInnes came by to tell us about Mabel's father, he asked how I hurt my hand. I said I jammed it between some crates in the store."

"Why'd you do that?"

"I don't know. I just didn't think it was any of his business."

"Jesus Christ, James. You never lie to the police," Sam said. He stirred two heaping teaspoons of sugar into his tea.

"I know. But I thought it was an innocent enough lie at the time. Do you think I should tell them now?"

Sam sat quietly for a few minutes remembering his father's advice. Share what you can, everything you can, without making it harder for your client. "I always figure it's best to be totally honest, especially with the police. But what good can come from it now? Hell, next thing you know, McInnes will be implicating you in Adshade's death."

James was about to take a sip of his tea, but put his cup down. "I don't know. Maybe it's better to tell them. What if they find out? It'll seem like I deliberately lied as part of a cover up."

"Honestly, unless you or Stanley tell them, how would they ever know?"

James shrugged, despite the unease he was feeling.

Sam added another spoonful of sugar to his tea. "Let's connect the boys to the fire and work on getting the assault charges thrown out. Shit. I wish we had the knife," he said.

James screwed up his face. "Christ! How can you drink that?" James asked.

"I like it sweet," Sam said. He dipped his spoon back into the sugar bowl, lifted it up, and slowly let the fine sparkling grains fall back into the bowl. "But three's my limit," he said, grinning.

James kicked Sam under the table. "I think the waitress has taken a shine to you. She keeps looking over this way. And I know she's not eyeballing me," he whispered.

Sam looked in her direction, then back at James. "I can't get past the hairnet. Besides, I'm pretty sure she's not kosher."

James wasn't sure how good a lawyer Sam was, but he liked the young man sitting across from him. Sam continued to drink his tea and watched James idly stir his. "Something's eating at you," Sam said. "Just thinking," James said. No point in telling the kid he was picturing himself being cross-examined by Mannie Chernin. *So, Mr. Cameron, are you prepared to swear under oath that Stanley MacIntyre was with you the entire night Johnnie Adshade was murdered?*

"About the case?" Sam asked.

"No," James lied. "Just thinking about how much grief Johnnie Adshade brought to so many people."

"Yeah," said Sam. "I hear he was a real bastard."

CHAPTER 8

Constable Dunphy dropped by Eddie's house. His toothless mother answered the door, saying she had no idea where he was, or when he'd be home. "He ain't here. I ain't seen hide nor hair of em in two days. Whatcha want with em?"

"Just needed to ask him a few more questions about the assault charges."

"What assault charges? Eddie wouldn't hurt nobody."

"He's just a witness in a case we're investigating," Dunphy said. She closed the door on him. He was sitting in his wagon, about to pull out when he saw Eddie limping towards home. He looked happy. He was talking and laughing to himself, until Dunphy got out of the paddy wagon and approached him.

"Hey, Eddie. Got a minute?" Dunphy hollered.

Eddie looked panicked. He didn't like talking to the police, especially without Billy. "Ma's waitin for me."

"I just talked to her. She didn't seem to think you were coming home any time soon."

"Am I in trouble for somethin?"

"No. Captain Collins just wants to have a chat with you about the Adshade case."

"Are we gonna fetch Billy, too?"

"No. The captain just wants to have a word with you."

Eddie turned back and looked in the direction he'd come from.

He wanted to bolt, but thought better of it. His lame leg wouldn't carry him too far.

"Captain just has a few questions. That's all. C'mon. I'll give you a lift home when you're done."

Dunphy put an obviously nervous Eddie in the questioning room. He then went to McEwan's desk and picked up the switchblade he kept in his top drawer.

Captain Collins entered the stark room.

Dunphy was leaning against the wall, facing Eddie.

"Thanks for coming down, Eddie. No need to worry about anything, son. Just have a few questions to tie up a few loose ends on the Adshade case."

Eddie looked back and forth between Collins and Dunphy. "But I told Sergeant McInnes everythin."

"I know. But something's come up. Just wanted to confirm some details. Stanley said Billy pulled a knife on him."

Eddie didn't say anything.

"Did Billy have a switchblade on him the night you were assaulted?"

"No," Eddie said confidently, knowing he gave it to Billy.

"In fact, Billy claims he doesn't even own one. Is that correct?"

Eddie nodded.

"You're sure?"

"Um sure," he said, squirming in his chair. "I never saw em with one. And me and Billy are best friends."

"See, Eddie. We found a knife at the scene," Captain Collins said, slapping McEwan's blade down on the table.

"That's not Billy's knife!" Eddie blurted. "Billy's knife doesn't have a white—" He stopped and looked at the Captain. "Ya tricked me," he said. His lower lip began to quiver.

"It's okay, son. We know you've been covering for Billy. You don't want a man to go to jail for defending himself, now do you?"

There was no reply.

"Eddie… you're in a spot of trouble here. You can either tell us the truth, or I'm afraid the judge is going to lock you up on a number of serious charges, including misleading the police. So, can we count on your cooperation?"

Again, no reply.

"Eddie? Look at me."

Eddie raised his head, but kept his eyes down. "I need to pee."

"Look at me, Eddie."

Eddie finally looked up at Captain Collins, who was smiling back. "Eddie," he said, in a soft voice, "things could get a lot worse unless you tell us the truth. Can we count on you? Eddie? Can we count on you to tell us the truth?"

"Yeah," Eddie whimpered. *Billy was going to kill him.*

"Let's start with the fire. Did you and Billy start the fire?"

Eddie chewed on his filthy nails. "Fire?"

"Yeah, the fire that killed Stanley's ponies."

Eddie pushed his fists into his crotch. "I need to pee."

"You can pee in a minute. Did you and Billy start the fire?"

Eddie looked behind Captain Collins and saw Constable Dunphy put his hand over the head of his baton.

"I really need to pee," he repeated, rocking back and forth is his chair.

Captain Collins slapped his hand on the table. Eddie jumped. "I'm just going to ask you one more time. Did you—"

"Yes!" Eddie confessed.

"Why?"

"Johnnie told us to."

"Johnnie Adshade?"

"Yes."

"Why?"

Eddie closed his eyes, trying to remember what Billy told him. "I don't remember."

"Come on, Eddie. You remember."

Eddie opened his eyes. "Johnnie said Stanley was doin things to his daughter."

"Did you and Billy hear Stanley threaten Johnnie?"

Eddie just kept his head down. He pressed his eyes shut, again. "I dunno."

"Eddie! Did you and Billy hear Stanley threaten to kill Johnnie? Eddie!" Collins shouted. His face was red.

"No," Eddie said meekly.

"Speak up, son."

Dunphy tapped Collins on the shoulder and nodded to the puddle under Eddie's chair.

"No," Eddie repeated. "Can I go now?"

"Did Stanley tell you he killed Johnnie?"

"I think so," Eddie said. He looked to the door.

"Well, Eddie. He either did… or he didn't," Collins said.

"Billy said he did. I was scared. I gotta go now."

"Eddie? What did *you*, hear?"

"I wanna go home. I peed myself."

"Not quite yet. Did you hear Stanley admit to killing Johnnie?"

"I thought Stanley was gonna kill us."

"So, you didn't hear him threaten, or admit to killing Jonnie?"

"No," Eddie said, putting his head down on his outstretched arms and sobbing.

CHAPTER 9

Margaret was minding the store when Mary Catherine walked in pushing the baby carriage, with Luke and Mark at her side. "Hello, Mrs. Cameron. Is Mabel here?"

"Yes," Margaret said, walking to the kitchen to tell Mabel she had some visitors.

Mabel peeked around the doorway. "Hi guys. How ya doin?"

"Hi, Mabel. The boys were wondering if you had any more cans to arrange," Mary Catherine said, putting her hand on Mark's shoulder as he leaned into her.

"No doubt lookin for more penny candy," Mabel said, walking toward them and mussing Mark's hair. She introduced Margaret to her friend and the boys.

"Mabel said you helped out yesterday. The boys did a great job with the cans," Margaret said. She smiled and bent down next to the baby. "How old is he?" she asked.

"Eight months."

"I'm four," Mark said, holding up his hand and spreading his stubby fingers.

"You're big for four. And very smart," Margaret replied. "And how old are you?" she asked Luke.

He dropped his head.

"Go on, Luke. Tell Mrs. Cameron how old you are," Mary Catherine urged.

"Eleven," he whispered.

"I think the canned good section looks great. But I'm thinking we need to sort that box of odd-sized nails and screws over there," she said, pointing it out to them. "Luke, do you think you and your brother can do that?"

He didn't look up. "I guess so."

CHAPTER 10

Captain Collins was back in his office. "Dunphy," he hollered.

"Sir?"

"Go tell Eddie's mother he'll be staying with us for a while. Oh, and get her to pack up some clean clothes. Then see if you can track down Mannie Chernin and ask him to drop by."

Dunphy started to leave. "Yes sir."

"I'm not finished," Collins growled. "Grab McEwan and go pick up Billy Guthro and throw him in the lockup, away from Eddie."

Dunphy turned back to the door.

"Just a minute. After you track down Mannie, go find Sergeant McInnes and tell him to get his sorry ass down here," Collins barked.

Dunphy waited for further instructions.

"Move!" Collins shouted, immediately regretting that, of all his constables, Dunphy was the one bearing the brunt of his anger.

CHAPTER 11

Amour stood in front of the only three-story, freshly painted building on Commercial Street and looked up at the sign that read British Imperial Coal Company. She took a deep breath, thinking she had no choice but to face Mr. Donnely a second time. She willed herself to walk up the narrow stairway and down the hall adorned with the unsmiling images of past and present company executives.

She stopped at the spot where Roddy's photograph once hung. The bare white space now exposed, proof that a paint job was in order and that Roddy's transgressions had quickly spread throughout the halls. An older gentleman walked out of an office toward her. Amour put her head down, hoping it was no one who would recognize her.

I can't do this, she thought, turning back. She looked down from the top of the stairs. Michael Donnely and two men in business suits appeared on the landing below. Amour could feel her heart quicken, unsure of what to do. Michael turned his attention away from his colleagues, put his hand on the rail, and looked up.

"Mrs. MacPherson!" he hollered up. "Are you here to see me?"

"Good afternoon, Mr. Donnely. Yes. If you have the time?

"Certainly," he said, bounding up the stairs. "Follow me." He opened the door to his office and encouraged her to enter.

"Sorry," he said, rushing to remove a box from the one comfortable chair he had for visitors. "As you can see, I'm still not completely settled in."

"You have a lovely office," she said. It was smaller and much messier than the tidy surroundings Roddy once occupied a floor above.

Donnely walked to the window and looked out at the waves crashing against the high, rugged shore in the distance. "Not quite as lavish as my office in Boston, but the view here is incredible. Hard to believe there are men under those angry waters right now, digging their way along with pick and shovel." He shook his head. "Anyway, it sure beats looking at skyscrapers."

He turned to see Amour looking at the framed picture resting on the corner of his desk. "You have twins, Mr Donnely," she said, hoping to keep the conversation light.

"My nieces. It's an old photograph. They were six when it was taken. They're nine now."

"And is this your sister?"

"Yes. Martha," he said, walking around his huge mahogany desk and picking up the photograph.

Amour watched him study it. "She's beautiful. And the girls, too."

He smiled. "She died about a year after it was taken. Girls live in England with their father now," he said, putting it back in place.

"I'm so sorry," Amour said, worried she was once again making a mess of things.

"She brought the twins into the world without any complications whatsoever, but died giving birth to her third child. A boy."

"I'm very sorry. I didn't mean to—"

Donnely waved his hand in the air as if to say no harm done, walked behind his desk, and sat down.

"My brother, Johnnie, just passed."

"Then we share a like heartache," he said.

"It's been in the papers. They found his body a few days ago. We're still not sure what happened."

"So, you're home for the burial. I saw you at the depot and was about to reintroduce myself, but the young lady with you seemed anxious to leave."

"Oh? I wasn't aware you were there," Amour said, unsure of why she would lie about such a thing. "Mr. Donnely," she continued, anxious to get to the purpose of her visit, "I want to apologize for my behaviour the other day. I'm sure you must have thought that I was rude, if not totally daft, when I left before even discussing the matter that brought me here."

He smiled. "Mrs. MacPherson. I thought your departure was curious, but certainly not daft, or rude."

"Amour. Please? I prefer to go by my given name. You see—"

He held up his hand. "No need to explain. I'm just glad you're here now. In fact, if anyone should apologize, it's me. I hadn't seen the paper and wasn't aware of Mr. MacPherson's circumstances. I certainly didn't mean for you to feel uncomfortable as I prattled on about what a brilliant man he was."

She looked as if she were ready to cry.

"Can I get you a cup of tea?" he asked, sensing her discomfort.

"Thank you, Mr. Donnely. But—"

"Michael," he interrupted. "If I'm going to call you by your given name, then I think it's only fair you call me by mine."

Amour smiled, bowed her head, and stared down at her lap. "Roderick…" she said, stopping and squeezing the leather straps of her purse. She lifted her head and started again. "Roderick owns several properties that are currently being rented to employees of your company."

Michael looked surprised, curious as to why none of his colleagues mentioned this to him, given Roddy's name had come up so much lately.

"Well, he has deeded them to me. I'm hoping to dispose of them as soon as I can," she said, relieved she finally got to the business of her visit.

"But wouldn't they provide you with a steady income?"

"They would. But I wish to free myself from all ties to…" she hesitated, "to my past."

"I understand," he said, picking up a fountain pen and idly scratching it up and down his notepad.

"Anyway, I was wondering if your company might wish to purchase them. I'm prepared to sell at a fair price."

"How many properties are we speaking of?"

"Three. All near town," she said, knowing the location would be a selling feature.

"And the income they provide?"

She unsnapped her purse and handed him the deeds and a piece of paper detailing the monthly rent for each one.

Donnely looked them over.

"Do you think this is something the company might consider?" she asked.

"Consider? Yes. Purchase? I'm not sure. I would have to visit the properties to ensure they are in good repair."

"Of course," Amour said, grateful he didn't reject her offer out-of-hand.

"Do you have a lawyer to represent your interests?" he asked.

"Not yet. It's my next order of business."

"Very well then. I'll have the properties assessed, you get yourself a lawyer, and we'll take it from there."

"Thank you, Mr. Donnely… Michael," she corrected, standing and extending her hand.

He came around from behind his desk. "You're very welcome, Amour," he said, placing his hand in hers.

"Here! Let me get this," he said. He sprinted to the door and pulled it open.

"Thank you."

"You're welcome, Amour. So, we'll be in touch?"

Michael Donnelly watched her lower her head and walk quickly out of sight. He was hoping the rental properties were in good repair. For her sake, as well as his own.

CHAPTER 12

Sergeant McInnes was sitting outside Mannie Chernin's office when the burly prosecutor rounded the corner and made his way down the hall. McInnes jumped to his feet and walked toward him. He was grinning and holding a manila envelope.

"Why are you here?" Mannie asked, with his briefcase in one hand and his keys in the other. "I don't have much time. I need to be back in court within the hour." He turned the heavy key ring over in his hand, found the one he was looking for, inserted it in the Mortise lock, and pushed the door open.

"This won't take long. Just thought I'd stop by and make your day," McInnes said, waving the envelope in the air. He started to unbutton his jacket.

Mannie shot him a look. "I just told you, I'm pressed for time. Don't make yourself too comfortable."

McInnes looked around at the array of framed press clippings on the wall that were testimony to Mannie's ego and his prowess in the courtroom. "You'll need space for one more," McInnes said.

"One more what?" Mannie asked, throwing his coat over the chair McInnes was about to sit on.

McInnes nodded to the wall to his right. "One more headline. It's all comin together nicely. Sit down and I'll fill ya in."

Mannie didn't care for McInnes's intrusion, or his orders. "You must have shit for brains and it's coming out your ears. I told you! I don't have time. Just leave the envelope. I'll get to it later."

McInnes shook his head. Mannie was just a selfish prick. "Jesus, Mannie. Cut me some slack. I'm just tryin to make your job easier."

Mannie thought McInnes looked like he was ready to cry. He leaned back in his green leather chair and waved him on.

"Bottom line. The fire's a ruse. Billy's father swore that both Billy and Eddie were at home with him the mornin of the fire. And, get this. Stanley's got no alibi for the time Billy and Eddie say they heard him threaten Johnnie. Apparently Stanley's been fuckin Johnnie's daughter. And Johnnie didn't like it. The two had words. That's why Stanley threatened him. I had a witness come forward this morning. Claims she'll testify to the relationship between Stanley and the girl. Says it wasn't a happy one. She also provided a statement that blows Stanley's alibi for the night of the murder to smithereens."

McInnes placed the envelope on top of Mannie's desk. "It's all in there," he said, tapping it. "Ya know, I'm startin to think James Cameron is in this up to his eyeballs. Why else would he be lyin? Hell, for all we know, he could have delivered the fatal blow."

"It's one thing to go after a coal hauler," Mannie said, shaking his head. "It's quite another to go after a well-respected businessman."

McInnes shrugged. "I guess that's why we only hang poor men." He turned and walked out.

Mannie closed the door and returned to his desk. He picked up his sterling silver letter opener, slid it under the corner flap of the envelope, and ripped it open. He turned his chair to face the window and rested the heels of his shiny black Dacks on the sill. He read the first page, then looked at his watch. He had all the time in the world.

CHAPTER 13

"Hope they're not giving you any trouble, Mrs. Cameron," Mary Catherine said, sticking her head around the corner.

"Not at all. They're going a great job. They're earning their candy," Margaret said, watching Luke re-sort the misplaced screws his younger brother tossed into the nail box.

Mark heard 'candy' and walked around the corner with his hand out.

"Okay. Just one more honeymoon for you. And one for your brother. I don't want you to get a tummy ache," Margaret said, playfully pinching his belly. She put the candy in his open hand. He leaned in and wrapped his chubby arms around her knees. Margaret crouched down and hugged him. "You're a sweet boy," she whispered.

"Mabel? I'm going upstairs for a moment," Margaret called. "Keep an eye on the store."

"Sure, Margaret. Me and Mary Catherine got things covered."

Margaret welled up the moment she reached the top of the stairs. Images she'd tried hard to forget came back with a fury. Her baby's blue lips, as he struggled for air. James trying to take the breathless bundle from her arms. The thud of the sticky wet mud hitting the miniature coffin.

She laid down on her bed and cried. She stayed there for some time, before remembering her promise to James. She would try harder. She sat up, wiped her hand under her wet eyes, pinched her cheeks, and smoothed down her blouse. She took a deep breath, found what she had come for, and returned to the store.

"Mabel? Where are the boys?" she asked.

"They just left. The baby woke up in a foul mood. Left a stink to match," Mabel said, waving her hand under her nose. "Whatcha got there?" she asked, pointing to the book and rattle in Margaret's hands.

"Oh. Just a few old things I found for the boys," she said, opening a cupboard and tucking them away. "Hopefully they'll come by again soon."

"Hopefully," Mabel said, thinking Margaret looked like she had been crying.

CHAPTER 14

Mannie Chernin drove from his office to the station, relishing the thought of another murder trial. As far as he was concerned, they were far too rare. He mentally checked off the pros. He could prove the accused had motive, means, and opportunity. It was too bad he didn't have a more worthy opponent, but it would be fun just the same. He pictured his face and the headline on the front page of the local paper. *Chernin Wins Again. MacIntyre Sentenced to Hang.*

He pulled in front of the station, stopped briefly to joke with some officers, and walked into Captain Collins's office.

"Heard you wanted to see me."

"Mannie," Collins said, standing and shaking his hand. "Thanks for coming. I wanted to bring you up-to-date on the MacIntyre file." He told Mannie that Eddie admitted he and Billy started the fire, and that he didn't hear Stanley either threaten Adshade, or admit to the killing. "Oh. And Billy said he doesn't own a switchblade, but Eddie confirmed he does."

"So, you want to drop the assault charges against MacIntyre?" Mannie asked.

"Yes. Angus MacNeil is on his way down to file a statement about seeing Billy and Eddie running from the scene the morning of the fire. I want to charge them with arson, for starters."

Given the circumstances, Mannie agreed that most people in town would sympathize with the defendant for going after the boys and that a conviction would be unlikely. "Fine by me," he said. He stood to leave.

"That's great. I'll let Stanley know he's free to go."

Mannie held up his hand. "Whoa! Not so fast, Teddy."

Collins gave Mannie a confused look. "What do you mean?"

"We may not get him for assault, but we're holding him on suspicion of murder."

"Murder? You mean Adshade's?"

"Yes."

Collins jumped up and leaned across his desk, "On what grounds?"

"Ask McInnes," Mannie said, and walked out.

CHAPTER 15

Captain Collins was pacing back and forth when Sergeant McInnes tapped lightly on his open door. "You wanted to see me, Captain?"

"Have a seat."

"Everything okay?" McInnes asked, pulling the chair out and sitting down.

"No!" Collins snapped. "Why are you holding MacIntyre on suspicion of murder?"

"Cause… he's guilty," McInnes said. "Just need to verify a coupla things and we're off to the races. Or should I say gallows." He laughed.

"Listen, you smug little bastard. I don't know what you're trying to prove—"

"*Prove Captain*?"

"Shut up! The assault charges against MacIntyre have been dropped."

McInnes leaned back in his chair. "Yeah. Dunphy just told me."

"You didn't even look into the knife for Christ's sake. It took less than fifteen minutes to get Eddie to fess up. Your shoddy work is damaging our reputation. I have a mind to go to the Board of Commissioners and ask for your badge."

"Go ahead and try," McInnes said, putting his feet up on the Captain's desk. He knew his threats wouldn't amount to anything. Collins did too. McInnes's uncle was the deputy commissioner. In fact, half the men on the force were the sons, nephews, or cousins of corrupt commission officials.

Collins urged himself to stay calm. He leveled his voice. "Get your feet off my desk."

McInnes didn't protest.

"I reviewed MacIntyre's file. I see no evidence that would warrant holding him."

"Well, Mannie and I do." McInnes smiled, knowing the Captain wasn't privy to all the details he shared with Mannie.

"Based on what?"

"Like the bad blood between Stanley and Johnnie."

"Christ almighty! There was bad blood between Johnnie and half the men in this town," Collins said, roughly shoving papers across his desk.

"True. But how many of them admitted to assaulting Adshade a coupla days before he shows up beaten to death?" McInnes said.

"Medical examiner thinks it was a hit and run."

"He didn't rule out the possibility he was beaten to death. Said it coulda been with a heavy object. And don't forget, we got Billy's testimony that he witnessed Stanley threaten the deceased. Also claims MacIntyre admitted to killing him the night of the assault."

"Eddie claims he never heard the threat, or the admission," Collins said, clenching his fist.

"Yeah. I heard. Also heard you made the poor bastard piss himself. Eddie doesn't know if he's punched or bored," McInnes said, shaking his head.

"And you believe Billy? That lying little punk!"

"His broken nose and missin tooth are pretty convincin."

"Bullshit! Stanley went after them because of what they did to his ponies. Hell, I'd have done the same. And so would you."

"Yeah. Well, there's more to the story than ya know."

"Like what?"

"Stanley's sketchy alibi for the night of the murder."

"What? You don't believe James Cameron?"

"No. He's lyin through his teeth."

"And why would he do that?"

"I have my suspicions. Yer just gonna have to trust me."

Collins started to laugh. "Trust you? Jesus! I hear Billy originally told you it was the coloureds who killed Johnnie. How'd that work out for you? You're lucky folks didn't burn them out," Collins hissed.

"That was unfortunate. But, don't forget, I was the one who contained the situation."

"You contained a nasty situation you brought about. As far as I'm concerned, you've got your mind set on creating another."

McInnes leaned forward. "Listen, Captain. The mornin I went to the store to tell the Adshade girl her father was killed, Stanley and Cameron were pullin up together. Cameron tells me he spent the night at Stanley's and that the girl stayed with a friend. I betcha any money she was still back at Stanley's. Anyway, Stanley sees me out front and just drives off. Goes and gets the girl, and comes back about a half hour later. It was all very odd, the way they all acted. Like they were hidin somethin. Nobody seemed too surprised, or even broken up about hearin Adshade was dead. And Cameron's wife acted odd, too. Saw her husband and Stanley pull up after he spent the night away from home and didn't even acknowledge him. Just leaves and goes upstairs, even though the police are at her door. Like she knew her husband and his buddy were up to no good. Then, the girl comes in and walks right past me. Goes out back to the kitchen with Cameron on her heels. Dollars to doughnuts, he was tellin her to keep her mouth shut."

"You have absolutely no proof of that," Collins said.

"Maybe not. But there's lots more."

"Like what?"

McInnes looked at Collins and thought back to how he had tried to interfere in the Greene boy's case. He'd said enough. Probably too much. "Like, I said. You're just gonna have to trust me."

"Well I don't. You're wrong about MacIntyre. And Cameron. Dead wrong."

"No, Captain. You're blind. What's up with ya, anyway? Are ya still pissed about your friend? Ya gotta let that go. Ya know he killed his son. Can't say I blame him. If my son was a faggot, I'd want him to disappear, too."

"Get out of my office. Get out! Get out!" Collins screamed.

Sergeant McInnes walked into the hallway. "See ya in the mornin, boys," he said with a grin and a tip of his cap.

CHAPTER 16

Margaret was setting the table when James walked into the kitchen.

"Smells good," he said. "What is it?" He lifted the lid off the pot and sniffed the steamy aroma.

"Just soup. Mabel got the recipe from Amour. She said it's really good."

"Everything go well today?" James asked.

"It was a good day. We had a new customer from Number Eleven come by. He ordered four pies and picked up almost six dollars in canned goods. Oh, and Mrs. MacGuire dropped off the parcel that was at the Stamp and Post. It's on the counter. What is it?"

"I ordered more pie tins," he said.

"James? Mabel's working really hard, but she can't keep up with demand. I think you should hire another baker. Maybe expand the selection of baked goods."

"Did Mabel and Stanley put you up to this?"

Margaret gave him a curious look. "No. Why?"

"Because they both mentioned it to me."

"I think they're right."

"Maybe. But Margaret… I'll *never* hire Gladys Ferguson."

"I was actually thinking of someone else."

"Who?"

"Mary Catherine. That's Catherine with a C," she said, smiling.

CHAPTER 17

Collins knew he had made a grave mistake assigning McInnes the Adshade case. But it was too late to remove him. McInnes would just spread his allegations around town faster than ever, poisoning the public's view of MacIntyre and Cameron beyond repair. He'd seen him do it before. He'd leave him on the case, but keep a close eye on things.

"Damn it," he said. He grabbed his coat and headed toward the door.

"Captain?" Dunphy called after him. "What do you want me to do with Billy?"

"Tell him to make himself comfortable."

Collins drove by twice, each time almost coming to a full stop before speeding up and driving off again. "Doing what's right is never wrong," he repeated over and over to himself. He wondered if he'd be driving around in circles and contemplating ruining his career if McInnes hadn't mentioned Isaac. He wasn't sure if his motive was to help Cameron and the accused, or to get back at McInnes for destroying his friend's good name. He stopped and got out of the car. It's both, he decided.

James and Margaret were clearing the dishes when they heard the knock on the front door.

"Good evening, Mrs. Cameron. I'm wondering if I might have a word with your husband."

"Come in," Margaret said, swinging the door open for him to enter. "James! There's someone here to see you."

"Captain," James said. "I wasn't expecting to see you. This is my wife. Margaret."

"Mrs. Cameron," he said, nodding.

"Would you care for a cup of tea?" James asked.

"No. But thank you." Collins waited for Mrs. Cameron to return to the kitchen. "You wouldn't happen to have anything a little stronger?" he whispered.

James looked pleasantly surprised. "As a matter of fact, I do. Follow me," he said. He ushered Collins into the back room. "I'd tell you it's for medicinal purposes only, but I know you'd see right through me." He took the rum down from the shelf and poured two healthy glasses. "So, did the knife finally show up?"

"No."

"Oh. I just assumed that's what brought you here. You know, Captain, there was a knife. Sam and I saw it at Iggies. We just thought it better if you guys discovered it."

"Mr. Cameron. The knife's no longer an issue."

"So, if you're not here about the knife, what brings you by?"

Collins paused before answering. "Guilt."

"*Guilt?*"

"Yes. Guilt."

"I'm sorry. I don't understand?" James said.

"I should never have assigned Sergeant McInnes the case. Eddie recanted his statement. Also admitted to starting the fire. And, contrary to what Billy said, we know he owns a switchblade. The assault charges have been dropped."

"Thank God," James said.

"Don't get too excited. It's not over yet. Mannie and McInnes still think Stanley murdered Adshade."

James was about to take a swig, but froze. "That's insane," he said, louder than he meant to. He lowered his voice. "I was with Stanley the night Adshade was killed. Sergeant McInnes knows that."

"I know. But I'm afraid he's also intent on making a whole lot of trouble for you," Collins said, telling James about the suspicious behaviour McInnes said he witnessed the morning he came to tell them Johnnie was killed. "He claims you're lying for Stanley."

James shook his head in disbelief. "Captain. Everything that McInnes said about the day he came here to tell us about Johnnie is true. But I can explain it all. Everything else is pure nonsense. Stanley isn't involved with Mabel. And I'm not lying. I was with him the night of the second."

"I believe you. And I don't need any explanations. At least not yet. The less you tell me, the better. I could get in a ton of trouble if anyone knew I was sharing this with you. If I heard that one of my officers was warning a potential witness for the defence, I'd have them sacked."

"But you barely know me. Why risk your career telling me this?" James asked.

"So you can prepare yourself. I know how McInnes and Mannie operate. And I've seen what bad men can do to good men when left unchecked. It's no secret that I'm not high on McInnes. He's a real bastard. He's brash, incompetent, and blindly ambitious. Been after my job since the day he put on his uniform. You know what folks around here say. "If it weren't for the police—"

James finished for him. "We'd have the best justice system in the world."

"Even as a cop, I can't always say I disagree. In fact, I hold Sergeant McInnes responsible for the death of a dear friend. Isaac Greene."

James put down his glass. "Captain?"

"Ted, please?"

"Ted. You won't believe this. But I've been wanting to talk to you about the Greene case."

"What about it?" Collins said, squinting his eyes from the harshness of the rum.

"I think I know who might be responsible for the boy's murder."

Collins gave him a puzzled look. "What do you mean?"

James told him about the article in *The Post,* reprinted from *The Boston Globe.*

"I didn't see it. I rarely see the paper. But just because MacPherson allegedly molested a boy in Boston doesn't mean he murdered David."

"I know. But think about it. Roddy and Amour packed up and left within days of the Greene boy's murder. Why? Roddy had a great job. He was buying up houses just weeks before he left town. There was certainly no talk of him picking up stakes and moving. By all accounts, he liked it here. He was a big shot. Next thing you know, he's gone. And we both know David was—"

"Homosexual," Collins said.

"Yes," James said.

Collins smiled, remembering Isaac talk about his son. "David was a virtuoso, you know. Played the violin. He was really quite good .Isaac used to say that when David played *The Lark Ascending* on his violin, it'd bring a tear to a glass eye. In fact, he was saving every penny he could to send David to school in New York. He knew about his son, but he didn't love him any less. He was distraught when the ugly rumours started flying round town that he killed his own son. I should have done more to help."

James could see Ted's eyes fill up. He leaned in and put his hand on his shoulder. "I'm sorry. Your friend was obviously a good man."

They sat quietly, sipping their drinks, both weighing the sad outcome of a good family brought down by the malice of others. James reached for a makin. "And there's something else that's always bothered me about the way Roddy left. He was cheap. A tough negotiator. But when I went to see him about buying the Adshade property, he didn't even flinch when I offered him far less than it was worth. Just accepted it without any haggling whatsoever. And we signed on the spot."

"You own the Adshade property?"

"Yes. Well, it's in my name."

"Johnnie Adshade *rented* a property from you?"

"Not exactly. I never charged him rent."

"Why?" Collins asked, surprised by the revelation.

James told him why he bought the property and kept it a secret from Mabel and her father. Collins listened, impressed by the compassion of the man sitting beside him. Any doubts he harboured in coming to the store and divulging his conversation with McInnes quickly faded as he learned of James's generous efforts to help the daughter of an old friend. He liked and trusted the man sitting beside him, who he now knew, beyond a shadow of a doubt, was a good one.

"Anyway," James continued, "I know my suspicions about Roddy are only that, but I felt I should share them with you. There are just too many coincidences. And it would be a terrible thing to let people go on thinking Mr. Greene was responsible for his son's murder, if he wasn't."

Ted drained his rum and put his glass down. "It's been an interesting evening," he said. He stood and extended his hand. "You've certainly given me lots to consider. Thanks for the rum and for telling me about Roddy. You never know, you might be on to something."

James shook his hand. "Well, it may not amount to anything. But given Roddy's recent troubles, I think it might be worth looking into."

Collins nodded his agreement and buttoned his overcoat.

"Ted," James said, momentarily uncertain if he should go on.

"Yes?"

"There's something else I should tell you."

"What's that?"

"Stanley wasn't the only one to pay Johnnie a visit before he died."

"Oh?"

"Stanley broke his nose. I almost broke my hand," James said, holding it out in front of him.

Captain Collins sat down heavily on his stool. "Maybe I could use another rum?"

Friday, November 11

CHAPTER I

James nodded to Dunphy and walked toward Captain Collins's Office.

"If you're looking for the Captain, he's not here. His aunt took sick. He's gone to Boston," Dunphy said.

James knew full well that wasn't the reason Ted had gone to Boston.

"Perhaps I can help you?" Sergeant McInnes said, approaching from behind.

James's heart began to race. "I just dropped in to see Stanley."

"Well, yer not likely gonna find him in there," McInnes said, pointing to Collins's empty office. "Got a minute for a quick chat?"

James protested, saying he was pressed for time and had to be at the savings and loan for eleven. McInnes persisted. James reminded himself that he had no reason to fear McInnes. Yet he couldn't help but feel a growing sense of unease whenever he was in his company. He reluctantly followed McInnes back to his office.

"Have a seat," McInnes said.

"Thanks. I'll stand," James said, knowing it would make for a faster exit.

"Suit yourself."

"So, what can I do for you, Sergeant?"

"How about telling me about your relationship with the

Adshade girl."

"You know very well that she works in my store," James replied, cautioning himself to watch his tone.

"How long has she been in your employ?"

"Around six weeks. Listen, Sergeant, I'm sure you must have more important matters to deal with. I just want to check on Stanley and get—"

"This won't take long. Did ya know her before ya hired her?"

"I met her when she was a child. Her mother was a childhood friend of mine."

"A close friend?" McInnes asked, smirking.

"Yes."

"Her mother… that would be Johnnie's wife? Right?"

James smiled over his growing anger. That's very astute of you, Sergeant."

"So, how would ya describe your relationship to Johnnie?" McInnes asked, rolling a pencil between his fingers.

"You know the answer to that as well. Like most men in town, I had no use for him. But unlike most men in town, I didn't wish him dead. I have no idea what you are getting at, so I'll say good day." James turned toward the door.

"The night you stayed at Stanley's. What time did you arrive?"

James stopped. "I'm not sure. Sometime before six."

"And what time did you go to bed?"

James turned to face his persistent inquisitor. "I don't know."

"Before eight?"

"No."

"Before nine? After ten?" McInnes pressed.

"It was before nine. Look, if you have any more questions, my lawyer will be present."

"Oh, no need for that. Just tryin to establish a timeline. And you claim McInnes never left the whole time ya were there?"

"That's right," James said, anxious to leave. He moved closer to the door.

"Just one more thing," McInnes said, as James opened the door. "How'd ya hurt your hand again?"

James could no longer hide his exasperation. "I told you, Sergeant. I jammed it between some crates." James immediately regretted lying for a second time, but the deed was done. He walked out.

"Oh, yeah. Crates at the store," Sergeant McInnes called out.

James quickened his pace down the narrow hallway and past the front desk.

McInnes leaned back in his chair and smiled. "Crates at the store, my ass," he whispered. He was about to blow the case wide open.

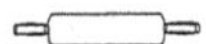

CHAPTER 2

Dunphy retrieved his keys from his belt and opened the cell door. Stanley sat up.

"How are you?" James asked, looking down the hall to make sure McInnes wasn't listening.

"Well rested."

"I see you finished the pie."

"Dunphy helped."

"Better than my grandma's. And she makes great pie," Dunphy volunteered.

"Sorry I don't have one for you today," James said. "But I brought you some fresh clothes. And this," he said, handing Stanley a dog-eared copy of *The Great Gatsby.* "Hope you didn't read it."

Stanley turned it over and read the back cover. "It's about a murder."

"Sorry about that," James said. "Wasn't a whole lot to choose from."

"Thanks, James. You know, you don't have to come by every day. I know you're busy with the store."

"Margaret and Mabel can handle the store. So, they dropped the assault charges," James said, sitting beside Stanley on his cot.

"Yes. I was fully prepared to go to jail for assault. Never figured I'd be facing a murder trial."

"Eddie recanted. And nobody will believe Billy. It's just Sergeant

McInnes being a prick. You'll be out in no time."

Stanley smiled. "Let's hope. So, did you tell Mabel you're her uncle? Or… half uncle?"

"No," James said. "There's no blood relationship between us."

Stanley looked confused. James told tell him that Percy, not Johnnie, was Mabel's father, and that he hadn't told Mabel yet. "It's also going to come as a shock to Amour. I figure she's dealing with enough right now," James said, filling him in on Roddy's arrest and his suspicions about Roddy killing the Greene boy.

"I never believed Isaac killed his son," Stanley said. "But, do you really think Roddy did it?"

"I know. Innocent until proven guilty. Right?" James said. "But he sure as hell left town in a hurry. And it was right after the boy was killed."

Stanley could tell James felt weighed down. He wondered if he should add to his burden. He knew he had no choice.

"I need to tell you something," Stanley said, wringing his hands.

James stood and looked at his friend. He immediately sensed that, whatever it was, it wasn't good. "Go ahead."

Stanley looked down at the floor, momentarily questioning his decision to confess. He lifted his head and looked directly at James.

"I took your car after you went to bed. I went looking for Johnnie."

James felt his heart pound and his legs weaken. "And?" he asked, not sure he wanted to hear the answer.

"I couldn't find him. I went to all the places I thought he might be. Steel's Hill, York Street, Iggies, Minto Street."

"Brookside Street?" James asked, through clenched teeth.

"No. I know this looks bad. But I swear I didn't find him," Stanley said.

James started pacing around the cell like a caged lion. "Jesus Christ, Stanley! What were you thinking! And what if you *did* find him? What then?" he hissed.

"I honestly don't know. I knew he was responsible for what

happened to my ponies and—"

"Your ponies!" James hollered, startling Stanley and bringing Dunphy around the corner to check on things.

"Everything alright in there?" Dunphy asked.

"Yes. Sorry," James said. He smiled and waved at the young constable who returned to his post. He turned on the man he thought he knew and leaned into his good ear. "Look! I know you loved your ponies. I suspected Johnnie as well. But sneaking out in the middle of the night and… Jesus! Ya know this doesn't just look bad for *you*, right? Christ! I should have stayed at Murphy's."

Stanley put his head down. "I'm sorry. But it wasn't just the ponies. When I picked Mabel up in the morning, she had blood on the side of her head. I figured Johnnie hit her again." Stanley now knew it wasn't Johnnie, but Billy and his accomplice who were responsible for the blood in Mabel's hair, but he wasn't about to expose Mabel's secret to anyone. Not even James.

"What? And you didn't tell me," James said angrily.

"I was afraid of what you would do. And you seemed to have enough to deal with, with Margaret and all. I just figured I could handle it on my own."

James looked away from Stanley. "Anybody see you?"

"I doubt it. It was a miserable night. I had trouble seeing the road. Probably only passed one or two cars. Look. If I ran him down, wouldn't there be damage to your car?"

James conceded that even his big, bulky Plymouth would likely show some sign of an impact with a two hundred and twenty pound man. "You'd think. Still, if the police find out you took my car, they'll say you hunted him down and beat him to death. Christ almighty! McInnes just finished grilling me. Asked if I was with you the whole night." James sat back down. "Shit. If this ends up going to trial, I swear I'm not going to lie. I won't lie under oath. Not for you, or anyone else. I just won't."

"I wouldn't want you to. Maybe I should call McInnes in right now and tell him everything. That way you're not—"

"Don't be stupid!" James snapped, wondering if he spoke too soon. "If you tell them you went looking for Johnnie, they'll conspire to see you hang. We're probably getting all worked up over nothing. You obviously didn't tell Sam any of this?"

"No."

"Good. He's skittish enough as it is." Both men sat quietly on the lumpy, vomit-stained mattress. Stanley stared at the bars that denied him freedom, relieved he had finally come clean. James looked at the floor, silently cursing his friend's stupid behaviour, and making a mental note to double-check for damage to his car. "Christ, Stanley! Why'd you even bother to tell me?"

"Because you had a right to know. I felt guilty. I wanted to be honest with you. Even if it comes out that I went looking for Johnnie, I won't regret telling you. You deserve to know."

James stood and put his hand on Stanley's shoulder. When Stanley looked up, James could see the regret, resignation, and worry on his face. He also saw a good man he knew he could trust. He left the station and walked toward his car, no longer feeling the need to examine it for signs of damage, or betrayal. He believed his friend.

CHAPTER 3

James was at the savings and loan. Sergeant McInnes was at the store.

Margaret peeked her head into the kitchen. "Mabel? Sergeant McInnes is here. He wants to have a word with you."

Margaret watched McInnes pick a hammer off the display counter and turn it over in his hands. "Nice one," he said. "By the way, how's your husband's hand?"

"It's coming along nicely."

"Jammed it between some crates, I hear," McInnes said, watching her closely.

Margaret nodded.

"Were you here when it happened?"

"No, Sergeant," Margaret said, feeling flushed. She was relieved when Mabel came around the corner, wiping her hands in her apron.

"Ya wanted to see me?"

"Won't keep ya long. Know yer busy. Wonderin if we can chat privately?"

He followed her into the kitchen. "I meant to ask, what happened to your forehead?"

Mabel kept walking.

He knew she heard him. "Your forehead?" he repeated, pointing. "What happened?"

"Oh? A dog knocked me down the mornin of the storm. Fell into a stick. Mr. Cameron had Dr. Cohen stitch it up. Don't hurt none."

He sensed she was lying. "Pie smells great. And I haven't eaten all day. Do ya sell it by the slice?" he asked. He put his cap on the table.

Mabel didn't care for the man. She reluctantly put a piece in front of him.

"Thank you," he said. He picked up his fork and shoveled a large forkful into his mouth. "I'm really sorry about your da. Terrible thing to lose someone so young," he mumbled. A chunk of apple fell out of his mouth and onto the table. "This is delicious," he said, picking it up. He tossed it on his plate and licked his fingers.

Mabel's heart was racing. *What could she possibly know that would be of any interest to the police.* "So, ya wanted to talk to me?" Mabel said.

As their conversation continued, she thought Sergeant McInnes seemed more interested in his free pie and small talk than anything else. His questions seemed innocent enough. How long she had worked at the store? Did she like baking? Was Mr. Cameron a good boss? Did she have a boyfriend? How well did she know Stanley? She wasn't sure what he was getting at and that's what unsettled her most.

"So, Miss Adshade?" McInnes said, smiling. "Did ya ever hear Stanley threaten your father?"

No, Sergeant."

"Yer sure?"

"I'm sure."

He knew she was lying. "Do ya recall if your father had some friends in on the evening of November first? It woulda been the night before he was killed."

Mabel put her head down, hesitating before replying. "Yeah. Da had a couple of buddies with him."

McInnes watched her reaction, more confident than ever the boys witnessed Stanley threaten Johnnie.

"Was it Billy Guthro and Eddie Lynch?"

Mabel didn't know why he was asking. He couldn't possibly know what they did to her. “Yes,” she said, pressing her hands together.

“In fact, Eddie told me you made him sardine sandwiches. Is that right?”

Mabel thought of her yellow vomit. Her hands began to shake. “Yes.”

McInnes smiled, knowing she was verifying Billy’s story. He tilted his head to the side and winked. “Damn, this is good pie.”

Margaret was standing on a step-stool dusting the shelves when James returned from town. “Everything’s in—” He stopped when Margaret nervously nodded toward the kitchen.

Sergeant McInnes was sitting across the table from Mabel. His empty plate, off to the side.

“Mabel? Sergeant? What’s going on?” James asked.

“Mr. Cameron. Have you tried this pie?” McInnes asked, turning in his chair and grinning at James. “Gotta be the best pie I ever had. Your girl, here. She sure knows how to please a man.”

Don’t let him get to you, James thought. “Sergeant. You’ve had your pie. Now if you don’t mind, I’m trying to run a business.”

“Not to worry,” McInnes said. He stood slowly and smiled at Mabel. “Just popped by to have a word with Mabel. Sure glad I did,” he said, patting his stomach.

Mabel felt she could cut the air with one of her bread knives.

“She tells me she loves working here and you’re a great boss. Not that that surprises me. Anyway, just wanted to ask her about her relationship with Stanley. She says he’s a fine fellow. Wouldn’t hurt a fly.”

“You should listen to her. She’s a good judge of character.”

“Also tells me Stanley drove her back and forth to work with your car after she ended up in your coal shed.”

James glanced at Mabel. “That’s right.”

“It’s very good of you to treat your employee so well. Lettin her stay the night. Arrangin for her transportation back and forth to work. Callin Dr. Cohen in to stitch her up. Don’t think I know too many employers who would do that for their employees. No wonder she thinks you're such a great guy."

"Look, Sergeant. Mabel just buried her father. I can't see how any of your questions have any relevance to the investigation."

"Sure. Just want to make sure we do our homework. But I can see yer busy," he said, standing and peering out into the empty store. He turned back. "Mabel? How about settin one of those pies you're makin aside for me. I'll drop by tomorrow and pick it up."

"Sorry. My orders are all backed up," she said, nervously looking at Mr. Cameron.

"Very well. Maybe another time," McInnes said. He picked his cap up off the table and walked out of the kitchen.

James followed him into the store.

"Goodbye, for now," McInnes said, as he headed for the door. He then nodded toward Margaret who was watching from behind the counter. "Mrs. Cameron," he said, doffing his cap.

"Sergeant," Margaret said flatly.

McInnes walked out, crouched down in front of James's Plymouth. He then stood up, running his hand over the grill and the hood. He was getting in his wagon, when he spotted James watching from the window. *Nice car,* he mouthed and smiled.

Mabel walked over to James. "I told him Stanley had nothin to do with Da's death."

"Problem is, he doesn't believe you."

"But why does he think Stanley killed Da?"

"Because he wants to," James said, his eyes following McInnes's car until it disappeared out of sight.

CHAPTER 4

Sergeant McInnes rushed to Mannie's office to get his reaction to the contents of the envelope and to report on his visit to the store.

"So, what do ya think?" he asked Mannie.

"I think we have a damn good case."

"Well, it just got better," McInnes said, excitedly taking his seat across from Mannie. "Mabel confirmed Billy Guthro and Eddie Lynch were at her place the night Billy said he heard the threat. Even said she made them sandwiches."

"And did she confirm Stanley was present?"

"No. But I could tell she was lyin. Got very quiet. Wouldn't look me in the eye. Even started shaking. She also lied about how she ended up with stitches. Said a dog knocked her down. Billy's right. She's terrified of Stanley. I think either Stanley's threatenin her, Cameron is, or they both are. One of them is responsible for the cut on her head. I'm sure of it. Ya shoulda seen Cameron's reaction when he walked in and saw me asking her a few simple questions. Hell, he practically threw me out."

Mannie doodled on his notepad. "Did you check out the car?"

"Yeah. No damage. But we both know Adshade was beaten to death. Medical examiner is all wet. Look, Mannie. I know ya find it hard to believe Cameron's a pervert, too. But, think about it. He's not lyin to protect Stanley. He's lyin to protect himself. I'm sure he's fuckin the girl, too. And I hear his wife's crazy," he said, twirling his finger at the side of his temple. "Had a breakdown after her son died a few years back. Barely leaves the house. Probably as frigid as the clampers in the harbour. The way I got it figured, ya got two lonely old geezers as horny as all get out. And they got this pretty little thing under their control who they can fuck at will. That's why Cameron's wife was so distant on the mornin of the third. She probably knew what they've been up to. And her husband stayin the night at Stanley's? Give me a break. The girl was there with them." He leaned back in his chair. "I swear, Mannie, when ya see Cameron with the girl, ya know it's a hell of a lot more than an employer-employee relationship. And I sure as hell don't buy that crap about him jammin his hand between some crates. I could tell he was lyin. Christ! Ya jam your hand between wooden crates and it'd be more than just swollen. Wouldn't the skin be broken? At least have a few scratches?"

"You'd think so," Mannie said.

"Damn right it would. But Cameron's hand doesn't have a mark on it. Just swollen. I asked his wife about it this morning. Said she wasn't home when it happened. And that's cause it didn't happen like Cameron said it did. I know it."

Mannie rested his chin on his hands. "We have more than enough to charge MacIntyre with capital murder. So let's just get that out of the way."

"But what about Cameron?"

"I don't know, Dan. I suppose anything is possible. But even if you're right, how do we prove it?"

"Oh, I'll prove it alright."

"And how do you propose to do that?" Mannie asked, balancing his pencil between his fingers and tapping its edges over the manila envelope.

"I already set the bait. Just need to get the girl alone when Cameron isn't hoverin over her."

"For God's sake, don't go spooking her any more than she already is. She needs to know she can trust us," Mannie said.

"Don't worry. I won't."

"And, Dan? Don't go sharing your thoughts with anybody else. No one. You hear?"

"I'm not stupid, Mannie."

"Good. And if your theory about Cameron turns out to be true, we'll let the drama play out in front of a packed courthouse," Mannie said, extending his hand to a beaming McInnes.

McInnes responded with a firm grip. "It's going to be quite the show, Mannie."

Deliver us From Evil

Saturday, November 12

CHAPTER I

Captain Collins waited outside Captain Bustin's office. He was anxious to get through the preliminaries, interview Roddy, and hopefully clear his good friend's name. He waited patiently for over two hours, but there was still no sign of his counterpart. He rehearsed the questions he would put to Roddy over and over again in his mind, as one constable after the other filed in and out of Bustin's Office. Finally, the captain of Boston's Twelfth Precinct opened his door and waved him in.

"Sorry to have kept you waiting, Captain. But I'm afraid you've come a great distance for nothing."

Collins stood. "But you agreed I could question—"

"The deceased," Bustin interrupted. "That's what all the fuss is about. I just got word, he's dead. Stabbed himself in the neck with a fountain pen. Took a few tries, but he eventually punctured the carotid artery. Boys said it was kind of ironic. I guess the blood spewed from his neck just like water from the Brewer in the Common."

Collins plopped down on the hard wooden bench outside Bustin's office. "Did he know I was here?" he asked.

"Yes. I'm afraid one of my officers let the cat out of the bag. Of course, no one expected the outcome. Just yesterday, he was full of bluster. Insisting the incident with the boy was all a big misunderstanding. Said the judge was going to throw the case out. Threatened to sue us for false arrest and *The Globe* for libel. Apparently, when he got word you were on your way to question him about a three-year old murder back in Canada, he became unusually quiet."

"Did he leave any kind of note?" Collins asked, suspecting he already knew the answer.

"No. But it's pretty obvious why he stuck himself."

"But we have no way of proving it."

"Guess not. But the good news is you don't have to wade through a mass of paper work, you avoid a costly trial, and the world has one less faggot to worry about," Bustin said, slapping Collins on the back.

CHAPTER 2

James watched Sam spin his teacup around in its saucer. "Are you okay, Sam?"

"I really hoped they wouldn't go through with this. I have no experience in court. I'm not cut out to be a criminal lawyer."

"Sam? Do you trust your father?"

"More than anyone."

"Well, he claims you have a sharp legal mind. He was the one who convinced me to hire you," James said. He neglected to mention he couldn't find anyone else. "He also said the only thing you need to be twice the lawyer he is, is a bit more confidence."

Sam looked both surprised and touched. "Papa told you that?"

"Yes. And he's right. You'll do just fine."

"But a man's life literally hangs in the balance," Sam said.

"Stanley knows that. And so do I," James said.

Sam shrugged. "I just can't figure out why Mannie's going to trial. He's gotta know something we don't. He obviously doesn't believe you. And you're a credible witness. He's accusing you of lying."

"Mannie's just being hoodwinked by McInnes and his cockamamie theories. Collins told me that's how McInnes operates. Always twisting the facts to support his crazy ideas."

"I know. But I thought Mannie was smarter than that. It's not like him to go forward with something he's not absolutely sure of."

James looked down and thought about his recent conversation with Stanley.

"James? You're not keeping anything from me are you?" Sam asked.

James shook his head. "No. Why are you asking me that?" he said, praying no one knew about the car and that this would all go away before he had to testify.

"You're sure?"

"I'm sure. Listen, Sam. No one will believe Billy over Mabel. Wait till you meet her. I told her you were dropping by later today. You put her on the stand and she'll convince the jury this business about Stanley is pure nonsense. And don't forget, we have Eddie's admission and Angus's testimony about the fire. The jury will see through Billy."

Sam looked up from his cup. "And we have your testimony."

James nodded.

The waitress with the hairnet approached with her large blue and white speckled teapot. "Care for a refill?" she asked, smiling down at Sam.

CHAPTER 3

Margaret was surprised when James introduced her to Sam. He didn't look old enough to have finished high school, let alone law school. The two went to the kitchen. Mabel was kneading her dough, while Mary Catherine watched, drinking her tea.

"Ladies. This is Stanley's lawyer. Sam Friedman. Sam, that's Mabel. And that's her friend, Mary Catherine," James said, pointing them out.

"Mary Catherine with a C," Mabel said.

Sam looked perplexed.

"Catherine spelled with a C not a K," James explained.

"Oh," Sam said.

"Mabel? Sam came by to talk about the trial."

"And some pie, I hope," Mabel said, picking one up off the cooling rack.

"Sure," Sam said. "That'd be great."

Mary Catherine stood up. "Should I leave?"

James looked to Sam.

"I see no reason for that," Sam said, smiling at her.

Mary Catherine took the pie from Mabel, sliced a quarter-sized piece, and put it in front of Sam.

"So, Mabel. The Crown will start calling witnesses on Monday or Tuesday, at the latest. As a witness for the defence, I'll be calling you to testify on Stanley's behalf. Likely the week after next." he said, taking a bite of his pie. He nodded his pleasure. "This is really good." He broke off another huge bite.

"I helped peel those apples," Mary Catherine said, pointing to Sam's pie. She jumped to her feet. "Can I get you some tea?"

"Sure."

Mary Catherine brought him his tea and pushed the sugar bowl closer to him.

"Thank you," Sam said, and added three teaspoons.

Mary Catherine reached for the cream bowl. "Cream?"

"Just a bit," Sam said.

She added more than a bit.

Mabel looked at her friend, thinking she had lost her marbles.

Sam licked his thumb, pressing it against the loose pastry flakes on his plate. "I don't normally eat the crust, but this is the best pie I've ever had."

Mabel beamed.

"Anyway, Mabel," Sam said, stirring his tea. "I'll just ask you a few straightforward questions. How long you've known Stanley. If you knew of any bad feelings he and your father might have had. Most important thing is to establish that your relationship with Stanley is strictly platonic."

Mabel turned to James.

"It means you're just friends… not…not intimate," James said.

"Sorry," Sam said, sensing Mabel's embarrassment "It's more of a… of a legal term."

"Well, ya better not be throwin too many of those at me. I got a hard enough time with every day words," Mabel said.

"I won't. I promise. I also have to establish you were not acting under duress," Sam continued.

Mabel turned back to James.

"Sorry," Sam said. "It means no one was coercing you. I mean, no one was forcing you to say or do anything against your will."

"I already told Sergeant McInnes no one's forcing me to do anythin. Hell, if it weren't for Stanley and his ponies I wouldn't even be here. I woulda froze to death in the shed."

"Great," Sam said. "Just remember, the only thing you have to do is tell the truth."

"That's all I plan to do," Mabel said.

"So, is there anything you need to ask me?" Sam asked Mabel.

"Like what?"

"I don't know… like how the trial works?"

"Way I figure it, ya put the questions to me and I answer em."

"That's right. And after I call you to testify, the prosecutor will ask you some questions."

"Well, it ain't like he's gonna get a different answer," Mabel said, shaking her head.

"I know you'll do just fine," Sam said.

"She'll do great," James said, putting his hand on Mabel's shoulder.

Mabel decided she liked Stanley's lawyer a lot. Apparently, Mary Catherine did, too.

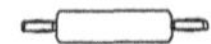

Sunday, November 13

CHAPTER I

James and Margaret went to the seven o'clock Mass at St. Anthony's where they both spent extra time on the kneeling pad. They listened to Father Vokey read from the book of John.

"If we confess our sins, he is faithful and just and will forgive us our sins and purify us from all righteousness."

Mabel went to her favourite place of worship, the brook. She walked down the steep, rocky pathway to the clearing that lead to the footbridge, stopping where she and Stanley had met around the same time the week before. There was not another soul in sight. She picked up a few pebbles and dropped them over the railing into the icy water below. Then, she closed her eyes and prayed. "Our Father who art in Heaven, Hallowed be Thy Name…"

She opened her eyes as it began to snow, looking up at the grey sky. "Dear Jesus, let him be safe," she said, for only her and God to hear. She pulled her collar up around her neck and made her way to Commercial Street. When she got to Senator's Corner, she walked up Main Street and then onto MacKeen. She stopped and looked at the imposing red brick building to her right. She walked in, grateful it was quiet.

"I came to see Stanley. Stanley MacIntyre."

"Follow me," said the one constable in sight.

Stanley was stretched out on his back, reading a book.

"Visitor," Dunphy announced, sliding the heavy door to the side.

Mabel jumped at the sound of it clanging open. She jumped again when it banged shut.

Stanley sat up. "Hi. I didn't expect to see you."

"I didn't expect to be seen. Not here anyways," Mabel said. She looked around at the small room with its dull, cement walls, "But here I am. Thought ya could use some company."

He smiled. "I couldn't have asked for better."

"Ya could if ya weren't cooped up in here. Ain't like they make it very welcomin. Ya don't even have a chair."

"Sit here," Stanley said, standing and pointing to his cot.

Mabel looked at his stained mattress. "I'm good."

Stanley sat back down. "So, did you forget something?"

"Whatcha mean?"

"No pie?"

Mabel turned when she heard the familiar voice and peeked out from the bars. Sergeant McInnes was talking to the young constable in the hallway.

"Thought ya didn't like my pie?" she said. Her eyes never left McInnes's back.

"Never said that."

"Did ya even try it?"

Stanley reached under his cot and pulled out the empty pie tin. "Best pie I ever had."

Mabel turned toward him. "Where'd ya get that?"

"James brought it in a couple of days ago."

Mabel thought of the day she saw James sneaking out with it. "So, *you* had my missin tin?"

"I had to share it with Dunphy," he said, leaning back on his elbows. He could tell she was distracted.

"I'll get ya one of yer own," she said, bending her head forward for a better view of the hallway.

"Better bring in a couple. Like to stay on the good side of my keepers. So, how are you?"

"Good. But my Uncle Roddy's in jail now, too. Not for killin anyone, but for somethin different. I know yer innocent. Not so sure bout him."

Stanley smiled. "I'm glad you believe I didn't do it."

"Of course not. And I told that sergeant, but he won't believe me. Dumb arse." She looked back out and saw McInnes walk out of sight. "Well, gotta go," she said. "I'll come back when I can stay longer. How do I get outa here?" she whispered.

"Dunphy," Stanley hollered. He reached down under his cot, picked up her pie tin, and brought it to her. "It was good to see you, Mabel."

Mabel picked up on the sadness in his voice. "You too," she replied, immediately regretting her decision to leave so quickly. "I'll come by again. I'll bring ya two pies… and a razor."

Stanley rubbed his chin. "Don't like the beard?"

"Ya mean ya grew it on purpose?"

"Not exactly."

"Well, it makes ya look even older."

"Then it will be gone first chance I get."

Mabel turned as Dunphy opened the door to let her out.

"Dunphy," Stanley said. "This is Mabel. She made the pie."

"Better than my grandma's," Dunphy said, reaching past her, sliding the door closed, and locking it.

Mabel turned back to Stanley, wrapping her hand around an iron bar. "I hope ya get out real soon."

Stanley smiled. "Me too. Thanks, Mabel. Take care."

Monday, November 14

CHAPTER I

Amour convinced Samuel Friedman Sr., that her case would require very little of his time and that she would pay him handsomely for his efforts. He merely needed to look over the agreement with the coal company and assist with the deed transfers, should the company find the homes in good repair and agree to her price. The two shook hands. Amour picked up her purse and stood to leave. "Oh, and Mr. Friedman? I was wondering if you could do something else for me?"

"And what's that, Mrs. MacPherson?"

Amour cringed when he called her by her married name. "I wonder if you could look into who owns the vacant shoe repair."

"May I ask why?"

"I may be interested in purchasing it."

"Why don't you sit back down? The property belongs to me."

Less than an hour later, Amour was sitting outside Mr. Donnely's office. So far, the day had been far more productive than she could have imagined. She already had a conditional agreement with Mr. Friedman to buy the abandoned shoe repair. She never expected it to be so easy to purchase such a prime piece of real estate, and for such a reasonable price. Its tragic history had scared off numerous potential buyers, but she was not one to be superstitious. It would take time, but eventually people would forget the past and flock there for her fine cuisine.

Mr. Donnely stood when she was led into his office.

"Do we have a deal, Mr. Donnely?"

"I thought we agreed you were going to call me Michael?"

"Okay then, Michael. Do we have a deal?"

"I believe we do, Amour. I just need to have the cheque requisitioned, your signature on a few documents, and we will send everything off to the lawyers to be put in order."

She extended her hand. "It was a pleasure, Michael."

"The pleasure was all mine."

She was about to leave, when he called to her. "Amour. This is not your shame to bear."

"Thank you, Michael. But I'm afraid it is."

CHAPTER 2

Mannie was cool, calm and confident as he stood in front of Judge Kennedy and described Stanley as a man quick to rage, with fists that were like deadly weapons. He told the court the accused admitted to hitting Adshade two days before he died, and that he also put a pummeling on two men, one of simple mind. He added that one of the two men MacIntyre assaulted, claims he was witness to the accused threaten, and then admit to killing the deceased. He said the bad blood between the accused and the deceased was not, as the defendant claimed, over a fire, but because he was having an unwelcomed relationship with Mr. Adshade's young daughter; whose own safety would be put in jeopardy if the accused was granted bail.

Unlike Mannie, Sam was as nervous as a cat. His voice cracked and Judge Kennedy had to ask him to speak up on more than one occasion. Sam maintained that Stanley was an upstanding citizen with no previous history with the law. And that he didn't deny assaulting the boys after learning what they had done to his ponies. He also said his client had an alibi for the night of the deceased's death. He further pointed out that Eddie Lynch had recanted his earlier statement and that, contrary to the prosecution's theory, the defendant was a *friend* of the deceased's daughter.

The ruling was swift. It was all over in less than fifteen minutes. "Bail denied," Judge Kennedy ordered, without further explanation.

James placed his hand on Sam's shoulder as the bailiff led Stanley out of the courtroom in shackles. They both turned at the sound of laughter. Sergeant McInnes was congratulating Mannie.

Sam and James waited for them to leave.

"I'm sorry, James. Mannie just intimidates the hell out of me," Sam whispered.

They left the courthouse and drove to the Five and Dime, which was busier than usual.

James knew the kid was blaming himself. He looked heartsick. "Sam, we knew it was a long shot."

Sam nodded. "Still, I get so damn nervous. I should never have become a lawyer. I'm not cut out for it."

"You did just fine," James said. He knew his words rang hollow. "So, Mannie won the first round. But it's the verdict that counts. And we're not going to lose."

CHAPTER 3

James left the Five and Dime just before noon, drove to the store, and put the closed sign on the door.

"Mabel? I've closed the store for an hour. I thought we'd sit and talk for a bit," he said, patting the chair next to him.

Mabel grew increasingly concerned when Margaret came in and sat beside her husband. She prayed she wasn't being let go.

"Is it about you ownin the shack?" she asked nervously.

"Yes… and Stanley. Remember I told you I knew your mother and that we were schoolmates?"

Mabel nodded, wondering how her mother, who had been dead for almost ten years, could have anything to do with the shack, or Stanley.

"Well, we were more than schoolmates. Your mother and I were very dear friends. The two of us, along with our friend Percy, who died in the war, did everything together. When your mother got sick, she asked me to come see her. You would have been around seven or eight. Do you remember coming in and seeing me at the table with your mother?"

Mabel shook her head. "Not really."

"Well, I remember you. Your mother knew she was dying. She was worried about you with your father off fishing and drinking so much. She asked that I check on you from time to time," James said. He began to tear up.

Mabel looked at him with a mixture of confusion and worry.

"Anyway," he struggled on, "I only went back once after that. The farmhouse was vacant. Neighbours told me your father took you somewhere, but they didn't know where."

Mabel turned to Margaret. "That's when I went to live with Da's cousin Frankie and his family."

Margaret smiled at her, remembering their conversation about the scissors. "You have to understand, Mabel. James didn't have a car back then. It would have taken him hours to get back and forth to Pleasant Bay."

James put his hand on Margaret's and squeezed it. She wasn't sure if it was to thank her, or to stop her from trying to defend him. She assumed it was the latter.

"Anyway, I had no idea what happened to you until you and your father came back to town after Roddy hired him to work at the Company Store. When I heard Roddy and Amour were leaving for Boston, I bought their place with some money your mother left in my trust. I made Roddy promise that he wouldn't tell your father that I took over ownership."

"And all that time, I was thankin Roddy for bein so generous," Mabel said. "Always thought it wasn't in his nature. But how'd Ma get that kinda money?"

"It was a few hundred dollars that your grandfather left her."

"Da had no idea?" Mabel asked, tilting her head toward James.

"None."

"I guess Ma didn't trust him to put the money to good use."

"She didn't. And she was worried about you."

"She was beautiful and smart," Mabel said, allowing herself to smile.

"She was all that and more. And you take after her. She'd be very proud of you."

"Not sure bout any of that. But glad ya think so. Rather take after her, than Da," she said. She blessed herself, regretting she'd spoken ill of the dead, and so soon. "But why didn't ya just charge Da rent?" Mabel asked, more confused than ever.

"We both know I would have been charging you rent, not your father. It was no secret your father hated me. If he found out I held the deed to the property, he would have packed you up, and you would've been back in Number Three in the blink of an eye. He certainly wouldn't have agreed to pay me so much as a penny, regardless of whether or not it brought him any comfort. Anyway, as far as I was concerned, it was your house to begin with," James said.

"But I remember you askin me bout the rent Roddy charged," Mabel said.

"I just wanted to confirm that Roddy kept his word to me and wasn't doing anything underhanded."

"Well, we know now he wasn't what ya'd call a good man," she said. Her neck began to turn scarlet as she thought of the charges against him. "But ya can count on me and Amour payin ya rent from now on."

James held up his hand. "I'm transferring the property to you. It's yours, not mine. Bought with the money your mother wanted you to have."

"But that's not—"

"No buts about it. When things settle down with Stanley, we'll get Sam Friedman to look after the details."

"Mr. Cameron? Did you put Mr. Mendelson up to tellin me bout the job at the store?"

"I did."

"I didn't get it on my own," she said, the disappointment evident in her voice and eyes.

James had planned on saving the good news for another day, but decided now was the time to tell her. "Mabel, I had no idea if you could boil water, let alone bake bread. But, honestly, you've far exceeded my expectations… *our* expectations. In fact, bar none, you're the best baker in town. So much so," James said, turning to Margaret, "that Margaret and I have decided to expand the bakery."

"Really?" Mabel yelped. She jumped up and threw her arms around his neck.

"Really," he said. "And there's more. We're going to hire someone to help you."

"And I know just the person," Margaret said.

Mabel's face fell.

"Mabel? Do you think Mary Catherine would be interested?" Margaret asked.

This time, Mabel threw her arms around Margaret. "I know she would. She'd be great. She's real good at bakin. And she can cover the register. She's really smart, ya know." Mabel was excitedly pacing around. "It's a blessin in so many ways. Now, Mary Catherine can keep the boys. She was afraid she was gonna lose em. Oh, my God, Mr. Cameron. I can't wait to tell her. After work I mean. Not like I'm gonna tear outa here this very minute, or anythin. Wait! Can I tell her? Or do you wanna? I shouldna —"

"Yes, Mabel. You can tell her," James said, smiling at his wife.

"And here I thought you were bout to fire me. Ya both looked so serious and all. Thank ya so much. Mary Catherine's gonna be beside herself."

"Mabel? Come back and sit down," James said.

Mabel noticed his demeanor had once again turned serious, quickly reminding herself that whenever she heard good news, bad news followed close on its heels. "I'm sorry. I got so excited by the news, I forgot ya wanted to talk to me bout Stanley."

Mabel sat in stunned silence as James described Stanley's visit to her father's the day after the storm, and then his own visit the following morning. "We knew your father, not Fritz, was responsible for the cut on your forehead. We were worried he'd do you more harm. Anyway, I let Johnnie get to me," James said, without further explanation.

"So, ya both had a fight with Da. I knew it wasn't the coloureds. But I never figured it was you and Stanley."

"That's how I hurt my hand," James said. He looked down at it and felt a rush of anxiety. He took a deep breath. "Mabel? Johnnie was responsible for the fire that killed Stanley's ponies."

Mabel's hand flew to her mouth. "Da set fire to Stanley's barn? He killed Stanley's ponies?" Her eyes began to fill up.

"No. He put two of his goons up to it. Billy Guthro and Eddie Lynch. It was payback for Stanley breaking his nose."

Mabel jumped up. She knocked her chair over and ran out the back door. James and Margaret ran behind. Mabel was bent over the back step, throwing up. The vomit clung to her chin. She wiped it away with her hand and tried to talk between sobs. "It's… it's my fault. If I wasn't so… so stupid… If I didn't…" She was coughing and struggling for air. "If I didn't provoke Da. If I didn't go to work in the middle of a storm… none of this woulda ha… hap… happened."

Margaret wrapped her arms around Mabel's bent body and gave James a worried look.

"Mabel! None of this is your fault. It's mine," James said.

Mabel started to cry harder.

"Mabel dear! You can't blame yourself for your father's actions. You did nothing wrong. Neither did James," Margaret said, trying to reassure them both.

"The ponies would still be alive. Stanley wouldn't… wouldn't be in jail. Ya wouldn't have hurt yer hand," Mabel sobbed. She was kneeling on the step. "No matter what I do, bad things happen."

It took some time for Margaret and James to convince her to come back inside where it was warm. Margaret went to make tea. James got the rum.

"Drink this," he said. Mabel took a swig and began to choke. Margaret handed her a wet dishrag to wipe her face, then turned to James. "I think we should close the store for the day."

James was in total agreement. He waited for Mabel to object. To his surprise, she didn't.

Mabel wiped her tear-stained face with the back of her hand and looked at James. "I need to see Stanley," she said.

CHAPTER 4

James and Mabel were getting ready to head to the jail when they heard the knock. "Sorry. We're closed for the day," James hollered. Again the knock, this time louder, with more urgency. James reached for the handle and roughly pulled it open to advise his impatient customer the sign said *closed*.

"What is it you want now?" James said coarsely. "We're on our way out."

Sergeant McInnes looked past James to see Mabel standing behind him. She had her coat on. He could tell she had been crying.

"Not interruptin anythin, am I? Lovers' quarrel?" he asked, grinning at James.

"Whatever it is you want, Sergeant, make it quick."

"Everythin okay, Miss Adshade?" he called out past James. "You look upset."

"I'm not feelin well."

"Of course," McInnes said, thinking it odd the store was closed, and that both Mabel and her boss seemed on edge.

James decided it best not to tell McInnes he and Mabel were on their way to the station to see Stanley. "If you don't mind, I was just about to take Mabel home," he lied, shooting Mabel a quick look.

"I'm sure Mabel won't mind if we have a brief chat," McInnes said.

Mabel didn't care for Sergeant McInnes when he sat across from her eating his pie. Today, she cared for him even less. "I know ya got the wrong man in jail," she said defiantly.

"How can ya be so sure?" McInnes asked.

"Cause I know he's a good man and wouldn't do no such a thing. He's been nothin but good to me."

"He put a pretty good poundin on two young fellows that are lucky to be alive. He also assaulted your father a couple of days before he was found dead in a ditch. Doesn't sound like a good man to me?"

"From what I hear, Stanley had good reason to do what he did to those boys."

"Do ya think he had good reason to assault your father? Kill him?"

"Mr. Cameron told me why Stanley hit Da. Way I figure it, Da had it comin. But Stanley sure as hell didn't kill him."

"And how would you know that? Were ya with Stanley the night your father was killed?"

"No. I was at the Toths, with my friend Mary Catherine."

James walked closer to Sergeant McInnes, trying to block his view of Mabel. "I think that's enough, Sergeant. She just told you, she's not feeling well."

McInnes stepped to the side and looked at her. "Well then, Miss Adshade, ya really can't say Stanley didn't do it now. Can ya?"

Mabel walked up to him. "I know he didn't. He's a good man," she said forcefully.

"Miss Adshade? Are you and Stanley involved? I mean, in an intimate way?"

"That's it," James hollered. He grabbed McInnes by the arm and pulled him toward the door. Don't come here again, or I swear I'll go to the captain about harassment."

McInnes pulled his arm free of James's grip. "Easy, Mr. Cameron. I'll be on my way."

Sergeant McInnes opened the door to leave, then turned back. "Oh. Just one more thing, Miss Adshade. Is anybody tellin ya what to say? Threatenin ya? Because if—"

James rushed toward Sergeant McInnes. He was about to shove him out the door, when Mabel spoke up.

"No. No one's threatenin me. And ain't nobody tellin me what to say."

"Good day, then," McInnes said.

James slammed the door in his face.

CHAPTER 5

Amour was at home, thinking about her plans to create the town's only refined dining experience. She was anxious to finalize the list of soups, delicate sandwiches, and petit fours that would be printed on a beautiful, leather-mounted menu, but knew there was still a mountain of work ahead of her. Still, she thought, she was way ahead of schedule.

Selling the rental properties and securing the shoe repair proved a lot easier than she had expected. Certainly, there was still a lot to do to ready the property, including structural changes to make it more airy. Perhaps she should consult James Cameron or Michael Donnely about reputable tradesmen. She would also need to purchase tables, chairs, linen, china, and artwork for the walls. And then there was the issue of securing a long list of ingredients she couldn't find at Mendelson's, or anywhere else in town. Her dream was about to happen. Soon, she'd be the proprietress of one of the finest establishments on the Island. Roddy, as cheap as he was, would always frequent similar eateries in Boston with his colleagues. He would treat himself at least once a week, coming home to rave about the delicacies. She had asked him if he would take her some time. *My money and your time, would be better spent on cooking lessons,* she recalled him saying. It was probably the only time she had appreciated his advice.

She was making a list of all the things she needed to do to open before Christmas when she heard the footfalls on the front step. She looked at the clock. Mabel was home early for a change. Then she heard the rap. "Amour MacPherson?"

"Yes."

"Telegram."

"Thank you," she said, unfolding it.

> *I regret to advise that your husband, Roderick MacPherson, died at his own hand while in custody. Stop. His body is at the city morgue awaiting instruction. Stop. Will await word on disposing of personal effects. Stop. Apologies for delayed notification. Difficulties locating your new address. Condolences on your loss. Stop. Captain F. Bustin, 12th Precinct BPD.*

Amour stared at the telegram. She felt nothing. She just wondered if his suicide would jeopardize the annulment. She should have never married him in the first place. As a young girl, she had been in love with the idea of marriage, children, and of being the wife of a powerful man. Now, childless at thirty-one, she realized how foolish she had been to waste all those years on a man that didn't love her. Couldn't love her.

She just found out her brother suffered a violent death. Now, she learns her husband commited sucicide. Only one of those discoveries made her sad.

CHAPTER 6

James was fuming after McInnes left. Mabel could see the anger in his eyes and clenched jaw. Their visit with Stanley would have to wait, neither wanting another encounter with McInnes. Despite James's pleas, Mabel refused to go home and went back to her baking. James went back to the store. Both silently went about their business. Both silently fearing the gathering storm.

Margaret walked into the kitchen as Mabel, lost in her thoughts, roughly kneaded her bread. Margaret knew she was hurting and tried to take her mind off Sergeant McInnes's visit and the shock of the news James had shared.

"Are you feeling any better, Mabel?"

"Ain't nothin like a good cry to set ya thinkin clearer. I can't change what happened. I can't turn the clock back, or bring Stanley's ponies back. Just gonna have to live with myself, knowin I meant no harm."

"Of course not," Margaret said. She struggled to find something else, anything, to draw Mabel out of her sadness. "Mabel, I was wondering if you had a chance to start *A Tale of Two Cities*."

"Tried, Mrs. Cameron. Sorry, *Margaret*. "But I didn't get too far into it. It just beat me down. Couldn't pronounce half the words. And certainly didn't know their meanin."

"Perhaps, it's a little beyond you at this time. I'll look for one less… intimidating."

"That'd be great," Mabel said, thinking about how badly she had misjudged Margaret.

"Maybe, when you're reading, you could copy out the words you don't understand, or know how to pronounce. Then we can work on them together."

"I'd like that. Ya shoulda been a teacher."

"I always wanted to be," Margaret said.

Mabel lifted her head from her kneading board. "So why didn't ya?"

"I had to put my plan to be a teacher aside when I married James. Schools don't hire married women. All the teaching jobs go to men, or single women."

"Well, I betcha woulda been good at it. Yer so smart and good with kids. Like how ya are with Luke and Mark. *And* the baby. Mary Catherine said Mark has taken a real shine to ya."

Margaret felt a lump forming in her throat. "I hope they know they're welcome here any time." She turned her back to Mabel and dabbed her eyes with the sleeve of her blouse.

"I'll let Mary Catherine know when I see her tonight. She's gonna be over the moon when I tell her yer gonna hire her. Soon as I finish up here, I'm runnin straight over."

"You know, someone's going to have to look after Mark and the baby through the day. And Luke, when he gets out of school. I certainly don't mind. In fact, I like having them around."

"Yer a Godsend, Margaret. Mr. Cameron too. First to me. Now, to Mary Catherine and the boys. Don't normally like to see time get ahead of itself. But not today. I can't wait to share the good news."

Margaret stood next to the counter and brushed some loose flour off the bread board into her hand. "Mabel… I was so mean to you. I truly am ashamed of my behaviour. I hope you can forgive me."

Mabel stopped kneading. "Ain't nothin to fergive. Gotta admit. I didn't take to you too much at first, either. But I do now. Just took you and me a bit of time to get to know each other, that's all."

Margaret smiled at her new friend. "So, do you want me to peel more apples?"

"No. No pies today. Just bread. We lost all that time this mornin. But ya can help me grease the pans. By the way, Margaret. Do ya think Mr. Cameron might consider gettin a telephone? I think it'd be good for business given more folks are gettin em and we're expandin n' all. Come to think of it, an advertisement in *The Post* wouldn't hurt, either."

CHAPTER 7

Mabel couldn't wait to get to Mary Catherine's. She tore out of the store exactly at five and ran most of the way. Mary Catherine and her mother were in the kitchen when they heard the pounding. They looked at one another, fearing a cave-in had buried another neighbour. They walked to the living room. Mary Catherine's father put down *The Post* and stood up as they appeared in the doorway. They nervously eyed one another, then the door.

"Mary Catherine!" Mabel yelled out. "Mary Catherine! It's Mabel."

Mary Catherine ran to the door and pulled it open. Mabel was bent over on the stoop, gasping for air. "What's wrong, Mabel? What happened?"

Mabel threw her arms around her friend's neck. "We're expandin the bakery."

Mary Catherine was relieved it wasn't more bad news, but puzzled by her excitement. "That's great, Mabel."

"And yer our new baker."

Mary Catherine let out a squeal. The two friends jumped in circles, laughing and hugging one another. Her parents and Mark quickly joined the happy celebration. Luke stood quietly off to the side, more interested in his feet.

CHAPTER 8

Mabel left Mary Catherine's with a full heart, a satisfied belly, and a plate of perogies. She couldn't wait for Amour to try them. They were her new favourite food. She stopped twice to pop one in her mouth. She wondered if Stanley would like them, and what he would have had for supper. Her happy mood suddenly turned sour as she thought of his predicament and her part in it. All will be good, she assured herself. There's no way they can find an innocent man guilty.

She made her way down Union Street and took a shortcut to Minto through the alleyway off Commercial Street. She would be glad to get home and out of the cold.

She opened the door. "I'm here. Sorry I'm late. Wait till ya taste what I got," she hollered, hanging up her coat. She walked the short hallway and rounded the corner to see Amour sitting on the couch. Sergeant McInnes was sitting beside her. Mabel's heart started to pound.

"Mabel? Sergeant McInnes dropped by to ask you a few questions," Amour said, giving her a puzzled look.

"I thought I answered all yer questions," Mabel said, with a tone.

"Most. But not all. I won't keep you long."

"I don't know what else I can tell ya."

Sergeant McInnes turned to Amour. "Perhaps we can have some time alone?"

Amour stood to leave.

"No," Mabel said. "Aunt Amour can stay."

Amour sat back down and wondered why *she* felt so nervous.

"Suit yerself. I'll make it quick. Mabel, you mentioned ya don't have a boyfriend and that ya never did. Is that correct?"

Mabel looked at Amour, then back at McInnes. "Yes."

"So you're not in a relationship with Stanley MacIntyre?"

"No. I ready told ya that."

"And you're not in a relationship with James Cameron?"

"*James Cameron?* Of course not! He's my boss! And he's married!"

Amour spoke up. "Sergeant? What has any of this to do with Johnnie's death? I can't imagine—"

"Mabel? Are you a virgin?" Sergeant McInnes asked.

Amour's stood up sharply. Mabel stared in disbelief. The perogies slid off the plate and onto the floor.

"Get out! Right now!" Amour screamed, thrusting Sergeant McInnes's overcoat into his chest. "Get out! And never set foot on our property again!"

Sergeant McInnes stood outside the shack, looking at the door. It was the second time in the same day he'd had one slammed in his face. He smiled, believing the angry reactions he provoked were further proof he was exposing the truth. Too bad the aunt was there, he thought. But hell, I got what I came for. Mabel wouldn't answer my question. She ain't no virgin.

Amour had her ear to the door and waited for him to leave. When she turned to speak to Mabel, she was nowhere in sight. Amour walked through the living room, past the kitchen, and knocked on her door.

"Mabel? May I come in?"

"It's open."

Mabel was sitting on the edge of her bed, looking at the yellowed picture of her, and her mother and father.

"I can't believe he asked you such a personal question, let alone fathom the reason why. He's a despicable man."

"He thinks I was intimate with Stanley and that's why he killed Da."

"Let him think what he damn well pleases. The truth always prevails."

Mabel put her head down, worried her shame would soon be fodder for the town.

Amour rested her hand over her niece's. "There's something I need to tell you," she said. "I got a telegram earlier today. It was from the Boston Police. Roddy killed himself."

CHAPTER 9

Margaret was in bed reading when James crawled in beside her.

"Seriously, Margaret? *Smokey the Cowhorse?*" James said, shaking his head.

Margaret ran her hand over the cover. "I love this book. I thought Mabel might like it, too."

"Mabel?"

"Yes, Mabel. I gave her *A Tale of Two Cities,* but it's well past her reading ability. Thought this might be better. I want to help her with her reading. She's very smart, James. You know, she might not want to bake bread for the rest of her life."

"Probably not. But I'm hoping you don't turn her into a scholar anytime soon. Remember, we wouldn't be expanding the bakery without her."

"I was thinking I'd give it to Luke when she finishes with it. I worry about him. He's so withdrawn. I've never once seen him smile. Not once. And he's so quiet."

"Unlike his brothers, he was old enough to remember his mother and father. A lot of tragedy for a boy so young," he said.

"James? Since you're going to be busy dealing with renovations to the store, maybe you can give him some small jobs? Cutting kindling… or stocking the shelves?"

James lay on his back, with one hand under his head, and thought of his dwindling finances. He had taken out a fifteen-hundred dollar loan to cover the cost of the renovations. He hoped that would be enough to cover the cost of materials and labour. Then, there was the added cost of Mary Catherine's wages. God, he thought, this had better work out, or *no one* will be working at the store.

"Well, what do you think?" Margaret asked.

James turned on his side and rested his head on her shoulder. "I won't be able to pay him much," he said, yawning.

"It's not so much about the money, but giving him something to keep his mind busy. He's a lost child," Margaret said. She looked down at James. His eyes were closed.

"James, she said, "when are you going to tell Mabel about her real father?"

"Soon."

"I really don't think you should wait much longer."

James struggled to keep his eyes open. "There's just been so much upset lately. It's not like I'm sharing happy news. I'd like to get past Stanley's trial first," he mumbled.

"Do you think Stanley will be alright?" she asked.

James didn't reply. Margaret eased his head off her shoulder, put her book on the bedside table, and turned down the lamp. She then turned to face him, running her hand over his greying temple. "I love you, James Cameron," she whispered.

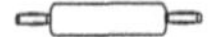

Tuesday, November 15

CHAPTER I

James and Margaret were having tea when Mabel walked into the kitchen.

"Good Morning, Mabel," they said.

"Mornin."

"How are you doing, dear?" Margaret asked.

"I'm alive and kickin, which is more than I can say for Uncle Roddy."

James turned quickly. "What did you say?"

"Roddy's dead. Killed himself," Mabel said.

James's shoulders slumped. "When?"

"Saturday. Amour got the telegram from Boston police yesterday."

Margaret blessed herself. "I'm so sorry, Mabel. And poor Amour."

James wondered if Ted had had a chance to question him. "Is Amour alright?" he asked.

"She's doin good. Ain't like he was a lovin husband, if ya know what I mean," Mabel said, dropping her eyes.

"Is she taking the body home?" James asked.

"No. Just gonna have him buried somewhere in Boston. No service. No nothin. Can't say as I blame her. Had so much goin for him and threw it all away. Still makes ya feel sad though."

"It sure does," James replied, his thoughts not on Roddy, but on

Ted, and Isaac Greene and his son.

Mabel didn't dare mention a word about Sergeant McInnes's visit and the personal questions he put to her, fearing what James might do. For now, it would be a secret she shared with her Aunt. Amour had wanted to tell James, but Mabel begged her not to, saying it would bring no good. Amour eventually relented, but vowed that if Sergeant McInnes showed up again, she would not only go to James, but to Sergeant McInnes's superiors.

CHAPTER 2

Mannie listened as Sergeant McInnes assured him the girl was no virgin.

"You have no doubts?" Mannie repeated.

"None. Wouldn't she tell me if she was?"

"Maybe she didn't like being asked?"

"No. That's not it. It's because she knows that if we prove she isn't, it will verify Stanley's motive for killin Johnnie. Just like Billy said. Who knows, maybe she really does like the guy and she's coverin for him. Ya shoulda seen the look on her face when I asked her. Stood there all wide-eyed with her mouth hanging open."

Mannie leaned back in his chair, chewing on the end of his pencil.

"Mannie. I still think we should charge Cameron."

"No!" Mannie answered flatly.

"Why the hell not?" McInnes asked, slumping back in his chair and throwing his arms in the air.

"Look. We got a solid case against MacIntyre. We know he hit Johnnie prior to his death. We got Billy's testimony, and we got this," Mannie said, holding up the envelope. "The most we have against Cameron is that he's lying. We've got nothing to substantiate that he's involved with the girl, or was with MacIntyre the night he went after Adshade."

"Hell! I know he was!" McInnes said, pounding his fist on Mannie's desk.

"Like I said. We'll get Cameron for perjury and let the rest play out in court." Mannie stood, walked to the coatrack and reached for his hat.

McInnes knew it was his cue to leave. He got to his feet. "Mannie, ever remember a double hangin in town?"

Mannie patted his fedora in place. "No. Not that I can recall."

"Well, I think we're about to make history."

Wednesday November 16

CHAPTER I

Margaret came downstairs and was immediately taken aback when she looked at her unshaven husband. He was being unusually gruff with a young boy who dumped his jar of pennies over the counter and onto the floor. James had tossed and turned all night, depriving them both of sleep. Likely worried about telling Mabel about her real father and growing impatient about Stanley's circumstances, Margaret thought. Her concern grew when Captain Collins walked through the door.

"Margaret! How about taking over for me?" James said, rushing from behind the counter to greet Ted.

"Captain Collins! See you finally came for your pie," James said, more loudly than necessary. "I believe Mabel has it out back. Follow me."

Margaret watched them enter the back of the store and close the door.

"Thanks, James. I didn't realize the store would be so busy. I got in late last night. Station doesn't know I'm back yet. I figured this was as good a time as any to get caught up. You okay? You don't look good."

"Didn't sleep the best last night. Mabel told me Roddy killed himself. Did you get to talk to him?"

"No."

"Jesus, Ted. I'm sorry."

"James, you were right. I *know* the bastard killed David. I just can't prove it. Boston Police said he was full of piss and vinegar, going to fight the charges and all that, until he heard I was on my way to question him. Stuck a fountain pen in his neck for Christ's sake."

"Jesus," James said, pinching his eyes closed.

"Apparently it was a bloody mess."

"Ted, you did everything you could," James said.

Ted lowered his head. "So, how are things going? McInnes giving you and Stanley any more trouble?" Collins asked, anxious to change the subject.

James momentarily considered telling him about Stanley taking his car and looking for Johnnie, but backed off. Sam didn't know. There was nothing to be gained from telling Ted. "He keeps asking how I hurt my hand. I think he knows I lied to him about it. Do you think I should tell him the truth?"

"Ordinarily, I'd say yes. But in this instance, no. I'm afraid it would do more harm than good."

"I don't know. I'm really worried it will come out. If they're asking now, they're going to ask when I take the stand. And I won't lie under oath. I just can't."

"Just don't rush into anything. I'm going to drop by the station when I leave here. I'll try and find out what's going on."

"Ted. I can't help thinking Billy and Eddie had something to do with Johnnie's death. One minute they're saying it was the coloureds and the next, it's Stanley. Maybe Johnnie reneged on paying them for starting the fire?"

"Billy, maybe. But not Eddie. He doesn't have the wherewithal. Honestly, I think it's a long shot. But I'll have a chat with Billy. See what he was up to the night Johnnie was killed."Margaret looked at the closed door her husband and Captain Collins huddled behind. She sensed he hadn't come for pie, but to share bad news. She was about to check on them when Mary Catherine walked in with Luke and Mark.

"Hello, Mrs. Cameron," Mary Catherine said.

"Well, hello. What a nice surprise."

Margaret rounded the counter, squatted down in front of Mark, took off his mittens, and blew on his fingers to warm them up.

"I just stopped by to thank you. Mabel told me you want me to help in the bakery. I can't wait. And…" her lips started to quiver, "now we can keep the boys."

Margaret stood up. "Did she also tell you I could help look after them while you're working?"

"Yes. But I couldn't possibly ask you to do that. Ma can take care of them. They're good company for her."

Margaret wondered if her face showed her disappointment. "Well, I'm sure your mother will need a break from time to time. So please, bring them along whenever you want."

"Thank you, Mrs. Cameron. That's really kind of you."

"So, Luke. Mr. Cameron and I were talking. He tells me he needs a big, strong boy to help out around the store. Do you think you'd like to do that? Maybe after school and on weekends?"

Luke looked up at Mary Catherine, but said nothing.

"Luke. Mrs. Cameron is offering you a job. What do you say?" Mary Catherine said, urging him to speak up.

He put his head down. "I guess so."

"I can't thank you and Mr. Cameron enough," Mary Catherine said. She put her arm around Luke's shoulder and drew him into her. "I'll work hard. We *both* will."

James and Ted emerged from the back. Margaret knew her intuition was right when James walked past Mary Catherine and the boys without as much as a word. She approached her husband. "I was just telling Luke about the job," she said, thinking he was being uncharacteristically rude.

He looked perplexed. "Oh, yes. The job."

Mary Catherine thought something was wrong, too. "If you don't mind, we're just going to pop into the kitchen and say hi to Mabel."

"Of course," Margaret said.

"Are you coming, Luke?" Mary Catherine asked.

Luke shook his head, no.

Margaret walked behind the counter and bent down to collect some licorice. "Luke. Would you like some…?"

He was already outside.

James was at the door saying goodbye to Ted.

"Forgetting something, Captain?" Margaret asked.

He smiled and gave her a puzzled look.

"Your pie?"

"Oh, yes. My Pie. Thank you."

James paused in the doorway of the kitchen. Mabel was playing *Pat-a-Cake* with Mark. He quietly walked in, picked up the one pie cooling on the counter, and returned to the store. He handed it to Ted.

Margaret waited for Captain Collins to leave. "More bad news, James?"

"We were talking about the Greene boy's murder."

"The Greene boy's murder?" Margaret repeated, wondering why that would be of any consequence to James.

"Yes. The Greene boy's murder. Roddy MacPherson killed him. We just can't prove it."

CHAPTER 2

Constable Dunphy brought Billy from his cell into the interview room.

"Sit tight. Captain's on his way."

"Hello, Billy. Enjoying your stay with us?" Collins asked.

Billy started to laugh, exposing the gap in his mouth following his encounter with Stanley.

Billy slouched in his chair. "Whatcha want?"

"Want to know where you were the night Johnnie was killed."

Billy started to laugh.

"Something funny, Billy?" Collins asked.

"Fuck. You guys really don't know what yer doin," Billy said, still laughing.

Collins's sat back in his chair, folded his arms, and waited for Billy to stop. His patience grew thin. "Just answer the damn question, Billy," he barked, reaching across the table, and grabbing him by the collar.

Billy knocked Collins's hand away. "So, when was that again?"

"You know damn well what day it was. But for the record, it was the night of Wednesday, November second."

"Oh, yeah. November second. Let me think," Billy said, drumming his fingers against his chin.

"Think hard, Billy. Because the way I have it figured, you were somewhere along Brookside Street, with Eddie… maybe a few of your other pals, putting a beating on Johnnie."

Billy dropped his hand on the table. "Now why would I do that?"

"I figure Johnnie didn't pay up after you and Eddie set Stanley's barn on fire. He stiffed you, so you went after him. So, tell me? Where were you on the night of the second?" Collins shouted.

"Seems to me…I was just down the hall."

Collins looked up at Dunphy. "What do you mean, just down the hall?"

"Check yer records, ya fuckin idiot. I spent the night in the drunk tank."

Collins left the station and drove back to the store. He told James it took less than five minutes to verify Billy's alibi.

James was stunned by the news. "I was sure it was them."

"Apparently not," Collins said, aware of the distress his news was causing.

James sat down heavily and considered the unexpected news. "If Billy and Eddie aren't responsible for Johnnie's death, who is? Christ, Ted. I don't have a good feeling about this."

CHAPTER 3

Despite Mr. Cameron's protests, Mabel walked home, grateful for the fresh air. As she neared the shack, she saw a shiny green car with a black, retractable roof parked in front. She opened the door, surprised to see a man in a lovely, navy blue suit having tea with Amour. Can't be from around these parts, she thought.

"Hello," Mabel said.

"Mabel, this is Michael Donnely," Amour said.

He stood to greet her. "My condolences on the loss of your father."

"Thank you." Mabel thought he looked vaguely familiar and gave Amour a curious look.

"Mr. Donnely used to live in Boston. He moved here a few weeks ago to work at the coal company."

Mabel unbuttoned her coat and unlaced Margaret's boots. "Now, I know why ya look so familiar. Yer the guy from the depot. Amour asked me if I knew who ya were. Remember, Amour? You asked who the tall, handsome fella—"

Amour jumped to her feet. "Mabel! Have some tea."

"Maybe in a bit," she said, wondering why Amour was giving her the stink eye.

"Mabel works at Cameron's bakery. She makes great bread," Amour said, kicking herself for telling Mr. Donnely she didn't remember seeing him at the bus station.

Mr. Donnely was smiling at Amour. "And pie. I stopped in a couple of days ago and picked one up. It was fabulous."

Mabel decided she liked Mr. Donnely a lot. "So, yer the guy who took Mr. Cameron's pie. Well, if ya think ya might want another one, ya better put yer order in."

"Okay. I'll take three."

"Three!" Mabel squealed, thinking he must really like her pie. "When do ya want em?"

"How about I stop by after work tomorrow? Around four?"

"Best I can do for tomorrow is two. And that's pushin it. Gotta look after my regulars. And my orders are already backed up."

"Okay, then. Two it is," Donnelly said, as he watched Amour wipe down the counter for the third time since he arrived.

"Great. There'll be two pies with yer name on em."

Michael looked to the door. "I've taken up enough of your time. I should be going." He made his way down the hall. Amour followed close behind. He had his hand on the doorknob and turned back. "I hope you'll forgive me for dropping by without notice. When I read *The Globe* this morning, I just thought you might… well, you might need someone to talk to. And remember, if you need any assistance with the arrangements, I have plenty of contacts in Boston who could help."

"Thank you, Michael. That's very kind of you. And I hope you'll let me know of any reputable tradesmen who can help with my establishment."

"I'll ask around and let you know."

"Well, good night then."

"Good night."

"Good night, Mabel," he hollered. "I'll see you tomorrow."

"See ya, Mr. Donnely."

Amour closed the door and turned to see Mabel grinning at her. "I like him," Mabel said.

"Yes. He seems like a nice man," Amour said.

"And very handsome," Mabel added.

Amour's cheeks were flush. "I suppose so."

"So, whatcha got cookin?" Mabel asked.

CHAPTER 4

Amour turned the lamp off and plumped her pillow. She wanted to go to the trial, but couldn't bear the thought of so many people looking at her and pointing out that stupid woman who married that despicable man. She thought of Michael and her reaction when she opened the door to see him standing on the step. She tried to recall if she had *actually* started fixing her hair as if greeting an unexpected suitor, or if it was just her mind playing tricks on her. And then getting caught lying about not seeing him at the depot. What could he be thinking? Michael was just being kind and she acted like a schoolgirl with her first crush. God, how could she have been so stupid.

Well, I was stupid enough to marry Roddy, she thought, remembering their wedding night. Her new husband slept on the sofa, claiming the wine at dinner made him sick. The next night, he was tired from work. Eventually, they reached the point where Roddy felt he didn't need to explain anything to her. The only time he ever showed the slightest interest in her was when they attended a company dinner or reception. He would smile at her, put his arm around her shoulder, and talk warmly.

She had heard of homosexuality, but had understood it to be a rare disease. She pressed her eyes shut as she recalled the first, and last, time she broached the subject of their lack of intimacy. She had set the stage, with candles on the dining table. Roddy seemed to be in a particularly good mood, having just purchased a new suit at an exceptionally good discount. He even bought her a new dress for the company's Christmas social. She reached across the table, put her hand on his, and said she wanted to have a baby.

Roddy glared at her. He then slammed his fist down so hard she jumped back, the plates rattled, and the candles tipped over. He called her a foul, fat pig, and said only a whore would be so forward. He hissed that he would be the one to decide when, or if, they ever had a child, and stormed out. After two days, she thought he had left for good, and that she had been abandoned in a strange city with no friends and no means to fend for herself. But he came home on the third day, carrying a dozen pink carnations. He had kissed her on the cheek and apologized for his outburst, before walking into his bedroom and closing the door.

Why, in God's name, didn't I leave? Harder to justify her reasons for staying now, she thought. Now that she knew the ugly truth about him. But not nearly as hard as seeing the best years of her life slip away. Not nearly as hard as being a virgin after eight years in a cold, childless, loveless marriage. She cursed Roddy, then herself, thinking she was responsible for her own misery. She alone, with her naïve aspirations of being the wife of a wealthy and powerful man, was responsible for her sorry state.

"I'll never make that mistake again," she whispered.

Thursday, November 17

CHAPTER I

"Please rise."

Judge Kennedy entered, making a dramatic sweep with his billowing black robe. His cherubic face, masked his stern demeanour. He looked around the small, cramped courtroom, sat down, and pounded his gavel.

"I see we have standing room only. I expect all of you to be on your best behaviour. If anybody here disrupts my court, I'll have the bailiff toss you out on your ass. The accused, Stanley P. MacIntyre, stands charged with capital murder in the death of John F. Adshade. He has elected to be tried before a jury of his peers. What say the defendant to the charges against you?"

Stanley stood and surveyed the twelve white men who would decide his fate. He knew all but four. "Not guilty."

After a few preliminary remarks to the jury, Judge Kennedy's eyes flew to a shoving match in the third row. He banged his gavel so hard the head flew off. It wasn't the first time.

"Yer Honour! I just stepped out for a minute to relieve myself and Gladys jumped in my spot," the frail, grey-haired woman pleaded.

"Mrs. Ferguson! Gladys! Forfeit your seat to Wilma. Right now!"

"But Your Honour—"

"Right now, Gladys. I know you have a personal interest in the proceedings, but Wilma was waiting on the steps before I arrived here this morning. That's her spot. Either move to the back of the room, or I'll have you removed altogether," he said, as the bailiff handed him a new gavel. Judge Kennedy tugged on its head, nodding his approval.

Gladys Ferguson stood and huffed her indignance, before finally surrendering to Wilma, who delighted in the comfort of her coveted chair and the generous applause of her fellow spectators.

"Now, gentlemen. As you know, I'm not one to waste time. Moreover, I promised Mrs. Kennedy I'd be home for supper. So let's get through the opening statements. Counsellor Chernin, please begin," Judge Kennedy said.

"Thank you, Your Honour," Mannie said. He gripped the lapels of his expensive suit and slowly walked toward the jury. He knew every one of the jurors by name and immediately set out to use it to his advantage.

"Bill, Gussie, Fess," he said nodding to them. "Ever know me to lose a case?" The entire jury shook their heads from side to side. "Of course not. I have prosecuted over seventy cases and I've never lost one. Not a single case. And you know why? Because I do my homework. Like you, I don't want to see an innocent man hang for something he didn't do. Of course not. None of us do. So I make sure the facts support the charge and that there's no room for doubt. And in this case, I am absolutely convinced that the accused, Stanley MacIntyre, beat Johnnie Adshade to death. Maybe not with his fists, which we all know pack a powerful punch, but with something equally as lethal. And I will prove to you, beyond any shadow of a doubt, that the accused not only had the means to kill, but motive and opportunity, as well."

Mannie paused and started to speak in a more subdued tone. "Now, I know many of you are familiar with the accused. Some of you no doubt think him a fine enough fellow. But how well do you really know him? Or think you know him?" His voice grew louder. "Trust me. There's a very dark side to this man," Mannie said, pointing to Stanley. "A very dark side." He raised his voice again. "And when that dark sides takes over," he said, suddenly pumping his fists outward toward his captive audience, "it erupts with a deadly fury."

He turned back to the jury and once again lowered his voice. "Yes. The accused has a very dark side to him. One that he has tried to hide from us. But not anymore. Not anymore. Because I plan to drag it out into the light of day." Mannie, once again, turned to Stanley. "I plan to expose the accused for what he is. A man who is incapable of controlling his emotions. A man with a history of violent rage." He turned quickly away from Stanley, pointing at Willie Morrison. "The kind of rage that can damage a man for life. The kind of rage that can kill a man. The kind of rage that killed Johnnie Adshade on the night of November the second. The kind of rage that will see him hang."

Mannie smiled at his adoring audience, thinking he would have made a good Baptist minister, if it weren't for the fact he was Jewish.

The courtroom was deadly quiet as Mannie walked back to his table and pulled his chair back to take his seat. The scraping sound of wood on wood surprisingly loud in the small courtroom packed to the rafters.

"Counsellor Friedman."

Sam stood. "Yes, Your Honour?"

"I assume you're going to make an opening statement."

"Yes."

"Well, what are you waiting for?"

"Sorry," Sam said. His mind went blank. He began flipping through the papers on his desk. He thought everyone in the courtroom could hear his heart pound. "Gentlemen of the jury," he began, gripping his lapels and walking toward them. Everyone broke out in gales of laughter. Sam's head fell to his chest and his hands dropped to his sides. They were laughing at him for mimicking his much older opponent. He wanted to tear out of the courtroom, down the street, and out of town.

"I'm sorry, Your Honour. If I can just have a moment?"

Judge Kennedy decided to give the kid a break. Sam returned to his table. He was as white as a sheet. He needed to wet his dry mouth. He put his hand on his glass, but decided not to chance it. He picked up his notes, put them back down, and thought of what his father had told him when he left for the courthouse. Make sure the jury knows you care about the truth, not winning. You need them to like you. And never let them see you sweat. Sam walked back toward the jury box.

"Hi, folks. I'm afraid I don't know many of you. I figure most of you are quite a bit older than me. You see, I'm not even twenty-three yet. And this is my first real case. I only got my license to practice about six weeks ago. So, unlike Mr. Chernin, I can't stand in front of you and say I've had a long illustrious career and never lost a case. So far, though, I'm one for one."

The courtroom laughed again. This time, with him. James wasn't sure if Sam had a strategy, or if he was just winging it, but he thought it was a stroke of genius to position himself as the underdog. He looked around the courtroom and suspected a good number of people were suddenly rooting for the kid. He hoped the men on the jury felt the same.

"I have to admit," Sam said, "I was taken aback by my noted colleague's opening remarks. But he got me thinking. He got me thinking about why we had to drag you all here today, tomorrow, and the day after that. Heck, who knows, we could be here for weeks. But why do we even need a trial? Why do we need a judge, or even a jury for that matter? The defendant must be guilty, because my esteemed colleague says he is. And because, as my esteemed colleague just reminded all of you, he's never wrong. He does his homework. And he never loses. It's as simple as that. Case closed." Sam raised his voice. "Gentlemen," he said standing in front of them. "My opponent doesn't want you to rely on your own good judgement. No! He just wants you to trust his."

Mannie jumped to his feet. "I object."

The ruling was swift. "Sit down, Mannie. You know there are no grounds for an objection."

The court laughed again. This time at Mannie.

Sam continued. "Gentlemen. The Crown will tell you there was bad blood between Stanley and the deceased. If any of you knew Johnnie Adshade, you would also know there was bad blood between him and dozens of other men in this town. Many, who unlike the accused, have no one to attest to their whereabouts on the night of November second. You will also hear that one of the Crown's key witnesses has since recanted his allegations against my client. Said he never heard the defendant threaten, or admit to killing the deceased. As for the other witness. Well, let's just say he has his own motivations for wanting the defendant locked up. And for the record, this is the same witness who originally told the police that it was a gang of coloured men who were responsible for Mr. Adshade's death. And where is this witness right now? He's locked up in the county jail awaiting trial for arson. Accused of torching my client's barn, killing his ponies, and robbing him of his livelihood.

And then…then we have the medical examiner's professional opinion. While he can't rule out the deceased wasn't beaten to death, after thirty years as a medical practitioner, it is his professional opinion that the cause of death is more consistent with that of a motor vehicle accident.

The Crown will also call into question my client's alibi. I can assure you, my client's alibi is as solid as any other man in this town who didn't care for Johnnie Adshade. In fact, it is foolproof."

"Gentlemen of the jury," Sam said pointing to Stanley. "I believe my client to be innocent. But you will be the judge of that. All I ask is that you presume he is innocent until such time as you are convinced, beyond a shadow of a doubt, that he is not. It's up to you, and you alone, to make that judgement." Sam then walked over and faced Mannie. "I'm confident, that after hearing all of the evidence, there will only be one person in this chamber who will continue to insist, no matter what the evidence concludes, that he is guilty. And that is because he believes he's never wrong," Sam said.

The courtroom was silent, but not for long. Someone started to clap and others joined in. Judge Kennedy called for order. "This is a court of law, not the Savoy Theatre." He slammed his gavel down. "Court will reconvene at ten tomorrow." He then stood and walked out, smiling to himself.

James watched Mannie approach Sam and whisper in his ear. He then waited for the aisle of departing specators to clear. He looked to the back of the courtroom and spotted Sam's father leaning against the wall. James nodded his approval, then made his way to the defendant's table. "Sam! You were great," James said, slapping him on the arm.

"Thanks. But we've got a long way to go."

"So, what did Mannie say to you?"

"Called me a fucking prick. Sai he was going to bury me, like he did my *Papa*."

"He's angry for sure," James said.

"Yeah, well so am I. God he's a pompous ass," Sam said. He was still shaking.

Sam's father approached them from behind.

"Papa! You're here?"

"I thought if you saw me it might make you more nervous," he said, shaking hands with James. He turned to his son, pulled him into his chest, and wrapped his arms around him. "I'm so proud of you," he repeated, over and over again.

"Thank you, Papa," Sam said.

James watched, thinking he would never get to enjoy such a father-son moment. He smiled just the same.

CHAPTER 2

"You better be fucking right about this," Mannie said, throwing his briefcase on his desk and roughly tearing at the buttons of his heavy, wool coat.

"Don't worry, Mannie. It's all good. Hell, put me on the stand tomorrow. Once the jury hears what I witnessed, there'll be no doubts. Not like you to be rattled," McInnes said.

"What the fuck are you talking about? I'm not rattled. Smartass kid just annoyed the hell out of me. Smug little bastard," he said, plopping down on his chair.

"So, am I up tomorrow?" McInnes asked.

Mannie shot him a look. "What the fuck is wrong with you? You'll get your turn. I need to establish means first."

"Nothing wrong with me. Just anxious to get things movin along. I just want to see those perverts get what's comin to them. That's all."

"Go! Go on. Get out of here!" Mannie said, pointing to the door. "I got work to do."

McInnes didn't budge. "Shit, Mannie. Ya wouldn't even have a case if it weren't for me. And we both know who'll be hoggin all the glory."

Mannie stood and walked toward him. "I'm sorry. You're right," he said, guiding McInnes to the door. "You'll get your moment in the sun. I promise. And, Dan. Don't worry. There'll be plenty of credit to go around."

"So, are ya callin me up tomorrow, or not?" McInnes pressed.

"Probably. We'll see," Mannie said, opening the door.

McInnes started out and turned back. "Mannie? I think this case will finally see me make captain."

"I'm sure of it, Dan," Mannie said. He closed the door, walked back to his desk, and with one fell swoop of his arm, cleared it of all its clutter.

"Fuck!" he yelled.

Friday, November 18

CHAPTER I

"Please Rise."

Judge Kennedy pounded his gavel. "Let's not waste any time. Counselor Chernin, please call your first witness."

"Thank you, Your Honour. The Crown calls Peter Boyd."

Everyone watched as Ten-After-Six tried to stand up straight as he walked down the aisle and took the witness stand. When he sat down, the overflow crowd could only see the top of his head. Mannie merely asked him to recall where and when he made his *gruesome* discovery. Sam declined the opportunity to ask any questions, understanding Peter's version of events was not in question. In the end, it took Ten-After-Six less time to testify than it did for him to make his way to and from his seat.

Mannie then called Dr. Adams. Dr. Adams made it clear that the bruising on the deceased face clearly indicated he was in an altercation prior to the night of November second. He said the deceased injuries included a ruptured spleen, several broken ribs, a shattered patella, and a depressed fracture of the anterior cranial fossa that resulted in brain hemorrhaging. Despite Dr. Adam's best efforts to suggest the nature and location of the victim's injuries were consistent with what one might expect to see following a vehicle-pedestrian collision, Mannie forced him to concede that the injuries could have been caused by a vicious beating with a large object, such as a heavy board.

Judge Kennedy looked at Sam. "Counsellor Friedman? Any questions for this witness?"

Sam checked his notes. There was nothing left to ask that Dr. Adam's hadn't already made clear; he believed the death to be the result of a hit and run.

"No, Your Honour."

James rubbed the back of his neck. He was becoming more and more convinced Sam *was* right. *He really wasn't* cut out to be a lawyer.

"I guess it's back to you, Counsellor Chernin," the judge said.

Mannie stood, looked at Sam, and shook his head. "Crown calls Willie Morrison."

Willie nervously approached the witness chair and did as told. He laid his hand on the Bible and swore to tell the truth.

"State your name, please."

"Dirty Willie," he said.

The courtroom began to snicker.

"Please state your full name?"

"Dirty Willie Morrison?"

The snickers turned to laughter. "Enough," Judge Kennedy said, without the aid of his gavel. "He knows who he is. And we know who he is. Make this quick, counsellor."

Mannie launched in. "Willie? Can you spell your name?"

He slowly drew out every letter. "W... i... l… l… e… i M…s… i… ss... i... r… o… n."

"And you went to school?"

"Yeah. I went to school."

"Do you remember what grade you completed?"

He put his head down, trying to remember, when his sister, standing in the back, hollered, "Grade eight."

Judge Kennedy reminded the spectators they were not to answer for the witness, but acknowledged he'd accept the answer under the circumstances.

"You completed grade eight, yet you can't spell your name?" Mannie said.

"I just did," Willie said, nervously fidgeting.

James could see Stanley rubbing his temples. He felt as bad for his friend as he did for Willie, who was confused by Mannie's questions. He could tell there were some in the courtroom who also felt uncomfortable with what they were witnessing. But most, he thought, found it amusing.

Sam stood up. "Your Honour, is this really necessary? Practically everyone in town knows that my client… that my client was a boxer and that he and Willie—"

"Your Honour," Mannie interrupted, "I'm merely establishing the accused has the means to—"

"I know what you're attempting to establish, counsellor. But like the defence, I'm not sure it's necessary. I'll grant you minimal latitude. But I'm warning you, don't drag this out."

Ten minutes later, Mannie took his seat, grinning from ear to ear. He knew he established beyond a shadow of a doubt that Stanley had a temper, that he did permanent damage to Willie, and that he had the means to kill.

"Does the defence have any questions for the witness?" Judge Kennedy asked.

"No, Your Honour. I believe he suffered through enough," Sam said, glaring at Mannie.

"Very well. Counsellor Chernin, next witness."

"The Crown calls Captain Theodore Collins."

Sam spun around quickly and looked at James. James shrugged. He had no idea why Mannie was calling Ted. James's heart began to pound and his mind race as he thought back to their conversations. His hand and his fight with Johnnie. By the time Captain Collins was sworn in, James began to relax. The two made eye contact, and James knew he could trust this man as well as he could any other.

"Captain? I hear you're a boxing fan."

"I like to watch the odd bout."

"I understand you were present the night the defendant almost killed Willie Morrison?"

"Objection," Sam said, jumping to his feet, but not knowing clearly the grounds for his intrusion.

"On what grounds?" Mannie said, shooting Sam a look. "I merely want to establish that the accused not only had the means to kill, but that he is incapable of controlling his emotions."

"Overruled. Again, counsellor, make it quick," Judge Kennedy ordered.

"Captain, will you confirm that you were present the night the defendant almost killed Willie Morrison?"

"Yes. I saw them box. But I did not witness a deliberate attempt on the part of the defendant to—"

"To what? To rob a man of a promising career and to pretty much ruin his life?" Mannie said, walking to the jury.

"No. To permanently harm him in any way," Captain Collins answered, hoping to make it clear to the jury that he sided with the defendant.

"But the accused did. Didn't he?" Mannie said, throwing his arm in the air for dramatic effect.

"He didn't mean to. The defendant was being goaded. Willie was—"

"Just answer the question. Did you, or did you not, see the accused hit the last witness so violently he can no longer spell his name?"

Collins stared at Mannie. "Mr. MacIntyre—"

"Yes, or no, Captain?"

Collins audibly sighed. "Yes."

"And can you also confirm that in describing the bout to your colleagues, you stated the accused 'snapped?'"

Collins looked at James and didn't immediately answer.

"Captain? Did you say, 'the defendant 'snapped?'" Mannie repeated, slowly drawing out each word.

"I may have. But—"

"One last question. Again, a yes or no will do. Can you confirm that, when the accused damaged Willie Morrison for life, there was no title on the line, no money on the line, and that there were only a handful of spectators on hand to watch what was supposed to be a friendly sparring match?"

"Yes."

"No further questions, Your Honour."

"Counsellor Friedman? Any question of this witness?" Judge Kennedy asked.

Sam had planned on calling Captain Collins to testify about interviewing Eddie, but was thrown off guard when Mannie called him for the prosecution. He wasn't prepared for cross. "Your Honour, I may have questions for this witness at a later time. I am not calling into question his testimony regarding the fight he witnessed, but hope I can recall him to testify about interviewing a key witness for the defence."

Mannie was on his feet. "But, Your Honour! The witness is here now. If the defence wishes to ask him questions about anything related to this case, I would suggest he take the opportunity to do so now, and not waste Captain Collins's time by asking him to return at a later date."

"Actually," Judge Kennedy said, "I'm sure Captain Collins is as interested in seeing justice done as you are, Mr. Chernin, and that he won't mind returning."

Collins looked at Judge Kennedy. "I'd be happy to, Your Honour."

"Very well, then. Permission granted."

Captain Collins left the witness chair, giving James a look of resignation. When he approached the back of the courtroom, he saw Sergeant McInnes smugly staring back at him. Collins decided right there and then, that he had had enough. It was time to move to the country and buy that farm.

Judge Kennedy looked at the clock on the far wall. The Crown had already called four witnesses and the defence hadn't challenged a single one. He was beginning to think the trial would be over by the end of the day. "Counsellor Chernin," he said, nodding at Mannie, "let's get on with it."

"The Crown calls Billy Guthro."

Constable Dunphy escorted Billy to the witness chair. It was the first time James had laid eyes on the man. His nose was out of place, and the yellow and green bruises on his face were a stark reminder he had been on the receiving end of a brutal beating.

"Mr. Guthro? You were escorted here today by the police and you are in custody on charges of arson. Is that correct?"

"Yeah."

"And you know the accused?"

Billy looked at Stanley. "Yeah. I know em," he said dismissively.

"In fact, the accused is responsible for your broken nose and bruises. Is he not?"

"Yeah. And my missin tooth," Billy said, opening his mouth and pointing to the hole where it used to be.

The courtroom began to laugh.

"The accused maintains you burnt his barn and killed his ponies, and that's why he attacked you," Mannie said.

"That's a lie. And he knows it," Billy said.

"And can you confirm for the jury that you heard the accused threaten the deceased the day before he was murdered?"

Sam was quick to his feet. "Your Honour! The question of whether or not the deceased was murdered, or the victim of a hit and run, is still in dispute. As Dr. Adams —"

"Sustained. Counsellor Chernin, watch your language."

"Sorry, Your Honour. Mr. Guthro can you confirm you heard the accused threaten the deceased the day before his *highly* suspicious death?"

Sam threw his pencil down on the desk, grabbing it just before it rolled onto the floor.

"Yeah. I heard him threaten Johnnie," Billy said.

"And where and when did you witness this threat?"

"It was at Johnnie's. On the first. Around five. It was just startin to get dark."

"Johnnie Adshade's, you mean?"

"Yeah. Johnnie Adshade's."

"And you are aware your good friend, Eddie Lynch, has since withdrawn his earlier statement? And that he now claims neither of you witnessed said threat?" Mannie said.

"Yeah. That's just Eddie. He's scared to death Stanley's gonna come after him again. Told me he'd rather go to jail for somethin he didn't do, than tell the truth and end up dead like Johnnie."

"Order! Order!" Judge Kennedy bellowed, as the courtroom started humming.

"And how long after you heard the accused threaten the deceased was it that he attacked you and Eddie?"

"It was the following Monday. Round ten at night."

"So, six days later, he just attacks you out of the blue?"

"Yeah."

"And where was this?"

"Outside Iggies."

"Mr. Guthro? Isn't it true that even though you heard the accused threaten the deceased the day before he was found dead in a ditch, you didn't immediately think it was him?"

"That's right."

"In fact, you went to the police and said it was a group of coloureds?"

"Yeah."

Mannie walked to the jury. "So, you heard one man threaten to kill another, he ends up dead the very next day, and yet you and Eddie Lynch go to the police claiming it was the coloureds. Why is that? Don't like coloured people?"

"Got nothin against the coloureds. Even had one of em over to my place one time. We thought that's what happened. Me and Eddie went to Johnnie's place and he was all beat up. He told us he was jumped by a gang of darkies from the Tar Pits and that he was gonna make em pay for it. We just figured they got to him first."

Mannie returned to the witness stand. "And this was the same night you heard the accused utter his threat?"

"Yeah. Stanley came in while we were eatin the sardine sandwiches Johnnie's daughter made for us. And he and Johnnie had words. Johnnie tells him to get out, leave the girl be, and never come back. Then Stanley shoves em down. Says somethin like, 'Ya won't be in my way much longer. I'm comin for ya.'"

Stanley shook his head and clenched his jaw. He was sorry he hadn't finish Billy off when he had had the chance.

"And where was Johnnie's daughter while this was happening?"

"She was watchin from the other room. Ya could tell she was real scared. She was kinda peekin round the corner. Didn't come out till after Stanley left."

"And then what happened?" Mannie asked.

"Then me and Eddie, we just left."

"And you never gave Stanley a second thought after Johnnie was found beaten to death in a ditch?"

"Not really. We figured Stanley was just being Stanley. We knew he had a temper. We figured he was just blowin off steam. And, like I said, Johnnie told us it was the nig… the coloureds who beat him up."

"But why would the accused wait five days after Johnnie's death before confronting you and Eddie? Why not the next day? And why would he bother at all, when the police were following another lead? Timing of his attack on you boys seems awfully strange to me."

Sam couldn't figure out what Mannie was up to. He seemed to be making the case for the defence. James and Stanley were thinking the same. Judge Kennedy knew better. He had seen Mannie in action too many times in the past. He knew Mannie was dispensing with the evidence he knew the defence would introduce.

"Yeah. But I don't think he came after us just because of the threat," Billy said.

"No?" Mannie asked turning to face his spellbound audience. "If it wasn't because you heard him utter the threat, it must be, as the accused claims, because you set fire to his barn?"

"No," Billy said defiantly, "I already told ya. That's a lie."

Mannie set the bait. It was time to reel in the prize. "Then why? Why would he attack you and Eddie six days after you heard the threat?" he bellowed.

"It was because of what we saw him do to the girl."

"Johnnie's daughter?" Mannie clarified.

"Yeah. Johnnie's daughter," Billy said.

"And what was it you saw the accused do to the deceased's daughter?" Mannie asked, glaring at Stanley.

"Me and Eddie, we saw the girl kneelin in front of him. His pants were down and he was holdin a belt over her head."

Stanley stood and screamed, "You lying little bastard! I should have killed you when I had the chance!"

"Order! Order! Order!"

James could barely hear Judge Kennedy pound his gavel.

"Control the accused! Take the witness back to lockup. This court is recessed until two."

Despite the bailiff encouraging people to leave, not a single person left their seat.

James turned and saw Sergeant McInnes leaning against the wall, staring back.

McInnes curled his fingers into his palm, cocked his thumb back, pointed his finger and mockingly pretended to shoot him. He walked away grinning.

CHAPTER 2

James and Sam sat in James's car outside the courthouse.

"It's all lies. Greasy little bastard. I could kill him," James spat.

Sam tore open his briefcase and whipped out his notepad. "Stanley's outburst sure didn't help. Jesus! Everybody in the courtroom heard him say he wished he had finished him off. Just confirms he can't control himself."

"Who could blame him! I'd like to wring Billy's scrawny, little neck," James hollered. He pounded the dashboard. "Fuck!" He immediately knew his hand hadn't fully healed.

"Calm down. I got less than an hour to prepare for cross and you're not helping," Sam said.

"Sorry," James said. He began digging in his pocket, hoping he'd find a makin. He looked up. Sergeant McInnes and Mannie were outside the courthouse, in deep discussion.

Sergeant McInnes seemed agitated. Mannie reached into his breast pocket and began taking notes. James wanted to kill them, too. He turned to Sam. He was no longer flipping through his notes. He was staring straight ahead. He looked catatonic.

"You okay, Sam?"

"I think Sergeant McInnes and Mannie are coaching Billy."

"I have no doubt of that," James said.

"I don't just mean going over his testimony. I mean telling him what to say. Like the part about walking in on Stanley and Mabel.

There was nothing in Billy's statement about any of that. I think the prosecution made some sort of deal with Billy. Maybe they promised to drop the arson charges if he helped nail Stanley for murder."

"Do you think the jury senses it?"

"No," Sam said, shaking his head, "I think they believe Stanley's guilty."

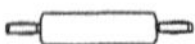

CHAPTER 3

"All rise."

Judge Kennedy reminded Billy he was still under oath, issued his predictable, but unheeded, warnings to the spectators, and called on Mannie to resume his questioning.

Mannie sauntered to the witness box. "Mr. Guthro? Just before recess, you advised that you saw the accused in a… in a compromising situation with the deceased's daughter."

"Yeah."

"And where and when did you witness the situation you are referring to?"

"It was at Johnnie's. Saturday, the fifth. It was about six o'clock."

James could see Sam lean into Stanley. Stanley shook his head from side to side.

"You went to Johnnie's place after he was dead?" Mannie asked, prompting the answer he knew was coming.

"Didn't plan on it. Me and Eddie were headin to the Colliery hockey tourney at the forum and saw smoke comin from the chimney. We figured we'd pay our respects to the girl, given Johnnie was such a good friend n' all," Billy said. He dropped his head.

"What did you do when you came across… the *situation* you described?"

Billy looked up. "I could tell the girl was upset… real upset. So I told Stanley to leave her alone. He just laughed. Said we could each have a go at her."

Sam put his hand on Stanley's shoulder.

"And then what?" Mannie asked.

"Then, I just asked Stanley to leave. He says it ain't none of my business. Tells me and Eddie to get the hell out. The girl was cryin. So I pulled my blade and kinda waved it around like this," he said, demonstrating. "He looked wild. Like he was ready to kill the three of us right there and then. But I stood my ground. Then he just zips up his pants, tells me and Eddie to watch our backs, and storms out."

Mannie looked at the jury for their reaction. They were stone faced. "Then what?"

"Then I comforted the girl. She was shakin like a leaf. I told her we should go to the police, but she begged me not to say anythin. Said she was afraid fer her life. Said she knew Stanley killed her da and didn't want to end up in the ground next to him. I had to swear to her I wouldn't tell the police. Eddie was whimperin like a baby. Kept sayin, 'he's gonna kill us too, Billy.'"

The courtroom was humming. "Quiet!" Judge Kennedy hollered as his gavel came down, missing its base and putting a sizeable dent in his oak desk. "Continue, Counsellor Chernin."

"And it was two days later that the accused attacked you and Eddie?"

"Yeah. We laid low the next day. Eddie was too scared to step outside. I went to his place on Monday. Told him he needed a little somethin to help calm his nerves. I convinced him to come to Iggies with me. Next thing ya know, we're wakin up all busted up."

"And isn't it true that when the accused viciously attacked you boys he admitted he killed Johnnie?"

"Yeah. Just after he sucker-punched Eddie. I said, 'Whatcha do that fer.' He said it was a warnin. Then he said 'if ya don't want me to do to you, what I did to Johnnie, ya better keep yer bleepin mouths shut.' Then he smashed *me* in the face. I got up, but he belted me again. Knocked me out cold."

"Thank you. I have no further questions of this witness," Mannie said. He stared at Sam as he took his seat.

"Counsellor Friedman, I expect you have some questions for this witness?" Judge Kennedy said.

"I do, Your Honour. But I was hoping… I was hoping that given the… the lateness of the day and the testimony of the last witness… I was hoping the defence could have the remainder of the day to prepare for cross-examination?"

Mannie jumped to his feet. "Your Honour. It's still early in the day. I would suggest we get on with things."

"I agree with the prosecution. We've got plenty of time for cross. Continue, counsellor," Judge Kennedy said.

Sam looked despondent. "Very well," he said, his voice cracking. The spectators nervously shifted in their seats. "Mr. Guthro? You are presently being held on charges of arson. Is that correct?"

"Yeah. But I didn't do it. I was at home. Ask my da."

"You know, Mr. Guthro, there's a witness who puts you and Eddie Lynch at the scene the morning of the fire."

Mannie was on his feet. "Objection, Your Honour. We're here to try the accused for murder, not the witness for arson. It would be patently unfair… no… *unjust…* to assume the witness's guilt on a charge for which he has not had an opportunity to mount a defence."

"But Your Honour! Mr. Guthro's testimony is directly related to my client's reason for assaulting the witness. An assault, by the way, my client freely admitted to. It had nothing to do with the deceased's daughter. I maintain it is material to this case," Sam countered.

Judge Kennedy sympathized with the young lawyer, but sided with Mannie. "Still, I believe the prosecution to be right. The witness is presumed innocent until proven guilty. The jury is to ignore any reference to the guilt or innocence of Mr. Guthro in regards to the pending arson trail."

Sam walked back to his desk and shuffled some papers around. "Mr. Guthro? Can you confirm that you are no stranger to this court and that you have previously done time for theft and public intoxication?"

"Don't pretend to be a saint," Billy said, slouching in his chair.

"Yes, or no?"

"Yeah. I got into some mischief. But I don't hurt no one, or threaten to kill em."

"Did you ever threaten Eddie?"

"Eddie?" Billy repeated, as if it were a preposterous question.

"Yes, Eddie Lynch? Ever tell him what to say, or you'd hurt him?"

"No. Me and Eddie are friends. And he ain't got no others. I know he's simple n'all, but he's like a little brother to me. I look out for em. I'd never hurt em."

Sam worried his questions were backfiring and that, instead of undermining Billy's testimony, the jury was starting to sympathize with him.

"Mr. Guthro? When the police were investigating my client for the assault against you and Eddie, did you not tell them you didn't own a switchblade?"

"I remember tellin em I didn't have one on me the night Stanley came after me and Eddie. Don't ever recall tellin em I didn't own one. Lots of people know I pack one for protection."

"So, you and Eddie are afraid for your lives. You're worried my client is going to come after you, and yet, two days after he allegedly told you to watch your backs, you aren't carrying your knife?"

"I thought I had it. I changed my coat just before goin to Eddie's. I fergot it."

"And you *never* told the police you didn't own one?" Sam repeated.

"No. Why'd I do that?"

Sam walked back to his table knowing he wasn't making any headway. He picked up his notes. "Mr. Guthro? As you know, Eddie Lynch has recanted his earlier statement. Said he was with you at Johnnie's the night you claim you heard the threat, but that Stanley wasn't there. That your testimony is all lies?"

"Like I said, he's scared Stanley will come after em again."

Sam needed to go after something else. "Mr. Guthro? I read

the statement you gave to the police. Can you explain why there was absolutely no reference to you mentioning you witnessed the accused in a compromising situation with Miss Adshade?"

"That's cause I just told em this mornin. Like, I told ya. The girl begged me not to say anything. So I didn't. Then, I got to thinkin. As long as Stanley's locked up, he can't do her no more harm. But if he gets away with murder, she'll end up dead like her father. Thought I wasn't doin her any good if he walks and that it was my civic duty to tell em everythin, even if it meant I broke my word."

"So, you sat on this information until you were just about to testify? Rather convenient, don't you think?"

"Like, I said. I made a promise to the girl. Don't feel good bout breakin my word, but I think she'll be grateful in the end."

"Mr. Guthro?" Sam said, leaning into him. "Have either the police or the prosecution promised you anything in return for your testimony?"

"Objection, Your Honour," Mannie said, jumping to his feet. "I assure you—"

"Sit down, Mannie," Judge Kennedy ruled. "The witness may answer the question."

"Ain't no one promised me nothin," Billy said, staring at Sam. "I'm doin this to protect the girl and to make sure that pervert," he said pointing at Stanley, "don't do her no more harm."

"Thank you, Your Honour. I have no further questions for this witness at this time," Sam said, holding Billy's glare.

The courtroom started buzzing again. Judge Kennedy banged his gavel. "I believe the jury has had enough to gnaw on for one day," he said, remembering it was corned beef and cabbage night and feeling a little peckish. "Court will reconvene Monday. Same time. Counsellors Chernin and Friedman, if I can see you in my chambers?"

Mannie and Sam walked into Judge Kennedy's dimly-lit chamber. His desk was bare, except for a notepad, pen, and desk lamp. Piles of papers were stacked on two side tables, as well as the floor. "Have a seat, gentlemen. Counsellor Friedman, Mannie has made an appeal to sequester James Cameron, and I agree with him."

Sam wasn't entirely surprised, but made an attempt to have Judge Kennedy's decision reversed. "Your Honour, James Cameron is an upstanding citizen. A man of God. I assure you he would not—"

Judge Kennedy held up his hand. "I have no doubt of any of that. But given he is a key witness for the defence and will be providing the alibi for the accused, I have no choice but to grant Mannie's request."

James sat in his car outside the courthouse, anxious for Sam to come out. Finally, Sam bounded down the steps and jumped into the passenger seat. James was beside himself when Sam explained the judge's ruling. He told James there was no appeal and that he could return to court after he testified.

They were on the way to the store to talk to Mabel about Billy's testimony. James suddenly slowed down, pulled to the side, and made a U-turn.

"What are you doing?" Sam asked.

"I'm driving you to the station. I need you to get Captain Collins to come to the store after five."

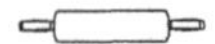

CHAPTER 4

Margaret was hovering over Mark, who was sitting on the counter, colouring. James and Sam walked in. She took one look at them and knew yesterday's good news, was *yesterday's* news.

"Not good?" she asked, taking their coats.

"No," James said, shaking his head. "Sam and I need to have a word with Mabel."

Mabel and Mary Catherine were sitting at the table when they entered the kitchen. Mary Catherine tucked her hair behind her ear.

Mabel jumped to her feet. "How did everythin go today?"

"Not great," James said.

"Mabel, one of the men Stanley assaulted claims you were present to hear Stanley threaten your father," Sam said.

"Well, he's a God damn liar," she said, quickly turning to James. "Sorry, Mr. Cameron."

"No need to apologize," he said. He pulled out a chair and sat next to her.

"I'm gonna go there first thing in the mornin and set em straight," she said, her face red with anger.

Sam explained that the court was recessed until Monday, the prosecution calls its witnesses first, and then he gets to call his. He began to tell Mabel about Billy's claim that he walked in on her and Stanley, but became flustered, leaving it to James to find the right words.

Mabel wanted to kill Billy. "He's a fuckin, filthy, pig," she hissed. This time with no apology. She grabbed James's sleeve. "Do people think it's true?"

James and Sam tried to assure her that that wasn't the case, but with little luck. James watched her twist her tea towel. Her knuckles were white and her face, no longer red, but ashen. "I gotta put things right," she said, looking at James. "Stanley'd never do such a thing."

"I know, Mabel," James said.

Sam looked at Mary Catherine. She was holding her hand over her mouth. He then turned to Mabel. "It'll be alright. I promise. No jury would believe Billy over you."

No one had any tea.

"I should get going," Sam said. "James, you'll drive me home?"

"Of course. I'll give Mabel and Mary Catherine a lift, as well."

"But it's not five yet. I got two loaves in the oven and I haven't tidied up," Mabel said, waving her hand over the counter strewn with flour and unwashed bowls.

"Margaret and I can see to that. No more baking today," James said.

James and Sam waited at the door while Mary Catherine and Margaret struggled to put Mark's boots on.

Mabel came out of the kitchen and handed Sam a pie.

"I want my tin back," she said, and walked outside.

CHAPTER 5

James closed the store and anxiously waited for Ted to show up. It was now going on six. He was pacing back and forth when he saw headlights appear at the top of Caledonia Street. The car turned onto School Street. "Finally," he sighed. But the car continued on. He was looking out the window for another car to appear when he heard the knock.

"Ted."

"I thought it best to park down the street," he said, taking off his coat.

"Thanks for coming."

"Sam said it was urgent."

The two walked to the back of the store. James described being barred from the court as he poured two generous rums.

"I know it's a lot to ask. But I'm hoping you can be my eyes and ears. Sam told me you could come and go as you please."

"I can. But I'm not sure what good it'll do if I'm reporting everything after the fact."

"It's just that, I don't know… I'd feel better knowing you were there. You might pick up on something Sam misses. Don't get me wrong, he's doing good. Real good. But he's up against a bunch of crooked thugs. Sergeant McInnis, Mannie, and that lying little prick, Billy."

Captain Collins took another swig of his rum while he mulled over James's appeal. He didn't think much, if any, good could come from it. He put his rum down and picked up his coat. "What time is court on Monday?"

James stood up. "Ten."

"Judge Kennedy always recesses for lunch. Likely at noon. I'll be at the produce section at Mendelson's around quarter past. Who knows, I might bump into you there," he said.

Monday, November 21

CHAPTER I

Captain Collins arrived at the courthouse to see a large crowd waiting for the doors to open. A fight broke out between two men at the end of the line. Ten-After-Six thrust himself in the middle in an attempt to break it up. Both men swinging wildly at each other, missing Ten-After-Six, whose bent body eluded their punches. Captain Collins made a dash toward them, but held up when the bailiff opened the door, the fighting stopped, and the crowd rushed forward.

Sergeant McInnes sat in the back of the courtroom, thinking how much he loved the view from the witness chair. He tried to contain his excitement, knowing he wouldn't have to wait much longer. At first, he was angry with Mannie for not calling him off the top, but he now realized it was a stroke of genius. Mannie was right. He'd be a strong follow-up witness and keep the momentum going. *Finally*, he whispered, as the bailiff opened the door to Judge Kennedy's chambers and yelled, 'All rise.'

Mannie winked at Sergeant McInnes as he approached the stand. After he had him describe his experience as a respected officer of the law, he asked him to recount his visit to Cameron's store the morning of November third. McInnes said he went to the store to tell the deceased's daughter, Mabel Adshade, that her father had died under suspicious circumstances. He said he was immediately troubled by everyone's behaviour. He said he was in the process of advising Mrs. Cameron of the deceased's death, when the defendant and Mr. Cameron, who claimed they spent the night at the accused's home, drove up. He added that Mrs. Cameron walked off without acknowledging her husband. He then informed the court that the defendant didn't stop to inquire why the police were present and that he immediately drove off. He then said it was at least a half an hour before he returned to the store with the deceased's daughter.

Mannie interrupted from time to time, repeating McInnes's testimony.

"And what was Mr. Cameron doing at this time?"

"It seemed like he was anxious to leave. Like he was trying to avoid me. He insisted I let him tell Miss Adshade about her father, then he waited outside for her and the accused to show up."

"Then what?"

"Then, Mr.Cameron and Miss Adshade walk in the store. I stood to greet her. To tell her about her father. But she and Mr. Cameron both ignored me. They just went directly to the kitchen."

"How long were they gone?"

"At least ten minutes. Maybe fifteen."

Mannie walked to the jury. "And what happened next?"

"Mr. Cameron walks out of the kitchen holding her arm. Looked to me like he had a pretty tight grip on her. Anyway, I proceeded to tell her the facts as I knew them. Her father was found dead in a ditch and that he had bruisin on his face. That his body was with the medical examiner and the death was suspicious."

Mannie rested his hand on the banister of the jury box. "And can you describe Miss Adshade's reaction?"

"She seemed more nervous than sad. Didn't cry or anythin. It was almost as if nothin I said came as a surprise."

"You mean she was aware someone wanted to kill her father? Perhaps had heard someone threaten him?"

"Either that… or she already knew he was dead."

Mannie turned to see the spectators whisper to one another.

"But how could she have known he was dead? The accused

certainly couldn't have told her. You said he didn't bother to stop when he saw you at Cameron's store. That he just dropped Mr. Cameron off and continued on his way."

"He would have known if he was the one responsible," McInnes said.

Judge Kennedy called for order.

Mannie pressed on. "And the accused was present when you told Miss Adshade what happened to her father?"

"Yes."

"And what was his reaction."

"He was sittin on a crate near the window. He had his eyes peeled on her. He just sat there and puffed on his pipe. Like, I said, it was all very strange."

"Did you notice anything else that seemed… odd?" Mannie asked, playing out their well-rehearsed strategy.

"Yes. The deceased's daughter had a bandage on her forehead. And Mr. Cameron's hand was swollen."

Sam knew what was coming. Damn. I should've let James tell them about his hand.

"And did you get an explanation for what caused their injuries?"

"Mr. Cameron said he jammed his hand while working at his store. The deceased's daughter said she was attacked by a dog on the mornin of the storm. Said she fell into a stick."

"Seems plausible. Does it not?"

"On its own, yes. But, like I said, it was the combination of things that made me think things weren't right."

"But, as strange everyone's behaviour seemed, you didn't immediately suspect there was any connection between Johnnie Adshade's death and the defendant?"

"No. Not at the time."

"So, when did you start to suspect the accused?"

"When Billy Guthro and Eddie Lynch walked into my office all busted up and said they witnessed the accused threaten to kill the deceased."

"And the accused never denied assaulting Billy Guthro or his friend, Eddie Lynch?"

"No. In fact, he actually seemed proud of it."

Sam immediately got to his feet. "Objection!"

"Sustained," Judge Kennedy said. He looked at McInnes. "Careful, Sergeant."

Mannie was pacing around the witness stand. "And did the accused tell you why he beat Billy Guthro and Eddie Lynch to the point of unconsciousness?"

"He claims Johnnie Adshade had them set fire to his barn."

"In fact, through earlier testimony, we know they're up on arson charges?"

"That's right."

"Now, with respect to the timing of the threat against the deceased, does the accused have an alibi?"

"No. He claims he was home and that he was alone."

"So, the accused admitted to assaulting the two witnesses who said they heard the threat?"

"Objection," Sam said. "Eddie Lynch has recanted his testimony."

"Sustained."

"So the accused admitted to assaulting two people, one of whom *insists* he witnessed the threat?"

"That's right."

"Is that all he admitted to?" Mannie asked.

"No. He also admitted he hit the deceased on October thirty-first, two days before he was killed."

Judge Kennedy called for order, again.

Gladys Ferguson stood and angrily wagged her finger in Stanley's direction.

Mannie continued. "So, the accused hit Johnnie even before his barn caught fire?"

"Yes."

"Did he say why?"

"He claims he visited the deceased to tell him his daughter was stayin at the Cameron's after gettin caught in the snowstorm. He said the deceased swung a pan shovel at his head. So he hit him, breakin his nose and knockin him out."

Mannie turned to face the jury. "Seems odd to me the deceased would swing a shovel at a man for simply letting him know the whereabouts of his daughter?"

"Yeah. Well, like I said, a lot of things seemed odd."

Mannie walked to the jury box. "The defendant, a former boxer with a known temper, admits to hitting the deceased just prior to his body being found in a ditch. He has no alibi for the night of November first, when the previous witness claims to have heard him threaten Mr. Adshade. And we have Mr. Guthro's testimony that he caught the accused in a questionable situation with the daughter of the deceased."

The murmurs in the courtroom started up. Mannie waited for them to subside and walked to the witness stand. "I assume, Sergeant, that you questioned Miss Adshade about her relationship with the accused?"

"Of course. She claims she was not involved with the defendant, or any other man. But I believe she is actin under duress and that the accused, and possibly others, are threatenin her."

Sam rose more slowly this time. "Objection. Again, Your Honour, this is pure conjecture. What evidence does the witness have to substantiate the deceased's daughter is lying or being coerced?"

"I assure you, Your Honour, the testimony of Sergeant McInnes is relevant in establishing the motive of the accused. And the testimony to follow will substantiate his claims," Mannie said.

"Overruled. I'll allow the testimony to stand, but caution the prosecution and witness against further testimony based on speculation."

"Sergeant? You are aware that while Billy Guthro said he heard the accused threaten the deceased on the night of November first, Eddie Lynch has since withdrawn his statement."

"I am."

"Yet you believe Mr. Guthro?"

"I do."

"And why is that?"

"Well, first I believe my captain, Captain Collins, who interviewed Eddie behind my back, went a little too hard on him. I don't think he appreciated how… how *fragile* Eddie is. Ya see, and I don't mean to sound cruel, but Eddie's… well, he's a little backwards. I think he was just intimidated by the Captain's questions, got confused, and didn't fully understand the consequences of his actions. In fact, I understand he peed his pants during the interview," McInnes said, staring at Collins.

"Is there anything else that has convinced you Mr. Guthro is telling the truth when he said he heard the threat?" Mannie asked.

"Yes. Miss Adshade confirmed Billy and Eddie were at the house the night Billy claims the threat was made. She even said, as Mr. Guthro has testified, that she made them sardine sandwiches."

Stanley and Sam huddled together as the courtroom began to loudly stir.

Judge Kennedy slammed his gavel down. He then recessed for five minutes, allowing time for the court to quiet, and for him to relieve himself. He returned with another stern warning that he would close the proceedings to the general public if there were any more outbursts.

"Good, then. Please continue, Counsellor Chernin," he said to the delight of the impatient gallery.

"Sergeant, you've obviously done a thorough investigation and make a compelling argument that would warrant the charge of capital murder against the accused." Mannie turned from McInnes and pointed at Stanley. "But this man's life hangs in the balance. And as incriminating as your testimony is, much of it is circumstantial. Is there anything more you can tell the court that has convinced you, beyond a shadow of a doubt, that the accused is responsible for Johnnie Adshade's death?"

"Yes. After Billy Guthro and Eddie Lynch reported the threat against Adshade, I started thinkin back to my visit to Cameron's store on the mornin of the third. And then I remembered the car."

"The car?" Mannie repeated, loving the sound of the hushed audience.

"Yes. Mr. Cameron's car. When the accused and Mr. Cameron drove up to the store, it was caked in mud. It was in the wheel rims and splattered over the bumpers and door panels."

Sam leaned into Stanley. "Where's he going with this?"

"I can explain the mud," Stanley said.

Mannie continued to play out the drama. "So the accused drove up in a muddy car. I sometimes drive a muddy car. That doesn't make me suspicious does it?" Mannie asked. He listened to the muffled chuckles and smiled.

"No. But Mr. Cameron told me that he spent the night at Stanley's. That they arrived by six, had a few drinks, played some cards, and went to bed before nine."

"And?" Mannie asked.

"And the roads were dry that day. The only way the car would have dried mud on it the next mornin was if it was bein driven well after nine, when the rain started and the roads got muddy."

"Perhaps the car got mud on it the next morning when they drove to the store?"

"Not possible," McInnes said, eager to drive another nail in Stanley's coffin. "See, the temperature dropped sharply around midnight and it turned to freezin rain. The roads were frozen solid within a coupla hours. That means someone was drivin Mr. Cameron's car well after he claims he and Stanley called it a night."

Sam slouched in his chair and closed his eyes. Jesus! What was happening?

Mannie smiled at the jury. "And this was the same night Johnnie Adshade lay dead in a ditch?"

"The same night," McInnes said.

"One last question, Sergeant. Did you promise Billy Guthro anything in exchange for his testimony?"

Sergeant McInnes spoke loudly and clearly, "Absolutely not."

"Thank you, Your Honour. I have no further questions for this witness."

"Counsellor Friedman. Over to you," Judge Kennedy said.

Sam was thrown by McInnes testimony about the muddy car. Stanley had said he could explain it. And James was adamant he had been with Stanley all night. He wouldn't lie. Everything's moving too fast.

"Counsellor Friedman," Judge Kennedy said more pointedly.

"Yes, Your Honour?"

"Do you wish to cross examine the witness?"

Sam stood, turned, and looked at the clock hanging above the double doors on the back wall. He couldn't believe it wasn't even eleven o'clock. "Your Honour? I was hoping… in light of the time… if it would be possible to recess for lunch?"

Judge Kennedy looked at the clock. "I'm afraid we have another hour to go. Please proceed."

Sam walked slowly to the witness stand. He had to show that McInnes had rushed to judgement and that he was less than thorough. "Sergeant? Isn't it the case that my client told you that Mr. Guthro pulled a knife on him the night of the assault and that he kicked it out of Mr. Guthro's hand?"

"Yes."

"And isn't it also true that you didn't even bother to look for the knife? Because, right from the get-go, you've been taking Mr. Guthro at his word and trying to make his accusations fit your theory?"

McInnes smiled. "Actually, I didn't think the knife was relevant. The accused didn't have any stab wounds. The boys, on the other hand, were beaten to a pulp. Frankly, I didn't see that it would make a lick of difference. I also believed my time would be better spent followin up on other leads."

"But Mr. Guthro lied when he told you he didn't even own a knife. Did he not?"

"Honestly, I don't recall him sayin he didn't own a knife. Just that he didn't have one on him the night he was viciously attacked by your client."

Sam was angry and flustered. He walked to his table, looked down at his notes, thinking every eye in the place was on him. He was right. He turned and walked back to the witness chair.

"Sergeant? Don't you think it odd that Billy Guthro and Eddie Lynch didn't report the so-called threat until after my client discovered they were responsible for setting fire to his barn?"

"Objection," Mannie screamed.

"Sustained."

Sam kept going. "They sit on it for days and do nothing. Then, all of a sudden, they're not pointing at the coloureds any more. They're pointing at my client."

"Like Mr. Guthro testified. They originally thought it was the coloureds. It wasn't until after your client attacked them that they realized how seriously deranged he was. And that maybe his warnin to the deceased wasn't so innocent after all."

"You never once considered they might be trying to discredit my client in an effort to evade the arson charges?"

"Briefly. But then my own observations, along with all the other mountin evidence, suggested they were bein truthful and that their allegations were bang on," McInnes said calmly.

"But, Eddie Lynch says it's all lies. There was no threat. No admission of guilt on the part of my client. The only thing Mr. Lynch says is true, is that he and Billy Guthro started the fire at the deceased's request."

Mannie stood. "Objection. My colleague's comments are straying beyond—"

"Sustained," Judge Kennedy swiftly ruled.

"Sergeant? Billy Guthro claims Miss Adshade heard my client threaten her father. Did you ask her about it?

"I did."

"And?"

"And she denied it. But she did verify Billy was at her house the night he claims he heard the threat."

"But you don't believe her?"

"Like the previous witness, I believe she fears for her life."

"So you take the word of an arsonist—"

"Objection!"

"Withdrawn. A *suspected* arsonist, with a record for stealing and public intoxication, over the deceased's daughter?"

"I believe she's being forced into lyin."

"So, I suppose you don't believe Mr. Cameron either, when he says he was with the accused the night Mr. Adshade was killed?"

Sergeant McInnes saw the opening to create his own drama. "Oh, I believe he spent the night there. I'm just not sure if it was after the accused killed Adshade, or they both did."

The courtroom erupted. Judge Kennedy pounded his gavel. "Order! Order!"

Mannie was furious the little prick stole his thunder.

Sam rushed to the bench, begging Judge Kennedy to adjourn for the day.

Mannie came up from behind, "Your Honour? We have lots of time left. Well over an hour. My time is important. I booked the entire day."

"I'd remind you, counsellor, my time is important, as well," Kennedy shot back. He turned to Sam. "Sorry, son. You can either continue to question Sergeant McInnes, or Mannie will call his next witness.

"Thank you, Your Honour," Mannie said.

Sam stood with his head down. He wished he had never taken the case.

"Counsellor Friedman," Judge Kennedy said with a note of sympathy in his voice, "you do know that you can ask to recall the witness?"

"Yes, Your Honour. Thank you. I have no further questions at this time."

Judge Kennedy dismissed Sergeant McInnes. "Counsellor Chernin?"

"Crown calls Minnie Atkinson."

Sam spoke to Stanley. He had no idea who she was. Everyone turned as the doors at the back of the courtroom opened and Minnie Atkinson walked proudly down the aisle, dressed in her Sunday best.

"Mrs. Atkinson, please tell the court where you live," Mannie began.

"Eight Minto Street."

"You live next door to the deceased and his daughter?"

"I do."

"And do you know the accused?"

"Can't say I know him personally, but I've seen him round plenty."

"And where was that?"

"At the Adshades. Saw him comin and goin all hours of the day and night."

"And was the Adshade girl with him?" Mannie asked, walking to the jury.

"Yes. He'd pick her up in the mornin and drop her off at night. Also saw him lurkin round outside once or twice. Like he wanted to get in, but she wouldn't let him."

Mannie resting his large hands on the brass railing that offered jurors a lofty perch from which to decide the fate of the accused. "So, you've seen the accused pick her up and drop her off? Nothing so terrible about that, is there?"

"No. Nothin wrong with that. But it's the way they were together that caused me concern."

"And what *exactly* do you mean by 'the way they were together?'"

"I just got the feelin things weren't too good. He'd drop her off and she'd stand on the side of the road talkin to herself. Couldn't hear what she was sayin, but I don't think it was anythin good about the man. Saw him laughin at her one day. Then he just sped off. She stood there watchin the car and didn't look at all happy."

Stanley remembered that was the day he said he hadn't tried her pie. He leaned in and whispered in Sam's ear.

"So you think her behaviour suggested… suggested she might be afraid of him?" Mannie asked.

"Objection. The prosecution is leading the witness," Sam called out.

"Withdrawn. So, you believe relations between my client and the Adshade girl were strained?"

"Oh, I got no doubt of that."

"And on the night of November the second, the night the deceased passed, you claim you saw a suspicious car in front of the Adshade property."

"I did."

Sam turned to Stanley. "What the hell is she talking about?" he urgently whispered.

"I'm sorry, Sam. I took James's car."

Sam glared at him. "Does James know?"

Stanley decided he better come clean. "Yes."

Sam was seething. Stanley and James had betrayed him. He couldn't concentrate. He looked to the side wall, saw Sergeant McInnes studying him, and quickly turned away.

"And how, Mrs. Atkinson, did you come to notice the vehicle in question? And why did you think it suspicious?"

"I got up outa bed cause I felt a chill and my good-fer-nothin husband never secures the latch. I knew the door had blown open with the wind and the rain n' all. Then, I spotted the car. I didn't think anythin of it at first. Just thought it was parked there for the night, or broke down. Then, all of a sudden, I saw this orange glow. I watched as it would come and go. And I thought it strange. That's when I realized someone was sittin out in the dark, in the pourin rain, smokin a pipe."

"And what time was this?"

"It was just past eleven," she said, tilting her head, and smiling at her friend in the second row.

"Do you know the model of the vehicle in question?"

"Don't know one of those contraptions from the next," she said.

"And do you have any idea who was sitting in the car you saw parked outside the Adshade property on the night Johnnie Adshade was killed?"

"Never saw their face. But the vehicle was just like the one the accused drove the Adshade girl round in."

"Thank you, Your Honour. I have no more questions for this witness," Mannie said. He walked toward the defence table, leaned in, and whispered in Sam's ear. "I warned ya, kid."

"Any questions of this witness, Counsellor Friedman?" Judge Kennedy asked.

"Yes, Your Honour." Sam was about to stand and quit right there and then. He looked at the clock. It was the longest day in his life. He'd finish out the day, then go see Judge Kennedy. He looked at his notes, none offering any clues as to what to do next.

"Counsellor Friedman," Judge Kennedy said, nodding for him to proceed.

"Mrs. Atkinson? On the night you saw the vehicle in question, you say it was pouring rain?"

"Yes."

"Were there any lights on the street?"

"No."

"Yet, you spotted a *black car* in the rain at night?"

"Yes. It was all shiny. Musta been the light from the moon."

"The light from the moon? On a night it was pouring rain?"

"That's right."

"In the pitch black of night, you could tell it was the same kind of car Mr. MacIntyre occasionally drives?"

"I know what I saw. I also know the accused smokes a pipe," she said, straightening her shoulders.

"So, is that it, Mrs. Atkinson? The accused smokes a pipe, so you assume it was his vehicle out front?"

"I know it was."

"And what kind of vehicle is that again?"

"A big, black one."

The courtroom started to laugh.

"Any idea how many men in this town smoke a pipe and own a big, black car, Mrs. Atkinson?"

"Of course not!"

"Objection, Your Honour."

"Sustained."

"Mrs. Atkinson? Are you aware my client was driving Miss Adshade to and from work because she had frostbite and was ordered by her doctor to limit her walking?"

"How would I know that?" she asked indignantly.

"Well, you seem to be an authority on everything else that's happening in the neighbourhood," Sam said sharply.

"Objection."

"Withdrawn. Can you confirm that your testimony is based on suspicion? And that you have no direct knowledge relating to any conversations between my client and the deceased's daughter?"

"Well, I know what I saw. And what I saw tells me the two had a relationship. And it wasn't a happy one."

"Just answer the question," Sam said, more roughly than intended. He knew better than to treat the grey-haired woman staring back at him with hostility, but fear and frustration displaced all logic.

"No. I guess not."

"No further questions, Your Honour."

Minnie Atkinson dismounted the witness chair, proud that she had fulfilled her civic duty, and delighted by her starring role in the most popular show in town.

Judge Kennedy looked at the clock. "It's close to noon. We'll recess for lunch and resume at one- thirty," he said, preferring a hot lunch at home with his wife, to a cold sandwich alone in his chambers.

Mannie requested they reconvene at two, citing an urgent personal matter he had to attend to. He wasn't about to tell Judge Kennedy it was because he needed to time to track down his next witness and use the element of surprise to his advantage.

Judge Kennedy saw no reason he shouldn't linger over tea and dessert. "Two it is," he said, banging his gavel.

The bailiff took Stanley back to the holding cell, while Sam sat shell-shocked at his desk. He felt like crying.

Despite the extended lunch hour, practically no one in the gallery left. They had come prepared with their brown bagged lunches, their knitting needles, and their tongues laced with the latest gossip.

Captain Collins was on his way out the door when McInnes stepped in front of him. "So, Captain? How's yer day goin?"

CHAPTER 2

James arrived at Mendelson's by eleven forty-five, in case the court recessed early for lunch. He walked up and down the aisles with his empty basket. He looked up from the potatoes and waved to Larry Mendelson. He knew his behaviour must appear suspicious, so he picked up some blood pudding, a box of saltines, and a red apple, that he bit into. He heard the door open. It was Ted. James picked up a turnip and waited for Ted to join him. They greeted each other as if it was a pleasant coincidence they would be shopping at the same time.

"How did it go?" James whispered, anxious for the news.

"We should go to my car," Ted said. "It's parked in Murphy's lot. I'll be there in a few minutes."

Ted purchased three apples. He was about to leave when Mr. Mendelson walked up to him holding James's basket. "He forgot what he came for," he said smiling. "And when you see him, tell him he owes me for the apple he's eating."

Ted opened the door to his Ford, threw the apples in next to James, and climbed in. "You didn't buy anything. And you didn't pay for that apple you're gnawing on."

"Sorry. I'm distracted. What happened?"

Ted told James that Sergeant McInnes laid out a pretty compelling circumstantial case, and that he brought up the cut on Mabel's head and his swollen hand. "James, he suggested you might be involved in Johnnie's death."

"Miserable bastard. Christ Ted! How do I prove I wasn't?" James asked, bringing his fist to his mouth. "Damn it! I should have followed my gut and come clean about hitting Johnnie."

Ted sat sideways with his back against the driver's door and his hand resting on the steering wheel. "Well, if memory serves me correct, I told you not to. So, I haven't helped matters."

"Don't go blaming yourself, Ted. It was my decision."

"Actually, it's the testimony about your muddy car that's more troubling," Ted said, repeating the testimony of McInnes and the Atkinson woman.

James couldn't believe what he was hearing. His head was spinning as he considered the implications for Stanley, then himself. "Christ! Sam must be fit to be tied. He's probably already quit. And who'd blame him."

"So, how did the car end up with mud on it?" Ted asked.

James shook his head. "Stanley went looking for Johnnie after I went to bed."

"And you knew this?"

"No. Not at first. He told me a few days ago. Ted, he didn't have to tell me. But he did. I know he didn't do it. Christ! I should have come forward about my hand, hitting Johnnie, and the car. Fuck!"

"I'm afraid it's too late now," Ted said.

"Did you know Stanley took your car the last time we talked at the store?"

James looked contrite. "Yes. I'm sorry. I should have told you. Stanley admitted looking for Johnnie. But he didn't find him. Ted, he wasn't looking for retribution for his ponies. He thought Johnnie was still beating Mabel. When he picked her up for work, she had blood in her hair."

"And what if Stanley did find Johnnie?" Ted asked.

James looked at him and took a deep breath. "He said he didn't know what he would have done."

"James, I believe you're a good man with good intentions. I'm no longer so sure about Stanley."

James turned quickly to face him. "Then you're wrong! I know him. He wouldn't do it. Ted, no one believed you when you said Isaac Greene didn't kill his son. But we both know you were right. This is the same thing. Police railroading people into believing things that aren't true."

Ted dropped his head, thinking about how McInnes had lied on the stand about the knife and about the rumours he'd spread about his dead friend. He'd have Sam ask him about the knife when he was recalled and hopefully prove McInnes lied. "I admire your faith in your friend. But you can no longer vouch for his whereabouts on the night Johnnie was killed. Jesus, James, the evidence before the court will be hard to surmount. Just don't dig yourself in any deeper."

James sat with the back of his head resting against the seat. His eyes were closed. "I guess it's all up to Mabel now," he said.

"Looks that way. But, James, if the jury believes the Crown's theory that she's lying because she's afraid of Stanley, *or you*, for that matter, then even her testimony might not be enough."

James nodded.

"Look, I better get going. I need to stop at the station before I go back and see what other surprises Mannie has in store for us."

James leaned forward. "So you're not giving up on us?"

"No, James. I did that once and lived to regret it."

CHAPTER 3

Sam looked at the clock that didn't seem to move fast enough, got up from his table, and walked through the side doors into the holding area.

"I'd like to see my client, Stanley MacIntyre," he said to the young constable reading a comic book. Sam was led down the hall and waited outside Stanley's temporary quarters for the heavy door to slide open.

Stanley looked up at him. "I'm glad you're here."

Sam waited for the familiar clang and some privacy. He stared at Stanley with a mixture of hurt and disdain. "You lied to me," he said.

"I didn't tell you the full truth. But I didn't lie."

"Don't fuck with me. You said you didn't kill Johnnie," Sam hissed.

"I didn't," Stanley said calmly.

"Well, you no longer have an alibi, *or* a lawyer. I'm going to see Judge Kennedy to advise him I'm no longer representing you."

"I don't blame you," Stanley said. He sat on his cot with his elbows on his knees and his head down. "But I no longer need one. I'm going to confess."

Sam threw his arm in the air and started to laugh. "See? That's what I mean. I can't trust anything you say. One minute you claim you're innocent. The next, you're going to confess."

Stanley turned on him. "Well, I'm damn well not going to let James go to jail, or hang, for being a good friend. We both know Mannie's going to nail him for misleading the police. And God knows what else. McInnes is already trying to implicate him in Johnnie's death. I'm going to tell them what they want to hear. I took James's car, found Johnnie, and beat him to death with a two-by-four. I'll make it clear James had no idea about any of it."

"They'll hang you," Sam said.

"Better one, than two," Stanley said. He stood and held out his hand. "I don't have the means to pay you for your services, but I'll arrange to transfer my property to you. It should cover the bill. If there's anything left, give it to James. And thank you, Sam. I appreciate all that you've done. You are a good man and a fine lawyer."

Sam shook Stanley's hand, walked to the door, and looked through the iron bars to the grey wall on the other side. What kind of man would sacrifice himself for a friend, he thought. Or think about paying his legal bills, when his lawyer quits on him, leaving him to face the noose. Sam thought of how James described him. *He's a good man. I know he doesn't have it in him.* And then, Mabel. *He's been nothing but kind to me. I would have froze to death if it weren't for him. Billy's a filthy, lying pig.*

Sam turned around and sat back down next to Stanley. "I'm furious with you. And James. But maybe I'm rushing things a bit. My father always says there's no shame in losing, just quitting."

"Thanks, Sam. But I can't let James get in any deeper. It's time to call it quits."

Sam was more convinced than ever that he needed to defend this man to the bitter end.

"Stanley, you're forgetting something. You're forgetting we have Mabel. Let's at least let her do what she's been itching to do. Defend you."

CHAPTER 4

James walked the short distance from Murphy's to his car and drove home. He couldn't stop thinking about what Ted had said. If the jury believed the prosecution's theory that Mabel was acting out of fear, her testimony might not be enough.

He needed some time to think. He pulled in front of the store and walked in. Margaret was waiting on a young couple. She smiled at James, then nodded for him to turn around. Constable Dunphy stood to greet him.

"Mr. Cameron?" he said.

"Yes?"

"Sorry, sir. But you're being called to testify. I've been asked to bring you to the courthouse."

Now?" James asked. "I don't understand. Has the prosecution wrapped up?"

"No. That's who sent me to fetch you."

James couldn't believe it. "Can they do that?"

"I'm afraid they can. I have a subpoena."

"But I'm not prepared… or dressed for court."

"You look better than most witnesses I've seen. I'll drive you there and take you back."

James was reeling. "I'll drive myself."

"Actually, sir, I'd appreciate it if you would let me drive you," Dunphy said.

Margaret watched and worried. She knew James was upset.

James turned to his wife. "I've been summoned to court."

"I'll come with you," she said, rounding the counter.

"No, Margaret. Stay here. I'm sure it's just some sort of formality," he said, knowing it wasn't.

James sat in the back of Dunphy's car. They were on Caledonia Street. "I know he's innocent," Dunphy said.

James looked up from his lap. "What?"

"I said, Stanley's innocent."

"Can you prove it?" James asked, shaking his head.

"No. But I saw the Adshade girl at the jail. If she feared for her life, why would she go visit the guy threatening her?"

"Will you testify?"

"Why do you think I insisted on driving you?" he said, glancing back at James. "Ya know, I told McInnes about the girl visiting Stanley. At first, he threatened me. Said if I told anyone, he'd have my job. Miserable little prick. Then he comes back and apologizes. Says you likely forced her into it, to throw us off."

James leaned forward and patted Dunphy's shoulder. "You're a good man, Dunphy. Thank you. I'll tell Stanley's lawyer," he said, wondering if it was still Sam, or if he had quit by now.

"I'll also tell the court McInnes lied about the knife. I heard Billy say he didn't own a knife. So did McEwan, although he's not likely going to say anything against McInnes. Anyway, not sure if any of this will do a hell of a lot of good, but it can't hurt."

They pulled up to the courthouse. James got out, rounded the front of the car, and walked up to the young constable. "I wish there were more good men like you."

"Likewise," Dunphy said.

They entered the courthouse. The courtroom doors were closed. Dunphy led James into a small office. "Afraid you'll have to bide your time in here till court reconvenes. I'm sure it won't be long. Good luck."

CHAPTER 5

"Please rise."

Judge Kennedy took his place and immediately began to question his decision to have a second helping of rabbit stew for lunch. He farted, grateful his thick, black robe would contain the evidence of his offense.

"Counsellor Chernin? Carry on," he instructed.

"Crown calls," Mannie paused… "James Cameron."

Sam slumped back in his chair when James was led in. Fuck you, Mannie. You bastard, he thought.

Stanley leaned into Sam. "I don't want this to go—"

"No," Sam said curtly.

James placed his hand on the Bible and swore to tell the truth, the whole truth, and nothing but the truth. He sat down.

"Mr. Cameron? Would you describe the accused as a friend?" Mannie started.

"No," James said, his voice cracking from the nerves constricting his throat. He looked directly at Stanley. "I'd say he was a *good* friend."

"Very well. And would you agree you're here as what we call a hostile witness?"

"I'm here to testify to what I know. To tell the truth."

Mannie smiled. "Of course you are. In fact, you're here to provide the alibi for accused? Isn't that right?"

"Yes," James replied, clearing his throat for the second time.

"How long have you known the accused?"

"About ten years."

"And he spends a lot of time at your store?"

"Yes. He stops by regularly."

Mannie leaned closer to James. "And you know the deceased's daughter?"

"Yes. She works as a baker at my store."

"And how long has she been in your employ?"

"Going on two months."

"Can you confirm that you hired the deceased's daughter even though she had no previous experience as a baker?"

"I did."

"And can you confirm that you didn't interview any other candidates for the job?"

James wondered how he would know this, then realized it must have been Gladys Ferguson, who was nodding her approval of Mannie's questions.

"That's correct."

"And why is that?"

"Because I was a good friend of her mother's."

"The mother is dead? Died about ten years ago?"

"Yes."

"And yet, after all those years, you still thought about the welfare of her daughter?"

"Yes."

"You and the deceased's wife must have been *very* good friends?"

"We were."

"Were you more than friends? I mean, did you have intimate relations?"

"No."

"Did you want to?"

James was getting angry and Mannie knew it. "Did you want to have more than a friendship with the deceased's wife?"

"I was young. I had a boyhood crush on her," James said, lowering his head and squeezing his hands together.

"And how would you describe your relationship with the deceased?"

"I didn't care for him," he said, thinking no one needed to know he was talking about his half-brother.

"Would you say you hated him?"

"I'd say… I strongly disliked him."

"Were you sorry to hear he was dead?"

James paused. "No. But that doesn't mean I wished him dead."

"You weren't sorry to hear the deceased was dead? Was that because he married the woman you had… *a boyhood crush on*?"

"No. Because he was a brute who didn't treat his wife well and regularly hit his daughter."

"So, on the night the deceased was murdered? Sorry, Your Honour. On the night the deceased died under *suspicious circumstances*, where were you?"

"I was at Stanley's."

"Do you make it a habit of staying at Stanley's overnight?"

"No."

"So, how often would you say you spend the night with the accused? Once a month? Twice a year? Five times a year?"

"It was the first time."

Mannie turned to the jury. "It was the first time you stayed with the accused. The first time in the ten years since you've known the accused, and it just happens to be on the night Johnnie Adshade was killed. Did you have your vehicle?"

"Yes." James knew what was coming, but didn't know how to stop it. "I had some rum and just got tired."

"How much rum?"

"I'm not sure."

"You're not sure?"

James hesitated. "I don't remember."

"Would you say you were intoxicated?"

"Yes."

"In fact, Sergeant McInnes told me that on the morning of November third you reeked of alcohol? A substance, I will remind the jury, is prohibited by law in this town. And the accused, was he drinking?"

"He had a glass or two."

"So why didn't Stanley just drive you home?"

"My wife and I had an argument. That's why I was staying with Stanley."

"Over what?"

James looked at Judge Kennedy. "Answer the question," the Judge said, as anxious as every other person in the room to pry into the private affairs of the reluctant witness.

"She misinterpreted my relationship with Mabel."

The courtroom started to stir. "Order," Judge Kennedy bellowed.

"And were you involved with her?"

"No. She's like a daughter to me. I made a promise to her mother to watch out for her. Margaret, my wife she…she just misinterpreted things."

Mannie turned to the jury. "So, you stayed with Stanley because your wife accused you of having relations with the deceased's daughter? The daughter of a woman you once cared deeply for?"

James didn't answer. He didn't need to.

Mannie continued. "Who who went to bed first? You or Stanley?"

"I did."

"And what time was that?"

"Just before nine."

"And the accused?"

"I don't know."

Mannie walked back to his table. Things were going exactly as he had hoped. "So, you went to bed before the accused and have no idea when he did. Was it possible the accused could have left, even taken your car to go look for the deceased?"

"Look, I know Stanley. He's not capable of hurting anyone."

"Tell that to Willie Morrison, Billy Guthro, and Eddie Lynch. Again, was it possible for Stanley to have left his home to seek out Johnnie without you knowing?"

"I'm a light sleeper."

"Even after, as you say, you were intoxicated?"

"Yes," James said, feeling his mouth go dry and wishing he had some water. He knew the moment of reckoning was fast approaching.

"I gather you have some experience…I mean, when it comes to being inebriated?" Mannie said. He looked at the jury. More than a few of them had their eyes cast downward. Best to leave this one alone, he thought.

James squeezed his hands into fists.

"So, you arrived at Stanley's around six, drank for a couple of hours, and spent the night?"

"That's right."

"And Stanley was there the entire time you were?"

James looked at Stanley. Stanley smiled, gave him a knowing nod of encouragement, and put his head down, waiting for the courtroom to explode.

"Yes," James said.

Stanley's head shot up. He leaned into Sam. "What's he doing?"

"Protecting his friend," Sam whispered.

Stanley looked at James and mouthed, *no.* It was already too late.

Captain Collins stood at the back of the courtroom, remembering James telling him he wouldn't lie under oath. He wished he had been as trusting and loyal a friend to Isaac, as James was to Stanley.

Mannie continued. "Mr. Cameron? On the night in question we have a witness who claims they saw a car similar to yours parked in front of the Adshade's home, and that the man driving it was smoking a pipe?"

"It wasn't my car," James responded. He knew he had already committed a mortal sin by swearing a falsehood before God. Whatever damage he could do to his soul, was done. There was no turning back.

"And you claim that there is absolutely no possibility that the man in the car Minnie Atkinson testified she saw on the night the deceased was killed was your good friend Stanley MacIntyre?"

"None."

"How can you be so sure? You claim you were intoxicated and went to bed before the accused."

"Because the keys to my car were in my pants pocket when I went to sleep and they were there when I woke up."

Stanley couldn't bear to look at his friend. He was overwhelmed by James's loyalty, but angry at him for lying. He wanted to stand and shout that he was guilty, that he killed Johnnie, and be done with it. He rubbed his temples, knowing that he was heading to the gallows, and James to jail.

Mannie knew James was lying, but he didn't have him pegged for being stupid. He turned and smiled at the jury, repeating James's testimony. It was time to go for the kill.

"Sergeant McInnes testified that when you and the accused pulled up on the morning of the third, your car was caked in mud?"

"Is there a crime in that?"

"No. But there is for perjury," Mannie shot back. "You see, Mr. Cameron? The only way your car could have had mud on it, was if someone was driving it in the rain. And the rain didn't start until well past nine. Well after you claim you and the accused were tucked in for the night."

James would put his faith in a merciful God and his trust in Mabel. "I took the car," he said, staring directly at Mannie.

Again, the courtroom was buzzing. Mannie started to feel bad for thinking McInnes jumped the gun in accusing James of being involved in Johnnie's death.

"*You* took the car?" Mannie repeated, the surprise in his voice evident to everyone.

Sam could feel Stanley's elbow dig into his side.

"We have to stop him," Stanley said.

"It's too late now," Sam whispered.

James could feel his heart race and struggled to show a calm exterior. He looked Mannie in the eye, speaking slowly and evenly. "Yes. I woke up and felt guilty about my argument with Margaret. I decided to go home. But when I got there, the place was in darkness. I was afraid I would frighten her, so I turned around and went back to Stanley's. I think the rum clouded my thinking."

"And what time was this?"

"I don't know. It was late. The roads were wet, but it had stopped raining. Maybe eleven, or a little later."

"You previously testified you were at Stanley's the entire night."

"No, sir, *I did not,*" James said. "You asked me if Stanley was there the entire time I was. And he was."

Mannie leaned in closer. James could see the blue veins bulging at his temple.

"But you conveniently neglected to mention that you left?"

"No. *You* neglected to ask if I did. I was only gone for about fifteen minutes at most. Certainly not enough time for Stanley to leave his place, track down Johnnie, beat him to death, and climb back into bed. I answered the question you asked of me."

Mannie was as mad at himself, as he was at James. He needed to be more precise in his questioning. He needed to nail the bastard.

"You do know you have sworn an oath to tell the truth and that, it's not only a sin to put your hand on the Bible and tell a falsehood, it's a crime punishable by law?"

"I do," James said, bracing himself for the next question.

"Mr. Cameron? On the morning of November third, the morning after Johnnie Adshade was killed, Sergeant McInnes noted you arrived back at your store with the accused, and that your hand was badly swollen. How did you say you came to hurt it?"

James looked down. He believed that God would forgive him for selflessly lying to protect an innocent friend. He wasn't so sure he'd forgive him for lying to protect himself.

"I hit Johnnie Adshade."

"Order! Order! Order! The witness may stand down. Everybody

out! Court dismissed until tomorrow at nine," Judge Kennedy said, pounding his gavel. He eventually gave up, threw it on his desk, and walked out.

Stanley gave James a look of despondence, mixed with guilt and regret, as the bailiff whisked him out the side door.

Mannie threw his papers in his briefcase and snapped it shut. He walked up to James as he was stepping out of the witness box. "I don't care who you are. No one in my town gets away with murder."

James approached the defence table. "Sam," he said tentatively, "I'm glad you didn't quit. I'm sorry we didn't —"

"Didn't what?" Sam said, turning sharply. "Trust me? Fuck! You two hung me out to dry," he hissed; his boyish features evaporating into thin air. "I almost quit. Only reason I didn't was because Stanley was going to confess. And for some crazy reason, I don't believe he did it."

"*Confess*," James repeated.

"Yeah. So you wouldn't get in any more trouble. Then you go and create your own. What the hell were you thinking?"

"I'm sorry, Sam. You have every reason to be angry," James said.

"You're damn right I do!" he said, followed by a string of words James could only assume were Yiddish curses.

They both turned at the sound of the double doors opening. It was Sergeant McInnes.

"Not disturbin you boys, I hope," he said, rummaging around in the back. He bent down and picked up a small, black notebook. He waved it in the air. "Wouldn't wanna forget this. Oh, and Jimmy? How's that hand of yers?"

They waited for him to leave. Sam looked around to make sure no one else was within earshot. "I thought you said you weren't going to lie under oath. 'Sam. Sam. I won't lie. I just can't,'" he whispered angrily.

"I'm sorry. It's just…just the evidence was piling up on Stanley. It was a split-second decision. I just thought that if we undermined the testimony about the car, Stanley would have a fighting chance.

I know Mabel's testimony will put the rest of the prosecution's case in doubt."

They turned again as the cleaning lady entered with her mop and bucket.

"Sam? Let's go to the store where we'll have some privacy? I'll fill you in on what Dunphy told me. We can prepare for tomorrow."

"What did Dunphy tell you?"

"I'll tell you at the store. You can have some of Mabel's pie."

"I need some time to think. I'll meet you there in an hour."

"Good," James said. "And, Sam, I really am sorry. So, I'll see you shortly?"

"Yes," Sam said. He opened his briefcase. "Damn it."

"What?" James asked, turning back to him.

Sam waved him on. "Nothing. Just remembered I forgot Mabel's tin."

CHAPTER 6

Dunphy was driving James back to the store when they spotted Mabel on School Street. "Pull over," James said, rolling down the window. "Mabel? C'mon back to the store. I'll drive you home."

"I'll drive her home," Dunphy volunteered.

"Thanks, Mr. Cameron. But I'm lookin forward to the walk. Things go good today?"

"It was an interesting day," James said.

Dunphy smiled, thinking it was a curious way to describe the day's events.

"I have to go back to court in the morning. Don't worry, I'll have the stove ready for you when you arrive," James said.

Mabel waved. "Good night, Mr. Cameron."

"Good night, Mabel."

James watched Dunphy drive off and started to secure the shutters.

Margaret poked her head outside. "Another bad day?"

"Afraid so," he said, dreading the thought of telling her what happened.

"Did you testify?"

"Yes. I have to go back in the morning," he said, walking past her and into the store. "Sam's coming by shortly. We need to go over my testimony. I'm going to wash up. I'll fill you in over supper."

James tried to get his emotions under control. He wished he

hadn't had to lie under oath, but he didn't regret it, either. He knew Stanley didn't kill Johnnie. It was the right thing to do. "Damn it," he said. He sat down heavily on the side of the bed and picked up Margaret's Bible. A bookmark opened to Isaiah: 43.

> *I, even I, am he who blots out your transgressions, for my own sake, and remembers your sins no more. Review the past for me, let us argue the matter together, state the case for your innocence.*

James knelt beside the bed, remembering the night he had begged God to make his son better. He hadn't answered his prayers then. He prayed this time would be different.

Dear God. Forgive me for doubting your merciful bounty and for my many sins. You are witness to my transgressions. Lord, I pray you know my heart was pure in intent and that I strive to live my life according to your will. I pray you see my willful sin was not against you, but the actions of Godless men. Dear Lord, forgive me. Grant me strength. Protect me, and those I love, from evil. And help us stay true to you and the teachings of your holy church.

He walked to the basin, splashed some cold water on his face, and returned to the kitchen.

Margaret stood at the sink, with her back to James, as he told her he had to testify to their argument and the reason for it.

"So, everyone in the courtroom knows we were having trouble and that I accused you of being unfaithful?" Margaret said.

"Yes. And I have no idea what will be reported in *The Post*."

"Dear Lord. Our private lives laid bare for everyone to read about," she said, staring out the kitchen window into the dark.

"I'm sorry, dear. I made a terrible mess of things."

Margaret turned, walked to the table, and sat beside him. "No, James. If I wasn't so quick to judge you and Mabel, this would never have happened. I have no one to blame but myself."

"Margaret, none of this would have happened if it weren't for Johnnie Adshade. We just got caught up in his ugly saga." He closed his eyes, knowing he still had to tell her he perjured himself. He worried she might be less forgiving than God and that no amount of novenas would satisfy her efforts to save his soul.

"Margaret, I lied under oath," he said bluntly.

Margaret put her head down and listened as he explained his lie.

"I'm sorry," he said.

She looked up at him. "So, how much trouble are you in?"

"I'm sure Mabel's testimony will convince the jury the charges against Stanley are just nonsense and that everything will be fine." He stretched his hand across the table. Margaret picked it up and brought it to her mouth. "You did what you had to," she said, and kissed it.

CHAPTER 7

Stanley picked up the sketchpad Dunphy had dropped off, trying to transfer the image from his mind onto the paper. He dropped it beside his bed, in favour of *The Great Gatsby*. He decided Gatsby wasn't so great after all and threw the book roughly across his cell.

He couldn't concentrate. His mind kept returning to James on the stand, lying for him. He laid down, doubled up his pillow, and turned on his side. He couldn't stop thinking of the anguish he had caused his friend, wondering why James had put such trust in him. For all James knew, he could be lying. He was torn by the gratitude and love he felt for his friend, but angry at James for betraying his own faith, his own convictions. Damn it, he thought. I didn't expect you to lie. I didn't want you to lie.

He tossed and turned on the squeaky coil mattress stained with the vomit and piss of those held for lesser crimes, and feared what was to become of them both. Wondering what other unwanted surprises would unfold.

He had no idea, that while he was praying for God to help his friend, Mabel was reading her summons to appear in court for nine the next morning.

CHAPTER 8

Mabel silently cursed Sam. "Why didn't he give me more notice? Now I'm gonna fall farther behind on my orders."

Amour shrugged and sifted through her wardrobe to find something decent for Mabel to wear. She had four different outfits spread out over the bed, but Mabel was reluctant to try on any of them, claiming they were all too lovely for the likes of her. Amour finally succeeded in convincing Mabel to put one on and to allow her to properly fix her hair. Mabel played along, till Amour reached for her makeup bag and approached her with a tube of lipstick. There would be no convincing this time. Mabel jumped from her chair, stripped down to her slip, and quickly threw her frock back on. Amour began to laugh as Mabel grumbled something about not looking for a man. It was a welcome, lighthearted moment that distracted them from the seriousness of the day to follow. Amour held the lipstick tube up, put the cap back on, and threw it on the bed. "You don't need it anyway. You're prettier than any model in any magazine." She studied Mabel, who was sitting on the bed, obviously lost in her thoughts.

"Don't worry about tomorrow. Just answer their questions truthfully and everything will be fine," she said. She walked over and tucked an errant strand of her niece's hair behind her ear. Mabel leaned forward and hugged her.

"I don't know how I'd cope without ya. Ya've been a godsend. But Amour, I ain't never gonna wear no lipstick."

Tuesday, November 22

CHAPTER I

Sam woke, his mind still clouded by the jumbled images of his dream. James had been his client, he was cross-examining Willie Morrison, and his father was the judge. He rubbed his eyes and looked at the clock. His heart was racing, knowing he would soon be back in court. This would be his last murder trial. Never again, he vowed. He brought the straight razor to his chin and brought it down over his invisible stubble. His hand was shaking. He tried to steady it with his other hand, but nicked himself. *Shtup,* he swore, dabbing at the stubborn bead of blood that wouldn't stop oozing.

When he went downstairs, his father was sitting at the kitchen table in dress pants and an undershirt, eating porridge.

"Your mother and sisters are at the synagogue. There's some shakshuska in the oven."

"Thanks, but it'd probably just come back up in court," Sam said.

Sam's father looked into his near empty bowl. "But I saved it for you. And you won't do your client any good if you get sick."

"Not doing him any good in any event," Sam said, struggling to get his rubbers over his shoes.

Sam's father pushed his porridge aside, picked up a tea towel, and took the hot pan out of the oven. "By the way, old man Chisholm came by to pay you. Money's on the table. I should get half of it. I had to listen to him rant about the MacGillvary kid for close to an hour. The old man said he stopped in to collect his damages, and he saw the kid's car pulling out. Apparently, it was all banged up. He says the kid's a menace."

"Papa? Do me a favour?" Sam said, buttoning his coat. "Can you make some inquiries? See if anyone reported another accident involving the kid's car?"

"Yes. But why?"

"Might be able to represent the other driver if the MacGillvary kid was responsible. God knows, I'm going to have to beg for new clients after the trial is over," Sam said from the doorway.

CHAPTER 2

James walked into the kitchen. Margaret was sitting at the table wearing the clothes she normally reserved for church and special occasions.

"I'm coming with you," she said.

"Are you sure?"

"I am."

He walked over and kissed her. "I'd like that."

James looked at the clock. It was after eight. "Not like Mabel to be late."

They waited until eight forty-five, before they closed the store and headed to the courthouse.

Margaret and James walked into the courtroom arm-in-arm. They could hear the murmurs, and watched as practically every head turned and peeled their eyes on them. Margaret spotted Gladys Ferguson, who swiftly looked away.

James led Margaret to her seat. "Thank you," he whispered and squeezed her hand.

"Please rise."

"Mr. Cameron? Please return to the witness chair," Judge Kennedy directed. "As you know, you're still under oath. Continue, Counsellor Chernin."

Mannie walked to the jury box, summarizing Sergeant McInnes's observations, and then James's explosive testimony from the day before. He pointed out that James had originally told the police a very different story about how he'd hurt his hand, and that he knowingly mislead the police when he told them he had been with the accused the entire time on the night of November second. He introduced the theory that James was not just a loyal friend of the accused, but perhaps had been with him when he brutally attacked the deceased, maybe even participated. Sam tried to object, but Judge Kennedy likewise was beginning to think it was a good possibility.

He then approached James. "Mr. Cameron? Yesterday you said that, along with the defendant, you also had a run in with the deceased just prior to his death. Could you please inform the court what caused you to strike the deceased?"

"I knew him to have a bad temper and to beat his daughter. I believed him to be responsible for a nasty gash on Mabel's forehead that Dr. Cohen had to stitch up. I asked Stanley to tell Johnnie that Mabel was at the store, safe n' sound, and that's when Johnnie swung a pan shovel at his head. The next day, I went back with Stanley to tell him never to hurt Mabel again, or I'd go to the police."

"Did the deceased's daughter tell you her father was responsible for the cut on her head?"

"No. She said she fell into a stick."

"So, you're claiming she was lying?" Mannie said, turning back to the jury.

"I believe she was trying to protect her abusive father."

"From whom?"

"From me. She knew I would speak to him about it. Maybe go to the police."

"Why didn't you go to the police?"

"I thought my warning him might be… more effective."

"Did he swing at you?"

"No."

"So, why did you hit him?"

"Because he said some vile things to me about Mabel and my wife. Accused me of things."

"What things?"

James put his head down. "He accused me of doing things to his daughter."

"And were you?"

"Of course not," James said. He felt his face get hot.

"But the deceased thought so? And your *wife* thought so?"

"The deceased was a…" James paused.

"A what, Mr. Cameron?"

"A vile man," James said, trying to put the image of his angry mother out of his mind.

"So, like the defendant, you snapped?"

"He provoked me."

"I think we can take that as a yes, Your Honour," Mannie said, looking from James to Judge Kennedy.

"I hit him once. Then Stanley and I left."

"Must have hit him pretty hard, given your hand was badly swollen the next day. Mr. Cameron? Isn't it true that after you and your wife lost a young son a couple of years ago, your relationship floundered?"

Stanley was on his feet before Sam. "You miserable, hateful bastard!" he shouted at Mannie.

It took several minutes for the courtroom to settle. "Your Honour," Sam shouted, "I have no idea what the prosecution hopes to gain by this line of intrusive and hurtful questioning, but *surely* it has nothing to do with the matter at hand."

James pinched his eyes with his thumb and forefinger, then looked at Margaret. She smiled and nodded. He knew she was feeling hurt and shame. He wanted to run to her.

"Sustained," Judge Kennedy ruled.

Mannie walked to the bench. "Your Honour, the deceased can't speak for himself. The witness just testified Mr. Adshade accused him of having a sexual relationship with his daughter. I'm merely questioning him about a matter that is common knowledge. Their relationship was strained and —"

"Counsellor! This is a court of law, not a torture chamber," Judge Kennedy fumed. "The witness has already testified he was not in a relationship with the deceased's daughter. Christ, Mannie, you really tick me off at times."

Mannie looked at the jury, then returned to the witness stand.

James wanted to grab him by the throat.

"Mr. Cameron? Were you present when the accused killed Johnnie Adshade? And did you help him?"

"I had nothing to do with Johnnie Adshade's death. Neither did Stanley."

"One last question. Have you ever threatened the deceased's daughter, either with physical harm, or dismissal, if she did not do as you said?"

"No. I would never hurt *or* threaten Mabel."

Mannie was satisfied he convinced the jury, along with Judge Kennedy, that Cameron was lying. His past relationship with the deceased's wife. His troubles with his own. His encounter with Adshade. The muddy car. His last minute confession that he wasn't at the accused's the entire night. Mannie was sure he had done more than enough. He'd get one conviction out of the way, then charge Cameron with perjury. And, if all went well, accessory to murder.

"Thank you, Your Honour. I have no further questions for this witness."

"Mr. Friedman?"

"Thank you, Your Honour," Sam said, approaching James.

"Mr. Cameron? Could you please tell us why you have taken such a special interest in Mabel Adshade's welfare?"

James recounted his visit to Pleasant Bay when Ellie was dying and the promise he made to her. He had difficulty speaking at times, his voice cracking when he recalled seeing her struggle to walk. He cried openly when telling the court that he had only returned once after that.

Mannie was convinced that it was all an act to garner the sympathy of the jury.

"In fact, Mr. Cameron," Sam continued, "you have a letter with you here today from the wife of the deceased, Miss Adshade's mother, conveyed to you by my father, Samuel Friedman, whom Ellie Adshade visited prior to her death?"

"I do."

"Could you please read it to the court?"

James reached into his inside pocket, carefully pulled it out, and gently unfolded it. His hands were shaking.

> *"My dearest James. When you read this letter, you will know that I am at peace. I hope you will forgive me for my many transgressions. I hope you understand why I failed to post the many letters I wrote to you and Percy while you bravely served our country overseas."*

He stopped to clear his throat.

> *"I have instructed Mr. Friedman to place in your trust a small sum of money that I hope you will use in whatever manner you feel appropriate to help my beautiful girl. I know that, when you get to know her, you will love her as I do. It is only you, and you alone, that I trust to carry out my final wishes. I fear Johnnie's demons would lead him to put it to uses that would not be to Mabel's advantage. Please know that I have always loved you dearly. May God bless you and grant you a long and joyful life. Until such time as the Misfits are reunited, you have my eternal gratitude and never ending love. Ellie."*

The entire courtroom sat hushed as James lowered his head. Sam waited for everyone to absorb the scene and for James to collect himself.

Mannie was concerned, but gave an air of confident detachment.

"Thank you, Mr. Cameron. Can you please read the date noted on the letter?"

"June eleventh, nineteen twenty-two."

Sam took the letter from James and handed it to Judge Kennedy. "Mr. Cameron? How much money did Mabel's mother entrust to you, and what did you do with it?"

"Just a little over three hundred dollars. I used it to purchase the Adshade property from Roddy MacPherson."

"And isn't it true, that unbeknownst to the deceased, you let him and his daughter live in a house you held title to, rent free for the past three years?"

"Yes."

"Why?"

"Because, I thought it was in Mabel's best interests. She had previously been living in a rat-infested flat with her father. I knew Ellie would like to see her… living in proper quarters."

"But why not just tell the deceased?"

"He wouldn't stay there with Mabel knowing the house was in my name."

"And why is that?"

"He hated me. He'd rather pay a handsome sum to live in squalor than live in a decent home I held title to."

"And why did you hire Miss Adshade without references or experience?"

"Because I felt guilty for not keeping my word to her mother. For not watching over her as I should have. I was trying to make amends."

"And how would you describe your relationship with Miss Adshade?"

"She's like a daughter to me."

Sam then questioned James about why he lied to Sergeant McInnes about how he hurt his hand. James told the court he thought it was an innocent enough lie at the time. He said when Sergeant McInnes showed up on the morning of the third, he immediately began asking him questions that he simply felt were none of his business. He said that when he found out the police were investigating the coloureds, he told Dr. Adams he was responsible for the bruises on Johnnie's face. That they both went to tell Sergeant McInnes, but things got away from them when they hauled Stanley in in cuffs.

"Yes, I lied to Sergeant McInnes. I regret that. But I told the jury the truth. I hit Johnnie for what he said to me and for what he was doing to his daughter."

"I have no further questions, Your Honour."

Mannie stood. "Permission to redirect, Your Honour?" Mannie asked, as he walked to the jury with a broad smile. He knew James's testimony had won their sympathy. He needed to poke it full of holes.

"Proceed."

"Mr. Cameron? Are you saying you purchased the Adshade property for a little over three hundred dollars?"

"No, that's the sum Ellie left in my trust. I invested it the *Light and Power Company* and almost doubled its value. I cashed in the stock and bought the property from Roddy on the condition he remain quiet about the sale."

"And can you prove ownership?"

"I can," James said, pulling the deed from his pocket and passing it to Mannie.

"So, how much did you pay Roddy MacPherson for the property?"

"Almost six hundred dollars."

"*Really? S*ounds like a ridiculously modest amount for a property in relatively good repair so close to town."

"I got a bargain."

Mannie huffed in exaggerated disbelief. "You got a *bargain* from Roddy MacPherson? Well, you must be the first man in town?"

Practically everybody in the courtroom laughed, including Judge Kennedy.

James looked at Ted, who was standing in the back of the courtroom. "I believe Roddy was anxious to dispose of the property and to get out of town in a hurry."

"And why is that?"

"I believe he killed David Greene."

The courtroom once again broke out into chaos. Judge Kennedy pounded his gavel.

James had no idea Mannie's questions would provide him the opportunity to hopefully clear Isaac Greene's name, but pounced on the opportunity.

Mannie threw his arms into the air. "Your Honour! I have no idea what the witness is trying to accomplish here," he said brusquely. "The Greene boy's case was put to rest years ago. The witness is deliberately trying to divert attention away from his own involvement in the case before us."

Judge Kennedy called for order and a half hour recess. Everyone remained glued to their seats.

James left the stand, walked up to Margaret, and kissed her on the cheek. "Are you okay, Margaret? I understand if you don't want to stay."

"I'm here for the duration," she said firmly.

Sam motioned for James to follow him and the two left to find a secluded spot to confer. They could see a long line of latecomers circle around the courthouse and up McKeen Street; all anxious for their chance to witness the drama unfold.

Sam kicked at the ground. "I think your testimony made a favourable impression on the jury. You certainly won their sympathy."

"Thanks. But I need more than their sympathy. I need them to believe me," James said. He put a makin in his mouth.

"I had no idea you were going to implicate Roddy in David's death," Sam said.

"Neither did I. Lucky break," James said, patting his pockets for his lighter.

"He was my cousin. Sophie, David's mother, was my grandmother's only sister. She left everything to my father when she died."

"I had no idea," James said.

Ted walked up beside them and opened his box of Eddy matches.

He struck one against the rough emery, cupped his hands, and leaned into James. “Thank you, James.”

“Don’t thank me, Ted. Thank Mannie,” James said, puffing circles of white smoke into the cool air. “I just saw the opening and took it.”

James then told Sam of their suspicions about Roddy and of Ted’s visit to Boston.

“We’ll never be able to prove Isaac was innocent, but at least your testimony has generated some doubt about his guilt,” Ted said. He turned to Sam. “I just saw your father. He asked me to give you this,” he said, passing Sam a note.

Sam opened it. *No record on file re MacGillvary and another vehicle.*

“Ted, I know this is a long shot, but I’m wondering if you might pay Jerome MacGillvary a visit. Find out how he smashed up his car,” Sam said.

“You mean the kid who forced the old man into the ditch?” Ted asked.

James pulled the makin from his mouth. “You don’t think he might be responsible for what happened to Johnnie, do you?” he asked excitedly.

“Probably not. But doesn’t hurt to ask a few questions. We know Stanley didn’t do it. So who did?”

CHAPTER 3

"Please rise."

"Counsellor Chernin? Any more questions for this witness?"

"Not at this time, Your Honour."

James was leaving the witness chair when Mannie called his next witness.

"Crown calls Mabel Adshade."

All eyes turned to the back of the courtroom as the double doors opened and Dunphy, with his hand on Mabel's elbow, escorted her down the aisle like an anxious father giving away the bride. James turned toward Sam and Stanley. They were as shocked as he was.

James dismounted the witness chair. Margaret stood, excusing herself as she eased her way between the cramped rows of spectators toward her husband. James waited, took her hand, and the two walked to the back of the courtroom.

Mabel was wearing a tailored coral suit that made her look much older.

"What's going on?" Margaret nervously whispered to James.

"I'm not sure," he said, squeezing her hand.

The bailiff held out the Bible. Mabel reached over and took it from him. The gallery started to laugh. The laughing intensified when Judge Kennedy instructed her to give it back and to place her right hand on top.

"Please state your full name," the bailiff said softly, feeling sorry for the pretty, young woman before him.

"Mabel Grace Adshade," she replied, more loudly than necessary.

"Do you solemnly swear to tell the truth, the whole truth, and nothing but the truth so help you God?"

"Of course. But I don't need no Bible to tell me to," she replied.

The bailiff stifled a grin.

Mabel settled into her chair, nodded to Stanley and Sam, and began searching among the onlookers for James. She saw a hand shoot up in the back. Margaret was waving to her. She smiled at them. She was surprised when it was Mannie who approached her and shot Sam a stern look.

"Miss Adshade, my sincere condolences on the sudden loss of your father."

"Thank you."

"How old are you, Miss Adshade?"

"I figure I'm either seventeen or eighteen. I'm not exactly sure," she said, still embarrassed she couldn't answer such a simple question.

"Very well, then. And you lived with your father on Minto Street for the past three years?"

"Yes."

"And you're a baker at Cameron's store?"

"Yes."

"Do you enjoy working at the bakery?"

"I love it. I love bakin, especially bread and pies."

"And I hear you're quite good at it."

"Thank you. But if ya want to place an order, I'm backed up. So, ya'll have to wait a while."

The courtroom started to laugh again.

Mabel began to wonder what everyone found so funny.

"And how long have you worked for Mr. Cameron?"

"It'll be two months next Wednesday."

"And you know the accused?"

"Yes, I know him. And I know he didn't kill Da."

"I think, Your Honour, we've established Miss Adshade is another hostile witness."

The courtroom, once again, started to laugh.

Mabel shifted uncomfortably in her hard chair.

"Were you with either the accused, or your father the night he was killed?"

"No."

"Then how can you claim he didn't do it?"

"Cause I know him. He wouldn't do somethin like that."

"And how long have you known the accused?"

"I met him when I started workin at the store."

"So, less than two months?"

"Yes."

"Hardly enough time to establish the character of the accused?"

"I'm usually pretty good at figurin people out. I just met you, but don't figure we'd end up bein such good friends."

Again, the spectators started to chuckle.

"Miss Adshade? Have either the accused, or your employer, ever threatened you?"

"Never. Stanley and Mr. Cameron have been nothin but kind to me. If it weren't for them, I woulda froze to death in Mr. Cameron's coal shed."

Mannie decided there was no ground to be gained in asking her about her last statement.

"Could you tell the court if you have a suitor?"

"No. No suitor."

"In fact, didn't you tell Sergeant McInnes that you've never had a boyfriend?"

"Yeah. The day he stopped in for some free pie."

"So, you don't have a boyfriend and you never did?"

Margaret tugged on James's sleeve. "Why is he asking—?"

James looked at her, then quickly back at Mabel. "I have no idea."

Sam wondered what Mannie thought he knew. "Objection, Your Honour. What does any of this have to do with her father's death?"

"I assure you, Your Honour, it's all very relevant," Mannie said, turning and smiling at the jury.

"I'll allow the witness to answer the question, but caution the prosecution not to draw this out," Judge Kennedy ruled.

Mabel thought back to Sergeant McInnes asking her if she was a virgin. She started to worry she might be asked again, with all these people staring and laughing at her.

"Miss Adshade?" Mannie urged.

"I'm sorry," Mabel said. She dropped her head, opened the black clutch on her lap, pulled out her prayer beads, and ran her thumb along the hard metal image of Jesus hanging on the cross.

Mannie and everyone else noted the change in her demeanor when pressed about having a boyfriend. The silence hung in the air as everyone waited impatiently for her response. Stanley slumped forward and pressed his eyes shut.

"Miss Adshade? Have you ever had intimate relations with the accused?" Mannie asked.

"No. And anybody who says I did is lyin," she replied firmly.

"Have you ever had intimate relations with James Cameron?"

"No," she said, this time with a glare that surprised even Mannie.

"And neither the accused nor James Cameron have ever threatened you?"

Mabel began to well up, thinking it was all her fault that the police thought Mr. Cameron or Stanley would do anything to harm her. She thought back to Fritz, the freezing coal shed, and Mr. Cameron sitting at her bedside, dimming the lights. "They didn't do nothin to me and they didn't threaten me. They're good to me."

"Miss Adshade? I assure you, you have nothing to fear from telling the truth," Mannie said, smiling.

"I am tellin the truth," she said, as a tear rolled down her cheek.

Mannie knew she was lying. It was time to wrap this up. "Miss Adshade? Would you agree to have a doctor of your choosing confirm you are a virgin?"

"Objection!" Sam hollered, as he and Stanley both jumped to their feet.

James hugged Margaret.

Sam pleaded with Stanley to sit back down.

"Counsellors! Approach the bench! Now!"

Mannie and Sam both started arguing with Judge Kennedy about the necessity of having Mabel answer the question. It went back and forth several times before Judge Kennedy lost his patience.

"We'll discuss this in my chambers. Court is recessed for the day."

Sam vehemently argued his case, but Mannie convinced Judge Kennedy that Mabel's answer would substantiate his claim that she had been taken advantage of and that she was lying out of fear.

"I'll allow it," Judge Kennedy ruled.

CHAPTER 4

James and Margaret tried to convince Mabel to come home with them, but she would have none of it.

"Come back with us, Mabel. I'll make you a bite to eat," Margaret pleaded.

"Thanks, but I'm not hungry."

James put his hand over Margaret's as she continued to press Mabel to come back to the store.

"Let her be," he said.

"At least let us drive you home," Margaret persisted.

"Thanks, but I'd rather walk," she said, and headed to the one place she knew would bring her some comfort.

"My heart breaks for her. Can you imagine that bastard asking her something so vile," Margaret said.

James gave his wife a surprised look. In the entire time he had known her, he had never once heard her swear.

Mabel made her way up the steep path. She stopped halfway to the top, sat on a flat piece of exposed shale, and kicked at the loose pebbles that cascaded downward. There was no turning back. She had to answer the question and reveal her shame. They think I'm not a virgin because I was intimate with Stanley, she thought. Well, they're in for a surprise.

She kicked hard, again and again, at the stubborn earth that held a large rock firmly in its grip. Eventually it gave way, bouncing its way down the hill, and splashing loudly into the icy water below. Mabel looked over at the footbridge. "To hell with them!" she screamed into the hollow below. I'll tell them I was raped. I'll shout it from the rafters if I have to. She stood, wiped her tear-stained face, brushed a light dusting of red dirt from the back of her borrowed skirt, and walked with purpose, back to the shack.

CHAPTER 5

Captain Collins went to the MacGillvary's. He looked around back but didn't see a vehicle. He knocked on the door several times, but there was no answer. He turned to leave when the door opened.

"Mrs. MacGillvary? Is Jerome home?"

"He's working at the lumber yard. Whatcha want him for?"

"Just had a question about his most recent accident?"

"Well, it didn't involve another driver if that's what ya think. He hit some ice on Highland Street and ran into a tree."

"When was this?"

"I dunno. A couple of weeks back."

"Thank you, Mrs. MacGillvary. Have a good day."

Collins drove to the Bugden Lumber Yard, spoke briefly to the owner, and waited patiently for Jerome to return from his deliveries. The truck finally pulled up. Jerome jumped down from the passenger's side. Mr. Bugden walked up to him and nodded in Collins's direction.

Jerome approached the car and leaned into the open window. "Boss says you wanted to see me," he said easily.

Captain Collins introduced himself. "I heard you had an accident?"

"Yeah. I paid Mr. Chisholm his damages yesterday."

"I'm not talking about the accident involving Mr. Chisholm."

Jerome straightened up. "Oh? Ya mean my run in with the tree?"

"I hear you hit an icy patch," Collins said.

"Yeah."

"When was this?"

"A coupla weeks ago. Look, Captain, I got a ton of lumber to load."

Collins looked at the young man's neck. It was breaking out in red blotches. "Where?"

"Where'd I hit the tree?"

"Yes."

"Ling Street."

"*Ling*?" Collins repeated, turning his mouth down and raising his eyebrows.

"Yeah, Ling."

"Your mother said it happened on Highland Street." Ted watched the red patches on Jerome's neck creep up his face.

"That's just, Ma. She gets confused."

"Mind showing me?"

"Where it happened?" Jerome asked. He laughed and looked back toward the office.

"Yeah. I hear your car is banged up. Must have done some serious damage to the tree?"

"Not really. It was a big spruce. Anyway, I'm not finished work. Can't this wait till tomorrow?"

"I already spoke to Mr. Bugden. He said I can borrow you for a few minutes. Collins leaned across the passenger seat and pushed the door open. "Jump in."

The two drove off. Collins was starting to think Sam's suspicion might not be that much of a long shot after all. "Where's your car now? Didn't see it at your place, or at Bugden's."

"Buddy of mine needed to go to the mainland. So I lent it to him."

"So, it's still running?"

"Yeah. Works fine. Hardly no damage."

"How long have you been working for Mr. Bugden?"

"What?"

"How long have you been working in the yard?" Collins repeated. He knew the kid was nervous, but quickly reminded himself that most people got nervous when questioned by the police; even those with nothing to hide.

"Almost a year."

"You following the MacIntyre trial?" Collins probed, turning his head sharply to see Jerome's reaction.

"No, not really," Jerome said. He looked back toward the yard.

"It's the talk of the town. But it looks like we got the guy."

Collins turned off Highland and onto Ling. "Just let me know when I'm getting close," he said, slowing to a crawl.

"It was dark. Maybe we passed it."

Collins pulled over to the side and shut off the engine. "Listen, son. There was no tree, was there? I've been up and down this street a thousand times before, and there's plenty of maple, but no big spruce."

"I dunno. Maybe, it *was* a maple."

Collins looked at him. "Jerome, don't make this any harder on yourself. I know you didn't hit a tree."

Jerome MacGillvary started to cry. "It was an accident. I wasn't speedin or anythin. I just came around the corner. I could hardly see anythin with all the rain. He was just there, standin in the middle of the road. I tried to stop. I swear. I tried. Me and Andy got out to help him, but we could tell he was already dead. I panicked. I was just in court with Mr. Chisholm. So me and Andy pulled him off the road and put him in the ditch. There was nothin we could do. I swear. He just appeared outa nowhere."

"But you knew an innocent man was on trial for his murder?"

"I'm sorry. I'm sorry. I'm really sorry," Jerome cried.

CHAPTER 6

Sergeant McInnes watched Collins and Dunphy usher the young MacGillvary kid into the interview room. What the dumbass kid do now, he wondered. He couldn't help himself. He opened the door. "Hey Captain? Won't be long now before we can put that whole MacIntyre mess behind us," he smirked.

Collins leaned back in his chair and smiled. "You're right, Dan. Won't be long now."

An hour later, Ted and Sam were racing to the store.

Margaret was in the kitchen when she heard them barge through the door. "Where's James?" Sam asked.

"He's upstairs."

"Is everything alright?" she asked.

Sam leaned in, surprising her with a kiss on the cheek.

She had her answer. "James! James!" she hollered.

James appeared on the upstairs landing and looked down. "What's going on?"

"James! It wasn't a long shot after all. We have a confession," Collins said, waving Jerome's statement in the air.

James ran downstairs, kissed Margaret, then Sam and Ted.

"So, is that it, Ted? The nightmare's over?"

"I have to speak to Judge Kennedy. But, yes. I'm sure it is."

"Does Stanley know?"

"Dunphy's brining him up to speed."

James grabbed his coat. "C'mon guys. Let's go tell Mabel."

Ted broke all the laws he was sworn to enforce. He sailed through every intersection at almost forty miles an hour, arriving at the shack within ten minutes.

Amour heard the pounding. She didn't get a chance to answer, either.

"It's over," James hollered, barreling through the door.

Mabel heard the commotion, scrambled off her bed, and ran into the room that rarely witnessed a happy moment.

"It's over," James repeated, wrapping his arms around her, and lifting her into the air.

Wednesday, November 23

CHAPTER I

Captain Collins sat on the bench outside of Judge Kennedy's chambers, waiting for him to show up. He had hoped to tell him about the confession the previous night, but by the time he got to the judge's home, the Kennedy's modest bungalow was in darkness. He knew Judge Kennedy to be a reasonable man, but he also knew there were two things he'd never tolerate; having his supper interrupted, or his sleep disturbed.

Judge Kennedy finally appeared in the hallway, brushing past Ted as if he wasn't there.

"Your Honour, I need to have a word with you."

"Not now, Collins. I'm already running late."

"But, Your Honour! It was a hit and run. We have the man responsible in custody and a signed confession."

Judge Kennedy looked like he could be knocked over with a feather. "Does Mannie know?"

"Not yet. I wanted to inform you first. Do you want me to get him and bring him to your chambers?"

"That's not necessary."

"But, Your Honour. We have —"

"A confession. I heard you."

"And you still want to proceed with the trial?" Collins asked, confused and worried.

"No. But I want to see Mannie's face when he loses his first case in front of a packed courtroom."

CHAPTER 2

The noisy courtroom turned to a dull murmur when James, Margaret, and Mabel walked in together. They each looked around the crowded room, took the seats Ted was holding for them, and watched Stanley be escorted in in shackles.

"I'm nervous," Mabel whispered to James.

"It'll be over soon," he said, patting her hand.

"Please rise."

Judge Kennedy looked out at the packed gallery. "Yesterday, before I recessed for the day, I had to make a ruling whether or not to require the witness, Mabel Adshade, to answer a question posed to her by the prosecution. I was conflicted. However, after carefully weighing the arguments of both the defence and the prosecution, I notified counsel that I was ruling in favour of the prosecution. The question Counsellor Chernin put to Miss Adshade was, in fact, materially relevant in determining, not just the veracity of the witness's testimony, but in establishing the quilt, or innocence, of the accused."

Mannie stood, buttoned his jacket, and grinned at Sam. He was anxious to wrap things up and pose for his picture for *The Post*.

"Sit down, Mannie," Kennedy ordered.

"But, Your Honour, I thought —"

"Sit down, Mannie," he repeated, more harshly.

Mannie sat.

"This morning, in fact just minutes ago, additional evidence has come to my attention. Evidence that is also materially relevant in determining the outcome of this trail."

Everyone was on the edge of their seat. Mannie had no idea what Judge Kennedy was talking about. He looked over at McInnes, who gave him the thumbs up.

"It has come to my attention…" Judge Kennedy paused, "the accused is innocent."

Mannie jumped up. "But Your Honour! Your Honour! We haven't heard all of the evidence."

Judge Kennedy looked at Stanley and Sam. They were hugging one another. He pounded his gavel. "Order! Order! Order!"

Mannie was red faced. "Your Honour? How could you possibly declare the accused innocent before the trial concludes? I haven't even finished with my last witness."

"Because, Mannie, we have a signed confession. It was a hit and run, just as Dr. Adams suggested. The jury is dismissed with the gratitude of the court. And, Mr. MacIntyre," Judge Kennedy said smiling, "you're free to go."

Mannie turned to see Sergeant McInnes being consoled by his aunt, Gladys Ferguson. He sat down heavily in his chair, put his head down, and listened to practically everyone within earshot, claim they knew Stanley was innocent all along.

Sam approached Mannie and extended his hand. "Counsellor? No shame in losing one after such a long and successful career. You're a worthy opponent."

Mannie shook his hand, but refused to look him in the eye.

Mabel waited for the bailiff to undo Stanley's cuffs.

"I'm really happy for ya," she said.

"Thank you, Mabel," he said, wrapping his arms around her.

She thought she could stay like that all day.

CHAPTER 3

James, Margaret, and Mabel sat in the car, anxious for Stanley to join them. When he finally walked out of the courthouse, Dirty Willie and Ten-After-Six were there to greet him. Stanley bent down on one knee to be at eye level with Peter. He then stood, hugged Willie, ran to the car, and climbed in the backseat next to Mabel. He smiled and reached for her hand; relieved, that this time, she didn't pull it away.

They stopped at the shack to pick up Amour and headed to the store for a celebration. Mary Catherine was pushing the baby carriage up Caledonia Street, with Luke and Mark at her side. Mabel rolled down the window. "Stanley's free! C'mon! We're havin a party," she yelled, waving her arm.

They were barely inside the store when Stanley approached James. "I'll never be able to thank you enough. I'm in your debt."

James slapped him on the back. "There are no accounts owing between friends. But if there were, the balance would be in your favour. Besides, it was Sam who put things together and Ted who got the confession."

"But it was you who stood by me from beginning to end, even though I gave you plenty of room for doubt. James, you lied under oath for me. You know I never wanted you to."

"To be honest, that's why I did. If you had asked me to, I would have said no. I have no regrets. None. I believe that as long as you act with goodness in your heart, you have God's blessing."

Stanley embraced him. "Then you are a well-blessed man, my friend." He reached into his back pocket and pulled out a folded piece of paper. "It's not much of a thank you, but I had some time on my hands."

James carefully examined Stanley's designs for the expansion and renovation.

"Measurements might need some tweaking, but I thought it might help move things along," Stanley said.

"This looks great. Honestly. I love how you've used the space. And Mabel's going to love the bakery counter in the front window," James said. He placed his hand on Stanley's shoulder. "Looks like we can get started tomorrow."

Stanley put his head down, knowing he could never possibly repay his friend for all that he had done for him. He looked back up at James, who continued to study the new layout. "I was wondering if I can trouble you for one more favour?" he asked James.

"Of course. I'm in a generous mood."

"Can I borrow a razor and a fresh shirt?"

Margaret watched James and Stanley walk upstairs. The trial had taken as much of a toll on James, she thought, as it had on Stanley. He looked far too thin.

Amour interrupted her thoughts. "This is the second time I've been here in as many days. I came by yesterday to tell you that Mabel would be in court, but found it closed for the day."

"Mabel is quite the young lady. And I hear you're quite the cook. She tells me you're opening a restaurant in town."

"Yes. At the old shoe repair. I had hoped to have it open for the Christmas season, but I'm afraid that might be too ambitious."

They both turned as Sam, his father, and Captain Collins walked in. Sam was about to close the door when he saw Mary Catherine approaching with Mark and the baby. He waved them in out of the cold, then waited for Luke, who was a good distance behind.

Sam's father looked at Ted and opened his coat, exposing a large bottle of rum. "Are you going to give me any trouble if I open this?"

"You'll be in more trouble if you don't," Ted said, swatting him on the back.

Margaret made her way to Mark. "Come with me," she said, taking his hand. She walked behind the counter, found what she was looking for, and handed him *The Cat Who Went to Heaven.* "You can take it home and have Mary Catherine or Anna read it to you. Or, you can leave it here, and when you come visit, I'll read it to you." He trotted off with it clutched in his hands. She then walked up to the baby carriage, shaking the rattle over John's belly. She laughed as his eyes widened and his chubby fists came together, empty-handed.

James watched her from the stairway as memories of her with their son came flooding back. He smiled, thinking he had forgotten what it was to feel happy.

The store turned raucous when Douglas arrived, along with Angus MacNeil who danced in with his fiddle. Jigs and reels drowned out the chatter.

Amour was by the door when she heard the rap. "*Michael,*" she said, "what are you doing here?"

"I came to return Mabel's tins and order more pie."

Mabel peeked out of the kitchen into the room and smiled to herself. "Count yer blessings," she whispered. This was not a day to worry about the backorders. She returned the flour she had just poured into her mixing bowl back into its huge, cloth bag. *I'll just come in early in the morning and stay late.* She joined the merrymakers in the store and saw Stanley coming downstairs, clean shaven and quite handsome in a crisp, white shirt. She wondered how she could have ever thought of him as creepy.

Margaret, James, Mabel, and Stanley began putting things back in place after the others left.

"Oh dear," James said.

"What is it?" Margaret asked.

"Mark forgot his book," he said, holding it in the air.

This is, indeed, a happy day, Margaret thought.

Thursday, November 24

CHAPTER I

James woke to the knocking. He looked at the time. It was almost seven. He ran downstairs and opened the door. It was Mabel and Stanley.

"Remind me to get you two keys," James said. He pulled his robe around him.

"I see you arranged for Angus and the boys to clean up my property. Thank you," Stanley said.

"They did all the work. I meant to go by and check on things. Did they leave the markers for Walter and Winnie like I asked?"

"Yes. Another reason for me to be indebted to you."

Mabel interrupted. "I need to warm up. I'm puttin on some tea. I feel like I spent my mornin back in yer coal shed. At least this time, I know it ain't my day off," she said laughing.

"I know it's Thursday… I just don't have a clue what day of the month it is," James admitted.

"It's the twenty fourth," Stanley replied.

"The twenty fourth," James repeated, wondering why the date stuck in his mind.

He walked upstairs, washed up, and swished his razor around the steamy water. *The twenty fourth…*

Margaret! Margaret! Wake up!" he said, shaking her.

"What is it?"

"It's Mabel's birthday."

CHAPTER 2

"Mabel? Margaret's upstairs and wants to see you," James said.

Mabel tapped on her bedroom door.

"Come in."

"You wanted to see me, Margaret?" Mabel said.

"I found a book you might like. It was one of my favourites," she said, handing her *Smoky the Cowhorse*. "Don't let the title fool you. I know you'll enjoy it."

"Thanks," Mabel said, flipping through the pages. "I'll start it tonight."

"Remember, if you come up against words you're not sure of, write them out and I'll help you."

"I will," Mabel said. She hugged Margaret and headed for the door. She was on the upstairs landing when she looked down to see James holding a cake, surrounded by Stanley, Amour, Mary Catherine and the boys, and Sam.

"Happy Birthday," James said.

"Happy Birthday, Mabel," the others chimed in.

"*Birthday,*" Mabel repeated.

"Yes, Mabel. It's your birthday," Margaret said, approaching from behind.

"But how do ya know?"

Margaret put her hand on Mabel's shoulder. "James got your birth record from the clerk's office. You were born November twenty-fourth, nineteen fifteen. It's your eighteenth birthday."

"*I'm eighteen.*"

"Uh huh," James said.

Mark couldn't take his eyes off the cake. He finally reached up and scraped his finger along the boiled white icing. Mary Catherine slapped at his hand.

"Well, young lady, get down here and cut your cake," James said, holding it out for inspection.

"And yer pwes…sants," Mark said, tantalized by the table laden with mysterious boxes wrapped in pretty paper.

"It's my birthday," she repeated. "I'm eighteen."

Mary Catherine held up a plate draped in a tea towel. "I'm afraid I couldn't wrap your gift."

"I hope it's what I think it is," Mabel replied.

"Then, I hope you think it's perogies."

The other gifts were equally as modest, but Mabel loved them all. A handmade card from the boys, a yellow apron from Stanley, a knit scarf from Amour, and a small picture frame from Margaret."

"I'm so blessed. All of this… *and* a cake! I'll never forget this day. Thank you all so much."

"There's one more gift, Mabel," James said. He handed her an unadorned paper bag. She reached in and pulled out a photo. "It's your mother. She would have been around your age."

The room was dead quiet as Mabel gently ran her hand over it. She looked up with tears in her eyes. "This is the happiest day of my life. Thank you, Mr. Cameron."

"That's me on the left."

"Ya were so handsome. I mean ya still are, but look at ya."

"And who's that with Ma on the right?"

"That's Percy. Our friend who was killed in the war."

"He has a nice smile and kind eyes," Mabel said.

"He had a kind heart, too," James said, his voice cracking.

Margaret squeezed his arm.

"Mark!" Mary Catherine screeched. They all turned to see him with a fistful of cake, and a mouth splattered in icing.

"Fine by me," James said, "I'm having pie."

CHAPTER 3

Margaret lay in bed with her head on James's chest and her hand stretched over his belly. "I need to fatten you up."

"No need to worry about that, now that I've been introduced to Mabel's pie."

"James? When are you going to tell her about her father?"

"Don't forget, I have to tell Amour, too. Not just about Johnnie, but what I said about Roddy. Maybe, tomorrow."

"They should know, now that Johnnie's buried and the trial is over. There's no reason not to tell them."

"It's still a hard thing to do, Margaret."

"I'll go with you. We can do it together."

He kissed her forehead. "I think I'll close the store on Saturday. I need a couple of days off. We all do. Maybe we can take in a matinee at the *Russell*. I hear that *Trouble in Paradise* is playing? What do you think?"

"I'd love to see a picture show. It's been so long," Margaret said.

"Then it's settled. Now all I have to do is tell Mabel she has to take Saturday off. For some reason, I don't think she's going to be too pleased."

"You know," Margaret said, "it might be a good time to ask Thomas and Eileen over for supper. I could make lamb. And I could ask Mabel to make us a pie."

James looked down at her. "I thought you didn't like Eileen."

"There was a time I didn't like anyone, or anything."

"And now?" James asked.

Margaret lifted her head off his chest and smiled up at him. "I count my blessings."

Friday, November 25

CHAPTER I

James, Margaret, and Mabel piled in the car.

"You're sure Amour won't mind if I stop in for her potato soup recipe?" Margaret asked, turning to Mabel who was sitting in the backseat.

"No. She'd love to see ya. She likes ya a lot. Likes you too, Mr. Cameron."

Amour insisted they stay and try her latest recipe. James polished off his first serving and glanced at what remained on the counter.

"You're welcome to more, James. There's plenty."

"Thanks. It's delicious."

Amour put seconds in front of her appreciative guest. "It's called *quiche*. Just a fancy name for egg pie."

James put his tea down. "I'm glad you invited us for supper. Not just for the fabulous food, but because there's something we need to tell you both." He leaned back in his chair and launched in. He began by talking about his relationship with Ellie and Percy, the day they shipped out, losing contact with Ellie, Percy's death, and his visit to Pleasant Bay. He then dropped the bombshell.

"Mabel, your mother was deeply in love with Percy. So much so that she had you. You're Percy's daughter."

Mabel sat speechless as Amour reached for her hand. "I know

this is hard for you, but I want you to know your father… your *real* father, was a good man. The best I've ever known. And your mother was a beautiful, kind woman, who loved you so much she would never give you up. She—"

"Da wasn't my da? Did he know I wasn't his?"

"I'm almost certain he didn't. Your mother told me he didn't," James said.

"And Ma really loved Percy?"

"Yes, she loved him. And he loved her."

"I never got to meet him," Mabel said softly.

"I know he would have loved you with all his heart. Just like your mother did."

"So, if I'm not Da's… Johnnie's daughter, I guess you're not my aunt," she said, turning to Amour.

"Mabel, none of that matters. I'll always think of you as my niece."

Mabel reached over and put her arms around Amour's neck, laying her head on her shoulder.

"There's more," James said. "Amour, Johnnie was adopted."

"Adopted?"

"Yes," James said. He closed his eyes. "And he was my half-brother."

Everyone sat in stunned silence, until Amour spoke up. "Was I adopted too?"

"No."

"So, your father was also Johnnie's father?" Amour said.

"No. *My mother* was Johnnie's mother. I don't know who Johnnie's father was."

Margaret spoke up. "I know this is a lot to take in. It's hard for women to have… to have a child out of wedlock. But it is far more common than you think. Some women don't see their pregnancies through. Others give them up. I even know of a prominent family in town where the mother of a child pretends she's her sister. Your mother obviously loved you and your father so much, she couldn't part with you."

"Ironic, isn't it," Amour said. "So many women having children out of wedlock and yet I was childless even after eight years of marriage."

Margaret reached over and squeezed her hand.

"So, did Johnnie know he was adopted and that you were his half-brother?" Amour asked.

"No. I only found out after he died. The clerk in the records office told me."

James looked at Mabel. "You okay?"

She nodded. "I never met my real father. Ma died when I was young. And the man I called Da all my life and raised me as best he could, wasn't really my da after all. I never got the sense he liked me, let alone loved me. Maybe he knew in his heart I wasn't his?"

"I don't think so," James said. "But we'll never really know for sure."

"Mr. Cameron?"

"Yes, Mabel."

"You don't have any more surprises do you?"

James looked at Amour, then at Margaret.

"Go on James, tell her," Margaret said.

"Amour," he said closing his eyes. "I believe Roddy murdered the Greene boy."

Monday, December 11

The store was in shambles. Stanley was tearing down the wall to the storage room, Luke was carting debris outside, and Mabel and Mary Catherine chatted away in the kitchen. James poured himself a tea and reached for *The Post*.

> *Local Officer Suspended, Under Investigation. Sergeant Daniel McInnes has been suspended from duty pending the outcome of an investigation that he falsified a witness's statement and incited said witness to commit perjury during the recent trial that saw Stanley MacIntyre acquitted of the murder of John Adshade, formerly of Minto Street. An unnamed source maintains McInnes promised to help William Guthro, a key witness for the Crown during the MacIntyre trial, elude charges of arson in exchange for embellishing his testimony. Guthro, along with Edward Lynch, are now serving two years in the county jail for arson. Guthro is still awaiting trial on charges of perjury. Captain Ted Collins refused comment when asked to confirm he was leading the investigation. Crown Prosecutor, Mannie Chernin, said, "The good people of this town can rest assured that I will thoroughly review any charges that are*

> *brought before me and that justice will be done. The last thing we need is for folks to start jumping to conclusions."*

"I'm home," Margaret announced, walking through the door and depositing her bags on the counter.

"How did it go?" James asked, flipping through *The Post*.

"It's going to be fabulous. Amour has gone out of her way to honour Mr. Greene's memory. The artwork is stunning. Nothing but shoes. Beautiful, colourful shoes of all sizes and shapes. And she has a counter with some of the old tools she found out back. Oh, and she had a plaque made. And that's not all. She also gave the money that Roddy left her to the synagogue, with a request they use a portion of it to fix up the Jewish cemetery. I understand it was a pretty tidy sum."

James looked up from the paper. "So what does the plaque say?"

"In memory of Isaac, David, and Sophie Greene. Rest in peace. We know the truth."

"That should get tongues wagging," he said.

"They already are. Everyone in town is suddenly claiming they never believed Mr. Greene killed his son."

James peered at her over the top of his glasses.

Margaret knew what he was thinking.

"You know, it's very brave of Amour to do what she's doing. She said she wasn't going to hide from her past anymore. I think Michael has helped her realize she has nothing to be ashamed off."

"They're seeing a lot of one another," James said, turning the paper over and spotting his advertisement. *You ain't had bread or pies till you had Mabel's. Delicious fresh-baked goods at great prices. Stop by Cameron's, 14 School Street, or Call 8638 to place an order.* He laughed to himself, thinking of the day Mabel and Margaret had argued over the wording. Margaret had insisted they not use the word *ain't.* Mabel insisting her name not be included. In the end, they'd compromised. "So is there a romance blossoming?" James asked?

"Amour says not. But I see the way they are with one another."

Luke came around the corner cradling a box in his arms.

"Hey, Luke! Do you like fishing?" James called out.

He put his head down. "I dunno."

"What? Never been fishing before?"

"Not that I remember."

"Well, how about I pick you up after church on Sunday and we go ice fishing?"

"Ice fishing?"

"Yeah. We dress warm, cut a hole in the ice, and fish," James said, acting out his words. "Maybe Stanley and Mark will come with us."

"I don't have a pole."

"I have an extra one. What do you say?"

"I guess so."

"Great. I'll pick you up around ten."

Luke started to walk away.

"By the way," James called, "you're doing a great job."

Luke kept walking.

Friday, December 15

James looked at his watch for the third time in as many minutes. "Margaret," he hollered upstairs. "We're going to miss all that wonderful food. I'm famished."

Margaret appeared on the landing.

She took his breath away. "You look… beautiful."

"You can thank Amour. She showed me how to do a French braid."

"It's not just your hair. You look absolutely stunning, from top to bottom."

"You don't look so shabby yourself."

He looked down at her high heels. "You'd better hope it doesn't snow."

"Or maybe I do and you'll be forced to carry me," she said with a wink.

They arrived at the once boarded-up shoe repair and joined the small gathering.

James took Margaret's coat, leaned into her, and whispered, "I was expecting to see more people."

"It's not open to the public, yet. Everyone here has been invited."

Amour walked up to greet them. "Welcome to Bistro l'Amour," she said with an exaggerated sweep of her arm.

"The place looks terrific," James said.

"Still lots to do, but we're getting there. Margaret's been a huge help. And thanks for making Stanley available. He's got a talent for design. Please, make yourselves comfortable and help yourself to the food. There are some libations in the back. Michael will see that you're looked after."

James looked at Ted, standing over the display of his old friend's tools. "So, what do you think?" James asked, shaking Ted's hand.

"It's wonderful. The art. The display. I know there will always be those who will think Isaac killed David, but I think most people now realize it was Roddy."

"I have no doubt of it. I see McInnes is finally getting his due," James said.

"He'll be spending Christmas in jail. Dunphy and I will testify he lied to the court about the knife. And Billy admitted it was McInnes's idea to invent the story about walking in on Stanley and Mabel."

"You have to wonder what made him so… so much of a prick," James said.

"Ambition, my friend. Pure ambition," Ted said.

"And what's our friend Mannie saying about all of this?"

Ted reached in front of James to sample one of Amour's offerings, popped it in his mouth, and licked his fingers. "Says if he was the judge, he'd throw the book at him."

Margaret joined them, followed by Ted's wife, Muriel, and Amour, who was beaming from all the praise.

Michael approached with a tray of drinks. "Oh, dear God," he said.

"What is it?"

"Look," he said, nodding to the window.

Amour turned to see a woman with her hands cupped around the side of her face, peering in.

"It's Lizzie MacNeil," Michael said.

"Should I invite her in?" Amour asked.

"No!" he shrieked, as everyone turned their eyes toward him.

He smiled awkwardly. "Sorry folks. I just remembered I forgot something," he said, quickly walking out of Lizzie's sight.

Mabel arrived with Mary Catherine and Sam. James looked at her and thought she was the image of Ellie. He helped her off with her coat. "You look beautiful," he said.

"Amour made me wear these," she said, pointing to her feet. "Don't know how good I'm gonna look when I fall on my face."

He pointed to the gramophone. "Does that mean you're not going to dance with me?"

"Hell, I can barely walk. And ya think I'm gonna dance with ya?"

"Well, if you don't want to dance with me, I guess you don't want to dance with that good looking guy who just walked in," James said.

Mabel turned around and nearly fell off her heels. Stanley was folding his coat over his arm. She couldn't believe it was him. He was dressed in a dark blue suit and wearing freshly polished shoes. She was laughing when she approached him. "Look at ya. Ya look… ya look—"

"Like a teacher?" he asked.

"Like a real gentleman."

"Well, you look pretty good, too. Like—"

"Like a baker?"

"No. Like you belong on a gentleman's arm," Stanley said.

Mabel played along, looping her arm around his. The two made their way to a table in the corner. Amour lifted the arm of the gramophone and carefully placed it in the narrow grooves of the spinning vinyl plate. Mabel watched Margaret and James effortlessly glide across the floor. Stanley watched Mabel. She turned to see him staring, and immediately felt awkward. He kept looking.

"What's up with you?" she said, elbowing him.

"Just thinking about how pretty you look."

"Shake yerself," she said, running her hand over her mouth to remove any lipstick that remained after Amour's forced application. She was anxious to change the subject. "They look so beautiful together," she said, nodding toward Margaret and James.

Stanley smiled. "I'm glad things are finally going better for them. I was worried after the baby died."

Mabel had always wondered why Margaret and James never had children and why there was a child-sized rocker in the bedroom she had stayed in. "They lost a baby?" Mabel said sadly.

"Yes, a boy. Died from the flu several years ago."

"I never knew," Mabel said, thinking about how good they were with the boys.

"Anyway, I think it's all behind them now."

"Stanley?" she said, no longer able to contain her curiosity. "How old are ya?"

"I'll be thirty-two in a couple of months."

"Oh," she said, thinking it sounded about right.

"Why do you ask?"

"Just curious, that's all."

"Anything else you're curious about?"

"How come yer not married? I mean, most men yer age have a wife and a half dozen kids by now."

"Guess I never found the right girl."

Mabel kept her eyes focused on the dance floor.

"I came close once," he said, anxious to continue the conversation he hoped would bring them closer. Mabel, her chin resting on her hand, turned her head toward him waiting for him to go on.

"Her name was Clair. She was the daughter of my trainer."

"What happened to her?"

He tilted his head to the side and thought about it for a moment. "Dirty Willie," he said.

Mabel's eyes widened. "She married Dirty Willie!" she said, slapping her hand on the table.

Stanley started to laugh. "No. I quit boxing after my last match with Willie and her father wouldn't let her see me anymore. Guess he didn't figure a coal hauler would be good enough for his daughter. They moved out of town years ago."

"Any regrets?" she asked.

"Only about what happened to Willie," he said. He stood and held his hand out to her. "Care to dance?"

"Care to have yer feet stomped on?" she said, playfully waving him away. "I never danced in my whole life."

It took a while, but Stanley finally convinced her to give it a try. He reached his arm around her waist, laid his hand on the small of her back, and gently drew her into him. He instructed her to put her arm up over his shoulder. He then clasped her right hand. Mabel wasn't sure if it was the wine that was making her feel flush, or her partner. She was hesitant at first and there were more than a few awkward stumbles, but Stanley's patient encouragement finally had them moving easily among the other couples.

Margaret watched over her husband's shoulder and whispered in his ear. "I look forward to their wedding."

James closed his eyes and smiled. "Me too."

Everyone was disappointed when Stanley left alone. No one more than Stanley.

August 9, 1935

John charged through the door with Mary Catherine's mother close on his heels. "I can't keep up with him. He wanted to see his brothers," she said, catching her breath.

"Look at you," Margaret said, opening her arms for him to run into. "Anna. If you want to leave him with me, I'd be happy to give you a few hours on your own."

"You sure?" Anna asked.

"I'm positive."

Anna looked around. "Where are Luke and Mark?"

"Luke's out back with James and Stanley. Mark's helping the girls. No doubt licking the batter off the spoons."

"I love the window display," Anna said.

"Mary Catherine certainly has a talent for decorating cake. We're so grateful she's with us."

"No, Mrs. Cameron. She's grateful to you. We're all grateful to you, and Mr. Cameron, for taking her on. She's loves it here. And you're both so good to the boys. Luke is finally coming out of his shell. You're like their grandparents."

Margaret smiled.

September 2, 1935

"Heat up the pans. We brought supper!" James said, proudly dangling four speckled trout high in the air. Mabel came around the corner. He could tell she was crying.

"What's wrong?" James asked.

"It's Margaret."

Mary Catherine stood behind her, wiping her hand under her eyes.

"Dr. Cohen is with her," Mabel said.

James dropped the trout to the floor and bounded up the stairs. He walked in to see Margaret sleeping and Dr. Cohen sitting beside the bed.

"Thomas? What is it? Is she alright?"

"I'm afraid she had a minor stroke."

James felt his legs buckle. He looked at her and could see no outward signs of her trauma. She was as beautiful as ever. He took her hand in his, raised it to his mouth, kissed it, and pressed it against his cheek.

"James, she needs her rest."

"Of course. Will she be okay?"

"It's too early to tell. Her speech is slurred and her right arm is not functioning properly, but I've seen this before and lots of people make a full recovery."

"But what caused it? Is it her headaches?"

"No," Thomas said. "I don't think it's that."

"Then what?" James asked, stroking Margaret's forehead.

"I think it's the baby."

"The *baby*!" James said, giving him a bewildered look.

"She didn't tell you? James, Margaret is almost three months pregnant."

November 22, 1935

Margaret sat in the kitchen sipping her tea. James peeked in at her.

"James, you're driving me mad. I'm fine," she said, with barely a hint of a slur. "Mabel and Mary Catherine are like mother hens. It's a wonder they get any baking done."

"Don't worry, Mr. Cameron," Mabel said. "She's back to her old self. Keeps gettin after me for leavin my gees off my verbs."

"You did it again, Mabel, just now," Margaret said, wagging her finger.

"That's cause I wanted to show Mr. Cameron I was tellin the truth."

"*Because*, not cause. And tell-*ing*, not *tellin*," Margaret said slowly, but precisely.

"Don't worry, Margaret. I'm just get-*ting* yer goat. *Ain't* I, Mr. Cameron?"

Margaret shook her head and started to laugh. She was going to have Mabel talking properly, even if it killed her.

James returned to the store. He had to stop waking up every ten minutes in the middle of the night to check on his wife and accept that Mabel and Mary Catherine would keep an eye on her in the day. She was doing much better than either he or Dr. Cohen had anticipated. She also seemed to handle the loss of the baby better than they expected. Likely, the result of preparing herself for the inevitable disappointment, he thought. She'd cried. They both had. But eventually, they came to grips with the fact they would be childless. He was sad, for sure, but he knew that carrying the baby to full term put Margaret at risk of suffering another, more debilitating stroke. Despite their best efforts, neither he nor Thomas could convince her to end the pregnancy. In the end, God took their fourth child from them and James thanked him for it.

Mabel studied James from the shelter of her kitchen. He was hunched over the counter with the newspaper sprawled out before him. She worried as much for him as she did Margaret. He seemed to bounce back after the ordeal of the trial, but Margaret's stroke and losing another baby, began piling the years on his thin frame faster than the passing of time. He was still handsome, but his head of thick dark hair was now mostly a thin, dull grey. She wiped her hands on her apron and approached him. As always, he greeted her with a warm smile.

"You know, Mr. Cameron, I'm here if you need to talk to anybody about what you're feelin. Feel*ing*," she corrected.

"Thank you, Mabel. I'm fine. Just a little tired."

"Why not let Mary Catherine handle the register and go get some sleep?"

"Not sleepy, really. Just fatiqued."

"Anyway, I wanted to let tell you that I'm here for you. Just like you've always been there for me."

"I haven't always been there for you Mabel. I should have —"

"Mr. Cameron, I love you and Margaret as much as I've ever loved anyone, and I won't hear you say any more shouldas. I just won't," she said folding her arms across her chest and giving him a stern look.

"We love you, too. We lost a son, but we both feel we found a daughter."

Mabel walked over and hugged him.

"Mabel," he said, "I think it's well past time you started calling me James."

May 2, 1936

CHAPTER 1

"Well, look who the cat dragged in. How are you, Sam?"

"I'm great, James. And you?"

"Life is good."

"And Margaret?"

"She's doing much better."

"You'll never guess who came by my office this morning," Sam said.

"Who?"

"Mannie."

"And how is my dear friend?" James asked, the sarcasm dripping off his tongue.

"Agitated."

"What's in his craw?"

"He's concerned about what's going on in Germany. This Hitler guy. Apparently he's not too fond of Jews. He's worried about some family members he has in Berlin. He got a letter from his cousin. Germans took away his license to practice medicine. Apparently, they're also rounding up all Jews and making them wear a star on their clothing. He wondered if my father heard from any of his relatives."

"Did he?"

"Not that he mentioned. Anyway, I'm sure it's nothing to be too concerned about. Mannie also said McInnes is getting out of jail in a few weeks. Told me to watch my back. Said he hasn't mellowed any."

"You don't seriously think McInnes will come after you?"

"I'm not going to lose any sleep over him, or Hitler for that matter. Is Mary Catherine here?"

"Yes. Go on back."

Mary Catherine had her head down and was applying icing to her cake. She was surprised when she looked up and saw Sam in the doorway.

"Sam? What are you doing here?"

"My case was postponed and I had some free time. Just thought I'd stop in to see if you want to go to the bistro tonight?"

"Tonight? Is it a special occasion or something?"

"Why? Do we need one?"

"No."

"Then, I'll pick you up at six," he said turning for the door.

May 3, 1936

CHAPTER I

Mary Catherine placed her hand on her cheek and batted her eyelids.

"What's up with you today?" Mabel asked. "You're acting all funny."

Mary Catherine wiggled her finger. "What's wrong with *you*? Are ya blind?"

"Oh, my God!" Mabel squealed, "Sam proposed! Let me see," she said, grabbing her friend's hand and bending down for a closer look. "It's beautiful," Mabel said, beaming.

"It belonged to Sam's grandmother."

"And your parents are okay, given your Catholic and he's a Jew?"

"There's a catch. I need to convert."

"You mean you're gonna become a Jew?"

"Yep."

"Just like that?"

"Well, not exactly. Got to do some studying and go through the rituals and all. But Sam said he'd help. It will take a while. Maybe a year or more. And I'll be given the name Sarah."

"What do you mean? You're not going to be Mary Catherine anymore?"

"Of course. Sarah will just be my Hebrew name."

"Well, thank God for that. I can't imagine calling you anything else. And your mother and father are okay with you turning Jew?"

"Ma took some convincing. But Da's fine with it. He told Sam he'd rather see me become a Jew than end up an old maid."

"What about the boys?" Mabel asked.

"I have to bring them up honouring Jewish traditions. But they don't have to convert."

"You mean they won't have Christmas?"

"No. They'll have Christmas and Hanukkah."

"Margaret! James!" Mabel hollered, running out of the kitchen. "Mary Catherine's marrying Sam. She's gonna become a Jew. And the boys are gonna have Christmas and Hanukkah!"

September 12, 1936

Stanley examined his balance sheet. His redesign of the store and then Amour's bistro, had generated interest from some of the town's other merchants and wealthier homeowners. Work was steady enough for him to buy a used truck and hire Angus MacNeil, who convinced Stanley he was a better carpenter than miner. After almost three years in business, he saved enough to buy the Andrews property, a vacated farmhouse overlooking the cliffs off Table Head. It required some serious attention, new windows and doors, a new roof, and a fresh coat of paint, inside and out, but he knew it was worth the effort. He put his coat on and headed to the store. He hadn't seen Mabel much now that he was self-employed and only occasionally popped by the store. Didn't see the point. The odd time Mary Catherine and Sam tried to get the four of them together to take in a movie, or to stop by the bistro for a bite to eat, Mabel usually found a reason to decline. It was clear she wasn't interested in him as anything more than a friend. He drove to the store, hoping to share his good news with her. Mabel was getting ready to leave for the day when he walked in.

"Haven't seen much of you lately," she said.

"Been busy with work. And I bought a property."

"Good for you," she said, buttoning her coat. "Where?"

"I bought the old Andrews place in Table Head."

"Don't know it."

"Big, grey farmhouse on the bluff. You can't miss it. It's the one closest to the ocean."

"*That* old place. I hope you got it for a song. It looks like it could blow over in a good gale." Her words were no sooner out of her mouth when she regretted them.

Stanley looked deflated.

"But I'm sure you can fix it up, given you're so handy and all," Mabel quickly added.

"It's actually not that bad. Has a big kitchen, three large bedrooms, and a nice bath."

"Any running water or electricity?" she asked, reaching for her mother's tote.

"I'm working on it. Just came from Light and Power. It will be hooked up before long. Want me to drive you home? We could swing by and I could show you."

They were on the way to Table Head.

"So how's the restaurant going?" he asked.

"Amour's happy. She's got a steady stream of regulars. Truth be told, I rarely see her anymore. We're lucky if we have our tea together in the morning. Oh, and Father Vokey was by the other day. She had her marriage annulled. Said she had pretty much given up on it. Anyway, according to Father Vokey, he pulled out all the stops. Personally wrote to the Pope. Imagine that!"

"See, it's not that bad," Stanley said, approaching his new home. "Beautiful view, lots of space for a garden, and a barn for horses."

"You're going to get new ponies?"

"Maybe. Want to see inside?"

"Might as well. I'm here, aren't I?"

Mabel walked in and looked around at the broken floorboards and wallpaper peeling off the walls. There was a three-legged table on its side and a gaping hole above the fireplace.

"So, what do you think?"

"I can see the potential," she lied. "But you definitely have your work cut out for you."

"I know. But I like working with my hands. I'm just gonna pick away at it. I think you'll be surprised when it's finished."

"I'm sure I will be," she said, running her hand over the narrow countertop covered in an array of tools and nails of every size.

"Want to help me paint and decorate?" Stanley asked.

"I'm not much at decorating, myself. But I could give you a hand with the painting."

"I'd show you the upper level, but I don't trust the stairs."

Mabel was relieved. She didn't either.

November 28, 1936

Stanley was gathering up the drop cloths and paint brushes, as Mabel surveyed the results of their efforts.

"You know, I thought you were crazy for buying this place. But it's turning out better than I thought."

"Ye of little faith," Stanley said.

"Listen to you, quoting the bible n'all. When are you moving in?"

"Soon. I just need to bring in my furniture."

"You got a new home, you should buy new stuff."

"In time."

"When's Angus taking over your old place?" Mabel asked, taking one of the drop cloths from him and folding it.

"Soon as I move out."

"So, are you going to drive me home after all my hard labour? Or are you going to make me walk?"

"Actually, I was hoping you'd stay for supper."

"*Supper*?"

"Yeah, supper. Why don't you wash up? It will be ready in no time."

Mabel returned ten minutes later to see an overturned box in front of the fire.

"Turn around, close your eyes, and don't open them till I tell you." Stanley instructed.

"Tell me when," Mabel said.

"I will."

Stanley laid a moth-eaten tablecloth over the box, stuck an unlit tapered candle into the mouth of an empty Frostie bottle, and threw two large pillows on the floor. He then ran to the kitchen. He quickly returned with a cookie sheet that he placed on his makeshift table. Everything was in order, but he let her stand with her back to him for a few extra seconds. He just liked looking at her without feeling compelled to turn away. He put his hands on her shoulders and spun her around.

"Okay. Open your eyes."

Mabel looked down, then quickly back up at Stanley. "Perogies! I'm glad I stayed."

"Me too," he said, reaching down and popping one in his mouth.

For Thine is the Power and the Glory.
For ever and Ever

June 6, 1937

James walked into the bedroom and found her on the floor, struggling to sit up. She was trying to say something, but her words were stuck in her head. They wouldn't come out. "Ames," she finally slurred through one half of her mouth. "Margaret!" he shouted. He lifted her up and placed her on the bed, then frantically ran downstairs to dial for help. He was back at her side within minutes. He couldn't see through his bleary eyes. He pinched them shut. She finally came into focus. He looked at her. He saw terror.

Mabel ran down the hospital corridor, almost colliding with a nurse carrying a tray of utensils. She charged through the door and into the sparse room; a curtain hiding the scene she dreaded she'd find. She pulled it back slowly and looked at James's swollen eyes and stubbled chin. He was holding Margaret's limp hand. Mabel wrapped her arms around his neck, but said nothing. She had nothing worth saying. She then walked over to Margaret, kissed her on the forehead, and began gently brushing her hair back off her forehead, just as she did the morning she'd found her dead mother, many years ago. She and James sat quietly until Dr. Cohen appeared in the doorway and called James into the hallway.

"Go," Mabel said. "I'm not going anywhere."

James stood slowly, but couldn't bring himself to let go of Margaret's hand. Mabel lifted it up and replaced it with her own. "Go on," she urged.

He walked in ten minutes later. Mabel didn't need him to share the news. She saw it on his ashen face and in his dull, red-rimmed eyes.

"The," he said, stopping. "The prognosis isn't… isn't…good," he choked between sobs.

June 29, 1937

Margaret came home three weeks later, in a wheelchair. She could barely talk and her right side was totally paralyzed. Mabel's heart ached as she watched James pick her up, rest her head against his shoulder, and rub his cheek against her hair. James had his eyes closed, thinking of the time Margaret wore it in a French braid and they joked he might have to carry her if it snowed.

He barely left her side as the days turned into weeks. Mabel had to practically force him to eat. Mary Catherine, along with Douglas and Luke, saw to the store. Stanley saw to the books. Mabel put her baking aside whenever she could convince James to leave Margaret's side. She would bathe her, comb her hair, and read to her.

"Margaret? Guess what I brought today?" she said, forcing her voice to sound lighter than her heart.

"Waw?"

"*A Tale of Two Cities.*"

"My fav… or… ite."

"And after we finish *this* tome, it's on to *Anna Karenina.* I figured you didn't want to hear *Smokey the Cowhorse* again."

"Noooo."

Mabel picked up the book. She was several chapters in when she looked at Margaret.

"Do you want me to stop? Are you tired?"

"Taaalk."

"You want to talk?"

"Twy."

"Okay," Mabel said, knowing what a struggle it was for her.

Margaret used her left arm to pick up her right. She put her lame hand on Mabel's.

Mabel tried not to cry.

"I," Margaret said, "I…" She closed her eyes to concentrate. "I… lof yeew."

Mabel's will didn't hold. "I love you too, Margaret," she said, as tears rolled freely down her face. "You've always been so good to me. All the things you did for me. Taught me to read and talk properly. Only thing you failed at was needlepoint. But that was my fault, not yours. I lost my mother, but I thank God every day for bringing me to you."

"Not always good… tooo… yeew."

"True," Mabel said, allowing herself to smile. "There was a time I thought you were a bitch."

The good side of Margaret's mouth curled up and she made a sound that Mabel knew was her new laugh.

James watched from the doorway. "Margaret? Are you up for some visitors?" he asked.

"Whoo?"

"The boys are waiting downstairs."

"Suur," she said, trying to sit up. Mabel helped her lean forward, put another pillow behind her back, pulled the blanket up to her chest, and placed Margaret's permanently clawed hand on her lap.

James returned with the boys a short while later. Mark walked in quietly and leaned against the far wall. John eagerly jumped up on the bed and snuggled in next to Margaret.

"Ames… can-dy."

"Margaret," he said smiling and shaking his head. "Those kids aren't going to have a single good tooth among them."

"Boo…ok," Margaret said to Mabel, gesturing to *The Cat Who went to Heaven,* which was never far from reach. Mabel passed it to

John, who began sounding out the familiar words to the delight of the woman who always loved reading to him.

James didn't return with the candy. Luke did. Mabel could tell he had been crying.

Margaret died that night as James lay next to her, holding her hand. He stayed like that till morning.

July 2, 1937

Mabel walked to the front of St. Anthony's Church and looked down at James. He was sitting between Mark and Luke, with John on his lap. Stanley, Mary Catherine, Sam, Amour, Michael, and Margaret's brother, Philip, completed the list of mourners in the front pew. She then looked out at the huge crowd staring back at her.

"A few years ago," she began, before stopping to gain her composure. "A few years ago, Margaret told me she wanted to be a teacher. When I asked her why she didn't, she'd said it came down to choosing between teaching and a life with James. It was never a question which one she would choose. What I pray she knows, is that she didn't give up one for the other. She was both. Both a devoted wife and teacher… an amazing teacher, not just to me, but to her boys, as she liked to call them, Luke, Mark and John. She taught me the Foxtrot, to add my gees to my verbs, and that there is no such word as *ain't*. She taught John the alphabet, to tie his shoes, and to print. She helped Mark with his math and reading lessons. She taught Luke about geography, making sure he learned about the country where his parents were born, and sitting with him for hours on end, explaining the parables of the Bible, or discussing politics and world affairs. But most of all, she taught us about kindness, about generosity, about strength, and about unconditional love."

She paused briefly and looked at James, uncertain if the words she had lovingly put to paper would bring him more sadness. He was smiling at her. "Of course, there was nothing Margaret wanted more out of life than to be a mother. God granted her only a brief time with the one child she and James brought into their world. Her dream of being a mother, like her life, cut far too short. So I pray she also knows, that for me and her boys, she was more than just our teacher; she was our mother, too.

I say this because each of us felt the kind of love we know exists between a child and a parent. And we know Margaret did as well. Today, I feel a loss that makes me ache in a place I never knew existed. I ache not just for the loss of Margaret, but for the pain I know James is left to endure. A pain that I know is far greater than mine, or anyone else who is left to mourn the passing of this wonderful woman. As anyone who has ever seen Margaret and James together will tell you, you couldn't just see the love they had for one another, you could feel it. Margaret's life wasn't always easy, and it certainly wasn't long, but it was full of blessings. She fulfilled her life's dreams. She had a husband who adored her, she was a teacher, and she was a mother. We will miss her dearly, but thank God for bringing her into our lives."

Mabel blessed herself and walked away from behind the lectern. She stopped, smiled at James, and hitched her skirt. She was wearing Margaret's boots. She then walked off the altar and hugged him.

"I love you," James whispered, kissing her cheek.

Margaret was laid to rest at sunset next to her baby son. James, Mabel, Margaret's boys, and the rest of the mourners who filled the front pew listened as Father Vokey intoned, "Ashes to ashes, dust to dust." Her simple grave stone read *Margaret Cameron, Child of God, Devoted Mother and Wife, Friend and Teacher. Born March 12, 1899. Died, June 29, 1937.*

James laid a single rose on her Coffin. Mabel and the boys laid daisies.

May 2, 1938

Mabel was sifting flower into her bowl. "It really was a beautiful wedding. I loved every minute of it. I'm sure that if I get to go to a hundred more, it'll always be my favourite," she said.

"Wait for your own," Mary Catherine said, mixing her batter.

Mabel closed her eyes, thinking any hope of donning a wedding dress were lost to her, forever.

"I was so proud of you. You wouldn't even suspect you're not a Jew," she said to her friend.

"But *I am* a Jew. A giyoret, to be exact," Mary Catherine said.

"Whatever that is. You know what I mean. The glass thing. When Sam stomped on the glass and broke it. What the heck was that all about?"

"It's a Jewish tradition. It symbolizes the destruction of the Holy Temple in Jerusalem two thousand years ago."

"Imagine, all the glasses that were broken since then. What a waste," Mabel said, shaking her head.

"I heard the boys had fun with Mr. Cameron while we were gone," Mary Catherine said.

Mabel peeked around the corner. James was greeting a customer. "They're good for him. The only time he seems truly happy is when they're around. I worry about him all the time. He's so thin and I can't tell you how often I go out back and find his ash can full of butts. And he's got this awful cough. Sometimes he starts and can't stop."

"He's still grieving," Mary Catherine said.

"I know. But it's been almost a year. It's like... he's just walking through life. Luke's been a big help, though. Coming by practically every day after school and keeping him company on weekends. I know James loves Mark and John, too. But he and Luke have something special."

Mary Catherine looked at Mabel. "Mr. Cameron will be fine. It's you I'm worried about?"

"*Me?*"

"Yes, *you*," Mary Catherine said.

"What do you mean?"

"I mean you're not getting any younger. You know, Mabel, Stanley really likes you."

"*Stanley?* Go shake yourself. He's just a good friend. Besides, he's a hundred years old."

"He is not! Anyway, I see the way he looks at you. Sam sees it too. He's a good man and very good looking, don't you think?"

"Oh, he's a good man for sure."

"And good looking?"

"He's not bad."

"And he has his own business and a nice home," Mary Catherine persisted.

"So?"

"So, maybe you should give him a chance."

"I'll give you a kick in the arse," Mabel said, returning to the task at hand. She lifted her doughy fingers from the sticky white mound on her kneading table, doused her hands in a fresh supply of flour, clapped them together, and thought how all hopes of marriage and children were lost to her forever. No man, not even one as good as Stanley, would want a soiled woman. No, she thought. There would be no husband or children in her life. They had been stolen from her the night Billy and Eddie showed up at the shack.

May 11, 1939

CHAPTER I

Mabel peeked under the blanket that covered the sleeping baby.

"Mabel, he's fine. It's done all the time," Mary Catherine said.

"I can't imagine. He must be in a lot of pain."

"He's sleeping like… like a baby."

"I don't know about this… what did you call it?"

"Bris. It's performed on all Jewish babies. All boy babies."

"Do they ever miss and, you know, accidently cut it off?"

"No," Mary Catherine said laughing. "The Rabbi knows what he is doing."

"And I thought stomping on the glass was strange. God knows what you're going to tell me next. I think I liked you better when you were Catholic. Seems a lot less dangerous," Mabel teased.

"Come on, before you wake him up."

The two friends walked back into the noisy living room. Mark was there, along with two of his friends, Sam's new law partner and his wife, and Sam's two sisters and their three children. Mabel reached for some punch and playfully stuck her tongue out at John, who immediately began to laugh. The door opened and Sam's mother and father walked in, hugging and kissing everyone in sight.

"Where's Irwin?" Sam's father bellowed.

"Papa! Quiet! He's sleeping," Sam scolded.

"What time is supper?" his father asked, rubbing his large belly. "I'm starving."

"It won't be long," Mary Catherine said. She looked at her husband, then pointed to the clock. Finally, they heard the knock.

"I was beginning to think you weren't coming," Sam said.

"What?"

Sam leaned into Stanley's good ear. "I said, come in. Come in and join my crazy family."

"I hope you don't mind, I brought you a little something," he said, holding out a brown paper bag. "Papa will love you," he said, taking Stanley's coat.

Mary Catherine joined them at the door.

"And this is for the baby," Stanley said, handing her a badly wrapped package. "It's not much. And it's not really very good, but I —"

"Did you do this? It's beautiful. I love it," Mary Catherine said, looking at a hand drawn sketch of two tiny ponies mounted in an ivory frame. "Look, Sam! Look what Stanley made for the baby."

Stanley smiled and looked over their shoulders, for Mabel.

CHAPTER 2

They were parked in front of the shack. Mabel was talking nonstop about how strange Jewish traditions were, when Stanley leaned over and kissed her. He pulled back to see her reaction. His heart fell. She didn't look happy.

"What was that all about?" she asked.

"Mabel, I think you know I have feelings for you."

"Well, I have feelings for you, too. Just not in that way," she lied.

Stanley put his head down, realizing that it had been a mistake to think her feelings would change with time. "I'm sorry. It won't happen again," he said. They sat awkwardly in the dark and silence. "I hope it won't make things awkward between us. I don't want to lose… our friendship," Stanley finally said.

Mabel was looking down at her hands. "It won't."

The silence crept back. Stanley contemplating what to say next. Mabel contemplating opening the door and running into the shack.

"Look," Mabel said, pointing to her neighbour's. "Nosy, old biddy."

Minnie Atkinson dropped the curtain meant to veil her prying eyes.

"Mabel, I think we both know things *will* be awkward from now on. It's only natural. Truth be told, I've had feelings for you for a long time and was hoping you felt the same. Now I have my answer."

"It's not like you won't be a fabulous catch for some other girl.

Just not me," she said, forcing herself to glance at him.

"So, if I'm such a fabulous catch as you say, what is it? Do you think I'm too old?"

"You're not that old."

"So, then? What? I could understand if you were interested in someone else. I know other guys have asked you out. And I'm pretty sure Michael's friend, Nelson, isn't stopping by the store every second day just for your pies."

"*He* happens to appreciate my pies. Not like some people I know. But no. There's no one else."

"Then what is it? I make a good living. I actually bought the Andrews property hoping that someday… someday you'd want to share it with me." He knew he was just making it harder on himself, and on Mabel. He needed to accept her decision and stop pushing himself on her.

Mabel put her head back down. "I'm sorry if I gave you the wrong impression. I didn't realize —"

"It's okay. I know where I stand."

"Thank you for understanding," Mabel said.

"Good night, Mabel."

"Good night."

Mabel stepped down from the passenger seat and watched him drive off. She walked into the dark shack, thinking Amour must still be at the bistro. She turned on the light and looked at the kitchen table, as images of Johnnie, Billy and Eddie flooded back. She climbed into bed, hugged her mother's pillow, and cried herself to sleep.

May 12, 1939

Mabel woke, surprised that Amour was not yet out of bed. She tapped on her door. "Amour? It's going on six." No answer. "Amour," she repeated again. She opened Amour's bedroom door. She wasn't home. She was getting ready to head to the store, when the telephone rang.

"I'm glad I caught you before you left for work."

"Where are you?" Mabel asked. "I was beginning to worry."

"I'm in a beautiful suite. In an inn up the coast."

"What?"

"Michael and I are on our honeymoon. We got married last night."

"You eloped! Oh, my God, Amour! I'm so happy for you."

"Thanks! I'm over the moon. I closed the restaurant for the week. I'll be home on Saturday."

"I'm really happy for you both. We'll have to celebrate when you get back."

"Thanks, Mabel."

"Say hi to Michael for me."

"I will. See you soon."

Mabel put the receiver back on its cradle. She started to cry. They were tears of joy.

May 28, 1939

"What is it, Mabel?" Mary Catherine asked.

"What do you mean?"

"I mean you've been so quiet lately. You don't seem yourself. Is it because Amour is moving out?"

"Of course not. I'm used to being alone. And Amour and Michael certainly aren't going to stay at the shack when Michael's got such a nice home."

"Then what is it? I know something's eating at you."

"I'm just worried about James."

"Really? I actually find he's doing better lately."

"He's still too thin."

"I think you're lying to me. I don't believe that's what's bothering you."

"I'm just tired. That's all."

"Well, you better rest up for Amour's and Michael's party. I can't wait to see their place. I bet Amour has it looking lovely."

"It's very nice," Mabel said flatly.

Mary Catherine pulled a chair out from the table and walked over to her friend. "Okay, sit and tell me what's going on with you. Or…or I'll think you're mad at me for something."

"I'm not mad at you," Mabel scoffed.

"Then for goodness sake, tell me? I'm worried about you."

"I think Stanley's mad at me. He hasn't been by in a couple of weeks. Not even to see James."

"He's probably just busy."

"No. It's more than that," Mabel said.

"Why do you say that?"

Mabel told Mary Catherine about the night he kissed her. "I didn't think he'd stop dropping by the store."

Mary Catherine began to lose her patience. "Well, you have nobody to blame but yourself. I don't understand you. You're like a couple when you're together. Why you don't want to date him is beyond me."

"I've just always thought of him as a friend."

"Well, obviously he thinks of you as more. You can't blame him for keeping his distance. He's hurt. I honestly think you care for him more than you let on. I'll tell you one thing. I'm sure you're gonna regret it when Stanley walks in that door with another woman on his arm."

"I'd be happy for him."

"The hell you would! You know it. And I know it. I think you should talk to him at Amour and Michael's party. Christ, Mabel! Neither of you are getting any younger. Next thing you know, my father's gonna be looking to find *you* a Jew."

June 2, 1939

CHAPTER I

James, Mabel, and Luke travelled to the party together. Everybody was there, including the Matthews, the Collinses, the Friedmans, Michael's colleagues, and Amour's growing staff. Everybody but Stanley. Mabel kept looking at the time, assuring herself he was usually the last to arrive. By ten o'clock, she realized he wasn't coming. By eleven, she was in the car and heading home with Luke and James.

"You're a good driver," James said to Luke, leaning forward and patting him on the shoulder. "Drop me off. Then take Mabel home."

James passed Luke a five dollar bill. "You can fill up in the morning. Good night."

"So, how's school going?" Mabel asked her young chauffeur.

"Good. Won't be long before I finish up."

"Then what?"

"I'll work at the store."

"Not going to continue your studies?"

"No."

"But you're so smart. James tells me you could go to any college."

"Not in the cards."

"Why?"

"I don't want to leave town."

"Is it a girl?" Mabel asked.

"No."

"I hope it's not James? Because, if it is, you know he wouldn't want you to limit your opportunities for him."

"I know. I like working at the store."

Mabel knew it was because he didn't want to leave James. "You're a terrific young man, Luke. James is lucky to have you in his life."

"I'm the lucky one," Luke said. He pulled in front of the shack. "Want me to go in with you?"

"Thanks. I'll be fine. Really, Luke, you should talk to James. I know he wants you to go to college."

Luke nodded and smiled.

Mabel entered the shack feeling low. She hung her coat on a hook in the hallway and latched the door. She then groped around in the dark for the lightshade. She reached under, found the cord, and pulled it down. The room lit up.

"Oh, my God! What are you doing here?"

"Well, I'm not here for your pie," Dan McInnes slurred.

CHAPTER 2

Stanley had driven by Michael's and Amour's a half dozen times. He had wanted to go in, but couldn't bring himself to. Instead, he parked his truck up the street and sat out front for almost an hour. His heart fell, when he saw them pile in James's car and drive off.

He drove home, cursing himself. He looked around his large empty house and poured himself a double rum. He closed his eyes and pictured Mabel knotting her blue and white, polka-dot kerchief at the back of her neck. He could still see her pulling it over her forehead to protect her hair from the light green paint she liberally applied to the grey walls. And he thought of the night they sat at their makeshift table, sharing perogies in front of the fire.

"Damn it," he said. He grabbed his coat and headed for the door.

By the time he got to the shack, he started to lose his nerve again.

CHAPTER 3

"I want you to leave. You don't need any more trouble."

"Ya do, do ya? Well, too fuckin bad! Cause I'm not goin anywhere. Been waitin for this opportunity for too long."

"What do you want with me?"

"I want ya to answer my question."

"What question?"

"Don't play stupid, ya fuckin slut," he said. He spun his gun around on the table. "You know exactly what I mean."

Mabel weighed her odds at making it to the door. "I have no idea what you're talking about. My aunt and her husband will be home any minute. So, you better leave now, or —"

"Don't insult my intelligence. Yer aunt and her big-shot husband aren't comin, and ya know it. They live in a big fuckin mansion. They wouldn't be caught dead in this dump."

"But they're coming by —"

"Shut the fuck up and answer my question," he yelled.

Mabel jumped. "I don't know what it is."

"Stupid bitch. I want…" he said, "to know who ya were fuckin. Cause I know yer no fuckin virgin. Was it Stanley? Was it Cameron?" He smirked and took a swig of rum. "Or was it both?"

They both turned when they heard the knock.

McInnes put his hand on his pistol. "Get rid of them."

"Is that you, Michael?" Mabel hollered.

"It's Stanley."

Mabel's heart began to pound.

McInnes stood with his gun aimed directly at her head.

"I'm just getting ready for bed," Mabel said.

"It won't take long," Stanley said.

"Like I told you yesterday. I don't want to see you anymore. Go now! Or I'll call the police."

"What?"

"Like I told you yesterday. I don't want to see you anymore. Go away!"

Mabel heard him walk down the steps.

McInnes staggered to the window and watched Stanley get in his truck.

My God, Mabel thought. He didn't hear me.

"So, I *was* right. Ya were fuckin that goon. Did ya just start to like it?"

Mabel said nothing.

"Ya ruined my fucking life, ya know. If it weren't for you, I'd be captain right now. And here I was, tryin to help you. And ya just screwed me over. Ungrateful bitch!"

"But Stanley didn't murder Johnnie. It was a hit and run."

"Doesn't change the fact he and that sick bastard Cameron were fuckin you." He sat back down heavily on his chair. "Ya must get off on it. Ya know, if ya like that sort of thing, I'd be happy to oblige."

Mabel looked around for her bread knife. "You're right. I know better now. We can go to the police, together."

He started to laugh.

"No! I promise. We'll go first thing tomorrow. I want to see them both get what they deserve."

"Actually, I got a better idea. How about ya do for me, what ya did for them," he said.

Mabel heard him unzip his pants. She felt sick. He turned his chair to face her, spread his legs, and began rubbing himself. She turned her head away.

"Get over here!"

She didn't move.

"Get over here," he said, pointing the gun at her. She walked closer and looked for something, anything within reach, to hit him with. She spotted the rum bottle. The same kind of thick, amber-coloured bottle that Billy and Eddie had once brought down on her head. It was the only thing in sight to prevent the brutal indignity from happening again. She would sooner die than be raped a second time.

"Don't waste your time. Knives are put away. Rolling pin's burnin in the stove. Now, get over here and start yer kneadin. You'll get a good rise out of me with a little rub and tug."

"I prefer the bedroom," Mabel said.

"Get over here."

Mabel moved a step closer. He put the gun down on the kitchen table, lunged forward, grabbed the front of her blouse with one hand, and her hair with the other. He pulled her head back and licked her neck. With as much anger as fear, she kneed him hard in the groin. He bent over and let go of her. Mabel threw herself on the table, knocking the gun to the floor. She grabbed the bottle and was holding it over her head, ready to bring it down on him. She stopped midair. He was pointing the gun at her.

"Put it down! Put the fuckin bottle down, or I'll blow your fuckin head off. I got nothin to lose. Bitch!

Mabel slowly placed the bottle on the table. McInnes swiped at it with his arm, smashing it against the wall. He walked over and slapped her hard across the face.

Mabel fixed her eyes on his. "I'll do what you want. Let's just go to the bedroom."

"Don't fuck with me." He stood with his pants hanging loosely on his hips. "Take off your blouse."

Mabel slowly opened one button at a time.

"Hurry up," he said, holding the gun to the side of her head.

"Please! Not here!"

He clutched the neck of her blouse and roughly ripped it open. Buttons flew off in every direction. Mabel's hands shook as he began lifting her skirt.

"I'm going to be sick," she said.

"Shush," he whispered. He crouched down before her, tore at her stockings, and started running the barrel of his gun up her leg. She needed to get him into the bedroom. She would stab him with Margaret's hooked needle, bludgeon him with Johnnie's kerosene lamp, or smoother him with her mother's pillow. She would die, but she would not be raped, again.

"What the fuck is this," he said, shoving the barrel in the hole above her knee. "Not the hole I was looking for," he laughed. He pushed the gun up her leg. "I got two loaded barrels. The one between yers. And the one between mine. Which one should we start with? This one," he said, digging the gun into her upper thigh. "Or…" he looked down at his bulging crotch, "this one in that pretty little mouth of yers."

"You're hurting me," she pleaded.

He stood up. "On yer knees."

She didn't move.

He brought his hand back and slapped her a second time. She turned to him, her face stinging. Her angry glare unchanged.

"Yer gonna love this."

Mabel closed her eyes.

"It's going to be so much better than those two limp, old …"

She heard the impact of the pan shovel against McInnes's head, opened her eyes, and watched him slump to the floor at her feet. Stanley dropped the shovel, led Mabel to the sofa, and wrapped a blanket around. He then hauled McInnes along the floor into the back porch. He grabbed him by the collar and punched him in the face, shoved him back down, and then kicked him hard in the groin. Mabel watched as he tore out the front door. He was back in seconds. He handed her his half-empty bottle of rum. "Drink up," he said, more harshly than he intended.

The two of them sat trembling in the quiet and waited for the police. They arrived in less than ten minutes. Sergeant Dunphy took a brief statement from Mabel, then he and two of his fellow officers carted a still unconscious McInnes out the back door. Stanley watched from the doorway. One constable picked McInnes up by the arms, the other by his feet. They swung him back, then roughly hurled him forward onto the floor of the paddy wagon; the same black paddy wagon he drove to Cameron's store the morning after Johnnie's body was discovered in a ditch off Brookside Street. Dunphy slammed the double doors shut, waved to Stanley, and drove off.

Stanley returned to Mabel's side.

"You're shaking," Mabel said, offering to share her blanket.

"Adrenaline."

"I thought you didn't hear what I said and that you weren't coming back," she said.

"I knew something was up when you said you didn't want to see me anymore. I had to crawl through your bedroom window."

"Why did you come in the first place?"

"I needed to see you."

Despite the events of the night, Mabel began to feel better. "Thank God," she said, pressing her eyes together to rid herself of the image that was running through her mind. "If you hadn't shown up … I don't know."

Stanley pulled her into him, took the rum bottle from her, took a swig, and passed it back. "Would have been better if I came by earlier. If I went to the party."

"Why didn't you?"

"Figured you didn't want to see me."

"I missed you. And I don't just mean at the party."

"I almost didn't come," he said.

Mabel shivered.

Stanley pulled the blanket more tightly around her shoulders. "You're in shock."

She put her hand over his. "You know, Stanley MacIntyre? This is the second time you've saved me."

He pulled his hand away and leaned back against the sofa. "Anything for a friend."

She smiled at him. "I care about you. You know that."

"But not enough to be with me. You know I'm in love with you," he said, thinking the rum had fortified his nerve.

Mabel could feel her heart speed up. She put her head down. "Yes."

"Then why? You say you care for me."

She looked at him, not knowing what to say. "It's late. You should go home."

"I'm not leaving you here *alone*! I'll sleep on the sofa."

Mabel felt relief knowing he'd be close by. "You can stay in Amour's old room."

"Fine," he said. He began pacing and running his hand through his hair. "This time I'll be testifying against him. He's lucky I called the police and didn't finish him off. You sure you're alright? You should drink up. It'll help you sleep."

Mabel walked over to him and surprised him with a hug. "Thank you. But I need to put this night behind me."

She turned to go to her room.

"Mabel? I deserve a reason."

She pushed her bedroom door open. "I wish I could give you one," she said.

Whether it was the rum, the adrenaline, or a combination of both, the words were out of his mouth before he could stop. "Is it because of Billy Guthro?"

She spun around. "You know?"

"Yes. I've known for some time."

"But how?"

"Eddie told me the night I went after him and Billy. It's not your fault."

"Who else knows?"

"No one. I haven't told a soul."

Mabel looked down at the floor. "Not even James?"

"No. It was your right to tell him. Not mine."

"And you still want to be with me?" she asked.

Stanley looked at the ceiling, sighed, and shook his head. "Yes," he said emphatically.

"Because you feel sorry for me? Is that why you want to be with me?"

"No, Mabel. I'm not trying to be a martyr. I'd be the one with the most to gain. I want to be happy. And I know that's not possible without you."

Mabel could feel her chest tighten.

"Will you at least sleep on it? I've waited this long. I can wait a few more hours. If your answer is no, I promise never to ask again."

Mabel turned and entered her bedroom. She had her back to him. "You'll have my answer in the morning," she said, and slowly closed the door.

She didn't sleep a wink. Neither did Stanley.

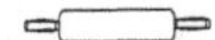

June 3, 1939

Stanley was waiting for the whistle on the kettle to sound. He had two cups set out on the table. If her answer was no, he'd keep his promise and move on. He felt anxious. He couldn't believe she wasn't up by now. Perhaps she was just putting off the bad news. He was impatiently pacing back and forth when her bedroom door finally opened. They looked at one another. Both waited for the other to speak.

"Yes," she said.

"Yes?" he repeated, looking for confirmation.

"Yes! What's wrong with you? Are you deaf or something?" she said.

June 19, 1939

James knocked lightly on the room that had once been a nursery to baby James and a refuge for Mabel. "Luke? Tide and time wait for no man. Fish aren't going to wait for us, either."

"I'm up. Give me a minute."

James was untangling his line when Luke appeared on the landing. James looked up at him, suddenly realizing he was no longer a boy. He must have grown a full foot over the past year.

"You're bleeding," James said, rubbing his own chin to show him where.

"I borrowed your razor. Hope you don't mind."

"You're welcome to anything I have. You know that. When did you start shaving?"

"This morning."

James put his arm around Luke's shoulder. "There's a knack to it, you know. You have to make sure the water is really hot and your blade is really sharp. You also have to use lots of soap and….."

They sat on the grass, with their legs dangling over the side of the bank. James was baiting his hook. "You seem unusually quiet. Anything bothering you?" he asked Luke.

"Not really."

"That means something *is* troubling you."

Luke cast his line into the still water below. "No. Just thinking about stuff. That's all."

"Like college? You know I was talking to Douglas and he said he could take on some extra shifts at the store. So I hope that's not what has you worried."

"I'm not worried about that."

"Than what?"

Luke's emotions got the better of him. "You," he said wiping his watery eyes.

"*Me*! Now why would you be worried about me? I'm fine."

"You need to eat more and quit the makins."

"You're starting to sound like Mabel."

"Well, she's right."

"Okay. I promise. I don't need the two of you nagging me," James said, elbowing his companion. "So, now that you know the store is looked after and I'm going to be on my best behaviour, are you going to look into continuing your studies? You know you don't need to worry about the cost. I have that covered."

Luke started to cry.

James put down his rod, leaned in, and hugged him. "What is it, son? What's wrong?"

"You're too good to me," he said, his voice cracking.

"That's because you make it so easy," James said. He reached into his pocket, pulled out the embroidered handkerchief Margaret had made for him, wiped his own eyes, and then handed it to Luke.

"When Ma and Da died, I didn't want to live," he said. I know Da killed himself. Kids at school used to ask me if I was a cliff jumper, too. Then I met you and Margaret. Don't get me wrong, Mary Catherine and her parents have been real good and I know they love me and my brothers. But, you and me, we talk about things. Do fun stuff together. You're the closest thing I have to a father. I lost one. I don't want to lose another."

James felt like he had a boulder stuck in his throat. "Luke, I never told you this before, but I lost a son." Luke turned to James who was looking off in the distance. "He was just a baby. Died from the flu. You lost a father. I lost a son. But here we are."

Luke looked down at his reel, not sure of what to say. He always wondered about the tiny rocker in the room where he and his brothers often slept.

"You know," James continued, "I think of you as my son. I sure worry about you like you are. You're a very smart young man. I just want you to get a good education and be happy. And I want you to know that after Margaret died, I took a few long walks along Table Head myself. I'm pretty sure that God brought us together for a reason. I think he knew we needed each other. That we could help each other. And he was right. We're both doing good now. Aren't we?"

"I guess so."

"I know so. And I know this. I'll be fine, as long as I know you are. You need to stop worrying about me and go to college. That's what your mother and father would have wanted for you. And that's what Margaret would have wanted, too. Agreed?"

Luke looked at the thin, grey-haired man sitting beside him. "Agreed."

"Good then," James said, remembering the day he had watched Sam and his father embrace in the courtroom. He'd thought he'd never get to experience that same kind of father-son moment for himself. He smiled, knowing he just did.

September 1, 1939

It was only after Stanley offered up a fifty dollar bill and a bottle of rum that Father Vokey finally agreed to perform the ceremony outside the church. "I'm sure the Lord will forgive me this one time, knowing I can do so much good with your generous contribution in aid of the poor," he had said. He then blessed himself, knowing that only two hours before, he had acceded to Mabel's wishes, after she promised her new husband would help with needed repairs to the manse, go to Mass on Sunday, and leave a generous donation in the collection plate.

The wedding was simple and intimate. James was Stanley's best man. Mary Catherine was Mabel's maid of honour. Luke, Mark, and John, along with Amour and Michael, Angus MacNeil, the Friedmans, Collinses, MacGuires and Mary Catherine's parents stood on either side of the footbridge, spanning the brook.

"And do you, Stanley Patrick MacIntyre, take Mabel Grace Adshade as your lawfully wedded wife?" Father Vokey asked.

Stanley put his hand to his ear pretending he didn't hear.

Father Vokey didn't get the joke and repeated the vow more loudly. Everyone laughed.

"I do," Stanley shouted.

"And do you, Mabel Grace Adshade, take Stanley Patrick MacIntyre as your lawfully wedded husband?"

"You bet I do," Mabel said.

"I now pronounce you man and wife."

Angus put his fingers to his mouth and let out a sharp whistle. Everyone else began to cheer. Stanley leaned in and kissed his new bride gently on the cheek. He was crying. Mabel leaned in and whispered in his good ear. "Took ya long enough."

They all headed to Amour's bistro for the celebration, where James began with a toast to the bride and groom.

"Today I feel joy. I feel like I am the proud father of the bride, giving away his daughter to the only man I know is good enough to be her husband. Stanley, I trust you to be the kind of husband to Mabel as you are a friend to me. Loyal, trustworthy, patient, protective, and kind. I love you both and I'm overjoyed that you finally came to your senses and realized what the rest of us have known for some time. If there is a hint of sadness in my voice, it's because Margaret isn't with us to toast this wonderful union. Before she died…" The words were lodged in his throat. "Before her last stroke, she told me that one day we would witness this happy occasion. In fact, she asked, 'What the heck is taking those two so long?'"

Again, everyone laughed. Stanley smiled at his new bride. "It wasn't my fault," he called out to even more laughter.

"So, let's all raise our glasses and toast this long overdue union of two very special people who are about to set out on a new journey together. A journey that, like all others, will have its ups and downs. May your path be lined with flowers and free of stones. And may God watch over you both and bless you with many children." James raised his glass. "To the bride and groom."

Mabel hugged James, as tears crept from the corners of her eyes. "I wish she was here, too."

"I feel as if Margaret and your mother are both here." James reached into his pocket and pulled out a small box wrapped in blue tissue paper and handed it to her. "Margaret wanted you to have this. I almost gave it to you after her funeral, but she made me promise to give it to you on a happy occasion."

Mabel gently removed the paper, pressed it into a neat fold and opened the box. It was a beautiful cameo brooch.

"It was her grandmother's."

"It's beautiful, James. I'll treasure it like I do my memories of her. Thank you," she said, stretching up and wrapping her arms around his neck.

"That's not all," he said. He turned and reached behind him. "I know she'd also want you to have this." He passed her a pastry box topped with a simple red bow.

Mabel lifted the lid and peered inside. It was a matching sterling silver hairbrush and mirror.

"Her mother gave it to her on our wedding day. I finally got around to sorting through her things."

Mabel put the box down and hugged him.

"Cheating on me already," Stanley teased. "Your toast was lovely, James."

Mabel wiped her eyes. "Stanley? Look what Margaret set aside for me," she said, holding out the brooch. "And, look at this," she said. "Aren't they beautiful?"

Stanley smiled at James. "She was a wonderful woman, James. You were a lucky man."

"Like you, my friend," James said, patting him on the shoulder.

James turned and walked away.

The newlyweds stood quietly. Stanley had his arm over his wife's shoulder. Mabel had her arm wrapped around his waist. Their mutual happiness momentarily interrupted by the loneliness they saw in their friend.

CHAPTER 2

They drove along the coast, Stanley's concern growing with every mile. Mabel was unusually quiet and kept her head turned to the side. He thought she might be worried about the wedding night. He reached over and put his hand on hers. "You okay?"

She turned to him. "I'm better than okay. Just look at all of this," she said, turning back to the window. "All the beautiful trees, the green mountains, and the colour of the sky and the water. How can anyone doubt there's a God?"

Stanley thought of all that she had been through and marveled at her unwavering faith. He smiled. "Not everyone sees through such forgiving eyes," he said.

They pulled into the parking area of the Inverary Inn; the same inn Amour and Michael had stayed at on their honeymoon. Stanley turned off the engine and looked at his bride. "I thought we'd get settled and then have supper. Amour says the food is great."

Mabel reached into her mother's tote and pulled out a half dozen ham sandwiches wrapped in wax paper. "I guess these will keep for another day."

Stanley was checking in. He peeked over at her. She stood wide-eyed as she took in the spacious lobby with its wall of windows exposing the ocean beyond. He knew she had never seen anything so luxurious and was glad he was the one sharing this moment with her. He hesitated, happy in the moment, simply watching her. He walked up to her and put his hand under her elbow. "All set?"

"It must be expensive," she said.

"It is," he laughed. They made their way down the hall. "Here we are," he said, putting the key in the lock and pushing the door forward. Mabel stepped in and looked around at the nicest room she had ever set foot in. It had a huge fireplace, a spectacular view of the ocean, and framed pictures on the wall. Bright green pillows, with gold tassels, rested against the beautiful wooden headboard of a massive bed hidden under a white, downy quilt.

"We even a gramophone," she said, laying her hand over it.

"I requested it," Stanley said, holding up a record and sliding it from its paper sleeve. He eased it over the pin and onto the plateau, cranked the handle, and carefully placed the needle in the outer groove.

Mabel laughed when the scratchy sounds of the revolving needle against the vinyl dissolved into, *When I'm looking at You.* It was the first song they had danced to.

"Care to dance?" he asked and held out his hand.

"Care to get your feet stomped on," she said, laughing.

Stanley sang to her as they danced.

Why is the sun brighter
Why is my heart lighter
What makes the promise of heaven truer
When I'm looking at you.

"You thought of everything, Mr. MacIntyre," she said.

"I also thought about dinner reservations. And as much as I could stay like this all night, we should get a move on." He kissed the top of her head.

They walked hand-in-hand into the dimly-lit restaurant. A dozen candlelit tables were draped in white linen.

Their waiter approached carrying two huge menus. "Good evening, Mr. and Mrs. MacIntyre. I have your table ready."

Mabel pulled on Stanley's sleeve. "How did he know our names?"

"He's the same guy who checked us in," Stanley whispered.

"Geez, it's even fancier than Amour's," she said, walking to their table and eyeing the long neck of a green bottle sticking out of a bucket of ice.

Stanley sat down, quickly jumped back up, elbowed their waiter out of the way, and pulled Mabel's chair out for her. She started to sit down and stopped midway, pulling the bottle up from the ice. She held it under the candle. "Cham…Cham… pang… nee."

Stanley looked at the waiter, then at Mabel. He smiled. "Champagne. It's a fancy French wine."

"Can we afford this?" she asked, her face registering concern.

"I didn't order it," Stanley said, taking his seat, and wondering why he had more than one fork.

Their waiter left. He came back a few minutes later, put two flute glasses down, and popped the cork. Mabel jumped. Stanley laughed and looked up at the sweaty man in his black coat and stiff white collar pouring the champagne. "Does it come with the price of the meal?" he asked.

"No. It comes compliments of an anonymous friend," he said, putting the bottle back on ice.

"James," they both said at the same time.

Their waiter smiled and rushed back to the lobby to check in a new arrival.

After more than a few minutes reviewing the menu, Stanley convinced Mabel to try the steak.

"Never had steak in my entire life," she said. She folded the menu over and leaned into Stanley. "It cost more than my new coat," she whispered.

"It's our honeymoon."

The waiter was back, sweating buckets. "May I take your order?" he panted.

Stanley gave Mabel an encouraging nod.

"I'll have the steak," Mabel said.

"And for you, sir?"

"The same."

"And madam, how do you like your steak?"

Mabel looked at him, then Stanley, then back at their waiter.

"Don't I get to try it first?" she asked, thinking working two jobs was getting the best of the poor man.

Stanley started to laugh as the waiter stood dumbfounded. Stanley leaned into her. "He means, well-done, medium, or rare?"

He then watched in amazement as Mabel polished off her own meal, and the remains of his.

They mostly sat in comfortable silence for rest of the evening, with the exception of Mabel going on at some length about how wonderful the food was, except for the pie.

When they returned to their suite, Mabel sat on the end of the bed and watched Stanley ready the fire. He was crouched down in front of the hearth. "Done," he said, as the paper shriveled into a feathery white ash and the wood began to crackle. He stood up, adjusted the damper, shut the lamp off, and joined Mabel at the foot of the bed. He picked up her hand, sliding his fingers between hers. "How are you, Mrs. MacIntyre?"

"Full," she said.

"I would hope so. I think I'd rather pay your board than feed you," he said and laughed.

Mabel got up and walked to the window. He walked up behind her, wrapped his arms around her waist and rested his chin on her shoulder. "You know, we don't have to rush anything. It's entirely up to you when… when we —"

"Do the nasty," she laughed.

"Well, yes. If that's what you want to call it."

"Are you nervous?" she asked.

"A little. And you?"

"Yes. I'm afraid I'm going to disappoint you," she said.

Stanley turned her around to face him. "I'm afraid that's not possible."

She leaned in and kissed him, thankful she had been unconscious the night Billy tried to steal this moment from her.

The only time they set foot outside their door over the next two days was to walk along the beach. Instead, they dined on Mabel's now stale sandwiches, danced in front of the fire, and made love.

September 3, 1939

Mabel was up before six. She quietly collected their things, packed their bags, and placed them by the door. Stanley woke to see her dressed in grey slacks and a pink sweater. She was watching the gulls circle over the shore. He propped his elbow up on his pillow and rested his head in his hand. "I love you, Mabel."

She turned, smiling. "I love you, too. But it's time to go home. I've got baking to do."

Stanley protested, suggesting they stay one more night. Mabel won out. They headed back to town.

When they pulled up to the store, James was out front, watching Douglas and Angus suffer under the weight of a huge sign they were trying to erect. Mabel stepped out of the car and looked at the faded sign lying on the ground. *Dry Goods Sold Here*. She then looked up at the new one, still precariously hanging sideways, as Angus yelled to Douglas to pull up on his end of the rope. She smiled when she read *Cameron's Bakery and Dry Goods Emporium.*

"Welcome home," James said.

Mabel stood speechless.

"This is my wedding gift to you. I remembered Margaret telling me you thought we needed a new sign."

"I used to dream you'd have a real bakery and this is the name I had in mind."

"I know. Margaret told me that, too."

Mabel was grinning from ear to ear. "*This*, the champagne, the beautiful gifts," she said. She leaned in and wrapped her arms around James's waist.

Stanley walked up to them. "Hey! The groom is watching, ya know."

Stanley hugged James.

"So, has Mary Catherine been able to keep up with the orders?" Mabel asked.

"Let's just say she's going to be glad to see you."

"Well, time's a wasting. I better get at it," Mabel said, leaving James and Stanley to supervise Angus and Douglas.

The sign in place, James took Angus and Douglas to the back of the store, where they each took turns toasting the groom. James and Stanley entered the kitchen a half an hour later. Mary Catherine was sliding a cake from its pan. Mabel was already rolling out pie crust.

"Mabel? There's a matter I'd like to discuss with you when you finish up. Your husband said I can drive you home."

"Sure, James," she said, her curiousity growing.

Mary Catherine beamed as Stanley kissed Mabel goodbye.

Six pies, four loaves of bread, and three cakes later, Mabel tidied up the kitchen while Mary Catherine waited by the front door for Sam to come for her.

James joined Mabel in the kitchen, put a shoe box on the table, and poured two cups of tea.

Mabel pulled out a chair and sat next to him. "You're certainly a man of mystery," Mabel said.

"Sam's father came by while you were away. He left this for you." He gently slid the box across the table. "Your mother left instructions for him to give it to you once you were married."

"What is it?"

James shrugged. "Open it."

Mabel was just about to lift the lid, when they heard the commotion out front. They ran into the store. Mary Catherine and Sam were hugging.

"What's going on?" James asked.

Sam looked distraught. "Britain just declared war on Germany."

CHAPTER 2

Mabel looked at the box on her lap as James maneuvered the car up the long, dusty path leading to the bluff overlooking the ocean. "Do you think we'll join the war?" she asked.

James nodded.

"Maybe it won't last long?"

"I doubt it. This Hitler fellow has been goose-stepping his way across Europe with little resistance. German people love him. And he's got the Italians, Hungarians, Romanians, and others on side. I hope you're right, but I fear we're in for another long war and thousands more casualties," he said, thinking of Percy.

"I've got some reading to do," Mabel said, lifting the lid of the box.

"It's an opportunity for you to see your father through your mother's eyes."

"I can't believe she set her letters aside for me."

"She loved you dearly. I guess she wanted you to know how much your father meant to her and why…"

"Why she had me," Mabel offered, knowing he was struggling to say, *out of wedlock.*

"Yes."

"Would you like to come in for supper?" Mabel asked.

"Thanks. But I'm just going to head home and tune into the radio."

"Good night," Mabel said, leaning over and kissing his cheek.

"Good night, Mabel."

CHAPTER 3

Mabel sat on the bed, opened the box, and carefully unsealed the letter on top, marked *Mabel.* Her chest tightened and her eyes filled, as images of her mother came flooding back. Her beautiful face and warm eyes. Her, patting the stool beside her, telling Mabel to jump up so she could see the beautiful blue water in the distance.

Stanley looked at his wife, knowing she needed time to herself. He smiled at her, walked into the hallway, and pulled the door over, careful to leave it open just a crack.

> *My Sweet Girl:*
>
> *I hope the years since my passing have been kind to you. Despite the circumstances that cause me to write this letter, my heart is full of gratitude knowing you are a young woman now, and that you have found love as a new wife. You are at the right time in your life for me to share news that I fear will come as a great shock. I pray you understand and will not judge me too harshly.*
>
> *The man you know as your father, is not. Your father is Percy MacPherson. Sadly, he died in the war before he knew he was going to be a dad. I know that, like me, he would have adored you, and that you would*

have loved him. Every time I looked at you, I saw his warm eyes, kind heart, and curious mind. I want you to know that we were deeply in love and that I feel absolutely no regret or shame about the choices I made, including marrying Johnnie. Johnnie was my only hope of keeping you and Percy with me.

I know this is a lot to ask, but Johnnie doesn't know he's not your father. So, I pray you will honour my memory by respecting our secret. No good can come from disappointing him anymore more than life already has. There is only one other person besides you who knows the truth. James Cameron. He's been a dear friend to me for as long as I can remember, and he was like a brother to your father. I know Johnnie's demons sometimes get the better of him, so I asked James to help watch over you. Knowing he is a man of his word, I expect that you have become good friends.

In the box, you will find the letters I wrote to your father while he bravely served his country overseas. I often wished I had sent them, but today I am glad that I have them for you. I hope you will read them and, over time, come to understand and forgive me. I know my time is short, but I thank God every day for the joy you, your baby brother, and Percy brought to my life.

I pray today, as I do every day, that God grants you strength and the power to forgive. Please remember to always count your blessings.

Yours in eternal love,
Ma

May 28, 1940

James felt sick as he watched a long line of men and boys gather outside the enlistment office and joke about vanquishing the Hun. He looked at their eager young faces, remembering how he and Percy also thought they were setting off on some grand patriotic adventure that they would one day share with their grandchildren.

"Mr. Cameron! Mr. Cameron!"

James turned to see Angus MacNeil and his two younger brothers.

"Angus? You're signing up?"

"We all are. Lauchie wanted to, too. But somebody has to stay home with Ma."

"I hope you understand what you're getting yourself into," James said. He wanted to take him back to the store and tell him about Percy and the young man caught up in the razor wire.

"Somebody's got to stop the Nazis before they start pullin into the harbour."

"I wish you well, son," James said, praying he would return home safely. He was getting into his car when he saw Sam and Douglas MacGuire leaving the office. His heart sank.

June, 21, 1940

James was reading the paper for news on the war when the door opened.

"Hello."

"Hello, Mr. Cameron. I was wondering if you might have any openings."

"You're Corliss's daughter?"

"Yes. Alice."

"Are you looking for work after school?"

"No. I'm finished school. I mean, I'm finished for now. I'd like to go back some day."

"I heard about your father's accident. How's he doing?"

"To be truthful, he's having a hard time. Hard enough to find work in this town with two legs, let alone one."

James realized Alice dropped out of school to help her family. "Are you any good at baking?"

"Ma says I am."

"And math?"

"My favourite subject."

James knew that with Luke away at college, Douglas enlisting, and Mary Catherine soon needing time off with another baby on the way, he and Mabel could use the extra help.

"Well, Alice, your timing couldn't be better. Come, I'll introduce you to Mabel and Mary Catherine."

October 19, 1940

"Please go home. Sam is leaving in a couple of weeks and Alice and I have everything in hand," Mabel pleaded.

"Are you sure?"

"I'm positive. I'll get more done if I know you're where you should be."

"Thank you," Mary Catherine said.

"Here let me try," Mabel said, watching her friend try and button her coat.

"God, at the rate I'm growing, you'd swear I was having twins," Mary Catherine said.

"Pie smells good. Hope you can spare a piece?"

"Luke! What are you doing home?" Mary Catherine squealed.

"I was hungry. Came for some pie. I see you're looking *swell*," he said.

They laughed.

"Why aren't you in school?" Mabel asked, hugging him.

Alice walked in the back door carrying a crate of apples. Luke rushed forward, took it from her, and put it beside the counter. Mary Catherine introduced them.

"Where's James?" Luke asked.

"He's doing inventory out back. He never mentioned you were coming?"

"I thought I'd surprise him."

James squatted and strained under the weight of a box of canned goods.

Luke watched from the doorway. “Looks like you could use a hand.”

James dropped the box, just barely pulling his foot out of the way.

“Luke! What are you doing here? Why aren’t you in school?”

October 26, 1940

Amour and Michael served the tea. Despite Mabel's best efforts to keep the mood light, everyone talked in whispers. The normally boisterous gathering of friends, subdued by the impending departures. James looked around the store. Sam was huddled over Mary Catherine in the corner, kissing his wife's extended belly. Mrs. MacNeil kept brushing her sons' cheeks, reminding Angus to look out for his younger brothers. Mrs. MacGuire was crying as Douglas kept saying, "Ma don't worry. Everything will be fine." Mary Catherine's mother and father sat quietly apart from everyone else, pushing Irwin back and forth in his stroller.

Alice appeared with a tray of sandwiches. She offered one to Luke. He wasn't hungry, but took one just the same. "Stay safe," she said. His heart skipped a beat.

James looked at Luke. He was standing with his arm protectively wrapped over his baby brother's shoulder. James was heartbroken when he had heard the news, but knew there no stopping him. Luke had already enlisted. He's so young, James thought, quickly reminding himself he had been about the same age when he and Percy signed up. James thought back to the shy, introverted, and lonely boy he'd first met. He was now a tall, confident, and handsome young man. Still, he thought, he's just a kid. It's the uniform that makes the boy underneath it appear much older.

Luke walked toward him. "If you're worried about losing your fishing partner, don't. Mark said he's going to take over until I come home."

James didn't say anything. He didn't think he could.

"I know you're worried, James. I promise. I'll be okay."

James remembered Percy saying much the same to his parents, knowing it was a promise Luke couldn't make.

Stanley walked into the middle of the small, solemn crowd and clapped his hands together. "Sorry, folks. But we need to head to the station now, or the boys will miss their train."

James turned to Luke. "I have something for you," he said. He reached under his collar and pulled Percy's St. Christopher medal out from around his neck. "Remember that I am praying for your safe return," he said with wet eyes.

Luke put it around his neck. "Don't worry. I'll be home before you know it."

"I love you, son. Godspeed," James said, embracing him.

"I love you, too," Luke said, kissing him on the cheek.

James didn't go to the station.

December 12, 1943

Mabel peeked around the corner and into the store. Alice was spending more time on the register than she was baking. James was back in bed. She looked at the pastry counter. The vast array of pies, raisin tea biscuits, brown bread, cakes, and scones she and Alice had frantically put out, was almost depleted.

Alice smiled broadly, handed her latest customer their change, and wished them a, "happy day." She quickly ran back to the kitchen, threw open the oven door to check on her oat cakes, and then back to the store to cheerfully greet another customer.

Mabel admired Alice, as much for her willingness to quit school and support her family, as for her baking abilities. She was thinking about how they could use Mary Catherine's help when she appeared in the doorway with Irwin and Ruth at her side.

"What is it?" Mabel asked. "You look like you've seen a ghost."

"Mabel? Where's James?"

"Why? What's wrong?"

"Luke is missing in action."

February 9, 1944

Mabel was in the doorway to the kitchen. James was in the store, standing next to the bakery display, watching the swirling snow. Mabel knew what he was thinking. She walked up to him and put her hand on his arm. He turned, smiled, and then wiped his eyes. "I'm sorry."

Mabel rubbed his back. "You need to have faith. I'm sure he's fine. He's smart and strong."

"It's been almost two months," he said, taking out his hankie and blowing his nose. "I'm sorry, it's just—"

"Just that you miss him."

"Bad enough he signed up. But a tail gunner? He'd be safer on the ground."

Mabel needed to distract him. "If this keeps up, it'll be two feet high before morning."

"You should have let Stanley come for you before it started to come down."

"I'd almost think you were trying to get rid of me," she said, trying to lighten the mood.

"Never," he said.

"C'mon. Let's have some tea," Mabel said, pulling on his arm.

"I feel like a rum."

"Okay. Tea for me and rum for you," she said.

Mabel tried to keep their conversation away from Luke and the war. "Did I tell you Stanley hired Willie Morrison and Peter Boyd? He says they're working out great. Oh, and Mary Catherine said Ruth is over the croup."

James was looking into his glass and swirling his rum around. "Do you ever wonder if there really is a God?"

"No."

He looked up at her. "Just like that? No."

Mabel smiled. "No. I have no doubts."

James leaned back in his chair. "What makes you so sure?"

"What makes you doubt? It's not like you," she said, with a smile conveying concern.

"I just can't fathom how a loving God could bring so much misery upon so many people. Good people. What he put you through. Your mother. Matthew Toth, his wife and sons. And now the damn war. I started to have doubts after Percy died. Then we lost baby James. Then I lost Margaret. I believe I'm a good man, yet I feel like God, if there is one, is punishing me."

"Or testing your faith?"

"But why?"

"Because you question it," Mabel said.

"But you don't? And your life's been no picnic."

"Well, despite some hardships, I feel pretty blessed. James? How could God test our faith if he didn't bring us a little misery along with joy?"

"But what about my son? Your brother? God took them before they had any understanding of good or bad, faith or doubt?"

"I think they were preordained by God to take their place beside him and they're happy at his side."

"And the rest of us are left to grieve."

"Yes. And to believe, or not believe. Margaret believed. Ma did, too. They both lost infant sons, yet they didn't doubt. They remained steadfast in their belief. I think God rewarded them for their faith by bringing them to their children."

"So, who's responsible for creating the wars and all the mean people of the world? People like…like Johnnie for instance. How do you explain someone like him? He had a good mother. He was raised by a family with more opportunities than most. He was blessed in so many ways, yet he was also a miserable you-know-what. Did God make him that way?"

"God gives us choices. Johnnie didn't always make good ones. I think it's sort of like John's colouring book. God," she said, moving her hand across the top of the table as if guiding an imaginary pencil, "gives us the outline of our life. It's up to us to colour it in. We can stay within the lines and make it as beautiful as we can, or we make a mess of it. Johnnie chose to scribble outside the lines."

James took a sip of his rum, thinking of how Ellie had described her as a child. Smart, curious, always finding joy in life when there was little to be found.

"But why? Why would God leave three young boys orphaned?"

Mabel shrugged. "So they could bring joy to others. Perhaps to restore the faith of those who doubt?" she said, resting her hand on his.

"I don't know. More and more, I think everything is just random. Ever notice how some folks bear more than their fair share of burdens. Good folks, I mean. I'm starting to think it has nothing to do with God. It's just the luck of the draw. You're either born smart, or you're not. You're either born with a caring heart, or you're not. You're either lucky, or you're not. I often wonder why I survived the war and Percy didn't. Why God would take someone with such a kind heart. A father- to-be."

"James? I know you're worried about Luke. It's only natural that you'd question your faith at a time like this. Your mind if full of fear. It's telling you to doubt. But I bet you're praying for his return."

James took a sip and smiled. "Every day."

"Why then? Why pray if you don't believe that there's a loving God to hear you?"

"You know, your father used to say that if the Misfits had siblings, we wouldn't have found each other. Your mother would argue that it had nothing to do with whether or not we had brothers or sisters. She'd say it was all part of God's grand plan. I guess you agree with your mother."

"Yes. And Percy, too. God's plan was that you would all be born without brothers or sisters. That's how you would come to find each other."

"You're forgetting I had a half-brother," James said, dipping his chin and fixing his eyes on those of the young woman he loved as deeply as any father could love a daughter.

Mabel smiled. "That God saw answer the prayers of another family."

James pursed his lips, flipped his outstretched hand palm-side up, and sat back in his chair, dismissing the thought Johnnie could be the answer to anyone's prayers.

"Alright then," Mabel said. "Let me ask you this. If you could have switched places with anyone else, but it meant you wouldn't have met Percy, Ma, Margaret, or Luke, would you have?"

"Or you?"

Mabel smiled. "Or me."

"No."

"So, despite what you're feeling now and the sad times in your life...despite your doubting faith, you're still pretty happy with how your life turned out?"

"Yes," James said. He smiled. "Margaret always said you were wise beyond your years. I love our chats."

They jumped at the sound of a loud bang.

"Damn! I forgot to secure the shutters," James said.

They walked to the front of the store and looked out the window at the snow whirling furiously under the street lamp. James reached for his coat. Mabel took it from him and put it back on the hook. "Why not just leave them as they are. You never know, there might be some poor, lost girl out there on her way to work, searching for a place to escape the storm."

"On her day off," he said, elbowing her.

"Looks like we won't be seeing too much traffic tomorrow," Mabel said. She wrapped her arm around his waist. He put his over her shoulder and they started upstairs.

When they got to the top, James turned to Mabel. "Thank you."

"For what?"

"For helping me repair my marriage with Margaret. For bringing Luke and his brothers into my life. For helping me see that I've been blessed me in so many ways."

She stood on her toes and kissed him on the cheek. "I should be thanking you. If it weren't for you, who knows, I'd probably be scribbling outside the lines."

She watched as he went into his room. He smiled and closed the door over, careful to leave it open, just a crack.

February 10, 1944

Mabel woke early with the wind still howling. She got up, removed her long, white nightdress trimmed with lace, and carefully folded it as if it was being placed in the window of *Marshall's Fine Ladies Wear.* She gently patted it with the palm of her open hand and thought of Margaret. She walked to the window and drew the curtains back to look out over School Street and the snowy street below. She then made the bed and walked toward the door. She stopped, looked down at the tiny chair sitting motionless in the corner and gently pushed it forward. It was rocking back and forth when she closed the door and headed downstairs to make the fluffiest, most delicious bread in town.

She had two loaves rising and a pie underway, but there was still no sign of James. It's good he's sleeping late, she thought. He's been looking especially tired, lately.

She was dusting her kneading board with flour when the phone rang.

"Hello," she said. "Are you sure? Absolutely positive? Yes!" She dropped the phone.

"James! James!" she hollered, tripping twice on the way upstairs. "They found Luke! They found Luke!" Her heart began to pound as she reached the top and the silence grew. She stood outside his bedroom. "James," she said more quietly. She slowly placed her trembling fingers on the door and pushed it forward.

"Oh, James," she said, holding her hand over her open mouth. She walked over, felt his cold forehead, kissed it, and brought his eyelids down over his dark brown eyes. She sat on the side of his bed, thinking of another storm almost ten years ago that had brought him to her bedside. She started to sob and slumped to the floor. She spotted an overturned fame between the night table and the large wrought iron bed James had once shared with Margaret. She turned it over. The sepia coloured photo was jarred loose from its frame when it had fallen to the floor. Mabel wiped her eyes, then carefully put it back together. It was a picture of James standing behind Margaret with his hand on her shoulder. A beautiful boy in a white christening gown sat on her lap. They were all smiling.

February 13, 1944

At his instruction, there was no funeral Mass. His wishes were simple. He wanted to be buried next to Margaret and his son, and that only his dearest friends attend the graveside service. Following internment, everyone was to return to the store for a sharing of happy memories. Mabel, Mary Catherine and her parents, Mark and John, Amour and Michael, Alice, Mrs. MacGuire, the Friedmans, the Matthews, and the Collinses looked on as Stanley walked over and stood beside the coffin. "God couldn't have given me a better friend. James Cameron was a man of honour and absolute goodness. Loyal, trusting, and generous. I loved him as much as I could any brother. And I will miss him until the day I die." He cleared his throat. "A reading from John, verse four. *Beloved, let us love one another, for love is from God, and whoever loves has been born of God. Anyone who does not love does not know God, because God is love. In this the love of God was made manifest in us, that God sent his only son into the world, so that we might live through him. In this is love, not that we have loved God but that he loved us and sent to the propitiation for our sins. Beloved, if God so loved us, we also ought to love one another. No one has seen God: if we love one another, God abides in us and love is perfected in us.*"

Stanley closed Margaret's Bible and walked with his head down toward Mabel. He wrapped his arm around her shoulder as Father Vokey, who was almost twice the age of the man for whom he recited the internment prayer, called out the all too familiar words. “Ashes to ashes. Dust to Dust.”

The gravesite was snow-covered and frozen, so the modest wooden coffin would be stored until the ground softened. “I’ll be back,” Mabel said, placing her hand on the cold, hard surface of the casket that held the man she loved as much as any daughter could love a father. “I’ll come back in spring. When the daisies are in bloom,” she whispered.

February 18, 1944

"He was a good man who will be missed," Samuel Friedman Sr., said.

"He was a wonderful man," Mabel said, clutching her purse on her lap.

Stanley put his hand over hers.

"Ordinarily, I would prefer to read the last will and testament with all of the heirs present, but given Luke is not here, I believe James would want me to proceed. Mabel, he has left the bakery to you, as well as his mother's Bible. He has left the store, as well as the apartment to Luke. In the event that either you or Luke die before the will is executed in full, the entirety of the property will go to the surviving heir. It's all very straightforward. There are some technical details in the event that either you or Luke wish to dispose of your share of the estate that I think are better discussed when Luke comes home. He has also left a sum of nearly thirteen thousand dollars, to be divided equally between Mark and John, with the wish they use it to pursue their education. Stanley. He left you his Plymouth."

"Thank you," Mabel said. She stood to leave.

"Mabel? That's not all. He left you this," Samuel said. He handed her an envelope. "I also have one for Luke."

Stanley and Mabel drove home in silence. They were both overwhelmed by the sadness of the day. Stanley put on the tea. Mabel opened the envelope.

Mabel, God blessed me when he brought you into my life. Ellie,

Percy, Margaret and I will be looking out for you. Live well my beautiful girl.

Mabel smiled, thinking of their last conversation. She tipped the envelope upside down. Two photos slid out and onto the table. One, was one of her laughing with Margaret in the kitchen. The other was of her, James and Margaret smiling in front of the store. It was taken just before they headed off for Mary Catherine's and Sam's wedding.

"He must have known the end was near," she said, resting her head on Stanley's shoulder. "I wish I had told him about the baby."

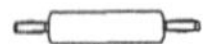

August 9, 1944

CHAPTER I

Mabel left Mary Catherine and Alice to the baking. She had looked in all of the usual places for the Bible, but never found it. Now was as good a time as any to try again. She went through all the cupboards and dresser drawers once more, but it wasn't there. She finally pulled the stool over and began removing boxes from the upper shelf of the wardrobe in James's bedroom. She smiled when she found *Smokey the Cowhorse* and *The Cat Who Went to Heaven.* She'd give them to Mark and John as keepsakes.

She then spotted what looked like a large box wrapped in a child's blanket. She pulled the blanket away. It was what she had been searching for. She eased it to the edge of the shelf and rested it against her chest. It weighed a ton. She then stepped off the stool, placed it on the bed, lifted its embossed leather cover, and turned the pages. She was immediately transfixed by colourful images of the Virgin Mother, Jesus on the Cross, The Last Supper, and The Ressurection, each protected by a delicate layer of onion-skin paper. It was the most beautiful Bible she had ever seen. She was about to close it over, when it fell open to a page that dislodged an unsealed envelope and two handwritten notes that had yellowed over time. One note was from James's third grade teacher commending him for his penmanship. The other, a condolence letter addressed to

Henritta on the passing of her sister, Louise. Mabel opened the envelope, pausing to admire the beautiful handwriting, perfectly set out in neat, straight lines.

> *My Darling Joe,*
>
> *I am so sorry I had to leave before seeing you. As I feared, mother discovered I am pregnant. They vowed to disown me if I keep our baby. I begged my parents to let me talk to you, but they refused. They're taking me to the train station tomorrow. Mother and I are going to the mainland until the baby arrives. I'm not sure where we'll be staying.*
>
> *Joe, It was awful what they said to me. They said I shamed them and called me unspeakable names. Well, I don't care. I love you more than anything and I'm heartbroken our baby might be taken from us. I wished we had run away as you suggested. I wish you could find steady work. Louise promised to give this letter to George so he can get it to you, but I fear she won't keep her promise. Father has put the fear of God into her, too.*
>
> *If you are reading this, please know that I love you with all my heart. If you love me as I do you, I hope you will find a way to come for me and the baby before it's too late. Please have George ask Louise where to find me.*
>
> *With my whole heart and soul.*
> *Love, Henrietta.*

Mabel closed the letter and knew the baby Henrietta spoke about was the man she used to call Da. But who was the father? Who was Joe? She walked back into the bakery, lost in her thoughts, when she recalled James talking about Dr. Adams being a childhood friend of his mother.

"Mary Catherine! The medical examiner, Dr. Adams? Do you remember his first name?"

"I think it's George."

"You ladies seem to have things in hand. I think I'll head home early."

"You should have left long ago," Mary Catherine hollered back. "Go home and relax. Put your swollen feet up."

Mabel put on her coat and waved goodbye. "I'll see you girls in the morning."

She took her time, walking the long way around. She went down Caledonia Street, avoiding the shortcut through MacLeod's field, across Brookside and up to Park Street, arriving at the footbridge spanning the brook. She stopped briefly, before making her way up York. She continued on to the intersection, turned right past Senator's Corner, and crossed the street to the medical examiner's office.

"Hello. I'm looking for Dr. Adams," she said to the young man who greeted her.

"Dr. Adams hasn't worked here for almost three years."

"Do you know where he lives?"

"Leslie's Lane. Big white house with a Red Maple in front. You can't miss it."

Mabel had to backtrack. She got to Leslie's Lane and had no trouble identifying the house. She knocked and waited.

"Hello. I was wondering if Dr. Adams might be home?"

"He is, but he's taking his nap."

"Perhaps I can come by another time?"

"May I tell him who was calling?"

"Mabel MacIntyre. I was a friend of James Cameron." Mabel was about to leave, when George called out to his wife.

"Who is it, Effie?"

"It's Mabel MacIntyre. She'd like to speak with you."

"Well, tell her to come in," he said, flattening his hair in place with his hand.

Mabel sat with Dr. Adams as he talked about James as a boy. She enjoyed his stories, but was anxious to see if he could help solve the mystery.

"I was wondering, Dr. Adams, if—"

"Call me George. I no longer practice medicine."

"I was wondering if you know who James's mother might have been seeing before she married his father."

"That would be Joe MacPherson. Fine guy."

"And they had a baby."

Dr. Adams looked surprised. "How do you know that?"

"James told me some years ago. So, I don't suppose Joe is still alive?"

"No. He died over twenty years ago."

Effie put some oat cakes and tea in front of them.

"Thank you. They look delicious," Mabel said.

Effie smiled and left them to their privacy.

"They are," Dr. Adams said, watching his wife retreat to the kitchen. He winked at Mabel and whispered. "They came from Cameron's bakery. Anyway, where was I? Oh, yes. Joe was killed in the pit."

"So what happened to Joe and Henrietta?"

He peered into his tea. "I guess, their parents, time, and distance wore them down," he said.

He looked back up at Mabel and recalled how Henrietta and her mother left town to escape the inevitable scorn of folks pointing their accusing fingers. "By the time they returned from the mainland, Joe and two of his brothers had gone off to work in the lumber yards in Maine. Mining jobs were at a premium back then, most were reserved for men with families to provide for. Two mines had closed. There was an explosion in one and a huge bump in the other. Lost twenty-six men. Anyway, Henrietta and Joe exchanged letters for awhile. Actually, I was their go-between for a few months, until I left for college. Then, we all kind of lost touch and went our separate ways."

"So, Joe never came back to town?"

"Oh, he came back two or three years later. But Henrietta was already married to Charlie by then, and James was on the way. Joe just got on with life. It all worked out well in the end. He married Rita and they had Percy."

Mabel stood up sharply. "Percy? Percy MacPherson? The same Percy MacPherson killed in the war?"

"Yes."

Mabel's mind was spinning. Percy was Johnnie's half-brother. James was Johnnie's half-brother.

"I'm sorry. May I use your phone?"

"Sure. But don't you want to have an oat cake? Finish your tea?"

CHAPTER 2

Mabel was going a mile-a-minute. Stanley couldn't keep up with her. "Have your supper," he urged, pointing to the pea soup that was growing cold on the table.

"I'm not hungry. I've been eating all day," she said, walking past him and into the living room. He knew better than to protest. Mabel slouched down on their pale green sofa, propping her elbows up on two large, white pillows embroidered with pink flowers.

"Stanley? Imagine, they both shared the same half-brother. Don't you see? They both wanted a brother," Mabel said. He didn't reply. She wasn't sure if he hadn't heard her, or if he was lost in his own thoughts about the irony of it all. She leaned forward, put another pillow behind her back, and spread her legs apart, allowing room for her bursting-at-the-seams belly to extend unencumbered. She looked into the kitchen and at her husband. He was slowly running his dry rag around the rim of a shallow, white bowl. A memory that seemed to come from a life-time ago guided her hand to her forehead. She slowly ran her fingers over the hint of a scar. Images of Johnnie storming out the door, James sitting on the side of her bed, Margaret's long white nightgown, and Dr. Cohen packing up his black bag flashed through her mind.

"I feel badly for all of them," she called out.

Stanley placed the bowl on the counter, lobbed his dry rag into the sink, and walked to the doorway of the living room.

Mabel was looking at the mantel above the fireplace, lined with books. A small rocker was off to one side and an empty coal scuttle off to the other. Johnnie's unlit kerosene lamp sat on a small table against the far wall. She then looked over at the small collage of treasured photos covering the pink and green flowered wallpaper. She dropped her head, brought her hand to her mouth, and began biting the ragged edge of a broken fingernail. "I feel badly for them. Especially Johnnie," she whispered.

"You feel badly for *Johnnie?*"

She turned, surprised to see her husband leaning against the doorframe with his arms folded over his chest.

"I do," she said, lowering her head.

He smiled and shook his head. "I'm sorry, Mabel. I can't. The way he treated you —"

"Still, if he knew where he had come from, perhaps things would have turned out differently. Don't you think it's sad he didn't know he had *two* brothers? I think that if he grew up knowing them, with their influence, he wouldn't have been so lost. So mean."

Stanley straightened up and walked toward the sofa. He picked up one of the large white pillows, threw it on the floor beside her, and knelt down by her feet. He took his wife's hand in his, wiggled his fingers between hers, and rubbed his thumb over her knuckles. "Mabel? I doubt it would have made a lick of difference. Some people are born good… and some aren't. And Johnnie certainly wasn't one of the good ones."

Mabel looked down at his fingers meshed with hers.

Stanley adjusted his position so he could rest his cheek against her belly. "On the other hand, if it wasn't for Johnnie, you probably wouldn't have given this creepy, old, deaf guy, who stunk of coal and tobacco, a second look."

Mabel started to laugh.

"It's true. If Johnnie…" he hesitated, "wasn't Johnnie, I probably would have never found you, and we wouldn't be here now, waiting for this little one to arrive." He ran the tip of his nose back and forth along her girth. Mabel squeezed his hand. She raised the other, arched it over his back, and began gently kneading the back of his neck. They stayed that way for nearly an hour, comfortable in their shared quiet.

A spark exploded in the fireplace, rousing Stanley from near sleep. He stretched his long legs,and got to his feet. "Time for bed," he said, holding out his hand. She put her arm over her belly. "You go. I'll be up shortly."

He bent down and kissed the top of her head, walked to the landing, then peeked back at her. She was awkwardly pushing herself upright with one arm buried deep into the soft pillow; the other stretched out for balance. She stood, crooked her arms around her waist, and arched her back. She turned to see Stanley watching her from the foot of the stairs and smiled. She waved him on, turned on the floor lamp, and peered at the image of her mother sitting in a straight back chair with Mabel on her lap. She had it committed to memory, but she needed to see it again before turning in for the night. "Count yer blessings," she whispered. She then leaned in closer, examining Johnnie's handsome face. She wondered if he somehow knew the child sitting on his wife's lap was not his own. Her eyes then shifted to the other images looking at her. James and Percy in their uniforms, each with an arm wrapped around her mother's waist. "You'll be a grandfather soon," she whispered, touching the image of Percy's face. She then looked at the photo of James, Margaret and baby James, all beaming into the camera. She laid her hand on her belly, and looked down at the unborn child that kicked and elbowed her from inside. "Just like your grandma always said, it's all part of God's grand plan." She reached under the lamp and pulled on the cord. The embers in the fireplace cast a flickering orange glow around the dark room. She felt both happy and sad, and then, the warm rush of water streaming down her legs.

Oct.13, 1944

Mabel looked around and thought about all that changed. The store looked nothing like it did when she first came here as young girl hoping for a job doing what she loved. And it didn't feel the same either. She looked up at the image of girl in the tam on the green and white can that occupied a coveted spot on the shelf behind the counter, recalling the time she had rolled the makins for James. She felt herself well up. She tilted her head back and chided herself, thinking her memories were taking hold of her emotions. Too much nostalgia, she thought, can cast a black shadow over the brightest day.

Still, she couldn't stop thinking about how happy James and Margaret would be on this day. It was over seven years since Margaret died, and almost eight months to the day since James had. Her mind then turned to Angus and Douglas, two young men with great promise who made the ultimate sacrifice. She thought of their mothers. Angus's mother died two weeks after learning her son kept his promise to protect his younger brothers, only to be gunned down in a vain attempt to save a British soldier. Douglas, who didn't set a foot on foreign soil, was no less a hero for his sacrifice. The ship carrying him off to battle was torpedoed somewhere in the North Atlantic, leaving hundreds of grieving mothers behind; among them, the once cheerful and outgoing, Mrs. MacGuire. Now sullen and withdrawn, she rarely left her house, other than to go to church.

Stanley walked over to Mabel, the baby wrapped in a pale blue blanket, rested his bald head on Stanley's wet shoulder. "You okay, hun?" he asked.

"Of course," she said. She brought her hand to her neck and touched Margaret's cameo, a reminder to herself that this was a happy occasion.

"Want to hold JC for a bit? Amour wants me and Michael to pour some… li-ba-tions," Stanley said.

Mabel took the sleeping bundle from his father. "Come here, you little monkey."

Amour approached.

Mabel was gently bouncing the baby. "I thought they'd be here by now," she said.

Amour put her hand on Mabel's arm. "He'll be coming through that door any minute."

Luke stood next to Stanley's car and took a deep breath. He looked at the black clouds gathering overhead and sniffed the cool, salty air into his lungs. *Hold it together. Hold it together.* He started walking in the direction of the store, then stopped. Mark, at least fifty feet ahead, turned to face his big brother. "Luke, it's going to rain and everyone's waiting. C'mon!"

Luke waved, put one leg out, and then the other. It wasn't the pain slowing him down this time. He looked up to see Mark with his hands in his pockets and kicking the ground. He hastened his pace.

They were standing on the wide, wooden platform that led to Cameron's Bakery and Dry Goods Emporium. "Thank God. Those clouds are about to burst," Mark said, pointing skyward. "I wouldn't wanna ruin my hair."

"Trying to impress the girls, are we?" Luke asked.

Mark grinned. "Just one."

"And who's that?"

Mark reached in front of his brother and threw the door open. "Her name is Alice. She works here."

Luke gripped his cane, put his head down, and pinched his eyes shut; overwhelmed by the moment. Mary Catherine wrapped her arms around his neck, kissed his cheek, and led him in by the arm.

"It's good to be home," Luke said, his voice breaking.

The welcoming was more subdued than jubilant, as everyone took in the frail, young man standing before them, hobbled by war.

Mabel walked up to him, holding the baby in one arm. She wrapped the other around Luke's waist. She felt as if she were hugging James. Luke had that same tall, thin frame.

"It's wonderful to see you," she said, giving into the tears she knew she could no longer contain. "Look at me," she said and started to laugh. She put her hand under the baby's arm and turned him to face Luke.

Luke transferred his cane to his left hand, brought his trembling right hand up, and gently cupped the baby's head.

"Meet JC. James Cameron MacIntyre," Mabel said.

"He's beautiful. Like his mother," he said. He leaned in and kissed her cheek.

Stanley walked up to them. "It's good to have you home, son," he said, patting Luke's arm. He took the baby from Mabel.

Luke bowed his head, reached under his collar, and pulled out the St. Christopher medal James had given him. "I wish he knew I was coming home to him," he whispered. He started to sob.

Mabel brought his head to her chest and stroked the back of his head. She was sobbing, too.

A few in the room put their heads down. Others looked on in silence. All were aware that the day's happy occasion, came with its share of sadness.

Sam's father turned his head from Luke and Mabel, and looked around the room. He jumped to his feet, drawing the attention of the small gathering.

"I'm starving," he bellowed.

"Me too," said John.

"Let's eat," Mark said, eyeing Alice, who was holding a plate of sandwiches.

Luke pulled away from Mabel and smiled. “I hope there’s pie,” he said.

“There’s always pie,” she said, leaning into him.

“First a toast,” Stanley said, as Michael and Amour passed out the drinks. Stanley lifted his glass and nodded at Luke. “Welcome home, son,” he said. “And to James and Margaret, who are here with us.”

June 26, 1945

"Why don't you hold the baby and let me drive?" Stanley said.

"Because I like to drive. And I know where we're going."

"Where are we going?"

"Hold your horses. You'll see."

Mabel drove another twenty miles before pulling over to the side of the road.

Stanley leaned against the car with the baby in his arms and watched her jump a narrow ditch, scramble up a small embankment, and begin wading through the tall grass. "Is this it? A big field?" he yelled.

She turned back toward him and the baby. "It's not just any field," she hollered, making a sweeping motion over the wide expanse. "It's the biggest, most beautiful daisy field in the world!"

From there, they drove to Pleasant Bay. Mabel pointed to where the farmhouse once stood. "That's where I used to live."

The outline of a collapsed roof was barely visible among the wild raspberry bushes and scraggly weeds.

"Do you want some time alone?"

"I won't be alone. Ma and my baby brother are here," she said, holding two bouquets of freshly-picked daisies.

"Take your time. Me and JC here are going to go have a drink. Aren't we, buddy?"

Mabel returned to the car about a half an hour later. "When

we sell the shack, I'd like to buy this place," she said, her eyes fixed on the sunlit knoll. Maybe put up a little cabin. Plant some cherry trees. What do you think?"

Stanley squeezed her hand. "Let's do it."

By the time they arrived home it was almost dark. Mabel was asleep with the baby on her lap. Stanley turned off the car and nudged her awake.

"I'm going to check on the ponies," he said. "I'll be in shortly."

Stanley entered the kitchen twenty minutes later and peeked into the living room. Mabel was on the sofa, hunched over JC. She had a daisy in her hand.

"Now this one…this one is Daisy Mae," she said, tickling his nose and pulling it back before he could grab it. "She's the prettiest one of all. She just came back from a far off place called China where she danced on a great wall. And this one… this is Dudley the Daisy. He's the strongest one of all. He lives in Timbuktu and it's said that he can move mountains with just one little finger. Oh, and this one," she said, sensing she was being watched. "This one is Daddy the Daisy. He's the kindest, bravest, most handsome one of all. He has a stable of grand steeds and lives in a magical kingdom beside the bluest ocean you'll ever see."

Stanley walked over and laid his hand on the back of her head. When she looked up, he bent down and kissed her.

"What was that for?" she asked, grinning.

"That," he said, smiling back, "*that* was for saving me."

Amen

Printed in the USA
CPSIA information can be obtained
at www.ICGtesting.com
LVHW090412111124
796237LV00001B/29

* 9 7 8 1 4 6 0 2 7 2 1 8 3 *